The
COLDWATER
WARM HEARTS
CLUB

The

COLDWATER WARM HEARTS CLUB

LEXI EDDINGS

KENSINGTON BOOKS
www.kensingtonbooks.com

KENSINGTON BOOKS are published by

Kensington Publishing Corp.
119 West 40th Street
New York, NY 10018

All Kensington titles, imprints, and distributed lines are available at special quantity discounts for bulk purchases for sales promotion, premiums, fundraising, educational, or institutional use.

Special book excerpts or customized printings can also be created to fit specific needs. For details, write or phone the office of the Kensington Sales Manager: Kensington Publishing Corp., 119 West 40th Street, New York, NY 10018. Attn. Sales Department. Phone: 1-800-221-2647.

Kensington and the K logo Reg. U.S. Pat. & TM Off.

eISBN-13: 978-1-4967-0404-7
eISBN-10: 1-4967-0404-5
First Kensington Electronic Edition: October 2016

ISBN-13: 978-1-4967-0403-0
ISBN-10: 1-4967-0403-7
First Kensington Trade Paperback Printing: October 2016

10 9 8 7 6 5 4 3 2 1

Printed in the United States of America

For my dear parents, who always loved and encouraged me and told me I could be anything I wanted to be. Unfortunately, they were wrong. I'll never be a size two.

Chapter 1

No one ever steps into the same river twice.
Maybe not. But you get your feet wet all the same.

—Lacy Evans, who's never really been
in trouble . . . until now

"Home is the place where, when you have to go there, they have to take you in. At least according to Robert Frost," Lacy Evans muttered. "But he didn't say you have to like it."

She didn't usually talk to herself, but she'd been on autopilot for two bleary-eyed days. After driving halfway across the country, she tooled into Coldwater Cove, Oklahoma, at six o'clock on a Sunday morning.

The town was one step up from rustic, a hundred steps down from trendy. It was the last place on earth she'd ever thought she'd live again. But that was before her business partner ran off with half a million dollars in client funds and left her holding the empty bag.

It was too early to pop into her parents' house. Mom needed her "beauty sleep" until eight at least. Dad was probably puttering about in the kitchen, making his abominable coffee, but if Lacy tried to slip into the house now, his booming welcome would be loud enough to wake the dead in the cemetery next door.

Besides, after what had happened in Boston, she didn't deserve a welcome. So she drove around the narrow streets, looking for evidence that time had passed since she was home last.

Coldwater Cove was a quiet little place where Arkansas tossed a rumpled blanket of hills and hollows over the Oklahoma state line. The air that morning was so still there wasn't a single ripple on Lake Jewel, the blue eastern boundary of the town. The tired peaks of the Winding Stair range brooded over the lake, their velvety foothills bathed in an Ozark haze. Nothing ever seemed to change here.

In a weird way, Lacy was glad. If nothing was different in her hometown, it was almost like Boston never happened.

The lights were on in the Green Apple Grill on the Town Square. Her stomach rumbled, a reminder that she hadn't eaten since those stale Twinkies in Peoria. She pulled up in front of the hurt-your-eyes green door. There were still no parking meters on the Square around the Victorian gem of a courthouse, so she got out, locked her Volvo out of habit, and went into the Green Apple. A trio of bells tinkled over the door.

"Have a seat. Be with you in a minute." The rumbling baritone came from a guy on the other side of a half wall that separated the kitchen from the rest of the place. His broad-shouldered back was turned to her. The grill hissed when he gave it a quick scrub-down with a damp rag.

Lacy slid into the nearest booth, hoping they still had Belgian waffles on the menu. Just thinking about melted butter and powdered sugar made her mouth water.

"Lacy? Lacy Evans, is that you?"

Jacob Tyler peered at her from the kitchen. Superstar halfback, homecoming king, voted most likely to succeed—he was Mr. Big Stuff when they were in high school. Lacy never expected he'd still be in Coldwater Cove, much less manning the Green Apple's grill.

"Hey, Jake. How've you been?"

"Can't complain. Besides, no one would care if I did."

Lacy doubted that sincerely. Jacob still had that devastating dimple in his left cheek and a megawatt smile. It was almost enough to make her forget the flotilla of broken hearts bobbing in his wake.

Almost. The last thing she needed was more man trouble on top of everything else.

"What can I do you for?" he asked.

"Coffee, and—please, God—waffles." They weren't listed on the plastic-covered menu affixed to the wall.

"For you, anything."

That was Jake Tyler's gift. He made a girl feel special. Only trouble was, he made *all* the girls feel special.

While he went to work on her breakfast, Lacy took a deep breath and enjoyed the sensation of not moving. When she pulled a tablet from her backpack, her hand shook a little. She chalked it up to lack of sleep. She refused to think of it as residual panic.

I'm OK. The people I borrowed all that money from have no idea where I am.

When she powered up her tablet, Bradford Endicott's face grinned up at her from the screen saver. She quickly deleted him, wondering why it had taken her so long. She was so over feeling anything for the guy but loathing. Deciding her belly was fluttering because she was just hungry, Lacy flexed her fingers and scanned the to-do list.

The first item to tick off was finding a place to live. Her stuff, such as it was, was on a truck en route from Boston. She had two days to call in a delivery address.

Lacy so didn't intend to spend any more nights in her parents' spare room than she could help. Granted, she deserved to suffer for being so stupidly gullible, but being reduced to the status of a perpetual twelve-year-old might be considered cruel and unusual punishment.

Her savings were far from bottomless, but it would be cheap to live in Coldwater Cove. If she was careful, she'd have a month or so to figure out what to do with herself. She'd be broke inside of a week in Boston.

More broke than she felt on the inside.

"I was sorry to hear about your troubles," Jake interrupted her thoughts. "So, how you holding up?"

"What do you mean?"

"You know. That business about the guy back in Beantown who absconded with your money."

It wasn't her money. It was their clients' money, deposits on special pieces, for design and renovation work yet to be delivered. And Bradford wasn't just any guy. He was her partner. She and Bradford had been all but engaged. Trusting him was the biggest mistake she'd ever made. She frowned at Jacob. "How did you—"

"Remember where you are, Lace," he said. "Your mom tells her hairdresser, who confides in her sister, who lets it slip to the UPS guy, yada, yada, yada. Then once something makes the Methodist prayer chain, it's better than going viral on YouTube." His smile faded. "Seriously, though, are you OK?"

She'd lost her business, her condo, and her professional reputation, but she was better off than Bradford Endicott would be if she ever laid eyes on him again. Lacy wasn't a naturally violent person. But if Belize ever honored the extradition request for him, she'd be more than happy to bloody his nose. Then she'd testify against him for ripping off their high-end design clients and running off to Central America with all the firm's liquid assets. *And* Ramona, their stiletto-wearing, hair-flipping, sure-to-rock-a-bikini assistant.

"I'm fine," she assured Jake. She wished she could assure herself. Switching off the tablet and stowing it in her pack, she couldn't think about what to do next. At least, not until she got some real food in her. "I didn't make it to the ten-year reunion. What've you been up to? I expected to see you in the NFL."

"College football convinced me my future lay elsewhere. Two concussions in as many months was too much. Not much point in a football scholarship if you get your brain rattled every week trying to keep it. I need all the gray matter I got."

"You did OK in school."

"Yeah, but only in classes where the answer was a matter of opinion."

Jacob smiled again and a shock of dark hair fell forward on his forehead. Lacy itched to push it back for him, but she scrunched her fingers in her lap instead. She should be immune to his brand of self-deprecating charm.

That's how vaccines work, isn't it? You take in a little of the virus, get comfy with it, and then you're safe from the full power of the real thing.

Still, her chest constricted a bit at his lopsided grin.

"Did a hitch with the Marines after that," he said.

"Semper fi."

"Oo-rah." He came around the half wall with a cup of coffee in one hand and a plate of steaming waffles in the other. She noticed his slight limp for the first time. And the fact that below his camo shorts, his left leg was titanium from the knee down. He caught the direction of her gaze. "Ran into an IED in Helmand province."

Afghanistan. According to Mr. Curtis, their high school history teacher, the land of the Khyber Pass was a place where plenty of countries had had their rears handed to them over the last millennium or so. "Jacob, I'm sorry."

"Don't be. I was one of the lucky ones." He set down the plate of waffles and coffee in front of her. A shadow passed behind his dark eyes. "Most of the guys in my unit didn't make it back."

Lacy buried her nose in her cup and wondered how to change the subject. Out of nowhere, she blurted, "So, did you ever get married?"

"Once. Didn't take. You?"

"Almost engaged. Once. Ditto." She forked up a bite of waffles. Deciding that carbs were better than men, Lacy sank into powdered-sugar bliss.

"Saving yourself for me, huh?" Jacob said as he settled into the booth opposite her.

"You've uncovered my evil plan." They laughed together. They both seemed to need it.

"Are you home for good?" he asked.

"I don't know." It was more like she was home for bad. Coldwater Cove was her penance. And her sanctuary. And the slow-paced, backwater vibe of the place was likely to drive her batty if she stayed longer than six months.

"Think you'll start your own business or will you need a job here?" Jake asked.

Hadn't Boston proved she wasn't much of a business-woman? "Since I'm not independently wealthy and I'm kind of addicted to eating and sleeping indoors, yeah, I need a job."

"I hear Wanda's looking for someone over at the *Gazette*. She'd jump at the chance to have you."

Lacy nearly choked on the waffle. She used to write part-time for the *Coldwater Gazette* when she was in high school, covering ball games and board meetings alike. Back then, everyone figured she'd become an investigative journalist like her uncle Roy. Instead, she shook off the dust of this little wide spot in the road and followed her passion to a design school in New England. She specialized in fusing Old World antiques and architectural features with industrial kitsch. Her work won awards, the important hang-on-your-brag-wall kind.

But that was before Bradford Endicott ran off with their clients' deposits and she had to liquidate everything to try to make it right. From the displays in their trendy Back Bay showroom to the equity in her condo and every last nickel in her IRA, everything she'd worked for was gone. Even after all that, she still had to sign a usurious note with some semi-unsavory characters for a balance that would eat her alive if she didn't find a way to pay it off pronto.

Even though she wasn't cut out to be a businesswoman, she'd never considered that she might have to dust off her reporter hat.

"I don't think I can work at the *Gazette* again. It would feel like going backward. Besides, my uncle Roy says small-town papers are a license to steal," Lacy said between waffle bites. The local rag filled its pages with puff pieces that ended with "a good time was had by all," and then charged the earth for advertising space. It was an insult to her uncle's journalistic soul. Since Lacy adored Uncle Roy, she thoroughly endorsed his opinion. "It's like Chinese food, only in print. After you read the *Coldwater Gazette,* your brain is hungry again in an hour."

"Yeah, well, it might pay the bills. Things change and sometimes you have to do whatever comes to hand." A hard edge cut through his tone. It hadn't been there before. Jake shrugged. "It was just a thought."

While she polished off the waffles and made appreciative noises at appropriate intervals, Jake filled her in on what had happened with some of their other classmates. Quite a few had moved on, but more were still in Coldwater Cove than she expected. There'd been marriages and shacking-ups, splitting the sheets and reconciliations. Kids had been born, houses built. Businesses had bloomed or withered. Everyone had been filling up their lives with people and things.

All Lacy had to show for her twenty-nine trips around the sun fit neatly into a relatively small shipping pod. She figured her worldly goods ought to be somewhere in Ohio by now.

"Everyone will be happy to see you back," Jake assured her.

She smirked. "On the theory that misery loves company?"

"After you've seen Kabul, Coldwater's not so bad," he said. "Besides, it's not the back of beyond it used to be. We've got cable and Internet on top of the *Gazette* to keep us up to speed. And whatever news they miss turns up on the Methodist prayer chain."

She took a swig of coffee. It wasn't as bitter as the brew she was used to. She'd become accustomed to coffee that gave her taste buds a smack. "Never figured you for a Methodist."

"Getting your leg blown off will make you rethink a lot of things."

Lacy nodded, but Jake looked away, signaling that was all he had to say on that topic. If she waited long enough, he'd probably tell her more. All her life, people had told Lacy the most amazing things, surprisingly personal things, simply because she was willing to sit in silence and wait for them to fill it.

But she didn't want to invade Jake's head. It didn't seem polite after he'd made her waffles and all.

The bells over the door jingled and a guy in sheriff's office khaki came into the Green Apple. Coldwater Cove was too small to have its own police force, so the county boys did double duty. He took off his hat. The tight brim hadn't done his dark-honey hair any favors, but Lacy's stomach lurched in recognition anyway.

It was Daniel Scott.

Back when Lacy was in school, it seemed every girl in Coldwater Cove had a not-so-serious fling with Jacob Tyler at one time or another. It was like a rite of passage.

You go through it and get your heart bruised. Sadder, but not much worse for the wear because even though Jake has moved on to the next girl, he's so darn likeable, you're still his friend.

Lacy was glad she'd gone through her "Jake phase" in fifth grade when their courtship consisted of holding hands during school assemblies. Once their budding "true love forever" ended abruptly after a new girl moved to town, Lacy's dad had mended her broken heart by signing her up for riding lessons. She stopped pining for Jake almost immediately. At ten or eleven, girls love horses more than boys anyway.

But Daniel Scott . . .

For one breathless summer before Lacy headed east to study design, Daniel was her soft, warm night and endless sky. Even though she was the one who moved to Boston, he was the one who got away.

"Saw the out-of-state plates and—" Daniel stopped mid-step. His eyes were as green as she remembered them, not muddy like a moss green, but vibrant like a spring morning.

"Lacy," Daniel said.

That was it. Just her name. It'd been over a decade since she'd seen him, yet something inside her hummed with re-membered longing. A slow-motion scene where they ran toward each other, arms outstretched, scrolled across her mind.

Down, Lacy. You are so seriously sleep-deprived. And Bradford Endicott should be enough to make any girl swear off men completely.

Instead of a slow-mo sprint, Dan walked over to the booth where she and Jake were sitting. They started the round of small talk again. It was basically the same ground she'd covered with Jacob, only Daniel didn't sit with them. A question tromped around on the tip of her tongue, but she bit it back.

The bells over the door jingled again. A group of folks dressed in church clothes filed in for the breakfast special before Sunday School.

"Gotta go." Jake slid out of the booth to take care of his customers.

"Me too." Daniel put his hat back on, and when he looked down at her, one side of his mouth lifted. She would have given her last penny for the thought behind that half smile. "It's good to see you, Lacy. Welcome home."

His lips parted as if he was about to say something else, but then he turned and walked away. Still looked pretty incredible doing it, too, but Lacy didn't need to ask that other question anymore.

She'd seen the ring on his left hand.

Chapter 2

*Once a marine, always a marine. I was born to
kick butt and take names, sir. I'll just have
a little more titanium in my kick from now on.*

—Jacob Tyler to his commanding officer,
after coming out of surgery for the
injury he received in Afghanistan

Back in Boston, the streets had been rimed with crusts of
dirty snow, the remnants of a late-season nor'easter. Lacy had
chased warmer weather half the way across the country and
arrived in Coldwater Cove in time for full-blown spring.
Crocuses and daffodils pushed through the red clay soil and
forsythias erupted in a yellow riot on every block.

In her parents' yard, the War of Squirrel Insurgency began
afresh.

Lacy had never actually seen the squirrels in action, but
her dad was convinced they broke off twigs from his oak trees
and threw them down into the yard for pure cussedness. Of
course, it didn't help matters that her parents' neighbor, Mr.
Mayhew, put out bird feeders that had the (hopefully) unintended effect of enticing even more squirrels to the Evanses'
yard. According to Lacy's dad, the feeders were supply depots
for the enemy. As she pulled up, the first casualties of this
year's opening salvo littered the grass.

Dad was out front, gathering fallen twigs from under the
ponderous oaks. Fergus, his little Yorkie, nosed around the
trunks, always alert for the stray "rat with a fluffy tail." Her
dad had been warned not to break out his shotgun in town

anymore, so Fergus was all the firepower he could muster against the furry foes.

Still, the battle must be enjoined each spring.

Again, Lacy was glad some things didn't change, however ridiculous they might be.

She was barely out of the car before her dad had her in a solid hug. Sometimes, her parents' affection was like being smothered by a blanket of molasses, too sweet to resist and too sticky to escape. But now Lacy sank into her dad's loving acceptance with gratitude, blinking away tears.

She was the baby of the family. On a scale measuring good behavior, Lacy fell somewhere in the lower middle between her perfect sister, Crystal, and her black sheep brother, Mike. It had been tough going through school with teachers expecting her to either be as brilliant and good as her sister or as wild and irresponsible as her brother. Lacy was never given the benefit of a totally clean slate either way.

When her dad patted her back, the years sloughed off, as she'd feared they would, and she was reduced to childlike dependence again. Amazingly enough, that wasn't as bad as she'd expected. For a few moments, she allowed herself the fantasy that she had ever been that innocent. Then she pulled away.

She was back in Coldwater Cove because she hadn't been careful, because she hadn't been professional. Because she wasn't . . . good enough to cut it in the big city.

"Lacy-girl, we weren't expecting you till this afternoon." Dad's resonant voice echoed off the stand of trees. If he'd been a trial lawyer instead of a tax and estate planning attorney, he'd have been a terror in the courtroom. His James Earl Jones–like tone would carry every argument. As it was, every self-respecting squirrel within earshot ought to have been shaking in its little rodent boots. "You must have driven all night."

"The car seemed to know the way and I didn't feel like stopping." Lacy had a fear of bedbugs, so hotels held zero charm for her, even if she could have afforded a higher-priced room, which she couldn't. And besides, once she was horizontal, it was anyone's guess whether she'd sleep. Bradford's face had a nasty habit of hovering at the edges of her vision just as she started to drop off.

"How's the Volvo running?"

Gas mileage and odd knocking sounds in her motor were topics of intense interest to her dad. To Lacy, they had the charm of being safe to discuss, so she gave him the latest report. That way, she didn't have to revisit the reason she'd run home like a scalded dog. Besides, if Dad wanted more details, he'd be sure to ask.

"Coffee's on." Dad unloaded her suitcase from the trunk and led the way into the house.

The home Lacy grew up in had been built in the 1920s. It was a lovely two-story Colonial with decorative dentils under the eaves, a carved wooden pineapple on the newel post at the foot of the stairs, wainscoting in the dining room, and crown molding throughout.

Really good bones.

Unfortunately, it was filled to the rafters with *stuff*. Not quite at hoarder levels yet, but every room in the place was crammed with furniture of various vintages ringing the walls. It would be hard to find space on those walls for even one more eight-by-ten photo. Occasional tables jutted into the hallways and every horizontal surface was covered with bric-a-brac, collectibles, and doodads.

Mom never met a garage sale she didn't like.

Lacy followed her dad into the kitchen and perched on one of the bar stools at the island. He poured her a cup of vile, dark liquid and, like a good penitent, she drank.

Her dad's coffee was a cross between Starbucks on steroids

and about six Red Bulls. Even though she'd been driving for thirty-some hours, the cobwebs in her brain began to dissolve.

Dad took a sip and made a face. "Well, that'll make a grown man tremble. Brewed it a might stout today, even for me. Let's sweeten it a bit." He took down a bottle of Bailey's from the top shelf and liberally dosed both their mugs. The creamy liquor emitted pleasantly alcoholic fumes. "Don't tell your mother."

Dad was of the opinion that the apostle Paul's admonition to Timothy to "take a little wine for thy stomach's sake" extended to distilled spirits as well. Mom was a more literal theologian. They argued the point on a regular basis, but without a definitive winner.

Lacy was the pragmatist of the family. Anything that made her dad's coffee drinkable was aces in her book.

"So how did you leave things back east?" he asked.

"I sold everything. The matter is settled to the DA's satisfaction." At least, she hoped it was.

"Did you have to take on some serious debt, daughter?"

What? Did he have some sort of weird dad-radar that pegged out when one of his kids got in over her head? She wasn't about to tell him that as part of the deal that kept her from being indicted along with the absent Bradford, the district attorney had required her to liquidate all she owned to make reparations. When that wasn't enough, she had taken out a huge loan for the rest with no idea how she'd pay it back.

"I'm OK, Dad," she said, more to convince herself than him. She'd had no choice really. It was accept the loan that almost miraculously became available from the O'Leary brothers or face jail time.

Lacy had lost everything. It made her chest ache every time she realized afresh that her trendy design studio was gone. In this economy, she wasn't the only one whose business had gone south, but her misfortune was the result of bad judgment rather than bad luck.

She really blew it when she took on Bradford as her business partner. As an Endicott, he was so well connected, so old money. Lacy figured he'd be able to bring in seriously well-heeled clients with discerning tastes. She'd counted on the patina of his Boston Brahmin status to cover the fact that she was from the sticks. As it turned out, it didn't seem to matter where she'd grown up. Once she'd completed a few projects, her designs were what brought in the work. Then "old money Brad" had used her to make off with a boatload of new money.

She was such a rotten judge of character. Maybe she deserved to lose everything. Lacy was grateful when her dad interrupted her increasingly depressing thoughts.

"What did they ever find out about that Endicott fellow?"

"The case is still open, but the trail is pretty cold. He made it to Belize, but the authorities there show no signs of wanting to return him."

At least, not until he spends all the money he wired to an account down there.

"Well, I was wondering if somehow the Irish mob was behind it. You know, putting your partner up to the scam." Lacy's dad had retired from a legal practice consisting mostly of drawing up wills and settling disputes over water rights. But in his heart, he was a big fan of true crime. He could rattle off the names of mob bosses as easily as some men spout baseball stats. She suspected he'd always wanted to work with an Eliot Ness type who spent his life putting away bad guys. "The police don't think you're in danger, do they?"

"If someone was angry enough to come after me, they'd have done it before now."

At least, that's what she wanted her dad to believe. She'd repaid her clients and suppliers. But if she missed a loan payment, someone might well come. The O'Leary brothers weren't the sort who accepted payment by check. She'd already arranged to wire funds monthly to her friend Shannon, who would leave the cash in an unmarked envelop at a certain bar in the North End. By borrowing from the O'Learys, Lacy probably *had* made a deal with an arm of the Irish mob, but what else could she do? She couldn't exactly waltz into a Bank of America and get an unsecured loan to cover a debt of this size.

She didn't think there was a connection between the mob and Bradford. Other than greed and the chance to lie beside Ramona on a tropical beach, she didn't know why he'd betrayed her.

Her father gave her a sidelong look. It was the same face he'd made when he caught her sneaking out of the house after curfew when she was fifteen. The expression was a mixture of skepticism over her excuses and frustration that he hadn't raised her better. The "look" hurt worse than a whipping.

Of course, Lacy had never had a whipping, but she imagined the "look" was still worse. It made her insides ache instead of her backside.

"Well, whatever's happened, you're always welcome here. You know that," her dad said with a shrug. "Your mother's been doing up the spare room and trying to empty a couple of drawers for you."

There was no question of getting a whole closet for her things. Even the one in the guest room was as full of her mom's "treasures" as the rest of the house. Her dad tipped back his mug, drained it, and poured himself another. Lacy marveled at his capacity for self-inflicted caffeine-buzz.

"You just stay as long as you like," he said.

"About that." Besides needing her space, and a chance not to feel twelve all the time, if anyone from Boston did come looking for her, she didn't want to lead them to her parents. "I'll be getting my own place right away."

"I understand, though your mother may not. She's been in a tizzy since you called to let us know you were coming. You can probably find something decent to rent in the *Gazette*." He pointed to the local paper, folded neatly on the counter. "No trailers, though. Promise me, Lacy. I won't have any kid of mine in one of those death traps."

"I promise." Growing up in Tornado Alley had instilled a healthy respect for solid walls and cinder-block basements.

Suddenly from the second floor, Fergus launched into a barking frenzy. The Yorkie bounced down the stairs ahead of Lacy's mom, like a furry little herald announcing to all and sundry, "The Queen is awake!"

Awash in a cloud of Estée Lauder, Mom gave her a big hug and kissed both her cheeks with resounding smacks. Then she palmed Lacy's face and eyed her critically.

"You've let your bangs grow too long, sweetheart," she said. "But never mind. We can fix it. You should see the cute new haircut Crystal got yesterday. Your sister looks like something out of *Vogue*."

"When did she not?" Lacy muttered.

"Come on. I'll crank up the curling iron and we can catch up while it heats."

Her mom had never given up the delusion that with enough primping, Lacy could be remade into the likeness of a country western star. She'd tried to tell her mother more than once that big hair was dead, even in Nashville, but she let herself be dragged up the stairs anyway.

Sometimes, resistance really is futile.

By 10:30, the church-folk breakfast rush petered out. They'd be back for bacon burgers and onion rings or the fried catfish Green Plate special once the last "hallelujah" was sung. The only customers left in the Green Apple Grill were members of a slightly pagan drum circle who met there for coffee and icebox rolls with religious regularity. While the rest of the town celebrated the Father, Son, and Holy Ghost, those old hippies were more likely to lift their spirits with a little weed they brought back from Colorado.

"Rocky Mountain high," Jake muttered. Then he asked Ethel, his decidedly long-in-the-tooth waitress, to refill the drum circle's mugs.

"Maybe I can sweet-talk them into that leftover coffee cake, too," Ethel said as she bustled off.

Ethel was a blue-haired wonder. She was old enough to collect both Social Security and her deceased husband's pension, so she didn't need the money she made at the grill. However, she did need the company and she liked working at the Green Apple. Even if her service was a little slow, most folks enjoyed being waited on by a grandmotherly sort who called them "honey," "sugar," or "darlin'."

At first, Jake thought it was because Ethel had forgotten their names, but she never forgot an order and didn't use a notepad to jot them down either. Once the meal was over, she convinced diners that because they'd cleaned their plates, they *deserved* blackberry cobbler with homemade walnut ice cream.

No doubt about it, Ethel was good for business.

Jacob gathered up the garbage and headed for the Dumpster in the alley. He shifted the bag onto the shoulder over his good leg. Too much weight on the wrong side and his stump would ache like the devil later that night. Sometimes it felt as if his absent toes were cramping and he couldn't massage them into submission. Then, too, even if everyone else "deserved" their piece of cobbler, Jake had to exercise and watch his weight lest an extra pound or two change how his prosthetic leg fit.

But he was dealing.

What he wasn't dealing with was the way folk treated him since he came back from his stint with the Marines. Oh, he was welcomed home and hailed a hero, right enough, but he'd never get used to those sidelong stares. The slight shake of the head when they glanced at his leg. Or the way a conversation would dry up as he approached—a sure sign he'd been the topic of gossip.

Or, most especially, the way women reacted to him.

Not that he was conceited or anything, but Jake knew he had a way with the ladies from the time he sprouted his first chin hair. He couldn't help it. He loved them and they loved him back.

Of course, he didn't love any of them very long.

Now they wanted to take care of him, like he was some pathetic invalid.

Except for Lacy Evans. She seemed to take his new leg as nothing particularly tragic, just something that had happened. She'd expressed as much sympathy as he could bear, which wasn't much, and moved the conversation on to greener pastures. He was the same guy. She was the same girl. They'd known each other since they were in kindergarten. Even back then, she'd caught his eye by showing off her underpants while she flipped around on the playground twirly-bars.

He slung the garbage up and into the Dumpster, where it landed with a dull thud, followed by the sound of a shattering pickle jar. Jake was instantly hyper-aware of his surroundings. The hair on the back of his neck rose to attention. He could have counted a gnat's eyelashes.

The jangle of the smashed jar seemed as loud as an explosion. The sound went on and on. It shivered down his spine and sent him back to his unit. He expected bits of glass to come flying out of the Dumpster. The real world phased out around him for a few heartbeats. Light flashed, blinding him, as the windows blew out of the Humvee. Blood trickled down his cheek.

Then his vision seemed to return. Barren hills with vibrant poppy fields in the hollows burst on his sight. Sandy grit filled every crevice and made his eyes sting. Fire shot up his leg. His buddy's scream was an ice pick in his ear. Everything was awash in angry red. He couldn't tell if it was poppies or blood.

A hoarse cry tore from Jake's throat.

"Hey, man, you trippin'?"

Rough hands seized his shoulders. They gave him a shake and the world turned round to its right colors again. Breathing hard, Jake found himself looking into the weatherworn face of Lester, Coldwater Cove's resident homeless vet.

Well, that wasn't strictly true. Lester didn't live in the town year-round. The former army grunt liked to winter in Brownsville, but he complained that summers in Texas were "hotter than hell." He was in no hurry for a preview of what he considered his final destination. So Lester always thumbed his way back to Coldwater Cove's green hills by the time the first azaleas were ready to bloom.

"No, I'm not tripping. I'm OK," Jake said, though his heart still pounded like a jackhammer. If someone had to catch him in a flashback, he was grateful it was Lester. Anyone else would go all frantic on his butt and demand he seek immediate help from a VA shrink.

Like I could get an appointment with one anytime this decade. Anyway, Jacob didn't want anybody poking around in his head. It got crowded enough in there with just him.

Then he noticed a pile of greasy-looking army blankets. Lester had made a pallet for himself by the Dumpster. "Look, you don't have to stay here in the alley. Samaritan House always has a few beds."

"Yeah, but they make me stay sober if I want one, and

where's the fun in that?" Lester bent over, gathered up his blankets, and stuffed them into a grimy knapsack. Only God knew when any of Lester's belongings, or the man himself for that matter, had last seen soap and water.

"Wait here and I'll bring you some eggs," Jake said.

Lester grinned. "That's more like it. Don't s'pose you have a little Jack Daniels to go with 'em?"

"No liquor license. Best I can do for you is coffee."

"Well, I won't say no to a cup of joe, the blacker the better," Lester said as he settled comfortably on the diner's back stoop. "You may be a jarhead, but you're a good'un."

Jake didn't consider himself all that good, but there was no reason to disabuse Lester of the notion. He went back into the Green Apple to whip up a breakfast scramble for the old man.

And made a mental note to let Daniel Scott know his father was back in town.

Chapter 3

*After God created the heavens and the earth, He
pronounced them good. Of course, He made squirrels,
too, but everyone's allowed at least one mistake.*

—George Evans, Esq., terror of fluffy-tailed
rodents everywhere

At 10:45 on the dot, Lacy's parents headed for church. She
begged off. Having been a recent star on the Methodist prayer
chain, she wasn't ready to face them en masse.

The house was so quiet Lacy could hear the occasional
creak of timbers settling on the foundation. She caught herself
pacing in time with the loud tick of the grandfather clock in
the foyer. Fergus followed her from room to room, hopeful
she'd land somewhere and provide him with a lap, no doubt.
But Lacy had been sitting too long and, even after an all-night
drive, the caffeine in her dad's coffee, plus the cup she'd had
at the Green Apple, ensured that she wouldn't be nodding off
anytime soon.

She needed to stretch her legs, so she headed out the front
door and down the street. If she went north, she'd be traips-
ing across Mr. Mayhew's front lawn. When she was a kid, he
was the neighborhood boogeyman. Fussy and argumentative,
he'd pop out on his porch brandishing a rake anytime one
of the Evans children put so much as a toe on his property.
His picture should appear in the dictionary next to the word
"curmudgeon."

Lacy decided that between incurring the wrath of Mr.

Mayhew and walking in the graveyard, the cemetery was the lesser of two evils.

The fact that the old territory cemetery was next to her house used to creep her out. If twilight descended while she was walking home, she'd run past the iron rail fencing that surrounded the rows of gray headstones and wouldn't stop until she was on her own front stoop. Of course, it didn't help matters that her dad kept assuring her it wasn't the dead ones she needed to worry about.

"It's them *live* ones," he'd say with a waggle of his brows.

At the time, Lacy hadn't appreciated her father's humor, but she'd learned to appreciate cemeteries since then.

In Boston, they were quaint and curious, with canting grave markers so old some of the inscriptions had been reduced to mere dimples in the stone. Important people's bones rested in the little churchyards along the Freedom Trail, people with names everyone recognized—Paul Revere and Sam Adams, John Hancock and Mother Goose.

Lacy recognized the names in the Coldwater Cove cemetery, too. There were Addleberrys and Bradens, Van Hooks and Sweazys—all big landholders and early settlers. Her grandparents on her father's side were also there, lying next to each other for all eternity. This arrangement undoubtedly made it easier for them to continue their playful running argument over who loved whom the most.

It occurred to Lacy that she knew someone else there, too.

Her high school classmate, Jessica Walker.

The Walkers were a prominent family in Coldwater Cove. They owned a good number of the buildings ringing the courthouse and held seats on the town council. When Walmart wanted to come to town, they fought like demons to keep it out, but eventually folks out-voted them and the big-box store moved in.

"Makes people feel like Coldwater has finally arrived,"

her dad had said, as if "low, low prices" were the ultimate source of a town's validation.

In addition to the Walkers' real estate holdings around the Square, the family occupied a choice portion of the burial grounds, too. Their headstones were grouped in the high northeast corner of the cemetery, so the dearly departed Walkers didn't have to worry about runoff from someone else's plot.

Lacy found Jessica there, next to a big bald cypress. Tired from the slog uphill, she sat down on the lush spring grass and leaned on the backside of the truly enormous WALKER headstone. Absorbed heat from the granite leached into her. A vision of Jessica doing handsprings for the length of the gym scrolled across her mind. Pretty, popular, and incredibly limber, Jessica had been captain of the cheerleading squad.

Lacy had played clarinet in the pep band. It was the only group she ever joined and even there, she was just one of the woodwinds. Nothing special.

If she could have traded places with anyone back in high school, it would have been Jessica Walker.

Until Jess drove her new car into Lake Jewel a week after her eighteenth birthday. With that sobering thought, Lacy decided maybe her problems weren't all that dire. At least, not at the moment.

Coldwater Cove had a way of slowing the world down. The earth sort of wobbled as it decelerated. Lacy decided no one would miss her if she stepped off that spinning ball for a bit. Her eyelids drooped shut, and she winked out, but she didn't get to nap long.

Low voices woke her.

"I'm telling you, she moved back home."

I'm right here. I can hear you, Lacy wanted to say. *Don't talk about me like I'm not on the other side of this honking big headstone.*

"In with her parents?"

The first person must have nodded because a brief silence was followed by a low whistle. "I never would have thought it. She really left him, huh?"

Bradford's the one who left, not me. They must be talking about someone else.

Lacy knew eavesdropping wasn't polite, but this was Coldwater Cove. Everyone was always in everyone else's business. She shifted her weight to one hip so she could listen more comfortably.

"Was it an affair, you think?"

"What else? I sure wouldn't kick Danny Scott out of bed for eating crackers."

Danny Scott. *My Daniel?*

"Come on, Georgina. Maybe it was Anne who had the affair."

"No, stupe. If it was her, she wouldn't be moving in with her parents. She'd be shacking up with whoever she's . . . well, you know."

"Sadly, I don't. I haven't *you know'd* in a long time."

The pair erupted in laughter. Then the one named Georgina announced that she had a tee time to make and left, but the other stayed on. Lacy heard the scrape of a trowel on a clay pot.

Someone was tending Jessica Walker's grave.

Getting out of this situation was going to be a good trick. Doing it without letting the person on the other side of the headstone know she'd been snooping on their conversation would be even better. It didn't help that all Lacy could think about was the fact that the ring on Daniel's left hand might not mean as much as she'd thought.

Of course, separated was still married. Lacy wasn't about to be cast as some sort of home wrecker. That would make her no better than the thoroughly hateable Ramona. But if Lacy wasn't ready to become as detestable as her traitorous office assistant, she needed to remind her wayward stomach. It did residual flip-flops whenever she thought about Danny Scott.

The gardener showed no sign of leaving, so Lacy decided to brazen it out. She yawned loudly and stood. Peering around the headstone—it was far too imposing a monument to peer over—she found Jessica Walker's fraternal twin sister, Heather, fitting a pot of yellow tulips into the brass vase next to the stone.

"Oh!" Heather said, shooting to her feet with a hand to her chest in surprise when she saw Lacy. "I didn't know anyone was there."

"Sorry. I drove all night to get home and I was just stretching my legs. After I sat down here, I guess I fell asleep," Lacy said as she came around to Heather's side of the marker.

It was a little weird for someone to be napping in a graveyard, but Heather shrugged as if it were no big deal. She folded her lanky frame back into a kneeling position to continue work on the tulips. Back in the day, long-legged Heather Walker had been a power forward on the Lady Marmots basketball team.

Lady Marmots. Now that Lacy had been away for a while, the team name struck her as beyond odd. Coldwater Cove's high school athletes had been known as the Fighting Marmots since the 1950s. The Marmots at least had the benefit of being politically correct since no one could possibly be offended by a glorified ground squirrel.

Except, of course, Lacy's dad. A squirrel of any stripe was enough to make his cheek muscles twitch.

"Heard you were coming home," Heather said.

"For a while." She hadn't given up on figuring out a way to pay off that note and rebuild her design business. *And when I do, no one remotely related to Bradford Endicott will even be allowed to gawk through the windows.*

"Got a place to stay?" Heather asked.

Lacy shook her head. "I need to find something pretty quick." She didn't add pretty cheap. It went without saying.

"Mrs. Paderewski has a one-bedroom on the Square. After you left, the town council required all the owners to refurbish the upper stories above the businesses. Mrs. P's rental is next to mine over Gewgaws and Gizzwickies," Heather said. Lacy recognized the shop as her mom's favorite junk emporium. "We'd be neighbors."

Lacy didn't connect with people easily. It was part of why she'd fled Coldwater Cove for the anonymity of a big city. But it was hard to resist Heather's friendly smile. "That sounds good to me."

So after helping Heather finish her grave tending, Lacy went home, called Mrs. Paderewski, and made an appointment to see the rental. Then she finished her nap on her mother's hundred-year-old settee. It was much more comfortable than the cemetery.

And Fergus finally found the lap he'd been looking for.

"Is up here. Come, come." It was a warmish Monday afternoon when Mrs. Paderewski motioned Lacy up the wrought-iron stairs on the back side of the brick building. The steps led to a second-story metal deck that stretched the whole length of the structure. Mrs. P's sensible shoes clanged on the iron work. For a round little woman, she hoofed it up the stairs pretty quickly. All those years of teaching piano to the tone-deaf children of Coldwater Cove hadn't hurt her spryness one bit.

"Is $575 a month," she said in her harsh Polish accent as she ushered Lacy into the apartment. "Water, heat, is all included."

Lacy didn't blame the piano teacher for branching out into real estate. Most of Mrs. P's students would never do her proud. Even Lacy had spent one summer squirming on the Paderewski piano bench for thirty minutes every Tuesday before her parents realized she'd do better with a clarinet. At least with a wind instrument she could only butcher one note at a time.

"$575?" Lacy said as she looked around.

In Boston, that wouldn't rent a closet. In Coldwater Cove, it'd bag a funky one-bedroom walk-up. The place didn't have granite countertops or stainless-steel appliances, but the kitchen was adequate, considering how infrequently Lacy cooked. Fortunately, the "refurbishing" Heather had told her about hadn't updated away the charm of the old building. The ceiling was still punched tin and the big farmhouse sink looked original and in surprisingly good condition.

"Is OK, $550 then," Mrs. Paderewski amended hopefully.

A peninsula with bar stools separated the kitchen from the rest of the open space. The old hardwoods creaked under foot as Lacy moved into the living room. Realtors called a room "cozy" when they meant small. This one qualified as both, but the floor-to-ceiling built-in shelves on one wall would help Lacy make the space work. There was no separate dining room. She'd have to shoehorn her bistro set into a corner.

She checked out the view of the courthouse. The old Opera House was on the corner to her right, next to the *Coldwater Gazette*. Across the Square, the Green Apple Grill was also within her line of sight.

The bedroom was small, but it would handle her sparse furniture, and the closet would do for her newly pared-down wardrobe. She'd sold her Jimmy Choos on Craigslist before she headed west. Where would she wear them in Coldwater Cove? Besides, if a special occasion did present itself, she still had the strappy Manolo Blahniks she couldn't bear to part with.

The bathroom had a deep claw-foot tub. Lacy checked the

water pressure. The pipes banged a bit, but the faucet flowed just fine. Hot water arrived before she counted to ten.

Lacy had looked at half a dozen semi-depressing places that afternoon before meeting with Mrs. P. She saw duplexes with linoleum floors that looked as if someone had been flamenco dancing in football cleats on them. Big dogs were invariably chained in the neighbors' backyards. This apartment was miles better than those and besides, this place spoke to her.

"I'll take it."

"Good." Mrs. Paderewski smiled. A bit of her bloodred lipstick had smeared on her upper incisors, making her look like a middle-aged Polish vampire. "Oh, I almost forget. Is $25 pet rent, too."

"I don't have a pet."

"Well"—Mrs. P waddled back to the kitchen—"now you do."

She followed as the piano teacher opened a door next to the refrigerator. Lacy had thought it was probably a pantry, but to her delight, the small space housed a stackable washer and dryer.

And a litter box.

A large Siamese glared down at her from the top of the dryer. How the cat had gotten all the way up there, Lacy had no idea. It yowled a greeting, which might be roughly translated as "Get your citified butt out of my apartment. I was here first." The cry was punctuated by a sharp hiss.

Lacy stepped back a pace. "I don't want a cat."

"You want apartment?"

She nodded.

"Then you want cat," Mrs. P said, folding her arms over her ample bosom. "Is package deal."

"What if I'm allergic?"

"Are you?" Mrs. Paderewski arched a pencil-thin brow at her.

Lacy's dad always recommended the truth. "It's easier," he'd say. "We forget lies. Tell the truth and you don't have to remember what you told someone."

"No, I'm not allergic," she admitted.

"Well, there you go. Is settled."

"But I can't have a cat. I've never had a cat."

It was a bit like being Republican or Democrat. Either you were a dog person or a cat person. Lacy's family was filled with dog people.

Dogs were faithful, friendly, and pathetically eager to please. Cats never let you forget the favor they bestowed on you by allowing you to serve them.

"Last tenant left her, poor thing," Mrs. P said, angling for a little sympathy for the creature. "She have no home."

"You could take it to the animal shelter," Lacy said. The way the cat bared its teeth at that suggestion, she probably ought to have it exorcised first.

"That I could not do." Mrs. P. lowered her voice to a whisper. "If no one takes cat after little while . . ." She drew a finger across her throat.

As if it understood and wouldn't forget the insult, the cat emitted a strange staccato meh-ing.

Lacy took a step back. "I've never heard a cat make a sound like that."

"Is OK. Is nothing. Siamese, they do it sometimes," Mrs. P said.

"What's it mean?"

"Is cat. What can it mean?" Mrs. P shook her head as if the animal hadn't just made a sound like a feline Gatling gun.

"Mrs. Paderewski, it's obvious you're a cat lover. Look at it, er, him. Oh, that's right. It's a her, you said. She's such a pretty thing." The cat flattened its ears to its head, obviously recognizing self-serving BS when it heard it. "Why don't you take it?"

"I would, but seven I have already."

Seven cats. Holy litter box. I hope she also has a seven-hundred-pound Air Wick.

"She tempt me, but no, I cannot," Mrs. Paderewski said. "But you can. She good company. You see. Cats, they no trouble. Food, water, litter, done. So, we good?"

Lacy looked around the apartment. It was charming, clean, and since it was located on the Town Square, she could indulge in the fantasy that she was still living in the thick of things like she had in her Boston loft. Everything else about the place was perfect.

How bad could a cat be?

She counted out her deposit and first month's rent in crisp Benjamins. "What's the cat's name?"

"Don't know. Last tenant call her 'eff-ing cat.' Is not nice." Mrs. Paderewski tucked the money into her cleavage. It would never see the inside of a bank. What the IRS didn't know evidently wouldn't hurt her. "So I call Effie. Is nice name. She like."

"Effie," Lacy repeated as Mrs. P made good her escape.

The cat growled menacingly. What Effie would really like was to be left alone.

"You and me both, cat," Lacy told her. "You and me both."

Jake gave his wet head a shake as he sat down to put on his prosthetic leg. His physical therapist had advised him to switch to tub baths instead of showers, but he'd never liked soaking in his own dirt. Hopping on a wet surface wasn't advisable, so he kept a set of crutches close. He had a teak bench in the stall to balance on if he needed it.

All in all, getting clean after a day behind the grill was a

complicated business, but what hadn't become more complicated since his injury?

Jake massaged his stump, checking for sores or the start of
one. The last thing he needed was a blister that might develop
into something worse. He didn't think he could bear going
back into a wheelchair.

There was something "in your face" about his titanium
leg. He liked it. He could have had one that looked real
enough to fool most folks, but he preferred the bare metal. It
was like shouting to the world, "If I'm tough enough to wear
it, you can be tough enough to look at it."

A wheelchair, on the other hand, made him invisible.
People, women especially, had averted their eyes when he'd
rolled down the German hospital corridor. Once he got his
leg, he felt like a man again.

Most of the time.

He stood and put his weight on the limb. The pin clicked
into place and the leg was his again. Then he tugged on a set
of sweats and wandered into his living room, wondering if
he'd be able to catch the last few innings of a ball game before
he fell asleep in front of the TV.

There was a time when he'd have hit a couple of bars after
work, maybe closed one down. It wouldn't have to be on a
Friday night either. Now, after all day on his feet, he couldn't
wait to get his leg up.

Dang, I even bore myself.

Then he made the mistake of looking across the Square
from his apartment above the Green Apple.

"Someone should tell Lacy she needs blinds," he muttered.

He could see her puttering around in her new place amid
all the boxes. Moving was all it was cracked down to be.

*She probably hasn't eaten supper. Her kitchen won't be set up to
cook in yet.*

Fortunately, his was. Jake headed down the back stairs

to the grill to check the fridge. There was still some meat loaf, even though it had gone over well with the early supper crowd. Since the Green Apple didn't have a liquor license, he closed up by 6:30 every day. Along with freeing up his evenings, it appealed to his sense of fairness.

Might as well let the local bar and its restaurant on the Square cater to late diners.

When he put the meat loaf in the oven to warm, the savory scent streamed into the air. He nuked some garlic mashed potatoes and fried okra. Once it was all steaming hot, he packed the food in an insulated catering bag along with some fresh icebox rolls. Then he decided to screw watching his diet for once and dished up blackberry cobbler and hand-packed homemade walnut ice cream for two. Lastly, he put a bottle of Yellow Tail merlot from his private wine stash into the bag.

His grill might not have a liquor license, but that didn't mean the apartment above the Green Apple was dry.

Jake headed out the front, setting the bells ajingle, and locked the door behind him. He nearly tripped over Lester, who'd staked out a spot on the sidewalk where he could watch the occasional car and more frequent pedestrian go around the Square.

"Easy there, marine," Lester said, smoke curling from his stubby cigarette. Jake was relieved to smell only tobacco. "Walk wary. Saw an enemy patrol cruise by about a minute ago."

"I'll keep an eye out." He was also glad to see that Lester hadn't relocated his pallet of dirty blankets to the front of the restaurant. "Think it might rain tonight. The Green Apple has a covered back stoop, remember."

Lester nodded. "Might take you up on it. Never know where the Cong is like to show up. Don't think they patrol the alley much though."

Cong. Poor guy thought he was still back in Nam half the

time. At least when Jake had a flash that took him to Helmand province, it was very much separated from the real world, and once he came to himself, he knew exactly where he was and what had happened. He could usually hide that he'd even had an episode. That counted for something in Jake's book. It gave him a measure of control.

For Lester, the past was all tangled up in the present and he couldn't seem to distinguish between the two. On top of that, his mental state was slathered with a thick coat of paranoia.

Thank God that's not me.

But sometimes Jake wondered if there might come a time when a flashback might fail to disperse completely. Or if he'd lash out at someone in the throes of one without realizing what he was doing. He shook off the morbid thought. No sense borrowing trouble.

Jake took off around the Square. Half a dozen middle-aged couples were headed to the Opera House, where the local big band would be playing standards until 11:00 p.m. That counted as a pretty late night for most of the wannabe swing dancers. Some skateboarders had set up a ramp on the courthouse steps. They'd flirt with head injuries until a County Mounty came by, gave them a stern lecture, and made them pack up their gear.

There were a few window shoppers wandering toward the ice-cream parlor that stayed open late hoping to catch folks coming out of the five-dollars-a-head theater. The Regal never screened a first-run show, but it was a good place for a guy to get real butter on his popcorn.

Jake shook his head. He used to think of the back row of that theater as his favorite make-out spot. Now greasy popcorn was the first thing that came to him. He had to get his mind off his leg and on a woman again.

Well, he was doing that, wasn't he? Lacy Evans was the

best opportunity that had come his way in a long time. She
was worth the effort.

Worth the risk.

He rounded the corner and ducked into the alley behind
Lacy's row of buildings. One of the sheriff's office cruisers
was parked back there.

Must be that enemy patrol Lester was talking about.

Jake glanced up in time to see Daniel Scott bounding up
the metal staircase to the iron decking that led to Lacy's new
apartment.

And there goes the Cong.

It made twisted sense that Lester would mistake his son
for an old army foe. The now homeless vet had abandoned
his family and Coldwater Cove near the end of Danny and
Jake's senior year. Jacob had tried to forget about what had
happened. He and Dan certainly never talked about that night
or what had gone on in the Scott home leading up to it, but
after the old man left, Danny's mom made a lot fewer trips to
the emergency room.

But screw the past. Jake was inclined to side with Lester
on this one. Everyone in town knew Danny and his wife
Anne were separated, but they were still married. He had no
business sniffing around Lacy Evans.

Jake started up the flight of stairs, his titanium leg clicking
with each riser. Time to engage the enemy. He had meat loaf,
blackberry cobbler, and—if he did say so himself—a killer
smile in his arsenal. Danny Scott had a slightly tarnished wedding ring and a handful of otherwise empty fingers.

"Game on, Cong."

Chapter 4

Marriage is a lot tougher than it looks. Given the domestic disturbance calls we get every day, it looks pretty darn hard.

—Daniel Scott, deputy sheriff

Lacy's furniture had been tentatively placed in the appropriate rooms. Boxes filled with her belongings were stacked on the kitchen counter, the small dining set, and her built-for-stout-not-for-looks coffee table.

"Coming," she called out when she heard a rap on her door. She was happy to quit unwrapping the box of coffee cups to answer the knock. So far she'd counted five broken ones.

When she opened the door, she discovered Daniel.

"What are you doing here? I mean . . . well, that sounded rude," she said. "I just . . . I thought you'd probably be manning the speed trap on Route 59."

"Mabry's got the laser gun tonight," Daniel said. The trap was designed to catch tourists in a hurry to connect with the scenic Talimena Byway. The locals knew the troopers would be there so they tended to behave themselves, but lookee-loos from other parts were none the wiser. It was no skin off the town fathers' noses if outsiders got to make not-so-cheerful donations to the county coffers.

"Can I come in?"

"Oh, yeah, I'm sorry." *Sheesh! I must have misplaced my manners somewhere around Cleveland.* Lacy waved him in and he took off his hat. He still had that determined set to his jaw. His shoulders were broader than she remembered and he needed a haircut, but he still seemed like the same Daniel.

When he met her gaze, she hoped to heaven her face didn't show the way her insides jittered. It was stupid really. He might look like her Daniel, but he wasn't. In all the ways that mattered, they'd both changed. A lot.

He's married, for pity's sake.

But her stomach didn't seem to realize it.

Daniel crossed around to the other side of the kitchen peninsula and hitched a hip on one of the bar stools.

This is good. It's safer to have that countertop between us.

"Are you getting settled in?" he asked.

"Sort of." She unwrapped the next cup and found that its handle was cracked in two places. "Oh, darn. This was my Grandma's." She wasn't usually attached to things, but there were a few pieces that meant something to her because they'd belonged to people she loved. She narrowly resisted the urge to swear over the loss of this one.

"Keep track of your breakage," Daniel advised. "You can get the moving company to reimburse you."

She sighed. "It's not their fault this box got dropped. In fact, I'll be relieved if they don't sue. I had to tip one of the movers an extra ten dollars on account of the scratch." She tried to fit the pieces of the delicate cup back together. A little of her dad's superglue might fix it, but it would never be the same. "And I'm not talking about the scratch he made on my coffee table."

"Why'd you tip him at all?"

"Through no fault of my own, I have acquired a cat. She came with the apartment," Lacy explained, gesturing toward

Effie, who leaped up, as if on cue, to perch on the other bar
stool next to Daniel. The cat daintily licked one of her front
paws. "Meet Effie the Deranged."

"Looks harmless to me."

"Maybe now, but trust me, she's the feline from hell. She
took a serious dislike to the movers. I had her shut up in the
laundry, but one of the men accidentally opened the door and
Effie came flying out. She landed on his face and cut a deep
gouge in his cheek. I couldn't blame him for dropping the box
he was holding."

After that, the cat had streaked around the apartment de-
fying Lacy's efforts to catch her. Finally, Effie scrambled up
the drapes in the living room and from there, made a prodi-
gious bank shot of a leap to the peninsula and then to the top
of the kitchen cabinets. She stayed there for the duration of
the move, spitting and yowling when anyone looked her way.

"Poor movers." Daniel eyed Effie with suspicion. "Guess
she was trying to tell them she preferred the place empty."

"I hope you've had all your shots," Lacy told the cat. Then
she turned to Daniel. "I guess I ought to take her to the vet to
make certain. But that supposes I can get close enough to put
her into a carrier of some sort."

Effie laid her ears back and hissed.

"She won't let you near her?"

"No, she allows me to feed and water her. I'm good
enough to clean the litter box, but heaven forefend I touch
her. Effie is a one-person cat who hasn't found her person yet."
With a slightly malicious grin, Lacy turned to the animal.
"Better start playing nice. If not, once I manage to corral you
in a carrier, I may never let you out."

Effie produced that staccato *meh*-ing noise again, as if daring her to try it.

"Ignore her," Daniel said, shifting away from the animal
on his bar stool.

"Good idea," Lacy agreed. "That's probably the worst thing you can do to a cat."

Obviously offended, Effie lifted her question mark of a tail toward both of them and jumped down from the bar stool. Daniel laughed.

Lacy's heart ached a bit to hear it. She'd always loved his laugh, maybe because she heard it so seldom.

"Always figured you for a dog person." He shook his head. "But I'm not here just to meet your new pet."

For a few seconds their gazes locked and Lacy remembered what it was like to tumble into those green eyes. Then she looked away. She struggled to remember why she'd needed to bolt away from Coldwater as soon as she could.

You didn't want an ordinary life. You couldn't bear to be identified just as someone's daughter or sister or even as Daniel's girl. You had to stand out. Had to be somebody. Look where it got you.

"I don't have anything to offer you." No joke. Not only was she still bruised from Bradford's betrayal, she hadn't been to the store yet. "How about some water?"

"Sounds good."

She needed to keep her hands busy in case they were trembling a bit, so she rummaged through the box again. "There must be something in here that isn't broken."

Lacy came up with two Boston Bruins mugs that had made the trip intact. She let the tap flow for a few seconds, and then filled them with the liquid the town was named for.

"I hear you're married now." She could have kicked herself, but the words were out there in front of God and everybody. *In for a penny, in for a pound.* "When did that happen?"

How did that happen? She knew it was selfish of her, but she'd always thought of Daniel as hers. That's how it was supposed to be. It wasn't rational, but while she'd lived and worked in Boston, she imagined everyone in Coldwater Cove frozen in place. She'd grown and changed, but she never imagined them doing the same. Daniel was still supposed to be pining for the girl who'd left him to follow her dream.

"Anne and I got married about three years ago, but we've been separated for a bit." He drummed the fingers of one hand on the countertop. "I shouldn't be talking to you about this."

Lacy forced herself not to reach across the countertop and touch his hand to encourage him to trust her. If it had been anyone else, she would have, but if she so much as brushed Daniel's skin, the sparks it would set off inside her might never quit firing. She settled for a verbal promise.

"It's me, Daniel. I won't tell a soul. You know I won't. I don't remember anyone named Anne in our class."

"She didn't grow up here."

"How did you meet?"

He loosed a long breath. It was obviously a relief to talk to someone about his marriage, even if it was the girl he used to love. "About a year after you left, Anne Littlefield moved to town. She lived with her dad in Tulsa until she graduated, but her mom and stepfather were here. So she moved in with them when she took the dispatcher job at the sheriff's office."

Lacy could imagine their courtship. It would have gone in fits and starts because Daniel wasn't smooth like Jake. He was the quiet one, but still waters run deep, her dad always said. At one time, Lacy had thought it would be worth a lifetime to figure out what was going on inside Daniel Scott.

"When I promised 'till death us do part,' I meant it," he said, "but about two months ago, Anne said she needed to take a break."

A pained expression passed over his face. Whoever this Anne Littlefield was, Lacy decided she must be crazy. With supreme effort, she swallowed back the smoldering question most likely to give her heartburn.

Why is he still wearing the ring if she left him?

She buried her nose in the cup and sipped her water.

"It's not her fault," Daniel said as if she'd asked. "Never think it is. I'm the one to blame for our problems." Then a smile lifted one corner of his lips. "Let me show you a picture of my boy."

Lacy swallowed hard to avoid spewing the water out her nose. "Your boy?"

"Yeah. Anne and I may not agree on much right now, but we both know Carson is the best thing either of us has ever done." Daniel pulled out his phone and showed her a shot of a sandy-haired, green-eyed toddler with the same serious expression as his dad.

Talk about the road not taken. If she'd not left for New England, this child might have been hers. An ordinary life might not have been so bad. "He's beautiful."

"He'll be a heartbreaker someday," Daniel admitted. "He's already full of the dickens."

"Where is he now?"

"Here in town with Anne. She's staying with her folks. I see him as often as I can."

Lacy mulled that over for a bit. Other than fending off the well-meant smothering of her overprotective parents, she didn't have any practical experience with the demands of a family. Managing marriage, kids, and a career would be a real juggling act. The fact that she only had a surly cat to care for suddenly seemed light duty in the relationship and responsibility department.

Daniel put away his phone and cocked his head at her. "Now it's your turn. What really happened in Boston?"

"Long story short, I screwed up."

"Your dad said your business partner got you crossways of some pretty serious people." His expression amended that to "seriously *bad* people."

Lacy's brows shot up. "Dad talked to you about me?"

Clearly, her father didn't think she was as out of the woods after the Boston debacle as she wanted him to believe. "I'm so going to have a discussion with him. About boundaries."

"Don't be too hard on him. He said you narrowly avoided prosecution over an embezzlement you had no part in. He's just worried about you." Daniel met her gaze in a way that made her insides shiver afresh. "So am I. Is anyone likely to follow you here to try and make trouble?"

"I hope not." Not as long as she made her payments. Requiring her to make full restitution to her clients was the DA's way of making sure she wasn't in on the scheme with Bradford. Bad as taking out that loan was, it was still a lot better than prosecution and jail time. "Coldwater is a long way from Boston. I didn't exactly leave a trail of breadcrumbs."

"Yeah, but if anyone's looking for you, they'll check your hometown first."

"I don't know how they'd discover where it is." She'd done everything she could to distance herself from Coldwater Cove while she was back east. She used her college address when she set up her business. If her accent made people ask where she was originally from, she'd claim the Midwest. That was ambiguous enough to suggest Chicago. Other than the Windy City, no one from Boston seemed to believe there was any place of note between the Berkshires and the Pacific coast anyway.

"If you're worried about it, turn off the GPS on your phone and stay off the Internet. Oh, and you might need to drop by the *Gazette* to make sure Wanda isn't running a piece about your coming home," Daniel said. "We may be in the boonies, but the newspaper's online now, too, you know. Anyone can Google you."

"Yikes." He was right. Dealing with the O'Leary brothers had scared her. She'd been thinking of Coldwater Cove as a sort of do-it-yourself witness protection program. "I'll pop by the *Gazette* office first thing in the morning before Wanda plasters a piece about my prodigal return all over page one."

He chuckled again. Lacy got the sense that he hadn't done that much lately.

"I'll try to keep an eye out for out-of-state plates, but we can't monitor everything." Dan fished in his pocket and came up with a business card. He wrote something on the back of it and handed it to her. "If someone bothers you, if you even get a feeling that someone's watching you, call me."

"Thanks." She slipped the card into her pocket. He'd written down his personal number but she didn't know what weight to give that information.

"I'll always come if you call," he said. Then he reached across the countertop and covered her hand with his. Sparks flew up her arm like a welder's arc. "I'm glad you're back in Coldwater, Lacy."

She'd come home because of a mistake. She'd never intended to be here again for more than the occasional fly-by on holidays. Hiding out in this small town was so not how she saw her life unfolding. But when she looked at Daniel, she realized that maybe this was her chance to have a do-over, to take that road she'd passed by before.

She evidently had a wicked little who-cares-if-he-is-married part of her heart. She probably needed to stomp that bit of her into submission lest she end up on the Methodist prayer chain again.

But what surprised her most was that part of her—maybe it was that wicked part—was glad she was back in Coldwater Cove, too.

Chapter 5

The trick to maintaining a beneficial relationship with one's
human is to never let on how much one needs the silly thing.

—What Effie the Disdainful means when she
makes that *"meh-eh-eh-*ing" sound

A solid knock on the door startled Lacy and made her yank
her hand away from Daniel. Guilt constricted her chest. She
glanced heavenward.

I haven't done anything wrong. Honest. I only thought about it.

But the knock at the door had broken the spell and Daniel
was putting on his hat again, adjusting the brim low over his
forehead. She wondered if places like Coldwater Cove had
their own thought police for the ethically challenged. If so,
she'd been well and truly busted.

"Lacy, it's me."

The voice on the other side of the door belonged to Jacob
Tyler. Feeling silly at the way her heart rate had shot up when
Daniel touched her, she breathed a sigh of relief that she'd
been spared from making a fool of herself over it and hurried
to let Jake in. She'd never have believed it, but she now considered the heartthrob of Coldwater Cove High completely
"safe."

At least compared to the married guy in her kitchen.

"Glad to see the stairs aren't a problem for you." *Lacy, you*
idiot. Could you be any more insensitive? If there'd been a way to

shove the words back into her mouth, she'd have done it, even if she choked on them.

He didn't seem to take offense. "I'm a little slower on them, but since my knee joint is still intact, I manage. In fact, my place is above the grill so I do stairs all the time."

Arms full, Jake moved past her into the small kitchen. A savory scent with a hint of garlic streamed in with him.

"Figured you wouldn't have time to cook." He found an empty place to set the insulated catering bag on her counter. Then he looked pointedly at Daniel. "Didn't expect to see you here, officer."

Officer? Daniel and Jake had been inseparable in high school, and they'd been friendly enough to each other in the Green Apple the other day. Neither of them looked especially friendly now. If they'd been dogs, both their ruffs would be straight up.

"I was just leaving." Daniel paused at the door. "Remember what I said, Lacy."

She patted the pocket where his card rested. "I'll remember."

As long as he's still wearing that ring, God help me to forget.

"Lester's back in town," Jake said without glancing Daniel's way. "Thought you'd want to know."

"Why? He's nothing to me."

Daniel and his dad had been estranged before she'd left for Boston, but she'd hoped after all this time, Daniel had made peace with the old man. For his own sake. "He's still your father."

"No, he's my sperm donor," Dan said curtly. "I don't have a father."

Once the door closed behind Daniel, Jake made a low noise deep in his throat. She couldn't decide whether it was a grunt of satisfaction or disgust.

"Meat loaf okay with you?" he asked.

Based solely on the heavenly aroma, Lacy suspected Jake's meat loaf was good enough to serve at a state dinner at the White House.

"More than okay. You brought enough for you, too, didn't you?" She took a couple of plates from the cabinet. The used Bruins mugs seemed to be the only survivors in the cup box, so she opened the box marked "glassware" and fished out two heavy Coke tumblers. She filled the glasses with water from the tap.

Her friend Shannon in Boston would have been embarrassed to offer a man who'd brought her meat loaf nothing but tap water, but Lacy felt no shame. Coldwater Cove didn't get its name for nothing. The artesian wells that served the town went deep. Even unfiltered, it was the best water Lacy had ever tasted.

"Yeah, there's enough for two," Jake said. "And blueberry cobbler with homemade walnut ice cream for dessert."

Jacob put the sweets in the fridge. Then he unpacked garlic mashed potatoes, fried okra, and fresh rolls. Judging from the yeasty, buttery smell, those rolls hadn't popped out of a can of refrigerated dough.

"When did you become Martha Stewart?" Lacy asked as she surveyed the feast.

"Martha?" Jake arched a dark brow at her. "Please. Emeril, maybe, but not Martha. Think we can do a little better than water, too."

He pulled out a bottle of merlot.

"Planning on getting me drunk and having your way with me, I see," Lacy said with a laugh.

"Let me know if it starts working." As if he was serving at a church potluck, he dished out heavy-handed portions for both of them.

By this time, Lacy had completely forgotten about the cat,

but Effie was evidently tired of being ignored. She leaped up onto the bar stool in the light-footed way of felines.

"Careful!"

"Of what?" Jake popped the cork and rummaged in her cabinets, looking for wineglasses. She hadn't found the box holding them yet. He settled for a couple of juice tumblers. "It's just a cat."

"Just an attack cat. After the way she mauled the movers, I'm in no mood to be trusting."

Then Effie began making a new noise, one Lacy had never heard from her—a loud, rumbling purr. The cat jumped down from the stool and twined sinuously between Jake's legs, rubbing both his muscular calf and the titanium with equal fervor. Finally, she groveled on the hardwood before him until he bent over and scratched her exposed belly. The cat writhed in pleasure.

"Effie, you little slut. You made a liar out of me," Lacy said. "She normally doesn't like anyone."

Jacob shrugged. "Seems to like me well enough."

"Guess she found her person," Lacy said. "Evidently, your charm works on females of all species."

He grinned up at her while he gave Effie a final long stroke. "Does this mean you'll let me rub your belly, too?"

Lacy punched his shoulder, sure he was kidding. They were just friends now. She carried the plates to her little bistro table. Jake moved the unpacked boxes off the top so she could set them down.

"This way we can see each other," he explained.

That was okay. Jake was easy on the eyes. As long as they kept things casual, she was all for spending time with Jacob Tyler.

Anything else was a proven hazard to a girl's heart.

The food was as good as its aroma promised. "Honestly, Jake, I never knew you could cook like this."

He flashed that ever-ready dimple. "Neither did I. But after I came home from Afghanistan, I had to figure out something to do pretty fast. I had a little put by and the Green Apple was for sale."

"And you figured, 'How hard could it be to burn a burger or two?'"

He swallowed a bite of meat loaf. "Something like that."

"But why here? Why come back to Coldwater?"

"Why not? It's home."

"Actually, I'm feeling a little homesick for Boston." *At least, the pre–Bradford Endicott Boston.*

"What would you be doing tonight if you were still there?" Jake asked.

"My friend Shannon and I might meet for drinks after work." Shannon Keane had been a student at the same institute where Lacy had studied design. Majoring in fashion, Shannon could not only draw beautiful clothes, she was a wiz with scissors and a sewing machine. Lacy could thank Shannon for most of the pretty things that would soon find their new home in her tiny closet.

"Do you think there are no bars in Coldwater?" Jake asked.

"I'm sure there are." The place she and Shannon favored was sleek and trendy, all chrome and polished wood. The tables in the Coldwater Cove bars were probably covered with red-checked cloths. The walls would most likely be bristling with dead heads, antlers, and large-mouth bass. But Lacy decided it wouldn't be polite to share her citified opinions about rustic décor. Jake might take offense. After all, the Green Apple Grill would never make the pages of *Architectural Digest* either.

"Then maybe after drinks," she went on, "my friend and I would go clubbing or take in a movie."

"The Regal's still in business here."

"I noticed," she said. "They're playing a movie I saw six months ago."

He shrugged. "We're a little slow out of the gate, but the movie hasn't changed because we wait for it a bit. And I'll put the Regal's popcorn up against anyone's."

"Granted. But I'm willing to bet any amount of money that Coldwater doesn't have a club scene," she said.

"You've got me there. The best we can do is the local big band. If you like to dance, it's playing over at the Opera House tonight."

"Are you asking me to go dancing?" Then she remembered his leg and felt all the blood rush to her cheeks in embarrassment. "Oh, Jake, I . . . I didn't mean . . . I forgot."

He shook his head. "It's OK. I haven't tried to dance since the injury, but that doesn't mean I can't. You don't have to walk on eggshells around me. I'm glad you forgot about my leg for a bit. It helps me forget about it, too."

She reached across the table and patted his forearm. Its musculature was rock hard. "Thanks. I shouldn't bore you by whining about Boston. I don't mean to be a pain."

"You aren't. I asked, remember."

"Well, then if it's any consolation, the next thing Shannon and I would probably do is wonder where all the good men are."

He grinned at that. Lacy had to admit that any town that could boast guys like Jake and Daniel was blessed in the man department.

"So you're saying your love life in New England was not what you were used to?" Something about his expression said he'd be more than a little glad if he was right about that.

Unfortunately, he was.

"Not even close." Bradford constantly nagged her to tone down her accent. And her opinions. But he'd dazzled her by dangling the promise of his grandmother's five-carat Harry

Winston. The thought that she might marry into an old-money family and have her rustic roots covered by the thick coat of Endicott sophistication was seductive stuff.

Not anymore.

She'd left Coldwater to stand on her own. It was probably a good thing she and Bradford never tied the knot. She'd have been assimilated into the Endicott fold and lost her uniqueness just as thoroughly as if she'd stayed in Coldwater.

"Guess the Baystate boys didn't appreciate my brand of Ozark snark," she admitted.

"Go figure."

"But at least I had the career I was born for and the excitement of the city." She glanced at Effie. The cat had claimed the stuffed chair, where she could make blinky eyes at Jake from across the room. With her front paws tucked under her, she looked like a furry loaf of bread with a cat head. "Now at the end of the day, all I have to look forward to is a bad-tempered cat."

Jake's mouth opened and shut as if he'd considered saying something and then thought better of it. "You still need to finish arranging your new place. Want some help with that?"

"No, that's OK. I'm kind of particular about where things go." Besides, she needed something to keep her busy while she figured out what to do next. "My folks volunteered to help me move in, but I nixed that pretty quickly. Dad doesn't need to do that much lifting and going up and down those metal steps repeatedly would not do his knees any favors."

It occurred to her that her dad's legs were in better shape that Jake's, but he didn't react to what she'd said. *Dang, will I ever stop putting my foot in my mouth?*

"Then there's my mom," she chattered on, anxious to quickly put any mention of men's legs behind her. "She'd be horrified at the paltry number of 'accessories' I own. She'd be over here with a trunk full of throw pillows before I could stop her."

Jake refilled both their wineglasses. Lacy didn't remember emptying hers, but she must have. Wine usually relaxed her. Ordinarily, she'd be asleep under the table in short order.

Instead she felt all fidgety inside, as if her thoughts were running in a hundred different directions.

"I'm a fan of uncluttered countertops myself," he said. "More room to work."

"Absolutely. Bare essentials, that's me. A coffeemaker and a toaster near an outlet is all I need left out, and if I can find a way to hide them while keeping them easy to reach, I do it," she said. "Everything else has its place in a drawer. No dust-catchers, please."

"What?" he said with raised brow. "No collection of tea-pots along the top of the cabinets?"

"I have a cat who treats that space like her personal board-walk. Can you imagine what Effie would do to anything I put in her way?" Lacy said. "Besides, a Warhol is all the decora-tion any kitchen needs."

She'd already pounded a nail into the wall and centered her copy of the iconic print of a Campbell's soup can above the sink.

"The rest of my apartment will be similarly spare once I clear out all the boxes." She polished off the last of her fried okra. That was something she couldn't get in Boston. She'd missed the distinctive dish. "Once Mom sees the place, she'll bring over an armful of her precious 'knickknacks and scarci-ties' trying to fill my blank spaces. She finds my style 'empty.'" Lacy sighed. "I'll have to fight to keep it that way."

"Emptiness can be restful."

She cocked her head at Jake. It was unusual for anyone else to get that until she showed them how it worked in her designs. "A blank space in a room is like a rest in a piece of music. It's a pause, a slice of silence. It lets the mind take in what surrounds it."

"Bet you figured that out when you were in the school band." He chuckled. "As I recall, the slices of silence were the best part of pep band."

She gave his forearm a smack.

"Hey, I'm agreeing with you. In a slightly unusual way." He raised his hands in mock surrender. "Too much stuff makes a place feel tight. Like there's no room to breathe."

So he did get it.

"Guess we're more alike than I thought, then," she told him. "I cull my stuff each spring. It's the only way to make sure I own my things instead of them owning me. The one exception I make is for books. There can never be too many."

She picked up both their empty plates and carried them to the kitchen. Then she dished up the blackberry cobbler, and put the bowls into the microwave to warm.

"I thought the built-in shelves would handle my collection," she rattled on, "but judging from the number of boxes marked 'books,' I'm probably going to have to buy another shelving unit and squeeze it into the bedroom somehow."

The microwave dinged. She took out the cobblers and scooped some of Jake's homemade ice cream on them. It looked and smelled like heaven in a bowl.

"I'm talking too much," she said as she carried their desserts back to the table. "Silence is restful, too."

"That's okay." Jake shrugged. "I like listening to you. Besides, if someone starts doing an imitation of a windup monkey, it's best to let them wind down on their own."

"A windup monkey!"

"Yeah, you know." He made motions in front of himself as if he were clanging a pair of cymbals. "A windup monkey.

You obviously have something you want to talk about, but you're not sure how to start. Instead of asking what's really on your mind, I figured I'd let you go on about whatever you want till you wear yourself down. Eventually, you'll come out with it."

Lacy straightened her spine, bristling. "What's really on my mind is that I don't like being called a windup monkey."

"Look, most guys who get wounded tend to suffer in silence, but every now and then when I was in the hospital, a jarhead would start blabbing a blue streak about everything and nothing—anything to keep from talking about what was really eating him." Jake scooped up a bite of dessert and then went on. "I'm just saying that stress is stress whether you get it on a battlefield or in a boardroom. You need a way to get rid of it. I didn't mean to tick you off, Lace."

But he had.

Mostly because he was right. She wanted to talk to someone about a lot of things—about how she felt about losing her beautiful Back Bay shop, about Bradford's betrayal, about Daniel and his on-again, off-again marriage, about how she was ever going to pay back that awful loan, and most especially, what would she ever find to do with herself in Coldwater Cove? Her list of challenges was overwhelming. But she couldn't tell him about any of that.

Life in Boston had taught her not to trust anyone, men in particular. Opening her heart was an invitation for it to be stomped on. She could only rely on herself.

"I hate to eat and ask you to run," she said, "but please finish your dessert. I have so much to do here and I'm the only one who can do it. I need to get back to work."

"Really? Is that how they do it in Boston?"

"Do what?"

"Dump unwanted dinner dates."

"Jake, it's not like that." And since when did this become a date? "But you're right. I do have a lot to deal with right now. I just can't talk to you about it."

"How about Danny?" Jake pushed away his nearly untouched cobbler. "Is he the one you can talk to?"

"No. They're my problems. I'll deal with them on my own without help from either of you," she said, upset that he was making her feel defensive when she'd done nothing wrong. "But you have to admit you've got a reputation for having the attention span of a gnat when it comes to relationships. Have you forgotten that, of the two of you, you're the one who is the player?"

"*Was* the player. I haven't been that guy for a long time." Jake rose and headed for the door with a seemingly lovesick Effie meowing after him. He stopped at the threshold. "Just remember one thing, Lace. People change. Danny Scott is the one with another woman on the string now."

The door banged shut behind him. Lashing herself with her long tail, Effie scowled at Lacy.

"Give it a rest, cat. Jake leaves all the girls sooner or later. Don't think for a skinny minute that you're any different."

Chapter 6

Why watch reality TV when I can work at the Green Apple?
There's a whole lot more "reality" going on at the grill
and it smells a good sight better than any TV show!

—Ethel Ringwald, waitress who's liberal with
both dessert portions and advice

"You were the best cub reporter I ever had, so I'm guessing you remember the drill. Your main focus will be writing general interest stories. You'll cover school activities, the Rotary Club, town council meetings, that kind of crap." Wanda Cruikshank, publisher, editor and Coldwater Cove media maven, stopped rattling off Lacy's proposed list of assignments long enough to blow a long stream of smoke at her office's dingy ceiling. Wanda was rail thin with leathery skin, a testimony to too much time in a tanning booth frying her outsides while too many Marlboros crisped up her insides.

Knowing how ridiculously easy it was to make the front page of the *Gazette,* Lacy had dropped by to make sure Wanda didn't run a piece about her return to Coldwater Cove. Somehow, the conversation had turned into an interview for the open reporter position.

"What about the crime beat?" Lacy asked, wondering if the job would put her in contact with Daniel too often for her comfort. He had promised to come if she called, but separated was still married. She wasn't going to mess with that.

No matter that Jacob Tyler thinks I will.

"The sheriff's office sends over their blotter, you know,

tickets, fines, and whatnot. We print them on page four once a week, but we don't generally do anything more with it." Wanda ran a hand through her impossibly dark hair. Sure enough, a thin strip of silver glinted in her part. "Our readers don't want hard news. They want feel-good stuff. If they want to be depressed, they can always watch CNN."

"Well, at least there's a bit of local politics in the council meetings," Lacy said. That qualified as hard news. It provided a sop to her conscience and might help her when Uncle Roy, the real journalist in the family, came down from Des Moines for a visit and demanded to know why she was selling out by writing for a small-town paper. "Can I do a design column?"

"Fine, kid. Go with that. Just remember who sells furniture and paint in this town and where they spend their advertising dollars. No directing *Gazette* readers to some dot-com site." Wanda smiled at her as if she were a not-too-bright child. "I'm sure you'll get the hang of it."

Then she offered Lacy a salary that would be an insult in Boston, but was considered a living wage in Coldwater Cove. It would keep body and soul together.

So long as she didn't mind renting out her soul from time to time.

"I'd liked to use a pen name for my byline," Lacy said, remembering Daniel's warning about someone Googling her. She explained—off the record, of course, and as cryptically as possible—about her unsettling business in Boston and the need to keep a low online profile.

"OK, but the pen name needs to be something locals will still get. Gazette readers like to feel they've got the inside track about town. What's your middle name?"

Oh, no. Anything but that.

Hand-me-down family names were a good way to remember someone special. Lacy understood that, but unfortunately, her dad had been really attached to his maiden great-aunt on his mother's side.

"Dorie," she admitted.

"Dorie it is, then. And your mom was a Higginbottom, wasn't she? We'll use Dorie Higginbottom for your byline."

She sighed. Her mom always claimed the best thing about marrying Lacy's father was getting to change her name to something as ordinary as Evans. Her dad liked to joke that if his last name had been Filpot he'd have never caught her.

"Oh, you'll be in charge of the 'Ago' columns, too," Wanda added.

"'Ago' columns?"

"Yeah, people like them a lot. Every Friday we run articles from past editions of the *Gazette*—you know, a hundred years ago, seventy-five years ago, fifty, and so on. Gives the historical flavor of the area."

I bet even a hundred years ago "a good time was had by all."

"Are back editions archived online?"

"You wish. Only starting about three years back. We got hooked up with that cloud thingy then. Before that, the *Gazette* is stored on microfiche and for the really old copies, there are paper files in the dungeon." Wanda meant the musty basement.

Words seldom failed Lacy. A few choice ones came to mind now—archaic, obsolete, and downright Paleolithic. But she couldn't say them out loud if she intended to take the job. She thought about her looming loan payment and swallowed hard.

"When do you want me to start?"

"Right now. A few things may be different since you were here last. Let me give you the nickel tour." Wanda shooed her out of her office.

The *Gazette* was housed in a limestone brick structure,

circa 1890. The ceilings were high and trimmed with dark oak crown moldings, a remnant of Victorian charm. The office was located near the Opera House. Lead glass windows on two sides allowed in a good amount of light. Unfortunately, sometime in the '70s, Wanda had done a remodel. She knocked down most of the interior walls except the ones that formed her office, and left the relic of a water closet untouched. Unfortunately, that room really could have benefited from a wrecking ball.

"This, if you'll remember," Wanda said grandly as she swept around a space that was chopped into sad cubicles by half walls upholstered in beige fabric, "is what we like to call the 'bullpen.' That's Georgina. She's our office manager. See her about setting up direct deposit and filling out your tax stuff."

Georgina looked up from filing her nails and shot them a toothy grin. When she said hi, Lacy recognized her voice as the same Georgina who'd been gossiping with Heather Walker in the graveyard on Lacy's first day back. Adorned with an eyebrow ring and an improbable pink streak in her hair, she must have been in middle school when Lacy graduated.

Knocking on thirty suddenly felt old.

"Deek here is our resident geek." The gangly fellow flinched when Wanda clapped a palm on his shoulder. "He takes care of the office network and manages our online *Gazette*."

"Lacy Evans." She offered him her hand.

From behind thick spectacles, he stared at her fingers for a few blinks but didn't move to shake them.

"The human hand is home to one hundred and eighty-two different types of bacteria." His voice crackled, the last gasp of a puberty that had gone on for too long and with too little positive effect. "And that's if it's a healthy hand."

"Oh, er, good point." Lacy resisted the urge to rub her undoubtedly germ-laden palm on her skirt.

Wanda continued the introductions. "You remember Marjorie Chubb."

Lacy nodded. The Iron Lady, so called for her iron-gray hair, had been in charge of the *Gazette*'s classifieds since the Flood.

"Besides doing the classifieds, I'm also the captain of the Methodist prayer chain, so I hear about everything that's important. If you ever need an idea for a story . . ." Marjorie laid a finger aside of her nose in the time-honored gesture of collusion.

Deliver me, O Lord, from the Methodist prayer chain, Lacy prayed silently and with fervor.

In the cube next to Marjorie was Tiffany Braden.

Of the well-landed Bradens.

She'd been behind Lacy in school by a couple of years. The pulled-together young woman was dressed in a tailored navy pantsuit. Compared to Tiffany, the rest of the staff seemed to have confused the concept of business casual with "business rumpled." A degree in something from Bates College hung in Tiffany's cube on the half wall.

Coldwater Cove was proud to be the home of the tiny private school with a reputation for academic excellence. Of course, some folks equated excellence with snootiness, but the Bates College crowd didn't care. Aside from its liberal arts emphasis while the rest of the world was going tech-happy, Bates offered degrees in a handful of obscure disciplines. Its graduates were pretty much guaranteed *not* to land a job in their field of study.

Her sister, Crystal, had stayed in Coldwater to earn her degree in medieval poetry before going on to become the dean of admissions for the college. What an exhaustive knowledge of Chaucer had to do with sorting through admission applications was a mystery, but Crystal made it work, as she did everything, perfectly.

Tiffany Braden might not be using her bachelor of arts in sock puppetry or whatever it was she'd studied, but she must have learned something.

"Tiff's our rainmaker here at the *Gazette*," Wanda told Lacy with undisguised pleasure. The young Ms. Braden sold advertising space to unsuspecting merchants in town and did it well. Lacy guessed that her Braden family connections had more to do with her sales than her degree from Bates.

"And here's you." Wanda steered Lacy into the cubicle in the corner, which had a decent window looking out on the Square and another with a view across the side street. Unfortunately, the Secondhand Junk-shun occupied most of that view. The shop full of dubious treasures was her mom's delight and the bane of her dad's existence.

Lacy checked her watch. "I really didn't expect a job offer today. The cable guy is coming by my place at three," she told her new boss.

The Internet that came with the TV package was her main interest. She intended to stay off social sites, but that didn't mean she couldn't keep up with things in Boston by lurking. However, if a strange person was going to enter her apartment at three o'clock, she needed to get there a little earlier to make sure her attack cat was securely shut up in the laundry.

Her Highness, Effie the Snarling, had been presented with a can of tuna last night after Jake left, but the cat didn't strain herself by showing any gratitude. Being the feline queen meant she wasn't required to acknowledge Lacy's existence other than as a food delivery system.

Evidently, primo albacore served on a Melmac plate was no more than her due.

"Get yourself squared away in your new place, then," Wanda said. "Stay as long as you can today to get acquainted with how we do things. We'll talk about deadlines tomorrow."

Lacy didn't feel guilty about leaving early. Sometime soon, she'd have to stay late. The previous occupant of her cube had left enough rubbish and files in the drawers and cubbies to fill a couple of big trash bags. After waiting a full five minutes for the tired desktop to boot, she decided to bring in her own laptop to sign in to the *Gazette*'s system tomorrow. Then with a bit of reluctant help from Deek, which he'd undoubtedly make sure involved no physical contact whatsoever, she'd set up her passwords and poke around the network.

The place smelled of ink and newsprint. Lacy inhaled the scent clear to her toes. She had expected to feel as if she were going backward by working at the *Gazette,* but surprisingly enough, there was a freshness about it instead.

Of course, that might have been because Wanda limited her smoking to her office. She kept the door closed so as to capture and enjoy the full benefit of her cigs for herself.

The office hummed, a low clatter of clicking keys as the people around her pounded out their work or at least mimicked the appearance of industry. Lacy started to feel as if she was where she should be. For now, at least.

Then she heard the whispers.

"I'm telling you, he's moving out of the house today."

Lacy leaned toward the voices, then stopped herself. *Dang! Shades of the cemetery.* She was getting to be a world-class snoop.

"Why? It's not like he has to share it with her."

Lacy suspected Georgina and Tiffany were the whisperers. She couldn't imagine Deek caring enough about another germy-handed human to indulge in gossip, and matronly Marjorie wasn't the sort who would stoop to it unless it was in conjunction with the prayer chain.

"I heard a rumor about why she left him. It explains why he's moving out of the house, too."

No names were mentioned, but Lacy wondered if they were talking about Daniel and his wife. He hadn't said anything about moving when he'd stopped by her place. She quit trying to straighten her desktop and pushed her chair closer to the beige cubical wall so she wouldn't miss anything.

Hey! I'm sort of a journalist. We're supposed to be nosy.

"I heard he lost the house in a poker game."

"Nooo."

"I wouldn't bet against it."

One of the pair—Lacy couldn't say which for certain—tittered over the lame wordplay. If Lacy were a gambler, her money would be on Georgina as the giggler. Upon hearing the laughter, Wanda, sensing not everyone's nose was being ground to nubbins on their grindstones, burst out of her office like an avenging angel.

"Am I the only one around here with a deadline?" she bellowed. "Back to work."

Lacy tried to focus on her desk again. Surely the gossips were wrong. She'd never known Daniel to gamble. Heck, he never even bought a lottery ticket. He was the poster boy for the straight-arrow type.

Or at least he had been.

People change.

"Thank you for that update, Jake Tyler. Now get out of my head," she muttered under her breath.

Her cell phone rang. It was her friend Shannon Keane from back in Beantown.

"Are you OK, Lacy?" she asked, concern making her Boston accent even thicker than usual. There was no trace of the *r* sound in her "are" at all. "There really is a place called Coldwater Cove?"

"Yeah, and it's really in Oklahoma. You know. One of those *I* and *O* states. I haven't fallen into some giant mid-continental sinkhole," Lacy said with a laugh. A soft one. She didn't want Wanda popping out of her office like a deranged jack-in-the-box again.

They talked about everything and nothing for a few minutes, and then Shannon got to the meat of her call.

"Deputy DA Hopkins came by today asking if I knew how to get in touch with you."

Lacy had changed her cell number and carrier before she'd left Boston in case someone decided to trace her with the old one. Only Shannon had her new number. "Hopkins? Doesn't ring a bell. Why did he want to talk to me?"

"He wouldn't say. I hope it means Belize is shipping back that waste-of-skin Bradford Endicott."

"I won't hold my breath."

"You better, girlfriend. Even though you did what you could to make restitution, there are still people around here who are mad enough to want someone convicted—deal or no deal. I hear Bradford's family is putting pressure on the DA to take the heat off their precious little scoundrel so he can come home without a warrant hanging over his head."

Lacy glanced out her window in time to see Jake entering Secondhand Junk-shun, bearing a taped-up cardboard box. Her conscience pricked her. He'd been nice enough to bring her supper and she'd practically thrown him out on his ear. It didn't matter how stressed-out she was—she was better than that.

"Did you hear me, Lacy?"

Shannon's voice made her jerk the phone back to her ear. "Yeah. No one named Hopkins was assigned to my case. Or Bradford's."

"Well, anyway, I told him I didn't know how to reach you," Shannon said. "Hey, you should be proud of me. I'm not even using my own phone to call you now."

"Good." Her dad's suggestion that Bradford might have fallen afoul of the Irish mob had stuck with her. "I'll wire you the first payment later this week. Be careful when you deliver it."

"No worries here. I'll be in and out before they know I'm there. Besides, nobody's gonna mess with me," Shannon assured her. "I know how to use a pair of shears."

That made Lacy laugh out loud.

Wanda's door swung open.

"Gotta go," Lacy said. "I'll call you soon."

She hit the button to end the conversation and stood before Wanda got up another full head of steam. "I'm heading out to visit some merchants to get ideas for that design column."

Wanda swallowed the reprimand she'd obviously planned and beamed her approval instead. "I knew you'd catch on quick. Let Tiffany know which shops you're going to mention in your article and she can hit them up for some ads to run alongside the piece."

Lacy nodded and headed out the door. She seriously doubted she'd find anything in the Junk-shun worth a single line. Even a line in a paper as fluffy as the *Gazette*.

But she seriously hoped she'd find Jake still there.

Chapter 7

One man's trash is another man's treasure.
Good thing. Otherwise, I'd be out of business.

—Phyllis Wannamaker, owner of Secondhand Junk-shun

Jacob carried the box of Fiestaware to the booth his mother rented in the back corner of Secondhand Junk-shun. He'd offered to put up a few shelves in the Green Apple for her more than once. If she sold her items there, she'd be able to save the rent, but his mom was determined to keep her booth in the junk shop.

Since his dad passed last year, his mom had been adamant about pulling her own weight and not leaning on her kids. Selling stuff in the Junk-shun was a relatively painless way to do it. His mother had inherited the household goods of both his grandmothers and three great-aunts to boot. Her supply of vintage glassware, derelict appliances, and aging furniture was nearly endless.

As he unpacked the box, the soft click of boot heels on the old hardwood and a familiar voice came from behind him.

"Hey, Jake."

Jake turned to see Lacy Evans smiling up at him as if she hadn't smacked him down big time last night. She was looking mighty hot in a flirty skirt, a sweater that hugged her curves, and a pair of bright pink cowboy boots. He grinned down at her feet. "Nice to see you can't take the country out of the girl."

She extended one cute little booted foot. "Mom brought these over this morning. I'd left them here when I moved east. Looks like they still fit. Besides, what else would I wear in Coldwater? Prada?"

When he was in Helmand province, all he could think about was getting back home to Coldwater Cove. Why did she have to give the town a back-handed slap every chance she got?

"Well, shucks, ma'am." Jake exaggerated his accent for effect. "What would a country boy like me know about shoes? You're lucky I'm wearin' any at all. We don't as a rule here in the sticks less'n we're going to meetin' on Sundays."

"Funny." She smirked and stuck out her tongue. "You know what I mean. I didn't want to look out of place when I was in Boston. I want to blend in here just as much."

"Never figured you for the blending type," he said as he unwrapped another soup bowl. "You lit out of Coldwater so quick the fall after graduation, it was like you couldn't wait to stand out."

"Yeah, I did, but what can I say? I've learned life's easier when you fit in."

Jake shrugged. With his stump and metal leg, in some ways he'd never fit in again.

"I didn't expect to bump into you away from the Green Apple like this," she said.

"I'm not chained to the grill, and anyway, Arthur still comes in to cook on Thursdays."

When Jake had bought the Green Apple from Arthur Quackenbush, part of the deal was that the wiry old fellow could come in and man the grill once a week for as long as he felt like doing it. Arthur had been cooking at the Green Apple since he'd opened it back in 1958. He wanted to keep his hand in the business and, Jake suspected, make sure the new owner knew his butt from a hole in the ground.

Even after Jake passed muster, Arthur continued to come in. If he burned a few things now and again, old timers and regulars still loved to see him there. Jake had added a number of new dishes to the list of options that were a mystery to Arthur. So the grill had a special, limited "Quackenbush Menu" on Thursdays.

"Oh. Well, it's good you have some time off," Lacy said. "You need a day of rest."

"Is that what you think this is?" he said as he continued to unload his mother's latest offerings. "Thursday usually turns into my day to finish all the things I didn't get done the week before. I didn't expect to run into . . ." He stopped himself before he said "a fancy-ass designer." If she didn't like being compared to a windup monkey, she'd really be insulted if he called her that. ". . . Into someone like you in a place called 'the Junk-shun' either."

"What do you mean by someone like me?"

"Don't get all touchy." So what was she doing there? Had she come into the Secondhand Junk-shun looking for him? If so, that meant he hadn't completely lost his touch where women were concerned. Something in his chest swelled a bit at the possibility. "I just meant I didn't think you were into antiques."

"You're right. I'm usually not unless they're European and a good deal older than anything here," Lacy admitted. She picked up one of the soup bowls he'd set out on the shelves he'd built for his mom. Lacy inspected the piece, turning it this way and that. "Very mid-century modern."

"Hmm. I'm sure that impresses the heck out of folks in Boston. Around here we just call them old bowls."

She rolled her eyes at him. He'd forgotten how blue they were. Then she turned her gaze to the red soup bowl in her hands again. The piece had little ceramic handles and what appeared to be a hand-turned foot on the bottom. "This Fiestaware is in terrific shape. Great color and near mint condition."

He nodded. "I like the blue one."

"You mean cobalt."

"Uh?"

"That's the name of the color. I'm partial to the chartreuse myself."

Jake frowned at the bowls. "I'm not color-blind, so I must be color-ignorant. Which one is that?"

"The green one, of course."

"Oh. Cobalt. Chartreuse. What do you call that one?" He pointed to the one she had in her hands.

She blinked slowly at him. "Red. What do you call it?"

He decided not to chance asking what she'd call the yellow bowl. It could act as camouflage for French's mustard. The only thing he evidently knew about colors was which ones he liked. The blue of Lacy's eyes sprang to mind, but he figured he'd better change the subject. He was hopelessly behind when it came to colors.

"Blame the bowls' good condition on my memaw Tyler. She didn't believe in dishwashers."

"How much are you asking for this set?"

"Not me. My mom. This is her booth. I'm just the gofer on Thursdays," Jake said as he wadded up the newspaper the crockery had been wrapped in and stuffed it back in the box. "She wants ten dollars a bowl."

"Ten dollars a bowl!"

"I imagine she'll take less for each if someone buys the lot."

Lacy's brows drew together as she studied the bowls. "I'll have to do some research, but I'm pretty sure she's underpricing her stuff. By quite a bit."

"Maybe if we were in Boston," Jake allowed. "In Coldwater, I bet everybody and his brother has this sort of thing in their attic."

"I won't take that bet." She chuckled and put the red bowl down next to the green one.

Nope, make that chartreuse.

"But since you brought up betting," she said, "have you heard that Danny Scott lost his house in a poker game?"

She was only after the straight skinny on Scott. Jake had started to feel more like his old self when he'd thought she might have come looking for him. That puffed-up something inside him deflated like a popped balloon. "Yeah, I heard about it."

"Is it true?"

He nodded. "It's why Anne left him."

"I don't understand. Daniel never had a gambling problem."

"Maybe he never used to," Jake said, "and I know you don't want to hear it, but a lot of things have changed since you left."

Like me not being with a woman since Afghanistan. Little things like that.

"You're right," she said. "You were right last night, too. I guess I've changed as well. Otherwise, I never would have been so rude to you. I'm sorry, Jake."

"No need to apologize." But he was glad she had. "You've been dealing with some pretty serious shi—"

He stopped himself short. He wasn't talking to a bunch of foul-mouthed jarheads. He was talking to the girl he hoped to impress with how much he'd changed for the better, titanium leg and all.

"Some serious stuff," he amended. "Just moving across country is enough to put most folks on edge."

Then the latent player in Jake recognized that if she felt the need to apologize, he had an advantage, if for only a moment. "But if you're really sorry, there is a way you can make it up to me."

"How?" She arched a suspicious brow.

"I'm supposed to open up the family lake house this afternoon. It's easier to do with two pairs of hands. There'll be time to do some fishing once we're done. And if we don't catch anything, I'll grill us some steaks." He flashed his best smile. It had rarely failed him. "Wanna come?"

"I can't." She glanced at her watch. "The cable guy is coming to my place in a bit and I have to be on hand to protect him from Effie."

Jake chuckled. "Poor misunderstood cat."

"You want her?"

He shook his head. "I'm really more of a dog person."

"Effie has that effect on people."

Jake prided himself on never hearing the first no when he asked a woman out. This was only strike one. "How about next Thursday? I can push opening up the house till then. My family doesn't really like to use the place until the weather heats up."

Spring-fed Lake Jewel lived up to the town's name. Until the air temperature hit the 90s and stayed there, swimming in the cold lake was only for the stout of heart.

And numb of backside.

"I don't know if I'll be off next Thursday," Lacy said. "I've got a job now."

When she told him she'd taken the position at the *Gazette,* he bit back a grin. Then he restrained himself from reminding her that he'd suggested that very thing on her first day home. He didn't think she'd appreciate either reaction.

Anyway, that was strike two as far as asking out Lacy went.

May as well go down swinging.

"Well, let me know when your day off is and I'll see if I can get Arthur to switch and cover for me at the grill then."

"OK. I'll find out tomorrow and let you know. I haven't been to the lake in ages. It'll be fun," Lacy said. "I'll check on that Fiestaware, too. I'd hate to see your mom get cheated on it."

Home run! He'd scored on asking her out. Whether he'd actually make if to first base with her while they were at the lake was another at bat completely.

"I'll pack my spare tackle box and rod," he promised. As she walked away, he imagined what she'd look like in a swim-suit. Too bad the lake was still far too cold to think about taking a dip, skinny or otherwise, yet. If he was lucky, maybe she'd wear a pair of shorts. . . .

"Oh, and Jake, just so you know"—Lacy stopped and turned back to him—"the women in my family may catch fish. We've even been known to whip up some beer batter and fry them on occasion, but we do *not* clean them. Not ever. It's a rule."

Jake smiled as he watched her walk away. He could live with rules like that.

Chapter 8

*Watching someone you love continue to destroy your
life together is like being stuck on a runaway roller coaster.
You thought the ride was going to be a thrill when
it started, but after a while, all you want is off.*

—Anne Littlefield Scott, mother of Carson forever.
Wife of Daniel, for now.

Dan shifted his weight from one foot to the other in front of
the screen door. His mother-in-law, Celia Hatton, was in no
hurry to let him in.

"Carson is still down for his nap," she whispered, finally
flipping the hook that held the door shut and motioning for
him to enter. The scowl on her face was enough to stop most
men in their tracks.

It didn't matter. Daniel would walk through fire for his
boy. Even a smoke-belching she-dragon like Celia couldn't
burn him as much as his own conscience did.

"Is Anne here?" He closed the door behind himself as
softly as he could.

"She's over at Walmart," Celia said. "They called her back
for an interview. If she gets the job, she'll be working at the
jewelry counter." The woman made a *tsking* noise. "Lookin'
at all those pretty things every day and can't afford a one of
them."

Daniel's gut cramped. He didn't want his wife to work.
Not that she couldn't, of course. She'd been the county dispatcher when they'd first met and did a bang-up job of it, too.

But once Carson came along, they'd made the joint decision that one of them should stay home with him. Since Daniel made more money, Anne happily took baby duty.

Now it grated on his soul that she felt she had to leave their boy and return to a job. A man took care of his family, but after what had happened, Anne wasn't willing to take a chance on his being able to provide for them anymore. But no matter how he felt about it, he had to say something positive with his mother-in-law glaring at him.

"Walmart would be crazy not to hire her. She's so pretty, she'd be good for business."

Celia narrowed her eyes and pursed her thin lips. "If she had a husband who knew how to take care of business, she'd be better off at home taking care of her boy, 'specially while he's so young."

She could give stinging lessons to a wasp.

"*Our* boy," Daniel corrected. "He's mine, too, you know."

"I know well enough. Do you?" Celia said with a sniff. "Wish you'd a thought about Carson and Anne when it mighta made a difference."

Daniel did, too. With all his heart. Even now, he didn't know how he'd let that poker game get so out of hand. He'd never lost more than a hundred dollars in a single game before. But on this particular night, he'd been on a hot streak. Stu Barger had brought some of his frat brothers down from Tulsa with fat wallets and pitifully easy tells. Dan had been winning for hours. So when someone suggested they throw out the table limit and let fly, he was all in.

He'd been holding a terrific hand, one of the best he'd seen all night. Four of a kind was almost a sure thing. If he'd taken that hefty pot, it would have been enough to remodel the little house his grandmother had left him. They could have turned the unfinished attic space into a new third bedroom and maybe added a second bath. Anne had been wanting to try for another baby, but as things stood, the place had seemed too small to grow their family in.

His four queens had winked at him as he scribbled out the IOU for the deed to the bungalow on Crepe Myrtle Street. Daniel tossed it onto the center of the table, certain he'd be tearing it up again in a second.

Then Stu Barger had laid down a small straight flush.

Daniel lost his house that night. And so much more.

His mother-in-law's lips tightened into a hard line and her nose wrinkled as if she'd smelled a particularly ripe poop. "Sit down there and I'll see if my grandson is stirring."

He sank onto the chair she pointed to, the hard-backed straight one closest to the door. Even from the first, Celia had never thought much of him. She didn't believe he was worthy of her pretty daughter. Maybe she was right. Ever since middle school, Daniel had had to fight to rise above the stigma of being Lester Scott's son, the town drunk with an evil temper and heavy fists.

Now Daniel wasn't sure he was any better than his dad. After he'd lost the house he'd shared with Anne in that stupid poker game, Celia had good reason to be disgusted with him.

She couldn't blame him more than he blamed himself. He'd never lost control like that before, but he hadn't been able to stop himself. The compulsion to see that poker hand through, no matter what the cost, had been impossible to resist.

Celia came back into the room. "He's still sleeping like an angel, and I'll not have you disturbing him. Come back in an hour."

"I can't." Daniel would be manning the speed trap near the Talimena Byway by then. He didn't mind the boring assignment. He counted himself lucky to still have a job after the sheriff heard about his stupidity. "I'll be here tomorrow morning to see my boy."

"Carson has a doctor's appointment at nine."

Panic squeezed Daniel's chest. "He's not sick, is he?"

"No. He's just due for another shot. Measles, I think."

"I'll be here to go with Anne."

"Anne may be working at Walmart by then, please God," Celia said, tossing her gaze heavenward for a moment.

Anne's stepfather worked for the town sanitation department. It was steady work, but her folks didn't have money to burn. Two extra mouths in the house hadn't made things easier for them or improved Celia's temper. Anne wouldn't take any money from Daniel, no matter how often he tried to press it on her.

"Don't know if Anne will be carrying Carson to the doctor or if I will," Celia said as she opened the door, pointedly inviting him to leave.

"I'll take him. If my son is going to the doctor, so am I. You can both come if you want to," Daniel said. No matter what Anne said, he was going to provide for Carson. If she wouldn't accept money, when he came in the morning he'd bring a bagful of groceries and diapers. Anne might refuse his help, but Celia wouldn't hesitate. She'd think it was owed.

Maybe that was the key. "Buttering the cow to get the calf," his granddad would have called it. If he could somehow bring Celia around, Anne should be easy.

As he walked back toward the cruiser, Anne pulled up in her aging silver Taurus. Looking as pretty as ever in a black skirt and pale green sweater, she climbed out of the car. He loved to see her with her dark hair just so and a dab of makeup to put extra color on her cheeks. Daniel wished it was him she'd gotten dressed up for. When she saw him, a tightness gathered at the corners of her mouth.

Shades of Celia. He shook that thought off. Anne was nothing like her mother. She was strong-minded, yes, but there wasn't a mean bone in her sweet body.

"Danny," she said with a nod.

"Did you get the job?"

Anne shrugged. "Don't know. There were a lot of people applying. They said they'd be making their decision by the first of next week."

Come back to me, Annie. I'll take care of you and our boy. I promise.

But he didn't say that. His wife was stubborn. Once Anne set her feet on a path, she was hard to turn. He'd have to come at her sideways.

"I dropped by to see Carson, but he's still napping," Daniel said. "I hear he has a doctor's appointment tomorrow morning. I'll come by to take you."

"I don't think that's a good idea."

"He's my son, too. It's my job to make sure he stays healthy."

Her big brown eyes were sadder than a puppy that just piddled on the floor. Except he was the one who'd made the mess. His stupidity had yanked the roof from over his son's head. Anne's sadness cut him more than Celia's rant had. Unlike her mother, Anne could make a man feel like a worm without a word.

"I moved out of the house today," he said to fill the void.

She nodded. The bungalow on Crepe Myrtle hadn't been much, but it was theirs free and clear. He mentally kicked his own butt up between his shoulder blades again. Losing a house in a card game was easily the dumbest thing a man could do.

"I rented a place over on Spruce Street." It was a duplex instead of a house, but it had two bedrooms and a bath and a half. It would do until he got back on his feet again. "There's a little yard where we can put Carson's swing set. I know it's not as good as the house, but—"

"Do you think all I care about is that house?"

"Isn't that what this is about?"

Anne shook her head. "It's not about losing our home. It's about you not even stopping to think what might happen to Carson and me because you can't resist the turn of a card."

"If I'd won, you'd have been happy enough. We could have—"

"No." She started walking toward the door. He fell into step with her. "Dan, whether you win or lose is not the issue. You've got a problem and you won't admit it."

His wife had left him. That was his problem. Admitting it wouldn't make her come back to him.

"I don't blame you completely," she said. "From what you've told me, your dad had some addictions. I guess I shouldn't be surprised when you turn up with one of your own."

"I don't have an addiction." He didn't smoke. He'd never done drugs, not even a single puff on a joint. He didn't drink unless you counted an occasional cold beer on a hot summer day. "And I'm nothing like my father."

It was one thing for him to wonder about how much he had in common with Lester Scott. It was another thing for Anne to suggest it. Revulsion made his stomach roll.

"You *are* like him in this, whether you know it or not. I checked a book out of the library and I've been reading up on it, trying to understand what drove you to play until you lost the house. They call it having an addictive personality. I'm not saying you're a bad person, Dan. I know you're not. Having the urge to gamble is not your fault. What you do with the urge is."

She started to open the door, but he stopped her with a hand on the screen.

"Well, if that's true, why don't you come home and help me deal with it?"

"If I did, would you promise never to gamble again? And I mean give up everything. No poker with the guys. No trips to the casino for slots. You even can't buy a lottery ticket. It would be like an alcoholic thinking he can stop with one drink."

He opened his mouth, but then closed it without speaking. In all honesty, he couldn't make that promise. Just the thought of never feeling the high of winning again made him take an involuntary step back.

Maybe he *was* no better than Lester. Abuse came in lots of disguises. Landing his family on the street was as bad as leaving bruises where they didn't show.

And maybe the damage was slower to heal.

Anne gently pushed his hand aside and opened the door. "Well, that tells me what I need to know."

"But I didn't say anything."

"Exactly." She went into the house and hooked the screen door between them. "I don't know why you're still here, Daniel."

"I'm here because I want you back, Anne. I love you."

"You have a funny way of showing it." She swallowed hard. "I heard your old girlfriend is back in town."

"So?"

"So someone made it their business to let me know you've been to see her."

Daniel closed his eyes and silently counted to ten.

"I swear, if gossip were an Olympic sport, Coldwater Cove would take the gold every time. Whoever told you I've been to see Lacy is not your friend," he said.

"So it's not true?" The hope in her eyes made his chest constrict.

"No, it's true, but it's not what you think."

Heather Walker was probably the one who'd made sure Anne knew he'd seen his ex. She lived in an apartment over Gewgaws and Gizzwickies, same as Lacy. On the night he'd dropped by, Heather had been out on the iron deck the two units shared, watering a tub of newly planted petunias. The sidelong look she'd shot him was so cool, butter wouldn't melt in her mouth.

"My visit to Lacy was totally innocent, honest," he said. "I was just checking on her. She's been through some tough stuff back east, you know."

Anne crossed her arms over her chest. "Oh, did someone gamble away her house, too?"

"Her dad asked me to stop by, so I did. Just to see if she's all right."

"And is she?"

Lacy was better than all right. She made him feel like he was eighteen again, when everything was sharp-edged and full of fire and so wretchedly important. When he looked at Lacy, he could still smell the tang of sweetgrass wafting in a breeze off the lake. He could feel the red earth beneath his back as the stars wheeled in a slow dance across the night sky. Lacy tempted him sorely, especially since he and Anne were on the outs.

But Lacy wasn't his wife. He'd vowed to be faithful to Anne until he was dust. If he did nothing else right in this life, he wanted to stay true to that vow.

Daniel had been almost relieved when Jake arrived and gave him a reason to make a clean getaway. A man couldn't be held to account for what he thought about, for what he was tempted by, but guilt stabbed him in the gut over thinking and being tempted all the same.

"I took a vow to love you, Anne, and only you," he said. "I haven't broken that promise."

Her chin quivered and her eyes glistened, but she was determined enough not to let a tear fall. Still, he could see she'd been afraid he was unfaithful. She couldn't depend on him. He felt as low as the soles of his boots.

"I wouldn't hurt you like that, honey," he said, willing her to sense how much he meant it. Winning her back was going to be harder than he'd thought. He'd broken her trust in one area and now she didn't seem able to trust him about anything. "I'll be back tomorrow at eight-thirty to go with you to Carson's doctor's appointment."

Before she could object, he turned and strode back to the cruiser. Sometimes, it was best to withdraw from the field and live to fight another day.

Anne watched Daniel pull away from the curb and drive slowly down the block. She was so hollow inside she didn't know how to name what she was feeling. Part of her ached to run after the cruiser and call him back. Part of her held firm. This was a fight worth fighting. She couldn't go back to him unless she won it.

"Did you tell him?" Her mother came up behind her and put a gentle hand on her shoulder.

"No."

"Lord knows I've no use for the man, but he deserves to be told. Might shake some sense into him."

"He'll find out sooner or later. Probably sooner." It wasn't a secret that would keep. When she was carrying Carson, she hardly showed at all until the end of her fifth month. But this pregnancy felt different. Like a balloon that had been blown up once, she suspected her tummy would pop out a lot quicker this time.

If Daniel knew she was pregnant again, he'd say anything to make her come home. But even if he did, how would she know if he really meant it?

How could she ever tell whether it was her he wanted or

if the only tie binding him to her was his children? After all, he was only coming back tomorrow morning for Carson's appointment. Especially with Lacy Evans back in town, Anne needed to know Daniel loved her for her, not just because she was the mother of his son. Not just because he was chained to her by a wedding vow.

If she and Daniel couldn't re-form their circle of two . . . if their love wasn't enough to get Danny through this gambling problem . . . how could they ever hope to create a safe place between them, a sweet little hollow for their children to take shelter in?

Chapter 9

There's nothing more relaxing for a man than spending
a whole day in the company of his own thoughts. Unless
it's spending a day in the company of his own thoughts,
a rod and reel, and the right kind of bait.

—Marvin Tyler, beloved husband of Mary,
father of Jacob, Laura, Steven, and Mark

Jake cranked up the oldies station as he and Lacy headed east
in his pickup on the highway that wound around Lake Jewel.
On the town side of the lake, there was an expansive public park. Part of the Bates College campus was snugged up
against its southwest cove. Once they passed the Coldwater
Cove marina on the north side of the lake, thick woods rose
up on either side of the drive.

Lacy had managed to get Thursday off from the paper,
the same day that he was regularly free from the Green Apple.
The fact that she was willing to arrange her life to suit his
schedule was a good sign. All week, he'd been looking forward to being with her at the lake house.

With any luck, he could turn Thursdays into a standing
all-day date.

Conversation flowed easily between them. Since his injury, it had been hard to talk to women for longer than he
could make a cup of coffee last. Invariably, they wanted to
hear him rehash what had happened to him in Afghanistan
and how he *felt* about it. Even if he could name what he was
feeling, what was the good in dredging it all up again?

Lacy treated him as if nothing had changed. If she had the slightest curiosity about his time in Helmand province, she kept it to herself.

Another good sign.

She was full of stories about her first week at the *Coldwater Gazette.* They were sure never to make the paper itself.

"Turns out, there's a running feud between Wanda and Marjorie Chubb for some unknown reason," Lacy said. "I don't remember them being at odds when I wrote for the paper before."

"They may have been and you didn't notice. High school kids are generally too wrapped up in themselves to pay attention to what's going on with the adults around them."

"Speak for yourself, Mr. Big Stuff," she said. "I was sort of invisible in high school."

"No, you weren't." *Mr. Big Stuff, huh?* He liked that.

"OK, name one thing you remember about me."

She'd been his best friend's girl and therefore off-limits. He and Daniel always had each other's backs, on the gridiron and off. But things were different now and he couldn't very well bring up Lacy's old boyfriend as an excuse for not remembering things about her in high school. He might be out of practice, but he was certain that was not the way to make points with her.

He pulled a nugget out of thin air. "I remember you played in pep band."

"Oh, yeah. What instrument?"

"How should I know? They all sound like kazoos to me."

She laughed. "I can see it now—the Fighting Marmots All-Kazoo Marching Band! They ought to book us for the Macy's parade."

Jake laughed with her. He couldn't remember the last time he'd shared laughter with a woman that wasn't forced.

"But anyway," Lacy went on, "according to Georgina—the Queen Bee of Gossips at the *Gazette*—there is no chance Wanda will ever fire her longest-standing employee."

"Why is that?" Jake asked.

"Not sure, but my theory is that since Marjorie is the captain of the Methodist prayer chain, she must know where all the bodies are buried."

Jake chuckled. "She probably does at that, but Marjorie means well. I know it seems like she's spreading gossip, but she really does care about people."

When he first came home and was adrift in the sea of changes his new leg had made to his life, Marjorie and her like-minded friends had prayed for him daily. And let him know they were doing so. It chafed at him in the beginning that other people thought he needed prayer.

But then it started to feel good to know that there were people who stopped what they were doing to think about him and what he was going through. Then once he settled in at the Green Apple, the gaggle of self-proclaimed prayer warriors sort of loved him into attending the Wednesday night chapel service for people whose jobs wouldn't let them go on Sunday morning.

He'd found a measure of peace there. And a community of folks who were willing to come alongside him while he found a way to feel like he belonged again.

"Oh, that's right," Lacy said. "You've gone all churchy on me."

"Nothing wrong with finding a little faith," he said. "Hey, what's your problem? You were raised in that church."

"Yeah, but I sort of outgrew it."

"Nobody outgrows the need for something to believe in."

"It's not about faith. It's just church itself. I mean, who needs everybody all up in everyone's business?"

"So it doesn't make you feel good to know you were being prayed for while you were in trouble back in Boston?"

"Of course not." She glared at him as if he'd sprouted a second head. "The prayer chain is just Coldwater's way of broadcasting my failures."

"Everyone fails at something."

"Yeah, I know. But it's almost like they're saying, 'Who do you think you are? See? We knew you couldn't cut it in the big wide world.'"

The prayer chain wasn't saying that at all. That attitude was coming straight from Lacy herself. *She* evidently didn't think she could cut it.

"What else happened at the paper this week?" Jake asked to change the subject. This was far too serious a topic for a first date.

She grinned. "I got the biggest kick out of some of the weekly notices sent to the paper. Did you see the one from the library?"

Jake shook his head. He didn't take the *Gazette,* but now that Lacy was writing for it, he needed to fix that immediately. "I must have missed that one."

"It went sort of like this." Lacy closed her eyes, the better to remember the piece verbatim. "'Head librarian of the Coldwater Cove Public Library, Rosa Mundy, reports that a certain patron has failed to return a book on time, along with two fishing rods. The borrower will be named in this report next week if the rods aren't returned before Saturday. Mr. Mundy is planning to enter the bass tournament at Lake Jewel and needs the gear.'" Lacy chuckled. "Notice Mrs. Mundy didn't seem a bit concerned about the book that's overdue. And what kind of library loans out fishing rods?"

"Oh, that's nothing. Henry Whiteside wanted to donate a chainsaw to the library once, but the town fathers put the kibosh on that. The town couldn't afford liability insurance for a loaner saw."

"Oh! Speaking of being able to afford something, that reminds me. I did some research on your mom's Fiestaware and I was right." From the corner of his eye, he saw she'd turned in her seat to face him so she could see his reaction. "How does eighty-five each sound?"

"Really?" he said, his brows arching. "That stuff is worth eighty-five dollars?"

"Only for the cobalt and mustard pieces," she said with a grin.

"Mustard, huh? How 'bout that? I figured that might be what you'd call the yellow one."

"You should have said so. See. You're not color-ignorant after all." Lacy punched his shoulder playfully.

The punch was OK by him. In Jake's experience, if a girl gave him a swat, he was more likely to score than if she didn't. Of course, that percentage was pre-Afghanistan.

"The red bowl is probably worth ninety-five because who doesn't love red?" Lacy went on. "And—hang on to your hat!—your mom might get even more for the chartreuse."

"The green one," he said, happy to show her he remembered her four-dollar word for that particular shade.

"That's right," she said approvingly, "the light green one. You mom could get as much as four thousand for the chartreuse."

"Four freakin' thousand dollars? For a soup bowl? When you said the green one was worth more than the red, I was thinking maybe a hundred." He never dreamed she meant a figure in the thousands. "Even eighty-five seems high for an old bowl. You're kidding, right?"

"I kid you not. Serious collectors will pay serious money for the right items. Chartreuse pieces in that particular style are rare, because the design was discontinued shortly after

Fiestaware introduced it in 1959. Factor in the excellent condition of your mom's bowl and buyers will be willing to pay a premium for it."

He shook his head. "Some folk have more money than sense. Of course, even if it's worth that much, if Mom puts that kind of price tag on her stuff at Secondhand Junk-shun, people will think she's crazy."

"Well, all right. I doubt you can get that price here," Lacy admitted. "But I have some contacts in Boston who would still do business with me. I bet I can find a collector for your mom's pieces. Want me to check on it?"

"Heck, yeah." If there was a chance his mom could bag that kind of windfall for an old bowl, he was all for it. "Mom's booth hasn't sold anything in a couple of weeks, but just to be on the safe side, I'd better call Phyllis Wannamaker and have her set those bowls aside."

Jake used the hands-free cell phone in his truck to place a call to the owner of Secondhand Junk-shun. When he explained what he wanted done, Phyllis acted as if she didn't understand and asked him to repeat himself.

"You heard me right, Phyllis. Don't sell *anything* from my mom's booth until I've had a chance to drop by tomorrow."

"But there's a gentleman and lady here that come down all the way from Kansas City and they want your mom's Fiestaware. In fact, they're standing in front of me right this very minute with the green one in their hands."

Jake hit the mute button with his thumb. "We called just in time." Then he clicked the mute again so he could talk to Phyllis. "Tell them it's not for sale. Tell them I brought the bowls in by mistake." Jake had a sudden inspiration and it happened to be true. "They belonged to my grandmother."

"Everything in your mom's booth belonged to some relation of hers or other."

"Yeah, but these are special. Thank the people from Missouri kindly, but my mom won't sell those bowls."

Jake heard a few moments of indistinct mumbling because Phyllis had probably covered her phone with her hand. Then she came back over the connection loud and clear.

"They say they'll double your asking price."

"I just bet they will," Lacy murmured.

"Not this time," Jake said to Lacy, then raised his voice so Phyllis wouldn't mistake his words. "What price can you put on a family memory, Phyllis? Tell those folks from Kansas City I'd as soon eat a bar of soap as take their money. Put Mom's bowls under your counter right now and I'll pick them up first thing tomorrow."

He'd have to duck out of the grill for a bit, but Ethel could be counted on to keep the coffee flowing. His geriatric waitress would happily push the fresh cinnamon buns until he got back. Ethel always claimed his rolls would give Cinnabon a run for its money.

"All right, Jake," Phyllis said in a miffed tone, "but just this once. You can't put things out for sale and then yank them back like that. It's not good business."

"Duly noted. OK, thanks," he said as if she hadn't just scolded him. "See you tomorrow."

"I mean it. Tell your mom not to expect this kind of service again. I've got my reputation to con—"

Jake punched the off button just as Phyllis began another rant.

"She sounded upset," Lacy said.

"She'll get glad the same way she got mad. Phyllis makes her money coming and going at the Junk-shun, you know. Not only does she charge all the vendors rent on their booth space, she takes a bite out of every sale, too."

"Really? How much?"

"Last I heard it was fifteen percent."

"Does she have any say on what sort of items the vendors bring in?" Lacy asked.

"Not as far as I know. Why? Are you planning to open a junk shop?"

"I'm not into yard sale castoffs." That about summed up most of the Junk-shun's wares. "I suppose if I could convince my mom to clear out the unnecessary dust-catchers in her house, we'd have ready-made inventory for a shop. But a girl has to have standards."

As long as her standards would include him, he was all for them. He glanced over at her and could almost see the wheels turning in her pretty little head.

"If I could make sure my shop was filled with quality pieces, I'd consider it," she said, so low it was almost as if she were talking to herself. Then she raised her voice a few decibels to bring him into the conversation. "You know, things like your mom's bowls. They're really good design—sleek and functional as well as pretty."

"Just because something's good doesn't mean people will like it," Jake said. "But I know what you mean. Every now and then I feel a little guilty over the menu at the grill. It's almost like grease and salt is its own food group perched at the top of the Green Apple pyramid. But if I was to try to add tofu and sprouts, I'd get a lot of pushback."

That was an understatement. The regulars might just burn the grill to the ground.

"You never know what will change until you try to change it," she said with a smile that seemed full of promise.

Well, he was trying to change something now, wasn't he? He glanced again at her profile. The tip of her nose turned up ever so slightly. He wondered what it would be like to be so comfortable with each other, he could drop a quick kiss on that little nose. Of course, her full lips would be better, but he'd settle for what he could get. He jerked his gaze back to the winding lake road.

Located where the road ended on the southeasternmost bank of Lake Jewel, his family's summer house butted up against national forest land. It was as far from the fashionable north and east shores as you could get. Those choice lots close to the Coldwater Cove marina were occupied by oversized vacation homes that belonged to folks who'd come down from Tulsa or up from Dallas for long weekends.

The Tyler family lake house wasn't exactly a house either. It was more like a fishing shack that had grown into a cottage through multiple additions over the years. There was only one bedroom unless you counted the bunkhouse, which was what Jake's folks had always called the half-finished attic room that ran the length of the structure and was home to four sets of sagging bunk beds.

Running water and an indoor biffy had finally been added about ten years ago. But just in case they had plumbing problems, there was still a little privy with a half moon on the door out back. It was camouflaged by underbrush at the edge of the stand of pines that ringed the place. The dock and boathouse had been his dad's pride and joy and were in better repair than the cottage.

"If a man has a lake to play on by day and a roof to turn the rain by night, what more does he need?" Marvin Tyler always used to say.

Well, if a guy was trying to make headway with an award-winning designer, a lake house that didn't look like a run of years of hard luck might come in handy.

Jake pulled into the graveled drive and parked the truck close to the cottage. He'd forgotten that the place could do with a fresh coat of paint. Why hadn't he run over and checked things out before he brought Lacy here?

She hopped down from the truck before he could make it around to her side to open the door. Spreading her arms wide, she drew a deep breath and then sighed in contentment.

"Just smell that pine and freshwater breeze. If we could figure out a way to bottle that air, we'd make a million dollars," she said as she walked down toward the dock.

She likes the place!

The dock plunked under their feet, each plank a different woodsy, twangy pitch, as if the boards had been roughly tuned. It was the song of approaching summer. From their vantage point on the dock, the westernmost peaks of the Winding Stair range rose on the other side of the lake.

"Why didn't you tell me the view was so incredible from here?" she asked.

"It's like a lot of things. If you see it often enough, you start to take it for granted. But I'll try not to. In fact, it's getting better by the moment."

The view of her neat little backside in those tight jeans made him very happy to be a man. Very happy indeed.

Chapter 10

Dating is like riding a bicycle. You never forget how,
but dang, if I don't feel a little wobbly about it all the same.

—Jake Tyler

Jake carried the cooler inside the cottage and transferred its contents to the short turquoise fridge. He'd brought soft drinks, cold beer, a couple of steaks in case the fish weren't biting, chips, and salad fixings. The furniture in the main room of the house had been draped with sheets to protect it from dust over the winter.

"It's like the Ghosts of Summers Past in here," he said as he pulled the cloth off a round oak table and mismatched chairs. A cloud of dust particles shimmered in the light that shafted through the big picture window.

"Wish your 'ghosts' could talk," Lacy said as she made a slow circuit of the space. "Bet they'd have plenty to tell."

Jake used his work gloves to swipe a few cobwebs off the wagon-wheel light fixture hanging over the table. "My family's had a lot of fun here over the years."

"Bet you have, too. What girl wouldn't love a moonlight cruise on the lake?"

"We can do that."

She met his gaze. Unfortunately, her expression was a little like a deer in the headlights.

"I didn't mean me. Actually, I can't stay past five or six.

Effie the Intolerable is even more difficult than usual when she thinks her supper has been delayed," Lacy explained. "Besides, I promised Heather Walker I'd go with her to the seven o'clock show at the Regal tonight."

Well, that shot him down pretty hard. He was being thrown over in favor of a cat she didn't even like and a girls' night out.

Jake had expected to have Lacy all to himself for the entire day and well into the evening. He'd refused to let himself imagine more than that. It had been a good long while since he'd been with a woman. He wasn't sure how Lacy would feel about the bare truth of his stump.

"So, where do you want me to start?" she asked.

How would it start? Jake let himself imagine Lacy, her skin all warm from too much sun tucked between a cool set of clean sheets.

"With the house-opening-up project?" she said emphatically because he'd zoned out for a tad.

He gave himself a mental shake to clear his head. That was better. No good would come from that sort of fantasy right now and a little work would take his mind off everything but the job at hand. He couldn't change the past and the future could be snatched away in a moment. Life was easier when he lived it one breath at a time.

"How about pulling off the dusty cloths and stowing them in the truck bed?" he suggested. The topper would keep them from flying out until he could take them to his mom's for washing. "I have some things to take care of. Back in a bit."

While Lacy was busy inside, Jake worked outside. He burrowed under the cottage in the crawlspace and checked all the pipes. Before the first frost last year, he had filled the system with an environmentally friendly antifreeze. But there was always a chance that something had gone wrong. After shining his flashlight under the kitchen sink and bathroom area, he breathed a sigh of relief. As far as he could tell, no pipes had frozen and burst during the winter.

He turned on the water at the main and crawled out from under the house. When he clomped up on the deck and came in through the front door, he nearly tripped over an ottoman that had been moved into his way. It took him a few moments of arm-flailing to regain his balance.

"Oh! Be careful, Jake. I'm sorry I left the ottoman there," she said as she hurried over to his side of the room. Lacy had been busy. She'd swept the broad-plank pine floors in the open space that served as living room, dining room, and kitchen. Now she was intent on dragging the furniture around. Clearly, she was trying to change the way the cottage layout worked.

Guess that's what I get for leaving a designer unattended in a place that seriously needs her attention.

"I hope your mom won't mind if I play with the furniture arrangement a bit," Lacy said, her color high. "I didn't mean for it to get so involved. I only moved one thing, but then that called for another. And another. And another, but don't worry. The ottoman isn't going to stay where it is now. I just need to see about—"

Lacy drew up short and eyed him from head to toe as if seeing him for the first time.

"Out," she said, picking up the recently used broom.

"What?"

"Look at yourself. You're filthy, Jake. Oh my gosh, you're covered with cobwebs and dirt." She made a face. "Even in your hair."

"That tends to happen when you're under a house." He ran a hand over his head.

"No! Don't do that in here. Out," she repeated, brandishing the broom. "Before I see something with more than four legs crawling on you."

She followed him onto the front deck and started sweeping him down, dusting off his shoulders, down his back and across his butt. "Well, that's a little better. Don't know what we can do about your hair though."

"There's a well with a hand pump in the side yard. Pulls water straight from the lake," he said. "Guess I can douse myself there."

"Okay, but if you got the water back on in the house, a full shower might be even better. Turn around." He obeyed and she gave his front the same rough sweep-down.

The old Jake might have suggested she join him in the shower, but he was trying to convince her he wasn't that guy anymore. He was interested in Lacy for a lot more than sex. When he thought about having a woman in his life now, it was about having something deeper. He wanted a connection, a safe harbor, and a relationship that lasted longer than a three-minute egg.

He really was done being a player. If someone had told him a few years ago that he'd be thinking like this, he'd have been sure they were crazy. But now, he wanted someone he could get to know and cherish—mind, body, and heart.

And someone who would know and cherish him, warts and all.

Though he wouldn't mind it if that someone was less heavy-handed with a broom than Lacy Evans.

"That's about as much good as I can do here," Lacy said. "Now, where's that well?"

Lacy pumped while Jake bent under the spigot. As the frigid water streamed over his head and neck, he realized he hadn't given enough thought to whether or not opening up the lake house was suitable activity for a date. He should have taken her to the Regal so she wouldn't have to go with Heather to watch whatever old movie was playing. He could have asked her to go dancing with him the next time the big band played at the Opera House. He wouldn't do much swing dancing, but if the music was slow enough, he expected he could manage a Texas two-step.

Instead he'd set himself up for a beating with a broom and a thorough baptism with some of the coldest water south of the Arctic.

"Enough!" he finally said, pulling away from the pump and shaking his wet head, flinging droplets about like a retriever coming up from the water.

"Not nearly enough," Lacy corrected. "You really do need a shower, Jake. There might be some creepy crawlies under your shirt. Are there any clothes in that old chest in the bedroom?"

He'd feel it if he'd attracted any wildlife, but whether the possibility bothered him or not, it clearly bothered Lacy. "Some of my dad's things are still there. Mom's never had the heart to clear them out."

Marvin Tyler always wanted the lake house well provisioned with the "necessaries," so he didn't have to waste weekend time packing a suitcase or stocking a pantry. Jake could hear his dad's voice in his head saying, "A six-pack of cold beer and a bucket of worms is all a man should have to bring with him to the lake."

"I'll find something clean to wear." Jake stomped toward the house and the coldest shower in recorded human history. No point in lighting the pilot on the water heater now. The old unit would take hours to warm up.

And after his shower, so would he.

Lacy watched Jake trudge toward the main-level bedroom. From the set of his shoulders, she could tell he was ticked off, but she didn't know how she could have done anything differently. If she'd gotten as filthy as he, she'd want a shower for sure. Just thinking about crawling around under the cottage gave her the willies. She shivered as she imagined the tickle of little buggie feet all over.

Suzanne Sugarbaker from those old Designing Women *reruns was so right. The man is supposed to kill the bugs!*

Jake returned with a handful of folded clothes and, without a word, disappeared into the small bathroom that jutted out into the room between the kitchen area and the opening that led to the bedroom. He shut the door behind him harder than he needed to, just shy of a slam. In a few minutes, there was a clanging of pipes from beneath the lake house and the water came on with a shushing sound.

A string of muttered curses emerged from the bathroom.

"Are you OK?" Lacy asked at the door.

Jake answered in a high falsetto. "I may never sing bass again."

"I didn't know you could sing."

"Well, you'll never know now." He switched back to his normal voice. "Man, this is cold!"

She couldn't do anything to fix that, and she was having trouble trying not to imagine Jake all wet and soapy.

Remember Bradford.

Her failed New England relationship had become her talisman, warning her against getting involved with a man again. Relationships were tricky. Design was simple, so she turned her attention back to creating a better traffic flow in the cottage. After a few minutes of trial and error, she had the round oak table and four chairs placed nearer the kitchen counter that ran along one wall so that when it wasn't used for eating, a cook could use it as an extra counter. It wasn't tall enough to be prep space, but it would hold finished dishes.

Lacy dragged the butt-bent couch away from the wall and repositioned it to take advantage of the view out the big picture window overlooking the lake. She repurposed an old trunk that was propped in a corner. It made a perfect "beachy" coffee table.

She was about to go on to place the most surprising thing she'd discovered among the "pre-attic" pieces—a Danish modern occasional chair—but something about the trunk caught her eye.

Someone had burned a chain of crude leaves along one of the old oak planks that made up the top. In one corner, the initials J. T. proclaimed that this was the dubious artwork of a young Jake Tyler. She ran her fingers along the ridges of the burned-in pattern, remembering the boy he'd been.

Not afraid of anything and proud as a tom turkey, he'd always been quick to accept a challenge. Like the kid in *A Christmas Story* who was "triple dog-dared," Jake would have been the one with his tongue stuck to a frozen pole.

She smiled to herself. Jake had also been the kind of kid who would stand up for others. They hadn't run with the same crowd in high school. Lacy wasn't part of the jock and cheerleader set. Pep band was her speed, but Jake never made her feel invisible the way some of her classmates did. One year their class had a foreign exchange student from Ecuador, and Lacy had befriended him. Since he'd understood only one word in three, he didn't know what a social zero she was and was easy to get along with. But some of the boys harassed him every chance they got. Jake cornered the bullies behind the football bleachers after school one day and gave them all black eyes.

His later history with the ladies aside, Jacob Tyler had been a pretty good kid.

When he strode out of the bathroom, she decided he cleaned up pretty well now that he was a man, too. His long, muscular frame did wonderful things for the faded pair of jeans and plaid work shirt that had been his dad's. His thighs filled out the jeans so well, she barely noticed his limp. His

wet hair was slicked back, dark and sleek as a seal. Lacy realized her mouth was hanging open and quickly clapped her
jaw shut.

"Want some help moving furniture?" he asked.

"Sure your mom won't mind?"

"If she does, I'll move it all back," he admitted. "Never get
between a woman and how she thinks her furniture should be
arranged, that's my motto."

Lacy grinned. "You will live long and see good days."

They worked together, shoving and lifting the rest of the
furniture into place. Lacy fluffed and placed throw pillows
while Jake shook out the rag rugs at both the front and side
doors.

When he came back in, she was draping a red throw over
the back of what she explained was a Danish modern side
chair. "This is a really good piece. Maybe a Peter Hvidt."

"A what?"

"Peter Hvidt. He was a mid-twentieth-century designer.
His work was famous for lines that were clean and elegant,
like this chair. Even though it appears light and airy, the layers
of laminate under the veneer mean it's still strong. 'Hell-for-
stout,' my granddad would have said."

"Is this another thing like those soup bowls? Worth more
than I think it is?"

She shrugged. "Could be. Of course, it's probably a knock-
off. I can't find a maker's mark, but the piece still has good
bones. It ought to be restored."

"You mean like sanding and restaining the wood?"

"No!" He'd just uttered sacrilege but he'd done it in ignorance, so she'd forgive him. Lacy ran a hand over the wooden
arm of the chair. "This looks like the original finish. The teak
can be cleaned, but gently. I don't think it's ever been oiled.
We could do that if you want, but anything else would take
away from its value."

Jake gave the chair a sidelong glance. "There's a cigarette burn on the seat. We never could get Dad to quit. I take it new upholstery wouldn't mess up any value the thing might have."

"Not at all," she said. "But good design isn't just about what a piece is worth. It's about what you choose to surround yourself with, and how you live with those things. How they function. How they make you feel."

"Never gave it much thought."

"No time like the present. What does this chair say to you?"

Jake frowned at it. "Not a thing."

When she made a noise of exasperation, he said, "Sit on me?"

"Really?"

"Sorry," he said. "I don't speak furniture-ese."

"Come on, Jake. Try. Do you like the way the arms curve? How does the thickness of the cushions make you feel? What about how the chair works in the room?"

"It's my *feeling* that if a chair will hold my weight, it *works* just fine."

Sometimes, you have to bow to the inevitable.

Jake would never get as excited as she did about the interplay of light and dark, proportion and line.

"So what do you need to redo the chair?" Jake asked.

"First, your mom would have to decide whether she wants to try to recapture the original style of the piece or do something that pulls it into this century a tad. Either choice is a good one *if* you pick the right fabric."

"Well, my mom's birthday is next month," Jake said. "How about if you pick the fabric and help me get this chair fixed up for her?"

"Sure. We can do the work on the wood ourselves, but I'll have to find an upholsterer who can do the piece justice. Put me in front of a sewing machine and I'm likely to stitch my thumbs together."

"I doubt that, but see who you can find to recover the cushions just in case." Jake caught up her hand and planted a quick kiss on the pad of her thumb. "A perfectly good thumb is a terrible thing to waste."

It seemed like a joke, but then he gave her a searching look. Before Lacy could decipher what she read in Jake's dark eyes, he dropped her hand. Then without another word, he hoisted up the chair and hauled it out to the back of his pickup.

Lacy scanned the room, satisfied she'd done the best she could with what she had to work with. It was just an old cottage filled with castoffs and rejects, but what the room lacked in beauty, it now made up for in functionality. She decided to think of the place as an ugly duckling. With the right design, the right pieces brought together to tell a cohesive story of the family and friends who used the place, the Tyler lake house could be charming.

But the kind of charm Lacy had in mind cost money and she doubted that Jake's widowed mother was rolling in it.

Lacy had one foot on the bottom step leading up to what Jake called the bunkhouse when he popped his head back in at the side door.

"We're done inside for today. I don't want you working anymore," he told her. "Since I have to get you back to town early, let's take that moonlight cruise now."

"But there's no moonlight."

"We'll improvise."

Chapter 11

Some people, they say to me, "You must be part cat, Mrs. P." All because I do not like the water. What's to like? Is cold. Is wet. Would rather be cat.

—Mrs. Paderewski, piano teacher, wannabe real estate tycoon, and cat fancier extraordinaire

Jake cranked the winch to lower the rowboat from its winter berth in the boathouse into the clear cold water. Keeping a tight hold on the rope attached to the bow, he floated the craft around to the dock. Then he tied it off and loaded the rods and tackle box in case Lacy wanted to fish. He started to hand her in, but without his help, she scrambled from the dock to the seat in the bow.

The forward thwart, he remembered from his Boy Scout days. He settled onto the center thwart, where he slipped the oars into the rowlocks.

"No motor?" she asked.

"Naw. My dad always said the sound scared off the fish."

"He was quite the angler, wasn't he?"

"The terror of anything with fins, that was my dad. At least, on a good day. Other times, he could only claim to be a drowner of worms." Jake pushed off from the dock and began rowing along the lakeshore, heading west. "He's been gone not quite a year. I still miss him every day."

"My folks told me he passed while I was in Boston. I'm sorry, Jake."

"Don't be. I didn't have him long enough to suit me, but

he taught me a lot in the time we had together." Marvin Tyler had always been there for Jake. His father had baited his first hook, tossed him his first football, and delivered either a pep talk or a kick in the butt whenever he needed it. Along the way, his dad had taught him everything he knew about being a man. "He gave me all he could and it was all I needed."

"Sounds like you and I were both blessed in the dad department," Lacy said. "My father was so patient with me. He tried to get me interested in law. Since neither of my sibs seemed to be headed that way, I was his last chance to groom someone in the family to take over his practice. Unfortunately, torts and codicils make me yawn. What a disappointment I must have been."

"I doubt that."

"You're looking at the only person in history to have been sent home from law camp."

"Law camp? Is there such a thing?"

"I'm sorry to tell you there is and it's as riveting as watching paint dry, which is probably how I came to fall asleep during every mock trial and inquest. I never understood why I couldn't have gone to Space Camp and gotten sick on the anti-grav machine instead." She flashed him a wry smile. "What sorts of things did your dad teach you?"

"Which tool to use for which job and how to take care of all of them." Jake's oar strokes fell into an easy rhythm as the boat surged across the clear water. "Not to irritate my brothers and sister more than they could bear. How to be a gentleman."

"A gentleman? Really? So, we have Mr. Tyler to thank for the smooth moves of the heartbreaker of Coldwater High."

Jake laughed. "That's not his fault. He tried to teach me how to treat a lady. It doesn't mean I learned."

"Oh, that's right." She trailed her hand in the water. "You do better in subjects where the answer is a matter of opinion."

"You remembered! You seemed so distracted that morning in the grill when you first came home, I wasn't sure you were listening to a word I said."

"I *was* distracted and . . . 'car-lagged' for lack of a better word, but when did Jacob Tyler ever have anything but a girl's full attention?"

He wondered if she was teasing. Her smile suggested she'd always paid attention to him. Maybe he hadn't lost all his smooth moves.

"After all," she said, "you do make the best waffles on the planet."

So much for his smooth moves.

Lacy leaned back, tipped her chin up, and closed her eyes, basking in the sun. If she were a cat, she'd have started purring. Then she sat up and shaded her eyes with one hand. Jake glanced in the direction of her gaze between long strokes of the oars. In soft blues and greens, rounded peaks rose above the sparkling lake.

"I know our mountains are really just little bumps on the earth compared to the Rockies or even the Berkshires," Lacy said, "but they sure look tall from here."

"As Dad always said, 'It's not that the hills are so high, but that the valleys are so low.'"

"I wish I'd known him. Your father sounds like a fount of useful information."

"Use*less* information, he'd have said. You should have seen him watching *Jeopardy!* He tried so hard to answer the questions, but he'd only get one right in ten, unless the clue had to do with geography. Then he was bang on the money. He was always studying an atlas just for fun."

As Jake turned the bow of the boat into a quiet cove and dropped anchor, Lacy sighed. "You know, I've heard people say that geography is destiny. Usually, they're talking about third world countries and the limited choices the people who live there have based on where they were born. But I wonder if it doesn't apply to us in a way, too."

"How do you mean?"

"Do you think maybe the reason I didn't make it in Boston is because I was born in Coldwater Cove?"

"You're blaming the town for that?"

"No, I'm blaming the town for the way I turned out—gullible and too trusting by half."

"That's not fair. Sure, part of who you are was shaped by growing up here, but you also get to choose what kind of person you're going to be no matter where you're born." Jake had encountered honorable and dishonorable people everywhere his unit went in Afghanistan. It wasn't fair to make generalizations based on where someone grew up. "Besides, it didn't sound to me like your Boston troubles were entirely of your own making."

"I chose the wrong business partner. That's on me."

Jake wondered if that was all the guy had been to her. She had claimed to have been almost engaged once. "We all make choices we wish we hadn't."

"And pay for them," she said pensively. Then she gave herself a slight shake. "I'm sorry for being so serious. I don't know what's wrong with me. It's a gorgeous day. I'm with the best-looking guy in the county. I shouldn't be wasting time kicking myself over the past."

"Best-looking guy in the county?" It was all he heard in that bundle of words.

Lacy splashed a little water in his direction. "As if you didn't think so, too. I'm your friend so I can be honest with you. Even in your dad's old clothes, you're still hot."

She thinks I'm hot, streaked through his brain, followed by, *Easy, dude. She also called herself your friend.*

If that wasn't the kiss of death, he didn't know what was.

"But anyway," Lacy went on, "I still can't help wondering

if things would have shaken out differently in Boston if I'd
grown up in, say, Amherst or Cambridge."

"Wherever you go, there you are."

"What's that supposed to mean?"

"You can decide to be happy anywhere."

"Really? How about Afghanistan?" Then her eyes widened and she clapped a hand over her mouth. "Forgive me. I
shouldn't have said that."

"You don't need to tiptoe around me, Lacy. I'm not that
fragile." Of course, his occasional flashback meant there was
something going on inside his head that was decidedly fragile,
but he had a handle on it. He had a cast-iron will. The past
wasn't going to intrude on the present if he could help it. "But
honestly, when I was hanging with my buddies, there were
times when I was happy even in Helmand province. It all
depends on who you're with. Say, did I ever tell you the story
about how my grandparents came to Coldwater? My mom's
folks, I mean."

Lacy shook her head and leaned back on the padded seat.
"That's an abrupt change of topics."

"It's really not. It's all about being happy wherever you
are."

"We'll see," Lacy said with grimace. "At the risk of giving
me conversational whiplash, go ahead."

"OK. Well, my grandpa Wilson was Army, all the way.
They lived pretty much everywhere, hopping from base to
base. So when he retired after his twenty-year hitch, he and
my grandma needed to find a place to settle and put down
some roots."

"So your mom didn't grow up here?"

"Not completely." Jake shipped the oars. Water droplets
ran up the smooth wood like a string of clear pearls. "She was
a sophomore in high school when her parents moved the family to Coldwater Cove."

"Did they have relatives in the area?"

"Nope."

"So why did your grandparents choose this town?"

"Well, you see, they met in Tulsa and got married right after he enlisted. They didn't have much time before he had to report to Fort Sill, so they honeymooned over a weekend in a little town near the Arkansas line. Grandma always said they started married life in a lovely place with a brand-new 'art deco' courthouse in the center of the square."

"Art deco? She knew design?"

"Sort of. She knew what she liked and what she liked was anything modern, which at the time was art deco, I guess. There were a bunch of new murals inside that courthouse that made her feel as if she were visiting a fancy museum. Even in a tiny place in Oklahoma, there was art and beauty and culture."

"Your grandma sounds like a woman after my own heart."

"She'd have liked you, too," Jake said. "Anyway, when he retired and they needed to pick a place to settle, she decided it would be good to go back to where they'd started, to the town where they'd spent their honeymoon."

"How romantic."

"Only trouble was, neither my grandma or granddad could remember the *name* of the town. They finally agreed that it started with *C*. After studying a map of southeastern Oklahoma, they decided it must have been Coldwater Cove."

"But Coldwater—"

"Let me finish," Jake said. "So they came to town and bought a house and had all their stuff shipped to their new address. After Grandma got her kitchen unpacked, she told my granddad she needed a break from moving. 'Why don't we go down to the Square and take a look at those murals in the courthouse?' she said. Art had a way of unraveling all her knots, you see."

"That's my idea of refreshing, too. When I was in Boston, I can't tell you how many times I'd get stuck on something and needed to push away from work for a while. So I'd hop on the Green line and take a stroll through the Isabella Gardner Museum. Nine times out of ten, the solution to my problem would present itself somewhere between the John Singer Sargent and the Titian."

"You and my grandma were kindred spirits," Jake agreed, and then pushed ahead with his story. "But when my grandparents got down to the Town Square, instead of the clean lines of a modern courthouse—"

"Your grandma was confronted by Coldwater's fussy old Victorian," Lacy finished for him.

Jake laughed. "That's right. 'Where the heck are we?' she asked my granddad. 'Darned if I know,' he fired back, 'but we already bought the house. We'll just have to bloom where we planted ourselves.'"

"So they moved to Coldwater Cove by accident?"

"Yep. Turns out the town they'd honeymooned in was Colton Springs, about fifty miles to the south. Actually, it was a good thing they didn't move there because that courthouse my grandma loved so much wasn't even there anymore. A few years after their honeymoon, a tornado came through and took it out along with most of the square."

"So all's well that ends well for your grandparents."

"Seems so. They were happy here together for the rest of their lives," Jake said with a smile. Then he sobered. "You can be happy here, too, Lacy."

She lifted her shoulders. "I don't know. Coldwater feels like it belongs to my past. I don't see a future for me here."

Jake always enjoyed a challenge, but he certainly had his work cut out for him with Lacy. He picked up one of the poles and opened his tackle box. "How about your immediate future? Do you see yourself doing a little fishing?"

"Sounds good." She flashed him a genuine smile. He was coming to need those smiles like he needed sunshine.

Then she cocked her head and eyed the crumpled-up oil-cloth on the hull of the boat between them. "Well, let's get this old rag out of the way in case I have to land a whale here."

Before he could stop her, she leaned forward and yanked it up.

Jake's dad was a pretty handy fellow, but he hadn't been one for an overly fancy fix if it might interfere with his fishing time. When his rowboat started leaking one day, he had simply wrapped a bung in oilcloth, wedged it into the spot, and then went on casting. The patch had held for going on five years, but it was no match for Lacy Evans.

Water gushed through the hole as the boat started to sink.

Chapter 12

Once again we've been told to "spring forward" for day-light savings time. It appears to me that the boys and girls in the statehouse who decide these things have neglected to consider the unintended consequences. How is an extra hour of sunlight each day going to affect my pole beans?

We gardeners vote, you know.

Signed, Alfred Mayhew, concerned citizen and avid hor-ticulturist, who feeds both birds and squirrels because it irritates the poowaddin' out of my neighbor, George Evans

—letter to the editor, the *Coldwater Gazette*

This is, bar none, the worst date in recorded human history. Totally FUBAR.

Jake tried to cram the bung back into the hole, but water gushed through too fast. He hauled in the anchor and rowed for shore with all his might. Lacy baled with cupped hands. It was a losing proposition. Water crept past their ankles and up their shins at an alarming pace.

"Can you swim?" he yelled.

"Yes, but surely we won't—"

Water lapped over the gunwale and they were swamped in seconds.

Fortunately, the bracingly cold water they slowly sank into was only about four feet deep. Jake grabbed her hand and, leaving the rowboat to settle on the lake floor, started slogging toward the shore.

"But what about the boat?" she wailed.

"It's not going anywhere, that's for darned sure," he said

as he trudged ahead, feeling his way along the sandy bottom. The sleeve on his titanium leg gave a bit as water began to seep in around his stump.

"It's all my fault," Lacy said with misery etched on her face. "I didn't see the plug until after I gave that rag a yank. Oh, I shouldn't have . . . why, oh, why do I always feel compelled to fix things?"

"Especially things that don't need fixing," Jake said crossly. To be fair, she couldn't have known his dad had jerry-rigged a repair with that bit of cork and cloth, but for once, why couldn't she have left well enough alone?

"I'm so sorry."

"Don't worry about it," he said woodenly. How was he going to explain this to the family? Everyone loved using Dad's rowboat. It was as if Marvin Tyler's spirit still hovered around the little craft in which he'd spent so many happy hours.

"But I can't help worrying," she said through chattering teeth. "When I'm to blame for something, I own up to it. I can't just let it go."

Some people go quiet during times of unexpected calamity, facing the unknown with stoic silence. Lacy Evans was not one of them. She lamented loud and long over the lost fishing poles, the oars, the padded and much-patched seat bolted to the front thwart, even the lures in the rusty tackle box. Nothing was excluded from her litany of woe.

They drew nearer to the shore. The water reached only mid-thigh at that point. Then the unthinkable happened. Instead of sand under his feet, Jake felt the suck of mud. He took another step with his right foot, but his left didn't move, stuck fast in the sludgy bottom of the lake. Then when he gave his leg a twist to pull it free, he felt, rather than heard, an ominous *click*. The pin on his prosthesis had come undone.

The only thing keeping his leg in place was the mud

his foot was stuck in and his dad's old jeans. The prosthesis weighed about three pounds. Since Lake Jewel was spring-fed, there was always some movement under the surface. If his leg came out of the jeans and got loose from the mud, it might be swept along in a current. He'd never find it. If he lost his leg, it would take months to replace, never mind costing *another* arm and a leg to boot. He would *not* go back to a wheelchair. Or even a pair of crutches if he could help it. He couldn't work at the grill like that.

Jake sat down in the water and grabbed his metal ankle.

"Go on ahead," he said.

"Why? What's wrong?"

"I said go on."

"No, not unless—"

"Lacy," he said sharply as he glared up at her. "My leg has come unfastened. I have to take it off the rest of the way here and then reattach it once I get to shore."

"When the boat started sinking, I forgot about your leg. You'll need someone to lean on, won't you?"

"No."

But she wouldn't take no for an answer, grasping his arm and giving him an ineffective tug. He wished he could be entirely sucked into the mud hole that had grasped his prosthetic foot.

"Leave me be. I mean it."

He hadn't raised his voice, but she must have heard the steel in his tone. Stricken, she turned away from him and made for the lakeshore.

"There's a path in the woods a few yards up that embankment," he said once she climbed out of the water. "Turn north and follow it. It'll take you back to the house."

Visibly shivering, she plopped down on a stump halfway up the embankment. "Not until you're out of the water, too."

She was right. Lake Jewel was so cold, if he didn't get out

soon, hypothermia was a real possibility even in spring. All his senses went on high alert.

A sudden rustle in the woods to the right pricked his ears and movement caught the corner of his eye. Heart pounding, he jerked his gaze a few yards down the shoreline and saw that it was only a whitetail doe coming down for a drink.

Feeling stupid for being spooked by a deer, Jake reached down and yanked his prosthetic foot out of the mud. Then he eased the leg out of the jeans. It was a relief to hold the titanium rod in his hand. Normally, Lake Jewel was clear enough to see ten feet down, but with the sinking rowboat and the way they'd mucked toward the shore, he and Lacy had churned up plenty of silt. If he lost his grip on the leg now, he'd be hard pressed to find it again.

He rolled in the water and started side-stroking toward shore. It was slow going. A pair of jays scolded overhead, their cries unnaturally loud. To his hypervigilant ears, it sounded like a warning. Like the high-pitched ululations of Afghani women . . .

Lacy was staring at him, her face white as those sheets in the lake house. He jerked his gaze away and focused instead on the flat rock outcropping at the water's edge that was his goal. Flecks of mica glinted in the sunlight. It was almost as if the rock was shining a searchlight on him, the better to illuminate his humiliation. He didn't want Lacy to see him like this. He couldn't let anyone see him. He wouldn't—

"Get down, Tyler," his commanding officer whispered fiercely. He yanked Jake down so roughly, he landed hard on his knees and then went flat on his belly.

He and the lieutenant had trekked for three klicks, forded the Helmand River in the dark, and now were humping it up a desolate hill. The plan for this recon mission was to use the night-vision gear in their packs to get a look at activity in the village over the ridge. Taliban fighters were suspected of hiding within the civilian population there, but Jake's CO needed accurate intel before sending in the whole unit to flush out the bad guys.

"There's a sniper out there," his CO said.

There was no moon, but Jake had never seen a night sky so filled with stars. They stretched in brittle pinpricks from one horizon to the other.

"A sniper can't hit what he can't see," Jake whispered back.

"This one can. If you break over that ridge standing up, you make a void in the stars behind you. It's a bullet magnet. That's how Stensrud bought it last month."

So Jake crawled. Slowly. Upward. Taking care not to make a void. Not to expose his position. Not to be seen.

Once he reached the top, he rolled onto his back, clutching his weapon in one hand. He couldn't turn loose of it or he might not find it again. It was so dark. Even the stars had gone dim. He—

"Jake?"

Someone else was there. Someone who was patting his cheeks. Whoever they were, they were sitting up beside him. Breaking over the ridge.

"No! There's a sniper. Get down," Jake said as loudly as he dared.

In the last firefight his unit had been in, his buddy Henderson had been right by his side when he took a bullet. Jake couldn't bear to watch the light go out of another pair of eyes. Not if he could help it.

Even though he couldn't see this new jarhead clearly, Jake grabbed him and yanked him down hard beside him before the enemy sniper could pick him off.

"Jake!"

He blinked slowly and found himself lying flat on his back on the rock outcropping at the lake's edge. Chest heaving, he gazed up at the canopy of a forest near to bursting into full leaf.

He wasn't downrange in Afghanistan. It wasn't night and that darn sure wasn't another jarhead he'd manhandled into a position of supposed safety on the rock beside him.

"Lacy," he whispered.

Jake realized that instead of his weapon, he held his prosthetic leg in his left hand. He'd had a flashback. Zoned out for a bit.

In front of *her*.

His belly spiraled downward. He'd rather she had walked in on him and caught him naked in that frigid shower. Cold water does a favor to no man, but it would have been preferable to this.

She'd caught his soul naked. She'd *seen* him at his most vulnerable. His weakness had broken over the ridge.

Lacy sat up and rubbed her upper arm. There was a red spot where he'd gripped her hard. It might even bruise. He'd rather take a beating than leave a mark on her.

"Jake, what in the world was that about?"

"Nothing. Get going back to the house. The walk will warm you up."

"Not until—"

"Look," he said, angrier with himself over hurting her than embarrassed about his prosthesis now. He needed to get away from her, but at this point, he'd have to convince her to do the getting. "I have to put my leg back on and I'd rather do it without an audience, if you don't mind."

He sat up and gave her his best leer. "Unless you'd like to strip, wring out your clothes, and let me watch while you put *them* back on. . . ."

That put her on her feet. She was trotting up the path and gone before he could get the hem of the jeans rolled up enough to reattach his leg.

Murphy was definitely in charge. Whatever could go wrong with this date, *had* gone wrong. Horribly, irrevocably wrong.

Lacy stomped through the woods, water squishing from her sneakers with each step. Her chest burned. Bradford Endicott might have stolen her reputation and her livelihood, but he'd never laid a hand on her in anger.

She'd never forgive Jake. Never.

Yes, she'd lost his father's rowboat, but she'd said she was sorry.

What was wrong with him?

Jake had been aggressive on the gridiron when they were in school and he had thrashed those bullies, but she'd never thought of him as the violent sort. This . . . "episode," for lack of a better word, wasn't like him at all.

At least, she wouldn't have said so. Still, a lot could change in ten years or so. Heaven knew she wasn't the dreamer she'd been back then, but she was still basically the same person. When Jake had grabbed her, she'd looked into the wild eyes of a stranger. She hadn't recognized him at all.

She picked up her pace, eating up the distance to the lake house in a quick dogtrot. Then a sudden thought stopped her cold.

"What if it wasn't him?" she whispered to herself. What had he said? It hadn't made much sense. Something about a sniper and getting down as if she were in danger before he grabbed her and hauled her to the ground.

Maybe Jake had had a flashback from his time in Afghanistan. A symptom of PTSD. She didn't know much about post-traumatic stress, but if anyone qualified for the disorder, a battle-tested amputee probably would. The anger she felt toward him began to dissipate. It was replaced by something else.

Not pity. Jake would be the first to reject that, she real- ized. No, it was understanding. Empathy. Lacy had a hard time connecting with others. If she kept to herself, no one could hurt or disappoint her. But Jake's weakness wakened something in her.

She felt an ever-strengthening tie to Jake. What if he hadn't meant to scare her any more than she'd meant to sink the Tyler family rowboat?

Of course, if Jake had these attacks of sudden fierceness with any regularity, she'd need to protect herself from them. Still, she'd help him if she could. She wouldn't turn her back on him.

That was why, when she slipped into the lake house to look for a blanket to wrap herself in, she made it a point to find two.

He half expected that Lacy had kept running and was now a quarter of the way around the lake, heading back to town. Instead, he found her curled up, knees tucked to her chest, in one of the Adirondack chairs on the front deck of the cottage. With an old quilt draped over her shoulders, she stared calmly out on the lake, not so much as glancing in his direction as he climbed the stairs to the deck.

An army blanket was folded on the chair beside her.

"For me?" he asked.

When she nodded, he wrapped the scratchy fabric around himself and sat down. The blanket absorbed some of the lake water that clung to him and emitted a wet woolly smell in exchange. Silence stretched between them. Neither of them seemed inclined to speak first, to fill the quiet as the sun beat down on them.

Finally Lacy turned to look at him and said in a whisper, "Does it happen often?"

He didn't pretend to misunderstand her, but he wasn't sure

how to answer her question. How many times did it take to make a pattern? How often qualified as often? One flashback was too many for him. He settled for a shrug.

"Do you want to talk about it?" she asked.

"No."

Birdsong erupted in the woods. A breeze set the trees whispering to each other. Now that Jake was warming up, he felt a little drowsy. He closed his eyes, letting the tension leach out of his body. At least Lacy hadn't run away from him screaming her head off.

"If you won't talk to me, are you at least talking to *somebody* about it?" she asked after a few minutes. "A doctor? A therapist?"

"No," he said wearily. "Are you seeing a financial adviser to help you get back on your feet after your trouble in Boston?"

"Touché." She stood, pulling the quilt tight around her wet jeans and T-shirt. "I guess you should take me home now."

"We haven't had lunch yet. It won't take long to grill those steaks," he offered, though part of him was relieved that she was ready to call it quits and declare this date officially dead.

"I'm not really hungry. Besides, I didn't bring a change of clothes. You may look good in your dad's old things, but I'd be swimming in them."

She thought he looked good. It was all he heard and he hugged it close. Not that Jake was vain or anything, but he'd been considered attractive for most of his life. It was hard to accept that women might not find him so now. Lacy was one of the only ones who still did. She'd even seemed to forget about his leg.

For a while, he had, too.

One corner of his mouth lifted as he rose and headed toward his pickup. He helped her into the cab of the truck.

Then he came around to the driver's side as quickly as a man with two good legs. He hauled himself in and revved the engine to life. She still had kind things to say to him. It was more than he'd dared hope.

But then hope faded as they passed the trip back to town in uncomfortable silence. After he pulled into the small parking lot behind her building, he started to get out to walk her up to her door, but she stopped him.

"Really, there's no need, Jake. It's a flight of stairs you shouldn't have to climb. We can say good-bye here."

Good-bye. That sounded final. But then she didn't open her door to get out.

"Something on your mind?"

She glanced at him. "Promise you won't be mad?"

"Lacy, I wasn't mad at you before. I was mad at myself because . . . I wasn't myself." The words he'd bottled up came tumbling out now. "I'm sorry I scared you, but I'm even sorrier that I . . . hurt you."

"I'll heal." A hand went to her upper arm. The red marks had faded. Perhaps she wouldn't bruise after all. "And you'll heal, too, Jake. But you can't do it alone. You need help. You need to talk to somebody about this. If not to a doctor, what about your pastor? Or another veteran?"

It would mean admitting he had a problem. Admitting he was weak. The only way he kept going was by telling himself he was still a marine. Still strong. Still dangerous. He could take whatever the world dished out and throw it back at the buggers.

But if his own mind was doing the dishing, where did that leave him?

Because she looked so concerned, he mumbled, "I'll think about it."

"Good." She hopped out of the truck, shut the door behind her, and then leaned on the open window. "Next Thursday, bring that chair we're redoing for your mom over to my dad's garage. We can work on it there."

Just like that. As if nothing had happened. He wished he could have pulled her back into the truck and kissed her. But after the way he'd manhandled her when he was in the middle of that flashback, he decided he'd better go slow.

"And maybe by next Thursday you'll have figured out who you want to talk to about . . . things," she said with a hopeful smile.

"Is that a requirement for us to spend next Thursday together?"

Her smile grew brittle. "Yes."

Jake swallowed hard. He didn't want to talk to anyone about it. He just wanted the flashbacks to go away without having to rehash it all. When he'd shipped out in that medvac copter, he was only skimming the surface of consciousness. He'd come to for a moment as the ground sank beneath him and he'd closed the door to Afghanistan in his mind. Now his time in Helmand province kept breaking through around the cracks, but talking to someone about it meant he'd have to pry open the door completely.

He badly wanted not to have to ask for help. But he wanted just as badly not to mess up this chance to be with Lacy.

"All right." If spilling his guts to somebody was the price of admission, he'd do it. "Since you want me to, I'll find someone to talk to."

"Thank you, Jake. But I hope you'll do it for you, not for me."

"OK." Why kid himself? He was doing it for her. "Then once we finish the chair for Mom, you'll have to come back out to the lake house so we can show it to her together."

His family was planning a start-of-the-season cookout in a few weeks. If he brought Lacy, it would get his family off his back about finding a girlfriend.

"After what I did to your dad's boat, are you sure you want me at the lake house?"

He wanted her all right. Anywhere he could have her. That was the one thing he was sure of.

"It'll be OK." He flashed his best smile and, wonder of wonders, she returned it. "If they can raise the *Titanic,* I ought to be able to figure out how to raise a rowboat."

Chapter 13

I watch Dr. Phil. I know folks are always trying to feel better about life by talking themselves blue over every little thing that ever happened to them. But to my mind, the best way to feel better about my troubles is to help somebody else get a handle on theirs. Everybody who has skin needs to give and receive some hugs. That's why I hand them out at the Green Apple, along with the raspberry tart.

—Ethel Ringwald, waitress at the Green Apple Grill

"I saw that movie back when I was in Boston, but my attitude was pretty bad then. I was hoping that had colored how the story hit me." Lacy and Heather Walker came out of the Regal Theater and headed toward their building across the street on the Square. "Unfortunately, my attitude wasn't the problem. The movie hasn't improved with time."

"I know what you mean," Heather said. "All rom-coms follow the same tired formula. The couple starts out hating each other with a purple passion. They're at loggerheads for the entire movie, and then when all seems lost, they suddenly discover they can't live without each other."

"Right? Why can't they make a movie where the couple starts out as friends or at least able to tolerate each other? Instant hate that changes to eternal love in ninety minutes or less is a little hard to swallow."

"Yeah, but we can't help hoping, can we?" Heather grinned as they turned down the alley that led to the iron staircase and deck they shared.

"So I'm guessing you're not seeing anybody," Lacy said.

Heather shook her head as they climbed the stairs. "I work such weird hours at the hospital, it's hard to meet someone."

"No workplace romance, then?" Lacy said. Heather was an RN in the emergency room at Coldwater General. "In my mom's soaps, hospitals are always hotbeds of romantic intrigue."

"I make it a point never to date a patient. All the doctors are either married or hopelessly old or both. And the only male nurse is sweet, but he's gay. There's a cute EMT who comes in sometimes, but he's always out again before I can shake free of the emergency he brings us."

"Too bad," Lacy said as they continued to climb. "How did you come to rent from Mrs. Paderewski? I thought your family owns most of the buildings ringing the Square."

"They do. Pretty much all of them except this one that belongs to Mrs. P. Oh! And the one that houses the Green Apple. Jacob Tyler owns that," Heather said. "My folks have renovated most of the second stories around the Square into residential apartments, though I think a couple of college kids use the one over the ice-cream shop as office space. They're trying to put together an IT start-up. At least that's what my dad hopes they're doing. They keep the shades drawn so he's not really sure."

"What else might they be up to?"

"Meth lab, online porn site, who knows? There's no end to my dad's ability to think the worst of people."

"Well, why didn't you rent that place from your folks instead of Mrs. P's unit? It would've spared them the agony of wondering what's happening behind the drawn shades."

"And why didn't you move back in with your parents?" Heather said with a roll of her eyes.

"Point taken." When they reached the top of the stairs, Lacy said, "I'd ask you in for a drink, but I can't vouch for your safety. My cat isn't very sociable."

"Is it your cat or did Mrs. P stick you with one of hers?"

"One of hers? She said Effie was left by the previous tenant."

"Naw, that's just her way of finding a home for one of her rescue cats," Heather said. "She bullies new renters into taking one and then charges them pet rent for the privilege."

Lacy huffed indignantly. "You might have warned me. Did she get you to take one, too?"

Heather shook her head. "I told her I had a goldfish so I couldn't have a cat."

"Wish I'd thought of that. Did you have a fish?"

"I do now," Heather said with a grin. "Come on in and I'll introduce you to Errol Finn. If you don't want sangria, I've got some decaf or herbal tea."

"Tea would be great," Lacy said as she followed Heather into her place. "Well, this is cute."

Heather's apartment was the mirror image of Lacy's. Her tastes ran more to shabby chic than the spare clean lines Lacy favored, but the place was neat and well pulled together. It was as restful as Heather's company, and Lacy needed restful after the time she'd spent with Jacob at the lake that afternoon.

"And here's Errol." Heather waved a hand toward the small bowl on the end of her kitchen counter. A little goldfish swam in slow circles around the perimeter.

"Bet he's a lot less trouble than Effie. I hope she's a good mouser."

Heather's eyes widened in alarm. "You have mice?"

"No, but I just keep hoping the cat has at least one redeeming quality. I never met a more aloof, more . . . *entitled* creature in my life—and bear in mind I've worked with the upper crust of Boston!" Lacy said. "The only good thing Effie has ever done is rub on Jake's prosthetic leg as if it were a real one."

"At least the cat has good taste in men. Jacob Tyler. Now

that's a topic I was hoping would come up. I heard you two were going out," Heather said as she put on the kettle. "Spill."

"Word travels fast around here. Even if it isn't on the Methodist prayer chain." Lacy sat on one of the two bar stools at Heather's counter. "But I wouldn't say Jake and I are going out. More like just spending time together. As friends."

Heather cast a skeptical glance her way and plucked a couple of mint tea bags from the tin. "Can any girl really be 'just friends' with Jake Tyler?"

"She can if she's trying not to get her heart broken. You know how he is."

"How he *was*," Heather corrected. "He's changed since we were in high school. And I don't mean just his leg, though I'm sure that'll do a number on any guy."

"I really don't want to talk about him." If Lacy did, it would feel like a betrayal. In the short time they'd spent together, she'd discovered a number of his secrets. She didn't want to let one slip.

"Okay." Heather switched topics and asked about her new job at the *Gazette*. Then when that subject dried up, Heather steered the conversation to Lacy's old job in Boston.

She seriously didn't want to talk about that either. "So, Heather, since you're a nurse, maybe you can help me. I'm thinking about doing a piece for the *Gazette* about PTSD." She was thinking no such thing, but it was a safer subject than Boston or Jake. "What can you tell me about the disorder?"

Heather cocked her head to one side as if scenting a deception, yet not quite able to decide what it might be. "Well, some experts describe PTSD as a natural reaction to an unnatural circumstance."

"What do you mean?"

"PTSD happens when a person has been subjected to a traumatic event. Something really out of the ordinary. An assault, a terrible accident, something life-threatening." The kettle sang out so Heather removed it from the burner. She filled their cups and dunked both teabags. "Statistically, women are more likely than men to experience PTSD."

"Oh? That's news. I always thought of it as an issue for the military."

"Well, that's true," Heather said. "It's definitely a problem for the armed services and has been since they called it 'shell shock' back in World War One. They described soldiers returning from the trenches as having a 'thousand-yard stare.'"

Lacy lifted her teabag and dunked it again. A minty aroma rose from the cup. A thousand-yard stare? While Jake was having that flashback, his eyes had been wild, but he didn't stare like that all the time. "How can you tell if someone has PTSD?"

"A doctor needs to make that diagnosis, but there are some strong indicators anyone can observe."

"Like flashbacks?"

"Yes, and nightmares. A change in personality. They become detached from the people they used to care about. Their symptoms start to interfere with work."

Jake was still involved with his family and he was the life's blood of the Green Apple. But while he and Lacy were together at the lake, he'd definitely had an episode when he didn't seem to know where he was or whom he was with.

"Shouldn't you be taking notes if this is for a piece in the paper?" Heather asked.

"Probably. But right now I'm just gathering a little background info. If I quote you, I'll run it by you before it goes to print."

Heather shrugged her assent. "Do you like honey in your tea?" she asked as she took a jar down from the shelf and spooned some into hers.

"No, I learned to drink it straight up. It's easier." And cheaper. In the early days when she was trying to get her business off the ground, she had economized any way she could. Lacy took a small sip so as not to burn her tongue.

She wondered how long it had been since Jake had lost his leg. He was home before his dad passed last year, so the blast that took his leg had happened before that. Since she was in charge of the "Ago" columns at the paper, no one would think it strange if she dug into the archives for that info. Surely there had been a piece about Jake's return home.

"You say PTSD is triggered by trauma. Do people show symptoms right away after the event?"

"Usually within a month. But not always. Sometimes it takes years to show up."

"Is it curable?" Lacy asked.

"It's treatable, which isn't quite the same thing. Sometimes, the symptoms go away completely the farther you get from the event," Heather said. "Then in other cases, the best you can hope is that symptoms become less pronounced over time. It's sort of like diabetics who monitor their blood sugar to help control the disease. Someone with PTSD can learn to live with it and keep away from triggers that launch an episode."

Lacy wondered what about being at the lake had triggered Jake's flashback. "But what if it's not treated?"

"PTSD can lead to depression, which is a lot more serious than people think. It's much more than just feeling blue," Heather said. "Then if patients self-medicate their depression with drugs or alcohol, it can end in addiction. And often in homelessness."

"Do you suppose that's what happened to Lester Scott?" He'd been homeless since he'd left Daniel's mother a few weeks before Lacy's graduation. Back when she was dating Daniel that summer, he hadn't been one to talk about what had happened with his father. But she'd made some pretty good guesses. No one should need to go to the emergency room as often as his mother had. And Daniel had his own share of unexplained bruises and broken bones over the years, too, until Lester limped out of their lives.

With a shiner and a cast of his own.

Lacy hadn't had much sympathy for the homeless vet. But now she wondered if he was a victim of PTSD, too.

"Oh! So this is about Lester," Heather said with obvious relief. "For a minute, I was afraid you were worried about Jake. He sure seems like he's adjusted well enough, but I thought maybe you knew something I didn't. Come on into the living room and let's get comfy."

Lacy carried her warm cup into the next room and settled in a corner of the over-stuffed sofa. She missed Shannon so, but Heather was quickly filling up that empty friend space. They'd taken different sorts of classes in high school—Lacy gravitating toward the arts and Heather eating up as much math and science as she could—so they really hadn't known each other well then. Now it felt wonderful to be able to relax with someone who was smart, perceptive, and not overwhelmed by drama of her own.

Lacy was determined not to burden Heather with any of hers. She knew in her head that was what friends were for, but it was still hard for her to let anyone into her private space.

"Say, I've got an idea for an article for the paper." Heather took the opposite corner of the couch. She set her teacup on the end table, kicked off her shoes, and pulled her feet up, crossing her ankles yoga style. "How about doing a piece on the Coldwater Warm Hearts Club?"

"The what?"

"The Coldwater Warm Hearts Club. That's what we call ourselves, though it's really not so much a club as, well, just a group of friends who meet for breakfast at the Green Apple. Tuesday mornings at seven-thirty. I'm just getting off my shift then, but it's before work or school for the rest of the gang."

Lacy set her cup down, too. "What do you meet about?"

"About how to help other people."

"Oh. It's another service club." Wanda Cruikshank had already assigned Lacy a piece on the Rotarians and their upcoming spaghetti dinner to raise funds for school supplies in Guatemala. Then just to make it fair, over the next few weeks, Lacy would have to do articles on the Lions Club, the Benevolent and Protective Order of Elks, and the PEO.

"Yeah, I suppose you could call us a service club, but we're not all that organized about it," Heather said. "We're different in another way, too."

"How's that?"

"Well, we do good like the members of those other organizations, but unlike them, we have an ulterior motive."

"Oh, my." Lacy sat up straight, intrigued. "That sounds slightly sinister."

"Not really. It has to do with the whole karmic, sowing and reaping thing. That's the reason we do good, you see," Heather said. "All the members of the Coldwater Warm Hearts Club have things in our pasts we're trying to work through. In my case, it's survivor guilt."

"Oh." Lacy remembered running into Heather on her first day home at the grave of her sister. "Because of Jessica."

Heather nodded and sighed. "She was the golden child. I was the also-ran. When she died, I was sure my parents wished it had been me who drove that car into the lake."

"Heather, I'm sure they didn't."

"I am, too. Most of the time." She took a long sip of her tea. "Guilt over being the one 'not taken' drove me nuts all through college and well past graduating from nursing school."

"So what got you through it?" Lacy asked.

"Do you remember Mrs. Chisholm?"

Lacy frowned. "Wasn't she the town librarian when we were in grade school?"

"The same."

"I remember she complained about everything. We were always too loud. We didn't handle the books carefully enough to suit her. We let the door shut behind us too hard. She was positively ancient when we were little," Lacy said. "Is she still alive?"

"And still complaining." Heather chuckled. "Being confined to a wheelchair hasn't sweetened her temper one bit, but she's lucky enough to still be in her own home. Her poor niece Peggy takes care of her."

"Sign her up for the Mother Teresa Award." Lacy raised her teacup in salute.

"Amen." Heather lifted her cup as well and clicked rims with Lacy. "Anyway, I could see how Peggy was flagging each time she brought her aunt to the hospital for this or that. So on my next day off, I offered to take care of Mrs. Chisholm so Peggy could have a little time to herself. I don't know what possessed me to do it."

"Martyr complex?"

Heather shook her head. "It was out of my mouth before I realized what I was saying. The old lady is just as difficult as she ever was. In only one afternoon, I was exhausted by her constant demands, but Peggy was so pathetically grateful, it was worth giving up my free day." A small smile lifted the corners of her mouth. "And I noticed something as I walked home."

"What?"

"I didn't feel crappy about me for a change. Compared to Peggy's burden, mine felt light."

Lacy chuckled. "You know that's why horror films are so popular, don't you? They prove however awful we think things are, they could always be worse."

"It was more than that," Heather insisted. "Feeling guilty for breathing is a full-time job, and believe me, I'd been gainfully employed for a long time. When I helped Peggy, I got out of myself for a while. I stopped feeling guilty about me while I put someone else first."

"And that put everything in a different light," Lacy said in sudden understanding.

"Right. After that, I started organizing regular respite days for Peggy, setting up a rotation of alternate caregivers. Then I experimented with other 'random acts of kindness.'" Heather made air quotes with her fingers. "In every case, I got more out of the deal than the people I helped."

"I'm not sure that's true, but it's good you felt that way," Lacy said. "So how did this experiment morph into a club?"

"I discovered there were other people who felt the same way—people who've got things they're trying to work through and have discovered that getting their minds off themselves is the best cure. Not that the club is a substitute for therapy or anything," Heather hastened to add, "but it certainly can't hurt. So now we meet to compare notes."

"What kind of notes?"

"We share who we've helped and how helping them helped us. See? Like I say. We have an ulterior motive," Heather said. "And if we need to, we team up for some projects."

"Projects like what?"

"Like shoveling for shut-ins last winter."

"Shoveling? Really? You got snow here?" Boston had suffered through a record-breaking winter last year. The Coldwater winters Lacy remembered were barren, but not white.

"Oh, yeah. We got four inches one time. With ice."

"Bostonians call three or four inches of snow a dusting."

"Yeah, but even New Englanders better take our ice seriously or they'll end up in the ditch." Heather tipped back her cup, and then headed for the kitchen for a refill. "Want some more?"

"No, I'm fine," Lacy said. But she wasn't fine. Not only

was she worried about Jacob having PTSD, the first payment on her loan from the O'Leary brothers was coming due in a couple of days. She'd scraped together enough to make that payment, but it would gobble up nearly all of her first paycheck from the *Gazette* to do it. How she'd stay current with that infernal loan and keep body and soul together was a total mystery.

Helping people and getting a warm fuzzy over it was all fine and good. But a warm fuzzy wouldn't solve her problem.

Lacy needed cash. Lots and lots of cash.

And she had no clue where she'd get it.

Chapter 14

If a problem can be solved with money, it's not really much of a problem, is it? Unless, of course, you have no money.

—George Evans, Esq., attorney at law and prosecutor, judge, and jury for squirrels of any stripe

When Lacy pulled into her parents' driveway, she discovered her dad working out on his front lawn with a spray bottle in his hand. Spritzing away, he circled one of the hundred-year-old oaks. She turned off the Volvo and climbed out.

"Lacy! There you are," he said in his usual booming voice. "Say, I saw that piece you did on the Rotary Club. Well done, daughter. Dorie Higginbottom, huh?"

"I thought it would be best if I use a pen name for my byline."

"Hmph! You might have picked a better one than that. Your mom hated her maiden name, you know," he reminded her. "Looks like the job is going OK though?"

"Yes, Dad. The job is fine." Writing for the *Gazette* didn't thrill her like a beautifully designed space did, but it paid the bills. Barely. Dad *would* think the article was good. Having been a Rotarian for ages, he was in favor of anything that publicized the group's activities. But the piece took no particular talent for Lacy to pull together. Just the facts with a dash of human interest about the Rotarians' upcoming project, the article had practically written itself.

When Lacy gave her dad a hug, she was nearly knocked

off her feet by the whiff of a pungent, and horrifically un-pleasant, odor. "Phew! Why does it smell like a moldy taco in a dirty bathroom around here?"

Dad brandished his spray bottle. "My secret weapon. It's do-it-yourself squirrel repellent."

"Smells strong enough to peel wallpaper." Lacy wrinkled her nose. "What's in it?"

"A pinch of this and a dash of that. I chopped up onions and jalapeños and garlic and boiled them half to death. Then I drained off the liquid into this spray bottle and added a little cayenne pepper for good measure." He gave her a sheepish glance. "And a bit of urine, too."

"Urine!"

"That's how animals mark their territory, isn't it? This yard is mine and I mean for those rascals to know it."

He glared up at a trio of reddish-brown squirrels on one of the limbs of the tree whose trunk he was spraying. Well out of range of his spray nozzle, the animals chattered down at him.

"You have to come down sometime," he yelled up at them, and then turned back to Lacy. "Once the little buggers get this on their feet, they'll give my trees a wide berth."

"I see Fergus is giving you one, too." The Yorkie was pac-ing the front porch, alternately whining and sneezing.

Her father had the grace to look embarrassed. "Poor little guy. Guess he got a bit too close when I was spraying. I'll have to give him a bath in a bit. Don't tell your mother."

"I'll add it to the list," Lacy said as she headed toward the house.

"No need to go in. Your mom's not here. My squirrel repellent . . . well, let's just say it repels more than squirrels. Your mother decided she'll stay with your sister until the smell clears out of the kitchen."

Lacy's older sister, Crystal, was Coldwater Cove's answer to Mary Poppins—practically perfect in every way. Instead of bolting away to a university after high school, she'd pleased their parents by staying in town to continue her studies at Bates College. Then she went on to become the exclusive school's dean of admissions. Crystal married Noah Addleberry, oldest son and heir of one of the town's founding families. In Coldwater society, the match was roughly equivalent to becoming a Kennedy by marriage. Crystal and Noah had two above-average children, two BMWs, and two pedigreed poodles, all neatly wrapped by a white picket fence around a two-story Craftsman.

Lacy had only seen her sister at their parents' home in passing since she'd returned. She could never live up to Crystal's standard and had given up trying.

"Mom asked me to come over when I had time to help her sort out what she should sell in a yard sale and what she should keep." Lacy couldn't wait to get her hands on the living room and clear out some of the extraneous stuff. But now that her mom was ensconced at Crystal's house, who knew when, or if, the Mother-of-all-Garage-Sales would get off the ground. "Doesn't she still want to have a sale?"

"Oh, yes. She's very keen on that. She's sure you'll find some real treasures among her things, just like you did for Mrs. Tyler."

"I'm probably banned from Secondhand Junk-shun for life over that." News about the rare Fiestaware had made the rounds. Phyllis Wannamaker, the owner of the Junk-shun, was still furious that Lacy had been able to find a well-heeled buyer among her former New England clients for the set of soup bowls. Jake's mother was floored when Lacy delivered a check for a little over $4,300 for them. Then Mrs. Tyler insisted on writing a check back to Lacy for fifteen percent of the amount.

"After all, I'd have paid Phyllis her cut if the bowls had sold at the Junk-shun," Jake's mom had said. "This is only fair. I insist."

Lacy hadn't wanted to take it, but in the end, she had and was grateful. It meant she didn't need to eat ramen noodles every night for the rest of the month.

"Dad, can Jake and I use your garage on Thursday?"

"Sure. What for?" he asked without glancing her way as he continued to spray down the trunk. This battle in the War of Squirrel Insurgency required his complete attention.

"I'm going to help him refinish a chair for his mom and he wants it to be a surprise."

"Okay. Sure. Just put the tools back where you find them. But speaking of surprises, I'm a little surprised you're seeing so much of Jacob."

"Why? Don't you like him?"

"It's not that. I like him fine. He's a good man. Works hard. Served his country and paid the price for it." Her dad stopped spritzing long enough to fix her with a searching gaze. "But didn't you always say Jacob Tyler wasn't the sort of fellow a girl could count on for long?"

"I did." It would do no good to remind him that years had passed since Jake was the town Don Juan. "But don't worry. Jake and I are just friends, Dad. We're not dating or anything. I just helped him open his family's lake house and found a chair worth redoing. That's all."

"Good. I'd hate to see you hurt again so soon after that business with Bradford Endicott." He started to spray the tree again and then stopped and stared at his secret weapon. "Say, if you think this stuff will remove wallpaper, it might take off old varnish, too. Want me to brew up another batch to use on that furniture you're redoing?"

"No," she said quickly. Putting that vile stuff on the Tylers' Danish modern side chair would be sacrilege, and more importantly, if her dad kept making squirrel repellent, her mother might never come home. "Don't make any more. We won't need any varnish remover for our project."

Lacy's dad continued to work his way around the biggest oak's trunk. A handful of twigs and acorns rained down on him. He jerked upright to glare at the squirrels, but the animals were just sitting on a branch, seeming to ignore him.

"Look at 'em. Butter wouldn't melt in their mouths. Let's see how cool they are once they climb down this tree." The bark glistened with the odiferous repellent.

"Well, I guess I'd better get going, then." Lacy needed to escape the smell. Her nose hairs were starting to curl.

"Oh, I almost forgot. Your mother said if you came by to help her go through her treasures, I was to say she wants you to call her cell phone so she can meet you at Gewgaws and Gizzwickies."

"Why? I thought the point of having a yard sale was to get rid of things."

"It is. To make room for new things, your mom says. Call her, Lacy. It'll make her day. And it'll make my day if those little rats would just . . ."

At that moment, the three squirrels bounded away from them, leaping from branch to branch, tree to tree until they chased each other down the trunk of an oak . . . in Mr. Mayhew's front yard.

"Dad, I think there's a flaw in your plan."

Lacy trailed her mother down the narrow aisle at Gewgaws and Gizzwickies with all the enthusiasm of a three-toed sloth. Unlike the Secondhand Junk-shun, this shop wasn't chopped up into small booths. Mom explained that while everything was here on consignment, just like at the Junk-shun, in Gewgaws and Gizzwickies similar items were displayed together regardless of who the vendor was. Only the color and style of the price sticker indicated the original owner of each piece.

"What if a price tag comes off?"

"Don't worry. Gloria will know who it belongs to," Mom

said. "She knows to the inch where everything is in her shop. One day I was in here after some kids had come roaring through the store. It all looked fine to me. Nothing broken, at least. But Gloria made a quick sweep, stopped beside a perfectly lovely arrangement of artificial fruit, and said, 'Would you look at that? Those fool kids have been messin' with the grapes.' She moved the bunch over a half an inch or so and was satisfied it was right again. The woman has a memory like a steel trap."

"Or OCD," Lacy muttered. Who cared whether plastic grapes were moved a smidge?

"Lacy Dorie Evans, I'm surprised at you." Her mom glowered at her. "That was unkind and uncalled for. I raised you better than that."

Lacy sighed. Her mother was right. It was OK when her snark was directed at herself. Not so OK when she unleashed it on someone else. "Sorry."

"That's better," her mother said as she meandered on. She paused before a display of vases and picked up the most ghastly of the bunch. No flower arrangement on earth would compensate for its horribleness. The ceramic monstrosity was totally out of proportion with a minuscule foot and a bulbous body. But the oversized gilded handles caught her mother's eye. Like a moth to flame, Shirley Evans was drawn to bling, in whatever form it presented itself.

"Mom, I really wish you'd wait until after your yard sale to start accumulating *more* stuff," Lacy said as she tried to ease the vase from her mother's grip. Mom wasn't having any of it. She hugged her find closer.

"You mean more *treasures,* not more *stuff,*" she said defensively. "Honestly, even if I do sell some of my things, you can't expect me to leave my living room as bare as that apartment of yours."

"No, of course not. I'd never suggest such a thing." *As if*

Mom would take my advice if I did! "It wouldn't suit you or the house. Your home is traditional, so if you want to keep true to the bones of the place, you need classic accessories. Like this." She picked up a crystal vase with a simple fluted shape. "It may not be Lalique, but it's not a bad imitation."

"How do you know it's not Lally-whatever?"

Lacy turned the vase over and showed her mother the smooth base. "No maker's mark. If there's no R. Lalique etched into the glass somewhere, chances are it's not a real Lalique."

"Seems real enough to me," Mom said.

To Lacy's relief, her mother returned the blingy vase to its place on the shelf and took the crystal one from her.

"I guess this'll be all right if you think it's the one I should have," Mom said with a sigh. "But you've become a terrible snob, Lacy. Do you know that?"

Lacy blinked hard. It was as if her mom had slapped her. "Knowing about fine things doesn't make me a snob."

"No, but sneering at the rest of us for enjoying what we like does."

Lacy opened her mouth, but no words came out. Would her mother give her sister Crystal a smackdown like that? No, because Crystal never did or said anything wrong. But even her brother, Mike, who was habitually in trouble, wouldn't get treatment like that from their mother. He hadn't come home in years. But if he did, Mom would be afraid to rock the boat with too much scolding.

The injustice stung. She was about to say so when Gloria came up behind them and slid a hand through her mother's arm, linking elbows with her.

"Shirley, how did you and your daughter slip in here without me seeing you?"

"You were ringing up a sale," Lacy's mom said. "You always have the prettiest things. They must just fly out the door all day."

"Look, Shirl, I know you're always on the hunt for roosters for your kitchen," Gloria began.

"George threatens divorce whenever I bring a new one home, but there's still a little room above my kitchen cabinets," Lacy's mother said. "If I don't point it out to him, he won't notice another anyway."

"What our husbands don't know doesn't hurt us," the shop owner said. The two women tittered together for a moment, and then Gloria went on. "Well, I just got in this new piece that I think you'll like even if it's not a rooster." She started toward the front of the shop, motioning for Lacy's mom to follow.

"What is it?"

"It's a life-sized ceramic hen," Gloria said. "She's brooding on her nest and, honest to Pete, she looks so real I catch myself wanting to check for eggs every time I walk past her."

Mom started down the aisle after the shop owner, but stopped when Lacy didn't trail her. "You coming?"

"Go on ahead without me," Lacy said. Whether it was snobbish or not, she knew she couldn't hold her tongue over a decorative laying hen, no matter how lifelike it was. "I want to take a peek at the wall art."

She used the term "art" very loosely, but that's what the sign said.

Along the back wall of the shop, Gloria had hung prints, paintings, and pictures of all sorts, from a velvet Elvis to a faded daguerreotype of someone's great-great-grandfather, a grand old gent who sported an impressive set of whiskers. Lacy had hoped looking at the pictures would settle her down, but inside, she still felt like a pot near to boiling.

Her relationship with her dad had always been strong, and more than a little conspiratorial. Mostly because Lacy was good at keeping her word *not* to tell her mother about his foibles. But she and her mother butted heads over everything under the sun and always had.

I am not a snob.

She strolled past the frames on the wall, mentally ticking off the deficiencies in each.

OK, maybe I am a little bit of a snob.

But it wasn't as if she was looking for something to criticize on purpose. She simply had discriminating tastes and she wasn't about to turn that off to please her mother.

The first print she came across featured some fellow pushing a girl on a swing. He had such a sappy expression on his face Lacy expected to see a spigot somewhere on the frame to siphon off the syrup. The next one was a poorly disguised paint-by-numbers effort of the *Mona Lisa*. Another was a jigsaw puzzle that had been shellacked onto a canvas and slapped into a frame. One piece was missing in the lower left quadrant. She decided it wasn't snobbish to object to that.

If you're determined to hang a puzzle on your wall, at least hang a complete one. Seriously.

Lacy's eye for fine things had made her successful in her career. Her clients had paid handsomely for her discernment. They *wanted* her to impose her decorating judgment on them. Then they'd claim afterward that she'd perfectly interpreted *their* sense of style.

She looked down the long aisle to where her mother was ooh-ing and ah-ing over Gloria's ceramic chicken. No doubt about it. That dust-catcher was going home with her mom. There was nothing Lacy could say to stop it. She sighed.

If Mom wants it, maybe I shouldn't try.

She turned back to the wall of pictures, schooling her face not to smirk or sneer or whatever expression it was that her mother objected to. If a life-sized hen peering over the edge of her kitchen cabinets made her mom happy, who was she to judge? After all, Lacy wasn't really a designer anymore.

She was a full-time reporter for a lackluster paper and a

part-time decorating snob. Disappointment settled over her like a heavy coat. She so hadn't seen her life going this way.

Then she saw something on the back wall that made the corners of her mouth lift.

There in the corner was a framed work that appealed to her sense of symmetry and color. With sinuous curves and thin lines, it had the look of an early Erté. His classic portfolio of fashion templates was legend.

Of course, this one had to be a fake. What else would be hanging in a place called Gewgaws and Gizzwickies? The idea of a genuine Erté languishing in someone's attic for decades before finding its way to a junk shop was laughable.

"But it seems real enough to me," Lacy murmured, unconsciously repeating her mother's earlier words. Its beauty raised her spirits. She didn't have money to burn, but it was marked only $25. The piece would look great in her new living room.

Just like her mother's new ceramic chicken, whether this painting was "real" or not, it satisfied her sense of composition and made her smile.

Lacy glanced down the aisle at her mom. Maybe that was the ticket to understanding her. Shirley Evans was emotionally invested in her *treasures,* almost to the point of ferocity. Lacy could understand that. She had a passion for symmetry and color and clean lines herself. Even if she couldn't understand why her mom picked the items she did, Lacy realized how she felt about them.

The value of a piece wasn't necessarily in itself. Its worth was determined by how it made you feel. Lacy tucked the painting under her arm and headed to the front of the store, where her mother was still in raptures over the broody hen.

Somehow, some way, I will *say something nice about that ridiculous chicken if it kills me.*

Chapter 15

I wish I was a dog. Then someone might take me in and
feed me and keep the rain off my head. And if I was a dog,
I'd dream of chasing rabbits, instead of the Cong.
That'd be even better than three hots and a cot.

—Lester Scott, Private First Class, Honorably Discharged, awarded
the Distinguished Service Cross and the Purple Heart. Left his
wife ten years ago. Never paid a dime in alimony.

When Jake stepped into the alley to take out the trash, he nearly tripped over Lester Scott on the Green Apple's back stoop. The homeless vet had been camping there since Jake had invited him to use the covered alcove in case it rained. Last night, Jake had left one of his pillows for the old man. He was glad to see that Lester had claimed it. The blue pillowcase peeked out of the fellow's pack, a surprising spot of relative cleanliness amid the general grime.

"How you doing today, Lester?"

"Fair to middlin', marine."

"Did Ethel bring you some lunch?"

Lester nodded and lit a half-smoked cigarette. "Love that Green Plate special. The meat loaf was A-okay, considering it was slapped together by a jarhead cook."

Jake ignored the backhanded compliment and tossed the garbage in the Dumpster. Then because the old vet sounded pretty lucid for a change and didn't reek of alcohol as much as usual, Jake sat down beside him on the stoop.

"Those cigarettes will kill you, you know," Jake said.

"So I heard. Last week, I decided I wasn't going to smoke

anymore." Lester shrugged philosophically, ignoring the butt hanging from his lower lip. "O' course since then, I haven't smoked any less either. Just depends on whether the cigs come my way, you see. I can't help it if I happen to find a half a pack here or there. A feller's got to deal with what comes to him, don't he?"

"Guess so."

Jake had to deal with what had come to his life or it'd swallow him up like Lake Jewel had swallowed his dad's boat. He knew if he didn't do something about those flashbacks, his chances with Lacy would go down the tube. He just wasn't sure what he was willing to do. Unlike his titanium leg, the flashbacks were a wound no one could see. Admitting he even had them made him feel weak. Like something was broken inside his head.

No, he told himself sternly. He wasn't weak. He wasn't broken.

But coping with the episodes that hurled him back to Helmand province was every bit as hard as learning to deal with his stump. He shoved the issue aside.

"Have you seen Daniel since you got back into town?"

"I got no call to. Reckon my boy don't want to see me much either." Lester blew a perfect ring of smoke into the air. "Can't say as I blame him."

"Lots of time has passed since you parted ways," Jake said. "Things can change."

"For some things, there ain't enough time in the whole world." Lester took one last drag and then stubbed the cigarette out before it burned his fingertips.

Jake figured Lester wouldn't want pity. Lord knew, he couldn't abide it when it was directed at him, but he did feel sorry for Lester Scott. Granted, the man was as contemptible an excuse for a husband and father as you could find. Lester had actually made his family's life better when he left them.

But he was still a vet and for that reason alone, Jake figured he deserved not to be written off completely. There was no telling what had happened to him while he was in Vietnam. Unlike Jake, who'd enjoyed a hero's welcome when he came home from the Middle East, Lester and his fellow Vietnam vets had been reviled and spat upon when they returned from that unpopular war.

Jake had promised Lacy he'd find someone to talk to before next Thursday. He hadn't promised it would be a shrink. Maybe if he told her he'd talked to another vet, she'd be satisfied. She didn't have to know the vet was Lester. He decided to come at the problem sideways to get the man talking. "You were in Nam, weren't you?"

The man nodded. "Part of the last unit to leave before the fall of Saigon. You serve in Iraq?"

"Afghanistan."

Lester grunted. "That where you lost your leg?"

Jake nodded.

"Guess that explains the way I caught you trippin' the other day. You was back there for a minute, weren't you?"

Jake stiffened. He wasn't as ready to talk about it as he'd thought. Not even to Lester. "I wasn't tripping."

"If you say so." Lester stretched out his legs and crossed his bony ankles. "Still, if you served, reckon you know well enough about being downrange. Back in Nam, bein' on base was as safe as a body could feel in that stinkin' place, but any time you left the gates, you were in Indian country. No tellin' who the enemy was. Makes a fellow a might jumpy, don't it?"

Jake frowned at the words "Indian country." His Native American buddy David White Eagle had served alongside him from day one at boot camp. White Eagle had died in the same explosion that took Jake's leg.

But he understood what Lester meant by "Indian country." Beyond the base, all bets were off. The typical rules of engagement didn't apply in Helmand province. The Taliban didn't wear uniforms to identify themselves as combatants. They hid among civilians. They used women and children as living shields.

"I know what you're talking about," Jake said. "Sometimes, it was hard to spot the real enemy."

"Damn right it was hard. Near impossible sometimes. I remember this one time when . . ." Lester fell silent.

"What?" Jake prompted.

Lester glanced at him and then looked away. "There was . . . this buddy of mine, see? He . . . well, he had this thing that happened over there and he wasn't never the same after that."

Jake wasn't fooled. The buddy was likely Lester himself. If Jake had an appointment with a VA shrink, he might have tried to pass off some cockamamie story about some other amputee he knew who had flashbacks. Now he realized how lame that bluff sounded. "What happened to this buddy of yours?"

Lester's eyes glazed over. "I need a cig. Got a smoke?"

Jake shook his head. "Never developed a taste for 'em."

"Just as well. They'll kill you, you know." Lester clammed up again, studying his cracked nails.

"You were saying . . . about your buddy?"

"Who? Oh, him, yeah." A muscle in Lester's cheek jerked. "He's messed up, man. A real head case. All on account of this one patrol."

Jake had thought he'd tell some of his story to Lester, but the old vet seemed to need to do the telling. Lester was carrying enough weight of his own. Jake couldn't drop his on him, too. "What happened over there?"

"Things were comin' apart pretty fast toward the end. Everybody was pouring into Saigon so they could get out and one day, instead of humping it on foot on patrol, we . . . I mean my buddy's unit, went out in a jeep to rendezvous with a convoy that was coming in. It was a pretty day, as I recollect, sunshine shooting through the jungle canopy in long stripes. Too pretty a day for war. And everything was going OK till we got stopped by this tree that'd fallen across the road."

He'd forgotten to distance himself from the story this time. Jake wasn't about to correct him.

"Wasn't no way to go around. Southeast Asia, leastways the part I saw of it, was all jungle. Green stuff grows so fast there, it's like to eat you alive if no one cuts it back, you know? Well, we start to get out of the jeep to see can we move the tree out of the way." Lester's voice broke. His eyes swam. "And then up pops this little boy."

Jake's gut churned. He feared where this story was headed.

"Couldn't have been more than eight or nine years old." The old man's chin quivered. "'Watch out,' my sergeant says. 'He's got a grenade!' Then I—I mean my buddy—he don't even think. He whips up his rifle and takes the boy out just as he's pulling the pin. One shot. Slick as snot."

Lord, have mercy. Jake had no words. Lester, however, seemed to have a few more.

"I remember the boy, he went down slow. Just sort of . . . crumpled, easy like. His little chin kinda dipped to his chest like he was falling asleep on his feet."

A tear left a salty trail on the old man's cheek. Then as if that one tear was enough to break the dam, Lester started to shake. He made no noise, but his chest heaved and he grabbed at his shirt front as if someone were trying to snatch his next breath from him. He wept without restraint.

Jake had no sense of time passing. Maybe none did. He just sat still beside Lester while the old vet grieved over a day too pretty for war, a day more than four decades old. Then finally Lester mastered himself, swiped his eyes, and sat up straight.

"That boy weren't old enough to know what he was doing with that grenade," he said, his voice husky with spent tears. "Some bastard taught him to pull the pin and give it a toss. And . . . some other bastard killed him for it."

Remorse rolled off Lester in waves. He'd hauled around the guilt of that day for all these years. Jake decided it'd take a better man than Lester not to stagger under the weight of it.

Some wars were a sad testimony to failed diplomacy. Other fights had to be fought, but even "good" ones took their toll on a warrior's soul.

"War turns us all into bastards," Jacob said softly. He put a hand on Lester's shoulder and Lester covered it with his own, grasping Jake's knuckles in a surprisingly strong grip. Jake wondered how long it had been since anyone had touched the homeless vet.

Lester pulled a ragged bandanna out of his pocket and blew his nose like a trumpet. "I ain't told you the worst of it though."

What's worse than killing a child? Jake couldn't bring himself to ask it aloud, but Lester plowed ahead without encouragement.

"The boy had got the pin out, see? And the grenade fell to the ground when he did. And who comes up with it, but his baby sister. She'd been hiding in the brush with him, see?" He swallowed hard, as if he might squeeze his Adam's apple tight enough to keep his next words from coming out. "Four, maybe five years old, she was. So tiny. But before she can give it a heave toward us, the thing blows her apart."

The anguish in the man's eyes made Jake's water in sympathy with him.

"So you see, I . . . my buddy, I mean . . . the blood of *two* children . . . that's on him." Lester held his hands before himself and studied the backs of them. The blue veins stood out like a road map of his troubled life. "Baby killers, they called us when we got home. Turns out, they were right."

Lester leaned forward and covered his face with his hands. He rocked slowly, shoulders shaking.

Jake had no idea what to say. What to do. There was no pat answer in the field manual for this sort of thing. But for God's grace, he might have been on a patrol in Afghanistan just like Lester's. What if he'd seen a kid burying the IED that tore apart his Hummer, the one that killed his buddies and took his leg? In the heat of a split second to decide, would he have done the same thing as Lester?

Jake decided there were some things he never wanted to know about himself.

Just then, Ethel poked her head out the back door. Lester straightened, his face suddenly like granite, but the waitress paid him no mind.

"A bus just pulled in, full of tourists headed out on a Tali-mena Byway sightseeing trip," she said. "I can hold 'em off with coffee and sweet tea, but we need you, Jake. Pretty darn quick."

The door flopped closed after Ethel as she hustled back in to deal with the sudden influx of Green Apple customers.

"I gotta go, Lester."

"That's okay, marine. You been chewin' the fat with me long enough."

Lester had done most of the chewing, but Jake didn't feel the need to point that out. How did a guy come back from something like that? Damaged, clearly. Overcome with guilt. No wonder he'd dived into a bottle and only came up for air long enough to be a horrible husband and father.

How could Jake help the man? He was no shrink, no counselor. He didn't have the training for this sort of thing.

So he decided to tackle a problem he could fix. If Lester would let him.

"Look." Jake rose to go back into the grill. "If you want to, you can slip in and go up the back stairs to my place and take a shower. I brought home a pair of jeans and a work shirt from the lake last week. They're folded on the foot of the bed up there. The jeans might be a little big, but they're clean and I bet with a belt, they'd fit you."

"I'll give it some consideration." One corner of Lester's mouth twitched. His gaze shifted suddenly to the right. He cocked his head as if he were listening to something. "My buddy says he still thinks as jarheads go, you're a good'un."

"Yeah, well, tell your buddy he got dealt a bad hand, but he saved the lives of every man in his unit." Jake stopped at the back door with his hand on the knob. "And that means he also saved the kids and grandkids they had after that day, too."

"He knows. He's thought about it once or twice, but I'll tell him again anyway." Lester's shoulders hunched. "I expect he'll still say he ain't sure it was worth the trade."

Chapter 16

I've always wondered why they call them "human interest stories."
As opposed to what? Animal interest? Vegetable? Just
make every story interesting to as many readers as you can.
That's how you sell papers. And that's all I ask.

—Wanda Cruikshank, editor of the *Coldwater Gazette* since 1973

Not everything reported in the *Coldwater Gazette* was vital enough to warrant a deadline. Most of what happened in town wasn't terribly earthshaking. In fact, a resident was likely to make the front page simply by calling in to report the first robin sighting of the season.

Lacy had started writing some of her stories, human interest and otherwise, at home in the early evening instead of at the *Gazette* office. Even though the town news was rarely urgent, the atmosphere at the paper usually was. Wanda Cruikshank thrived in chaos and arranged for it to swirl around her like a small tornado most of the time.

As a result, it was always too busy and loud in the office for Lacy to concentrate. Even if Wanda wasn't on a rampage over something, every time a decent train of thought chugged out of Lacy's mental station, someone would come in to fuss that their paper boy had tossed the *Gazette* into their hydrangeas again, or complain because their fifteenth letter to the editor about daylight savings time hadn't been printed yet. And if their readership gave them a break, Georgina and Tiffany could be counted on to fill in the gap with a running stream of gossip.

Granted, Lacy wasn't writing *War and Peace,* but she still wanted to do a decent job.

She'd positioned her desk in front of the bank of windows in her postage-stamp living room, giving her a bird's eye view of the Town Square if she wanted. She could also retreat from the world just by pulling down the Roman shades. Since the Green Apple was across the way within easy view, pulling the shade also helped keep thoughts of the grill's owner at bay. Jake was beginning to be many things to her.

Conducive to rational thought was not one of them.

So Lacy blocked out the world in general and Jacob Tyler in particular with the tug of a cord. Now she only had to worry about being sucked into that Erté-esque painting she'd hung on the same wall as the windows. Occasionally, she wondered if it could be genuine, but dismissed that as a pipe dream. If it was an Erté, its value would go a long way toward repaying the O'Leary brothers.

She shoved away the idea as improbable, took a sip of her tea, and settled to review her notes from an interview with Junior Bugtussle for a piece she intended to write. Junior wasn't the head of the family. That honor belonged to Senior, but he hadn't been able to come down to the *Gazette* office to meet with her.

"On account of his unfortunate incarceration," Junior had explained. "Seems there's been a misunderstanding with the state police about the family business."

"Oh?"

"Yeah, them dern revenuers misunderstood when they thought the Bugtussles was going to pay taxes on our moonshine."

Then Junior gave her the lowdown on the upcoming Bugtussle reunion.

The gathering of Bugtussles would be held at a rest stop

on the highway near the tiny town of Twicken on the same weekend in June as last year. Junior wouldn't give Lacy the actual dates. Everyone who was supposed to be there, he'd assured her, would know, without being told, when to show up.

"Don't want to encourage reunion crashers, you know," he'd confided.

Junior admitted that the Bugtussles had been warned by the sheriff's office to quit holding the reunion at the rest stop, but the place seemed tailor made for the event. It had all the necessaries. There was plenty of parking space, which was important because the Bugtussles loved their pickups. The rest stop had picnic tables galore so the grown-ups could hold their annual round-robin poker tournament after the main meal.

"Playing for toothpicks," Junior told her. "We Bugtussles don't hold with them fancy plastic chip thingies."

The rest stop also boasted a playground for the kids, which was crucial because the Bugtussle clan bred like rabbits. There were always lots of "young'uns" at the reunion. They needed something to do. After all, a rest stop near a place called Twicken couldn't be expected to have Wi-Fi.

And finally there was a sizable bank of flush toilets in case Grandma Bugtussle's potato salad got left out in the sun too long again.

"Why don't you go to a state park?" Lacy had asked Junior. There were plenty of pretty ones around that would accommodate a family the size of the Bugtussles.

"Well, we tried that one year, but then we had to send out directions, don't you know? Several truckloads of folks got turned around and missed the whole dang thing," Junior had explained. "Now we just use the rest stop because even the Bugtussles what come from a distance don't have no trouble finding it."

Head down, Lacy finished writing the story in about fifteen minutes. Then she gave her finished reunion article a quick proofread.

"Mark Twain was right," she muttered. "Truth *is* stranger than fiction."

Before Lacy could quit for the night, she still had a piece to write about the Lions Club and their plans to beautify the Town Square with barrels of petunias and geraniums on each corner. The club would purchase the containers and furnish the flowers. The only hitch was getting the merchants whose businesses were nearest to the barrels to buy into the daily watering and upkeep of the mini-gardens.

"That's where the power of the press comes in," Wanda had explained to her. "By publicizing the plan, we'll shame the business owners into agreeing to take care of the flowers . . . but by shaming I mean encouraging them in a way they can't refuse. In the nicest possible way, of course. Don't want them taking their advertising dollars somewhere else, you know."

Lacy found the concept of shaming, even "nice" shaming, morally questionable. But despite that needle to thread, Lacy figured the article would only take fifteen minutes to write once she set her mind to it.

The problem was setting her mind to it.

She raised her window shade. Down on the Square, tourists were filing out of the Green Apple and climbing back onto their bus. Every spring as far back as Lacy could remember, a brigade of blue-haired lookee-loos made their way up from places where spring was far drier and browner to see what the season was like in Coldwater Cove's cool green hills.

After the tourists had dinner at the grill, the bus would probably take them around Lake Jewel and up into the hills to stay at the Ouachita Inn, a restored nineteenth-century ranch house that looked like it would be more at home on an

Australian station in the Outback than the Ozarks. But it was surrounded by old bunkhouses that had been carved up into antique-filled private rooms and was as much a high point of the trip as the views on the Talimena Byway.

Suffering from an extreme case of "writing avoidance," Lacy continued to watch the tourists as the older gentlemen helped their ladies onto the bus.

One couple walked past the bus and halfway around the Square while their fellow travelers were loading up. Hand in hand, they stopped to gawk in the shop windows and take pictures of the Victorian courthouse, smiling, gesturing, and talking to each other the whole while. Granted, the Square was picturesque with its turn-of-the-last-century storefronts, but that was a small joy in the grand scheme of things. Certainly not cause enough for this couple's obvious pleasure. Then the pair ambled back to the bus, their heads inclined toward each other lest they miss what the other might have to say.

How long had they been together? Lacy wondered. Given their ages, maybe forty or fifty years. Or was this a second romance for them? Had they each laid their first spouse in the arms of God and now, late in life, a new love had grown?

Either way, Lacy was suddenly aware of how alone she was.

She had no one to share her joys, small or otherwise. No one she could make proud of her. No one she could build up. No one, as Sartre had said, to serve as a witness to her life.

Even if she and Bradford Endicott had made their quasi-understanding official and eventually tied the knot, she had never really thought about growing old with him. She couldn't imagine it. He'd always been all about "now." And he wasn't one to enjoy simple things. Everything had to be the best or he'd erupt in a full-blown conniption.

At the time, Lacy had overlooked that flaw in his character, telling herself it was how he'd been raised. An Endicott just wasn't the sort to settle for less than he thought he deserved.

A *small* joy? Preposterous.

But Lacy was beginning to appreciate them. Like going up to the roof deck above her apartment to watch the sun peep over the Winding Stair range and gild the lake with ripples of gold. The smell of coffee filling her little kitchen in the morning and being able to linger over a cup to start her day without the hassle of standing in line to buy an overpriced shot of caffeine. The comfortable feel of old denim on her thighs instead of squeezing herself into the latest haute couture she couldn't really afford anyway.

The tension of living in the city, which she hadn't realized she'd suffered from, sloughed off her a little more each day. Sometimes she went for a couple of days in a row without stressing about her next payment to the O'Leary brothers.

Her mother had always encouraged her to count her blessings. Wasn't a small joy the same thing?

But she still had no one to share them with. A lot of that was her fault. She'd never really been comfortable letting anyone close. Whenever anyone tried to break through to her tightly guarded inner self, she pulled away. It was part of why she'd fled from Daniel all those years ago. She was a far cry from perfect sister Crystal. Why let someone in to expose all that?

But she still felt her aloneness deeply.

Other than her parents, who didn't count in this respect, there was no one she mattered to. If she wasn't here, who would mark her absence?

Then suddenly Effie leaped up onto her desk. The cat plopped down, rolled onto its back, and presented Lacy with her unprotected tummy.

"What on earth has gotten into you?"

Had someone sneaked into her apartment while she was at work and substituted a real cat for the old one? Lacy reached out and tentatively gave Effie's belly a soft stroke.

The Siamese rewarded Lacy with a rumbling purr. Then the cat rolled over, sat upright, and rubbed her whiskered cheek against Lacy's forearm. Lacy scratched behind the animal's ear.

"Well, this is a wonderment. And by wonderment, I mean I wonder when you're going to turn on me and bite my fingers off," she told the cat.

But Effie seemed determined to make up for lost snuggling time. Uninvited, she climbed onto Lacy's lap and tucked her forepaws under her to form a vibrating ball of furry affection. Evidently, Effie had decided that Lacy had shown herself faithful in a few things—tuna, fresh water, and a clean litter box—so now the Siamese could reward her in many things— the comfort of a rumbling purr, unexpected friendliness, and the joy of being allowed to stroke sleek fur.

It was nice to have another beating heart in her apartment. Even if it was only a cat. Lacy decided she could risk liking Effie a little.

"A cat lady. That's what I've become. Next, I'll be skimping on my own grocery budget to buy squeaky toys and catnip for you," Lacy said with a sigh. "And if I should die alone in this apartment, you'll eat me, won't you?"

Effie just kept purring.

Chapter 17

Sometimes a body don't even realize he's lost until he finds a home. O' course, that don't count with me. I left home with my eyes wide open. If I'd stayed, everything that makes home worth having might have been lost.

—Lester Scott, a bundle of contradictions, more mistakes than triumphs, and a boatload of regrets. In a word, human.

Jake had rarely been so glad to flip over the OPEN sign and call it a day. Not that he was complaining. He suffered from a good kind of tired. The windfall of a bus full of customers was nothing to sneeze at. A few more of those and his ledger would look pretty happy for the month. But it made for a frantic time behind the grill when coupled with his regular supper crowd.

Fortunately, the Green Apple hadn't run out of anything important and everyone seemed happy with what was set in front of them. He'd need to do some extra baking in the days to come to make up for the dent those tourists had put in his store of pies. It might even be time to hire someone to give him a hand in the kitchen.

Maybe another server to give Ethel a rest, too, assuming she'd be willing to take a rest. Ethel went after everything like she was killing snakes.

"I'd rather burn out than rust out, honey," she always said whenever he suggested she take a few days of vacation. His geriatric waitress lived for the bustle of the grill. If fussing over his customers like a doting grandmother made her happy, who was he to argue?

Still, it wouldn't hurt to bring in a high school kid or a student from Bates College to work alongside Ethel through the busy summer months. Of course, she might take offense, thinking he believed she wasn't up to the job. But if he put her in charge of the extra server, Ethel might enjoy having someone to boss around.

Besides me.

It was worth trying. He'd drop by the *Gazette* office tomorrow and put an ad in the paper. The real strawberry in the plan was that it would give him an excuse to see Lacy before next Thursday.

After Lester's war story and the busload of customers, his day had been both heartbreaking and hectic. Just thinking about Lacy rested him.

With an absent smile he couldn't help, Jake ran a wet mop over the linoleum floor, giving the corners an extra scrubbing. He enjoyed the smells of his own cooking, but a good clean pine scent coming off the floors never hurt either. If cleanliness was next to godliness, Jake figured he had earned an extra star in his crown today.

After all, he'd managed to talk Lester Scott into taking a shower.

While he'd been finishing up the bus tourists' supper orders, the old vet had popped into the Green Apple's kitchen for a half a minute, wearing the old clothes that had belonged to Jake's dad.

"Thanks for the shower, marine, and the clean duds, too," Lester had said. His hair was slicked back and he'd used one of Jake's razors to shave off the salt-and-pepper stubble on his chin. The clothes were a couple of sizes too big for him, but all in all, Lester cleaned up rather well. "Usually, I have to turn up sober at the Samaritan House to rate a handout like this."

"It's not a handout. Just a hand. And if you want to camp

out on the couch upstairs for tonight, it'd be OK with me," Jake had said without looking up from the mess of chicken-fried chops he was cooking. He didn't want Lester as a full-time house guest, but maybe just this once. If the old vet got a taste of sleeping clean and dry again, perhaps he'd make an effort to return to a more normal life.

"We don't get many squeaky clean army grunts around here." Jake couldn't resist needling the vet from a rival armed service a little. "Seems a shame to send one out to sleep on the back stoop."

"Are you kidding me? I ain't soft enough to need a couch under my backside or a roof over my head, for that matter," Lester countered with a toothy grin as he headed out the back door. "What do you take me for? A marine?"

Even after the back door banged shut behind him, Jake could hear Lester's cackling chuckle.

Jake was glad the man could still laugh. After the war story Lester had told him that afternoon, it was a wonder.

He also wondered if he'd be able to convince Lacy that the conversation with Lester counted as "talking to some-body" about his own flashbacks. If Jake was honest, he knew it didn't. But lightening Lester's load by hearing him out had lifted some of Jake's burden, too. That had to count for some-thing.

Either way, he hoped his next date with Lacy would go better than the last one had.

It certainly could go no worse.

The linoleum was dry, so he returned to the front of the restaurant to turn down the blinds for the night. He looked out onto the Square as he reached for the cords. As if he'd conjured her by thinking about her, there was Lacy.

Dodging traffic.

There generally wasn't that much automobile traffic on the Square in the evenings, but a few carloads of high school kids were out cruising that night, racing their old beaters around the courthouse. The object of the game wasn't so much winning as being seen by the other "cool kids."

That's how it had been when he was in school. Seemed little had changed in more than a decade.

Usually, Jake ignored them, but not tonight. Not when Lacy was darting between the cars and pickups, chasing after a scruffy-looking little dog. Jake shot out the door in a hot second.

The mutt had probably started out white, but now its long, matted fur coiled in muddy ropes. Tongue lolling, it skittered back and forth in the street, not sure which way to run.

"Hey, you punks! Get out of here!" Jake yelled at the kids. "Or I'm calling the sheriff!"

He knew it would happen someday, but he'd never thought it would hit before he turned thirty.

OK. It's official. I'm getting old.

But those kids had no business driving so fast in town.

Now I'm even thinking like my dad.

But he still moved like himself. Jake hadn't been named an All-Conference college halfback for nothing. Even with his prosthetic, he could be quick when he had to. He dodged between a red Ford F-150 and a much-dinged-up Taurus, scooping up the dog as if it was a loose football and this interception would win the game. When he loped over to the courthouse lawn where Lacy was shifting her weight anxiously from one foot to the other, the look on her face was better than a touchdown.

"Oh, Jake, you saved him!" She threw her arms around both him and the squirming dog. "I saw the poor little thing from my window. I was so afraid he'd get hit by a car before someone could catch him."

"You might have gotten hit by one, too, you know," he said, shifting the wiggly ball of fur to his other arm. Just the possibility that Lacy could have been hurt trying to save a dog made his gut churn.

Then a sheriff's cruiser pulled into the Square and the cars and trucks filled with teenagers scattered like roaches when a light pops on. Daniel Scott parked his vehicle, got out, and headed their way.

Lacy didn't seem to notice Dan's approach, which was fine with Jake. Unfortunately, she was more focused on the little mongrel in his arms than on him.

"Is he injured?" She pushed the straggly fur out of the dog's eyes. Jake was relieved to see that he still had both of them under that mop of hair.

"I think he's just scared." Jake patted the furry head. "Now that he's not going to become road kill, what do you want to do with him?"

She blinked at him. "Do? I guess I hadn't thought that far. I just didn't want to see him hurt. We should take him to the shelter, I guess."

Daniel joined them, shaking his head. "That won't work. Animal Control won't take a stray unless they've picked it up themselves."

"Not it. Him. The dog's a him," Lacy corrected. "What do you mean they won't take him?"

"It's the shelter's new policy," Daniel explained. "They put it in place after Mr. Mayhew enticed Stella Upwhistle's Chihuahua out of her backyard one day. He turned it in to Animal Control, claiming it was a stray."

"What a rotten trick. Of course, my dad would say that a man who'll feed squirrels will do anything," Lacy said. "But still, why would he do such a thing?"

"He claimed the dog was a public nuisance," Jake said, not willing to let Danny into the conversation more than he could help. After all, he was the one who'd risked life and limb to save the hairy little bugger for Lacy. He didn't need Danny-come-lately messing things up. "Mr. Mayhew said the constant barking disturbed his sleep. Then Mrs. Upwhistle argued that she never put the dog out at night. After that, Mr. Mayhew admitted it was his afternoon nap the little yapper interrupted. Mrs. Upwhistle got an apology and her dog back and as far as I know, Mr. Mayhew hasn't had a nap since."

"Since that time," Daniel said, swooping up the conversational ball without missing a beat, "the shelter accepts animals dropped off by their owners if they can no longer care for them, but they won't take one labeled a stray unless the animal officers capture it themselves."

"But this poor little fellow is so obviously a stray." Lacy took the dog from Jake. "Under all that hair, there's really not much dog at all. He's no bigger than a minute." She cuddled him close. Whether he was filthy or not, she held him tight, speaking nonsensical endearments to the animal in a high, sweet voice.

Jake never expected to envy a dog, but there was a first time for everything. He guessed he could deal with four-legged competition, but he had a two-legged distraction to get rid of first.

"I've been talking to your dad some, and I think he'd like to see you," Jake told Danny. Since the old man had freshly bathed and shaved that day, there was no better time for it. Maybe a fence or two could be mended. It would do them both good to find, if not reconciliation, at least forgiveness. "Lester's out on the Green Apple's back stoop."

"No, he's not. And I've seen him already," Danny said, his face a hard mask. "He's in the county lockup. Walmart security caught him shoplifting about an hour ago and called me to come take him in."

Lester must have hoofed it straight to the big-box store

after he had his shower, Jake realized. Since the old vet no longer looked like a derelict, he'd probably tried to pass unnoticed and score some cold beer from the grocery section.

"I expect he earned himself thirty days of enforced sobriety, three squares, and a roof over his sorry head," Danny said, reaching over to pet the stray pooch. "You won't need to worry about Lester messing up your back stoop for a while."

"He wasn't any trouble. And you don't need to worry about the dog either. We'll take care of him," Jake said, giving Danny his best game face. In high school, they'd been inseparable, but they'd grown apart since then.

No sweat. Time moves on and moves people with it.

Daniel had been Lacy's only serious boyfriend in Coldwater Cove and had somehow botched it with her. Jake was in no mood to let the guy have a do-over. Besides, Danny had a wife and a kid to care for, if he could find his way back to them.

"That right, Lacy?" Daniel said. "You and Jake'll take care of the dog?"

"Unless you can pull some strings and help us get him into the shelter . . ."

"Sorry," Daniel said, looking as if he truly was. "I don't make the rules. I just enforce them."

"Then we'll take it from here," Jake said. "G'night, Scott."

Daniel popped his hat back on and headed for the cruiser.

That's right, Cong, Jake thought, falling back into Lester's characterization of his law-enforcing son. *Just keep walking.*

"This little fellow must be hungry," Lacy said, turning her attention back to the dog in her arms. "I can feel his ribs."

"He's also filthy. He's getting you all dirty." Jake took the stray back from her. The dog wiggled up high enough on his chest to slurp Jake's cheek with its tongue. He held him out at arm's length.

"Careful. You'll drop him. And be sure to support his

backside. Poor thing, he's just a mess, isn't he?" She shook her head. "Look at all those cockleburs on his tummy. Those will have to be cut out. He's underweight. He's unkempt. Doesn't that prove he doesn't belong to anyone?"

"You heard the county mounty. The shelter still won't take him."

"Well, we can't just turn him loose," Lacy said with a frown. Jake wished he could kiss away that line between her brows. "He'll be back in traffic again before you know it and next time, he'll get run over. Or he'll starve to death. Or—"

"OK, OK," Jake said. "So I guess you want to keep him."

"Me? No. I can't," Lacy said with a sigh. "I'd have to pay extra pet rent each month for him and buy dog food. I hate to admit it, but I can't spare the money to spend on another pet right now. Then there are vet bills to consider. He'll need shots, I'm sure. And I didn't notice, but has he been fixed?"

"Under all that hair, who can tell?" Jake wasn't about to check out a dog's junk. "I could help you with his expenses."

That was brilliant, if he did say so himself. It would make them co-owners. He and Lacy would have to spend more time together, playing with the silly little thing and taking their joint mutt for long walks every evening.

"Thanks for the offer, but that won't help," Lacy said. "The main reason I can't take him is that Effie would probably kill him. That cat is bigger than he is, you know. She tips the vet's scale at sixteen pounds."

"You're always telling tales on Effie," Jake said. "She seems harmless enough to me."

"That's because you charmed her. Believe me, she would not find this little fellow charming in the least. Some chew toys are bigger than he is." Lacy shook her head. "I simply can't take him."

She gazed up at him, her eyes sad and pleading. The stupid little dog gave him the same look. This powder puff wasn't the sort of pet most guys chose. A German shepherd, a Doberman, a barrel-chested bulldog—those were breeds a man could have at his side with pride.

Still, those two sets of pleading eyes . . .

"Let's get him cleaned up. Then we'll see." Shifting the dog in his arms, he started back toward the Green Apple with Lacy in tow. "You better come, too. I have a feeling this is going to be a job for two."

Chapter 18

Take all the showers you want. It won't clean up a person on the inside. Nothing made by human hands can do that.

—Jake Tyler, who's kicking himself for aiding and abetting an old drunk's shoplifting spree at Walmart.

Lacy followed Jake into the alley behind the buildings on the Green Apple side of the Square.

"We can't carry a dirty dog through the grill," Jake said as he led her to the back stoop, through the door, and up the stairs to his living quarters. "Don't want the health department after me."

There was little danger of that, even if he'd trooped a whole pack of dirty dogs through his restaurant. The Coldwater Cove health department consisted of the same overworked clerk who also served the paper-pushing needs of the county assessor and the treasurer. No one at the courthouse had time to make health inspections unless someone lodged a complaint.

Often and loudly.

Lacy believed she could tell a lot about a person by the way they organized their personal space. Or didn't. Of course, messy and disorganized didn't always mean something negative. Some of the most creative people she knew couldn't pick up a sock if their life depended on it. So as she climbed the stairs, she was both anxious and curious about seeing Jake's place.

Unlike her apartment, which was chopped up into small Victorian-style rooms, Jake's was a loft with a high vaulted ceiling that stretched from the back staircase to the long bank of windows above the Green Apple Grill's striped awning in front. An efficient kitchen was positioned in one rear corner with an island big enough to seat four as it separated the kitchen from the rest of the space. No stainless-steel appliances, no granite. The kitchen was functional and spotless, but not trendy.

Jake's neatly made bed was in the opposite corner positioned under a skylight. There was a partial wall behind the headboard that probably hid a walk-in closet, which was accessed from one side. The only interior door in the place was located opposite the entrance.

Probably the bathroom. Based on her estimate of the square footage behind that door, it was smaller than her bathroom. But then, guys didn't need much vanity space and tended not to go into raptures over claw-foot tubs.

In front of a leather sectional, a large-screen TV was the focal point of a wall filled with shelving. Along with books and a small set of hand weights, there were a number of trophies from Jacob's days as an athlete. Pictures of his parents and siblings and their families, of him and his marine buddies in desert gear, were propped on the shelves. In a corner niche, there was a small safe.

"You don't trust banks?" she asked, eyeing the safe.

"With my money, yes. With my Beretta, no."

Lacy's Bostonian friend Shannon had a horror of handguns, but Lacy wasn't shocked to learn that Jake had one. Not only was he a marine, he was from Coldwater Cove. And in this town, gun control meant when you take aim at something, you hit it.

"Now, where do you want to do this?" Jake asked, holding the wiggly dog away from his body.

She noticed he didn't set the dirty little thing down on his gleaming hardwood. His home was masculine, but not a man-cave. Jake was military clean and orderly. That squared with what she expected of him. The flashback she'd glimpsed was an aberration. This was the real Jake—solid, steady, and, she was beginning to hope, completely trustworthy.

Of course, after her experience with Bradford Endicott, she was skittish about trusting her "man judgment."

"I guess we'll have to use your tub and then give it a good scrub afterward," Lacy said.

"Can't. I don't have a tub. Just a shower."

"I can't say I'm surprised." She eyed the deep farmhouse sink in his kitchen. "That'll have to do, then, but let's see if we can cut away those burrs first."

Jake set the little dog down on the concrete counter of the island, opened one of the drawers, and pulled out a pair of scissors. He handed them to her. "You cut. I'll hold."

After a couple of minutes, Lacy realized he'd given himself the harder job. The little dog was nervous about Lacy's amateur attempts to groom him and tried to wriggle away from the sharp blades, but Jake held him fast.

"Easy, buddy," he said. "Lacy won't hurt you."

"I'm sure trying not to. Poor little guy. He must have been on his own for a long time to get this messed up." Some of the cockleburs were embedded so deeply, they were cutting into his skin. The dog whined softly. Taking care not to nick him, she snipped away the prickly weeds. Then she clipped off the excess hair hanging down in the dog's eyes and trimmed his scruffy beard.

"Even after we're done here, he's going to need professional help."

"Hear that, dog?" Jake said. "Lacy thinks someone besides me needs professional help."

Obviously, he was chafing under her insistence that he see

someone about his flashbacks. "I only meant you should take him to the Pampered Pup to get a good trim."

"You're pretty handy with a pair of scissors," Jake said as the dog began to settle. "Sometimes, a gentle hand is better than a pro who's just looking for a paycheck."

"I'm sure they're gentle at the Pampered Pup. My folks take Fergus there all the time, and that's a pretty strong endorsement. They consider him their 'fur baby,' you know. He's the little brother I never had," Lacy said, tossing him a sideways glance. "Since you're not big on professional help, does this mean you haven't talked to anyone yet?"

He didn't pretend to misunderstand her. "I've had a conversation."

"With a doctor?"

He shook his head and avoided her gaze. "Another vet."

Even though Lacy had suggested that as one of his options for help in dealing with his flashbacks, she wasn't sure it was the best course. If the other vet had issues of his own, it might only add to Jake's burden. But he was trying. That was something.

"That's good, Jake. I'm glad you're getting some help. But I hope you're doing it for you, not for me."

He made a *hmph*-ing noise. Of course he was doing it for her, the sound said. "So does that mean we're still on for Thursday?"

"Sure. Just don't ask my dad for any of his homemade furniture stripper." When he gave her a quizzical look, she waved off his unspoken question. "You don't want to know. It's the sad tale of an old squirrel-fighter who's desperate enough to try anything. I'd just as soon not spread the story around. Folks might wonder if my dad needs a little professional help of his own."

Jake shifted the dog into his left arm so Lacy could reach

the animal's other side. "May as well give him a complete haircut before the shampoo," he said. "Less to wash."

"I think he'll be cute once he's cleaned up."

"Yeah, that's what every guy looks for in a dog. Cute."

"Come on, Jake. You don't need a tough dog," she said. "You're tough enough already."

Jacob turned on his megawatt smile. She ought to be used to it by now, but his dimple was still devastating. Her knees really did wobble a little.

"I don't know," he said. "I'm beginning to think I'm becoming a big pushover."

"Why do you say that?" Satisfied with her work on the dog's coat, Lacy laid aside the scissors and filled the sink with warm water.

"Yesterday, Lester Scott was too grimy and obviously homeless to pass unnoticed in Walmart. Today, I let him use my shower and gave him those old clothes that belonged to my dad." Jake's lips pressed together in a hard line. "I doubt he'd have tried to shoplift if I hadn't done that."

"You were only trying to help," Lacy said. "You can't blame yourself for what someone else does."

"Well, hello, Kettle. This is Pot."

"What?"

"Isn't that just what you've been doing?" Jake pointed out. "Blaming yourself for something your business partner did in Boston?"

Her shoulders sagged. "Yeah, but I'm not the only one. The DA was ready to blame me, too."

It was a good thing no one in Coldwater Cove knew how close she'd come to being charged with embezzlement and outright theft. Only her willingness to make full restitution had convinced the DA that she wasn't in on Bradford's scheme. Even after she'd depleted all her resources, it wasn't until she took out the loan from the O'Learys that she was allowed to wiggle off the hook.

"Got any baby shampoo?" she asked, both because she needed it, and because she needed to change the subject.

"Not having a baby around, um, no. Why? Do you?"

"Actually, yes. I use it to remove eye makeup." It occurred to her that she'd been going much easier on cosmetics lately. In Boston, she never left the condo without a full face on—foundation, concealer, mascara, eye liner, shadow, the works. Now most days she made do with a little blush and a dash of lipstick.

"Well, I haven't used eye makeup since the weird Goth skit that goofy drama coach made the football team do for a pep rally once." He batted his dark lashes at her. "Little buddy will just have to settle for the shampoo I have on hand. Back in a minute."

He handed the dog to Lacy and went in search of the shampoo.

"Buddy," she repeated. "He's called you that a couple of times. That's a good name for you, my fine furry friend. Don't you think, Jake?"

"Not often enough evidently, since you roped me into washing a dog in my sink," came the reply from the bathroom.

"No, I meant what about Buddy for a name for him?" Lacy called back to him.

"I was thinking Speedbump."

"Jake, that's terrible."

"It's either that or Roadkill."

"No, not Roadkill."

"Why? It's what he'd have become if we'd left him in the street."

"That's no reason to give him such a mean name."

"It's not mean. It's unusual, like he is. As a mutt, he's unique, one of a kind. Plenty of dogs are named Buddy. I've never met one called Speedbump."

"Well, I guess Speedbump is better than Roadkill. Speedbump it is." Lacy gently placed the dog into the sink of warm water.

The newly christened critter didn't think much of the arrangement. He startled and quivered with nervousness. Whenever she dipped a handful of water on him, he gave a full-body shake, flinging droplets all over. By the time Jake returned with the shampoo and an old towel, the front of Lacy's navy T-shirt was drenched.

"Let me help," Jake said. "Maybe he'll stop shaking."

He poured a quarter-sized amount of shampoo into his palm. Then he stood behind Lacy, put his arms around her, and reached into the sink to scrub the dog.

Whether it was the addition of another pair of hands or the fresh scent of shampoo, Speedbump finally stood still and let them wash him.

Truthfully, Lacy sort of lost track of the dog altogether. She was too distracted by the heat coming off the chest of the man behind her. There was something undeniably pleasurable about having Jake so close. The strength of his arms around her, the way their hands slipped and slid against each other in the bubbles, the—

Lacy started to giggle.

"What's so funny?" Jake wanted to know.

"Doesn't this remind you of something?" She turned so she was caught between his body and the sink. "The pottery wheel bit from *Ghost*?"

The scene where the doomed lovers worked a disastrous pot on a wheel together, slathered in liquefied clay, had been lampooned plenty of times in later comedies, but the first time

Lacy had seen it, she thought it was one of the most sensual love scenes ever. Jake must have thought so, too, because his gaze met hers with undeniable heat.

He wants to kiss me.

And she wanted him to with an urgency that surprised her. She slid her arms around his neck and stood on tiptoe as he bent to meet her mouth.

Jake's kiss was a slow quest. His lips were strong and firm, but he wasn't pushing her. This kiss wasn't the torrid taking she'd read about in romance novels. She had nothing to compare it to since she and Jake had never kissed during the brief time when they were an item in fifth grade. But this certainly wasn't the practiced kiss she expected from him, given his reputation with women.

Instead of slick seduction, he seemed to be sending her a message. A tender one.

She tried to decipher it.

You are precious to me, his kiss seemed to say. *I want to know you, the real Lacy, deep down.*

At least, she hoped that was the message. That's what she wanted it to be. Needed it to be. The thought made a warm shiver reverberate through her. To be known and yet accepted. Wasn't that the heart cry of every soul on earth?

His kiss made her feel special, as if there was no one else in the world he'd rather be with at this moment.

Then she remembered that was Jake Tyler's gift. He made every girl he'd ever been with feel special. And no matter how hot he was, or how good his kiss felt, the last thing she needed was to be nothing more than a convenient hookup for him.

In fact, she wasn't ready to be *anyone's* hookup. More than just a kiss would complicate things all to heck, and her life was complicated enough.

Jake seemed to sense it. His kiss turned questioning. Vulnerable, almost.

Am I enough for you?

No, she was mistaken. Jake wouldn't ask that. He was Mr. Big Stuff, after all.

But what if he didn't see himself that way?

He should. Who cares if he only has five toes? He's still Jake.

She gave herself up to his mouth. It was a whole world of comfort, of pleasure, of . . .

If he was sending a message with his kiss, what was hers saying to him?

Accept me. I need you to.

I want to trust you, Jake. Don't make me wrong again.

He pulled her close.

Maybe I'm overthinking this. Why can't I just enjoy being held and kissed and—

But when Jake let go of Speedbump to wrap his arms around Lacy more tightly, the dog saw his chance. He scrambled out of the sink, gave a monumental shake, then jumped down from the counter and made a mad dash around the loft.

Lacy broke off their kiss and lunged after the little mop with feet. Jake gave chase, too, but having two people tearing around after him only gave the dog wings.

Speedbump darted. He zipped. He ran under the coffee table without needing to duck. Then the dog leaped from the floor to the coffee table, did a bank shot off the back of the sectional, and landed in the middle of Jake's bed.

Once there, Speedbump burrowed between the pillows and did barrel-rolls to rub himself dry on the navy-and-white-striped shams.

"Guess I didn't need a towel for him," Jake said wryly. "My pillowcases do just fine."

Lacy retrieved the towel from the kitchen island and tossed it to Jake. "Now is the time to set some boundaries for him."

"Oh." He shot her a teasing grin. "You mean like the boundaries you set for Effie."

"I wish." She rolled her eyes and shook her head. "Cats make their own rules. I don't know anything about how to deal with Effie other than to keep her in food, water, and clean litter. But my family has had a few dogs over the years."

"You're ahead of me in the pet department, then." Jake shrugged. "Dad was allergic to fur, so I was lucky to get gold-fish."

"The first thing you need to know about dogs is that they're pack animals. They need a leader. You have to show Speedbump you're the boss or he may decide he has to be in charge."

"Him?" Jake pointed at the ball of fur rotating between his pillows.

"Size doesn't matter in dog psychology. It's all about at-titude. I have a cousin who has a husky, a black Lab, and a dachshund, and, believe it or not, the wiener dog is the alpha of that little pack."

Jake frowned. "I'm not part of anyone's pack. I'm the hu-man and he's the dog and I'm not even sure he'll be staying."

"You won't turn him loose, will you?" Even if she couldn't keep him, she hated the thought of Speedbump wandering alone, unloved and unprotected.

"No." He scooped up the dog. It snuggled up under his chin and began giving him doggie kisses. Jake held him out at arm's length to escape the blatant show of affection. "Man, he's got the fastest tongue in the West. I think I should put an ad in the paper to see if someone has misplaced this little guy."

"I'll take care of that for you," she said with a stab of dis-appointment. She wished he'd keep Speedbump. When she was growing up, her family dogs had been a source of unques-tioning love and comfort. Jake could use some of that.

She could use some herself. Of course, Effie had been warming up to her and vice versa.

"I'll have to get some dog food for him," Jake said, sitting on the foot of the bed and vigorously rubbing the wet dog with the towel.

"You'll also need a couple of bowls for food and water, a collar and leash. Oh! And you'd better get a cushion and a small crate for him, unless you want company in your bed."

Jake gave her a searching look. "My bed hasn't seen any company in a long time."

Lacy swallowed hard. After that kiss, she could well imagine what it would be like to share Jake's bed. But she couldn't do it. It wasn't that she didn't trust him. Jacob wouldn't mean to hurt her. He never intended to hurt any of the girls he'd loved and left.

If she'd been able to separate that part of her from the rest, she'd have been sorely tempted to tumble between the sheets with him. Just the notion of lying down beside Jacob, the heat of his body, the scent of his skin mingled with fresh linen, the—

Lacy shoved those thoughts aside. The things that got drummed into a kid's head tended to stick there. Somewhere along the line, she'd been impressed with the idea that her body was unique and precious. A little holy, even. Lovemaking was more than just the joining of two bodies. It was a shared breath, a shared soul. She'd lost track of that back east, but now that she was older, sadder, and a little bit wiser, she knew it was true. If she went to bed with Jake now, she'd be giving him a piece of her heart she'd never get back.

And she needed every piece she had left.

She started backing toward the stairwell. "I gotta go. See you."

Then she turned tail and bolted out of his loft as if her pants were on fire.

They very nearly were.

Chapter 19

The first time I called 911, I was four years old.

"Does your mother know you made this call, sweetie?"
the dispatcher asked in a syrupy voice.

"No," I answered.

"Can she come to the phone?"

"She's in the other room. Daddy has a gun pointed at her head."

The dispatcher's tone shifted abruptly. By the time help arrived, my father's tirade had run its course. He was sprawled in his La-Z-Boy, watching The Tonight Show.

Mother brought him another beer as if nothing had happened.

She had plenty of bruises to back up a claim of abuse. It all could have ended right then if only she'd had the grit to press charges. "But I love him," was all she'd ever say about it.

If unconditional love really worked, Lester Scott should have been the best man who ever walked this earth.

—Daniel Scott, who isn't the best man to walk the earth either. The difference is, he's always known it.

The shift from hell was finally over. Daniel hung the cruiser keys on the hook for the next officer who'd drive it. Valentina Gomez, the county dispatcher whose sharp eyes missed nothing, gave him the once-over.

"Long day, Danny?"

"No longer than most."

"You're loco if you think I believe you. Sell that stuff someplace else, *chico*. No takers here." Valentina pushed away from her desk and leaned back in her chair. The khaki uniform did her ample figure no favors, but her friendly smile and pretty face made most folks forget about the straining buttons below her chin. "It isn't every day one of our officers arrests his own father. That had to be a tough collar. You doing okay?"

"I'm okay. No drama. No regrets. It's not like he's really my dad," Dan assured her. He hadn't even told his mother the man was back in town. He didn't want her to worry. Or worse, let Lester back into her life. "It's been a long time since I thought of Lester Scott as anything but a homeless bum."

A homeless bum who's still trying to shame and ruin what's left of our family.

"Well, *hermano,*" Valentina said, "that homeless bum has been pestering the guard to let him see you since you dropped him off for processing."

Lester had tried to talk to Daniel while he was escorting him to the cruiser. Once Daniel had him secured in the backseat, he'd shouted an abbreviated Miranda warning at him.

"You have the right to remain silent. If you know what's good for you, you'll use it."

After that, Lester Scott had sulked and studied his own knees the whole time. The trip from Walmart to the sheriff's office had never seemed so long to Danny. He couldn't wait to unload his prisoner and get back out on his shift.

"Has he been sentenced?" Daniel asked Valentina. It should be a slam-dunk. Thirty days, for sure. Unless Lester had some priors, in which case, his stay in the county lockup might be an extended one. Or maybe Daniel's prayers would be answered and his father would have an outstanding warrant from Texas. He'd be more than happy to extradite Lester's sorry butt all the way back to Brownsville.

Valentina shook her head. "He's just been arraigned. Judge Preston will see him for sentencing tomorrow afternoon, but we're holding him overnight. He could easily hightail it back to Texas, you know."

"I'm not that lucky," he muttered and turned toward the door.

"Five minutes," Valentina said. "Give the man five minutes and then you can race off to . . . whatever it is you have to race off to."

Valentina knew as well as he did that all Danny had to look forward to was Stouffer's pizza on a TV tray. He couldn't even pick up a few scratch tickets at the PDQ Mart on the way home. He hadn't played any more poker since Anne left, but according to her a lottery ticket was just as bad. It fed his addiction, she said.

But he had no addiction. How could he convince her of that? It was like trying to prove a negative. It couldn't be done.

Valentina had tried to encourage him, in ways both subtle and overt, to go for counseling with Anne. The dispatcher was working on husband number two, Tomas Gomez, attorney at law. After a stormy first marriage, this time Valentina's vows seemed to have taken effect. She was determined that everyone around her should bask in marital bliss, too.

"Come on, Danny," Valentina urged. "If you don't see Lester now, he won't give the night guard a moment's peace."

"All right," Daniel grumbled. "But only five minutes."

He stomped through the door marked AUTHORIZED PERSONNEL ONLY and told the guard to set Lester Scott up for a visitor. He could have taken him into the interrogation room, but he decided on keeping a plate of glass and phone wire between him and Lester. It was as close as he could bear to be to the man.

All through his growing up, Danny hadn't been afraid of the bogeyman or monsters under his bed. Not when he lived with a real live one. Half the time, his dad seemed perfectly normal. The other half, he was a hard-fisted demon. Danny never knew which one would meet him at the door when he got home from school. He got used to telling people he fell down a lot to explain the bruises.

Then when Lester lost his job at the electric company because he couldn't be counted on to show up for work regularly, he stopped trying to hide his drinking. Things went from bad to worse. Daniel's mother was a good ten years younger than her husband, but with the way he put her down constantly, she looked older.

Finally, a few weeks before his high school graduation, Danny had had enough. He couldn't think about moving on and making a life for himself if his mother was stuck with his father. Lester would kill her eventually. It was what abusers did.

That night, when Lester came home mean-drunk as usual, Dan was ready for him, lying in wait for his father in the garage. One way or another, the nightmare was going to end.

He beat his father to a bloody pulp.

Even now, his heart raced as he remembered how he'd felt that night. Scared. Determined. Out of control. Blood screamed through his brain. He always thought his father was a few bricks short of a load, but Daniel must have gone a little crazy himself that night. When Dan picked up a tire iron and would have ended Lester, Jacob Tyler appeared from the shadows and held him back while his father limped away. Dan was never sure whether to thank his friend for keeping him from killing his father or despise him for letting Lester live.

But either way, it was the beginning of the end of their friendship. Lester lit out for parts unknown before Dan had a chance to finish the job when Jake wasn't around.

Lester stayed away from Coldwater Cove for a few years— long enough for Daniel to get his degree in law enforcement and come home to take his place in the sheriff's office. Then the bum started straggling up from Texas during the summer months. Since he broke no laws, Daniel had watched him warily, but never spoke a word to him.

Guess Lester found a way to change that.

Led into the visiting cubicle by the guard, Lester plopped down in the chair on the opposite side of the glass. Both he and Daniel picked up the phone receiver on their respective sides. Silence filled up the space between them so completely, it crowded out everything, even air. Daniel was hard pressed to breathe. Intellectually, he knew Lester couldn't hurt him or his mom anymore, but that old kernel of fear was still about to pop inside.

"You want to see me. Here I am. Now what?" he demanded.

Lester met his gaze for a few seconds, and then looked away. "Among other things, I want to say . . . I'm sorry."

"I'd ask what for, but I told Valentina I'd only give you five minutes. We both know it would take a lot longer than that for you to list the things you should be sorry for."

The old man's eyes glistened. "You're right. And I'm sorry for tonight, too."

"Sorry for shoplifting or sorry you got caught?"

"Both."

"That's the first honest thing I've ever heard you say."

"I didn't mean to embarrass you, son."

"No." Danny slammed his palm down on his side of the table. "You don't get to call me that."

"Fair enough. Reckon I don't." Lester sighed. "You got a son of your own now, I hear tell."

Danny didn't say a word. There was no way he'd let Lester into his son's life. The man was a toxic swamp.

"Carson," Lester said. "That's his name, ain't it?"

If they hadn't been separated by thick glass, Danny would

have jumped down his father's throat. "How do you know that?"

"I seen him around. Your wife, she takes him to the park and lets him play in the sandbox there from time to time."

"Stay away from my family." Danny's knuckles whitened as his hands fisted involuntarily. He narrowed his eyes at Lester.

"I ain't come near 'im. Like I said, I just seen 'im. Ain't no law against a man looking at his own grandson, is there?"

Unfortunately, there wasn't. Since Lester had disappeared from their lives so completely after the beating Daniel had given him, his mother had never taken out a restraining order. The man wasn't a registered offender, so there was nothing to keep him from hanging out in a public park.

"Only thing is," Lester went on, "I ain't never seen you there at the park with 'em. Looks to me like you been staying away from your family, too."

"That's none of your business."

"No. It's yours and it appears you're not taking care of it."

That sounded so eerily like his mother-in-law, Celia, Dan wondered if Lester had been mooching coffee from her on her back stoop and shooting the breeze about him.

"You have no room to talk," Danny said.

"You got the right of it there, I'll not deny it. I screwed the pooch big time when it came to you and your mother. Sometimes, I look back and it's like my life happened to somebody else for a while. Like some stranger was living in my skin and doin' those terrible things."

"No, I'm pretty sure it was you."

Lester nodded. "It was. I'm not trying to make excuses. I own up to the past. I'm just telling you how it feels, knowing what I did and not being able to change it. I wish I coulda gave myself a good shake and knocked some sense into me or . . . well, like you said, five minutes ain't enough time for me to tell you all the things I'm sorry about," Lester said in a maddeningly calm tone. Then his voice dropped to a near whisper. "But it don't mean I ain't sorry for them all the same."

Lester was trying to play him. Dan was sure of it. "I'm not going to help you get out of jail."

"Never thought you would and I ain't asking you to. But I want to help *you*. If I can."

Danny scoffed.

"Reckon you're right to doubt. Never did help you much. And now I don't have nothing in my hands but ten fingers. All I can offer is advice."

"Pass." Daniel started to rise.

"Hear me out and then I won't bother you no more," Lester said, lifting a hand in what looked like supplication. Dan still mistrusted the man's motives, but the gesture stopped him from leaving.

"There's something broke in my brainpan, Danny. That's what I mean about the stranger in my head. I knowed it since I came back from the war. That ain't no excuse for the things I done to you and your mother but that don't make it less true that I was sick. Prob'ly still am. My fault is that I didn't try to get better. I wouldn't let nobody help me," he admitted. "Then I fell into a bottle and that took away any chance of making things better. And now my butt's sitting in jail 'cuz I made the choices I made."

"No argument here." The man deserved to die alone.

"The thing is, you're where *you* are 'cuz of choices you made, too. Don't throw it all away, son. Whatever it is that's keeping you from your boy and that pretty little wife of yours, it ain't worth it."

Danny started to hang up, but then he wondered aloud, "How do you know I'm the one to blame for our breakup?"

"When you live like I do, all you got is time. So to fill up the time, I watch folks. Where they go. What they talk about. Don't nobody think twice about saying whatever pops into their heads in front of me. It's like I'm not even there. . . ."

Lost in thought, Lester's eyes glazed over for a moment. Then he gave himself a little shake.

"Don't care what you say, watchin' folks is better than a play most days." Lester leaned forward on his bony elbows. "Anyhoo, I been keepin' tabs on your missus and there ain't any other man involved. I'd a seen him by now. Stands to reason you're the culprit. Tell me it ain't another skirt."

"No." A few stray thoughts about an old girlfriend did not count. "There's no one else."

"That's good. Otherwise, I'd stop bumping my gums right now on account of you bein' too stupid to help."

"What gives you the right to—"

"The right of a man that did everything wrong. I don't want you to end up like me. You know what the trouble between you and her is. You know what you gotta do. I see it plain as the nose on your face. Fix it, boy," Lester said with sudden fierceness. Then his shoulders slumped. "Otherwise, you're not lookin' through a pane of glass right now. You're lookin' in a mirror."

Dan slammed down the phone, called for the guard, and bolted from the room. He would have kept going until he was out of the building, but Valentina waylaid him again.

"Oh, Danny, I can see that didn't go well." She came around the counter and literally stood in his path. "I'm so sorry."

Not as sorry as Daniel was. He never should have let her talk him into sitting down with the man.

"Well, just one more thing and then I'll let the matter drop," she said with a pat on his shoulder. "Did you even read the report the Walmart security guy sent over?"

"No." He'd been in such a hurry to get Lester off his

hands and into custody, he'd punted the paperwork to the duty officer.

"Then you don't know what your father was trying to shoplift, do you?"

How many times did he have to say it? Lester Scott was *not* his father. "Beer, most like."

"No. He was caught with a little teddy bear stuffed in his shirt. A teddy bear," she repeated. "Three guesses who he had in mind when he tried to lift that."

"I don't want him thinking about Carson," Daniel said through clenched teeth. "And I sure as heck don't want him to use my son as an excuse to steal."

"Yeah, it was wrong. I know that. You know that. But at least Lester wasn't stealing something for himself," Valentina pointed out. "Doesn't that sort of change things, even a little?"

"No." Dan pushed around her and steamrolled out the door. "Not even a little."

Chapter 20

When I was in college, my sociology professor tried to convince us that no one ever does anything that isn't motivated by self-interest, not even things that are meant to benefit others. I argued with him about it at the time. Goodness is supposed to be its own reward. Now, I'm not so sure. I get so much back when I give, it does feel selfish sometimes.

But I'm not the sort to let a little thing like guilt stop me.

—Heather Walker, registered nurse and founding member of the Coldwater Warm Hearts Club

The trio of bells jingled merrily over the Green Apple Grill's front door at precisely 7:30 a.m. on Tuesday morning. Lacy let the door swing shut behind her. She clutched a pen and notepad. Wanda had warned her against using her tablet when she conducted interviews.

"Too high-tech for around here. Might put folks off and you want them talking, kid," Wanda had said. "Quotable stuff. That's always good copy."

As opposed to the community announcement posts that rolled into the *Gazette* office with regularity. Those were Wanda's fault. She encouraged her readership to submit short items of public interest so she could decide whether the event or announcement was worth assigning Lacy to do a full-blown story or if they'd just print the group's press release as it was taken down verbatim from a phone recording.

Like the little gem that came in yesterday:

Last Saturday, the Friends of the Opera House
voted to replace the carpet on the stairs going
up to the ballroom on the second floor. No, wait
a minute. That didn't sound right. The Friends
weren't on the stairs when they voted. That's just
where the carpet is. Anyway, it's getting replaced
on account of it becoming a mite shabby. The
carpet, not the ballroom. The community is invited to get involved. If you want to do anything
on the carpet, now's the time to do it.

After Lacy stopped laughing, she rewrote the piece to
make it clear that the Friends of the Opera House were solic-
iting financial donations to buy the new carpet, not encouraging the desecration of the old one. Then she thought about
it for half a minute before she deleted her new version. She
sent Wanda an e-mail encouraging her to print the original
announcement instead.

In Lacy's opinion, the quirky bits that cropped up in
nearly every edition of the *Gazette* were the only things that
made it worth reading. Besides, everyone in Coldwater Cove
would understand the intent of the original and if they do-
nated money to the Friends of the Opera House with one
hand while hiding a smile with the other, whom would it
hurt?

Wanda hadn't assigned Lacy to write a piece on the Coldwater Warm Hearts Club, but she was ready for her first meeting anyway. This stealthy group of do-gooders was ripe to
be subjected to a little investigative journalism. Surely they
harbored another motive beyond the "feel-good" reward of
helping others.

She just wished they met someplace other than the Green
Apple. After Jake's kiss last night, she wasn't ready to face him
so soon.

She felt ridiculously shy about it. As if he'd somehow caught her naked.

Lacy, you're such an idiot. It was only a kiss.

Only a kiss that had exposed her loneliness. Single. Solitary. Only-ness.

But if Jake had given that kiss a second thought, he didn't show it. He was hard at work before the grill, his broad shoulders turned from the rest of the place. The breakfast rush was in full swing, so maybe she'd be in and out before he even noticed she was there.

Heather Walker was already seated at a couple of tables that had been pushed together. A few others were gathered beside her.

"Lacy, come join us." Heather motioned to her and then turned to the others. "You all know Lacy Evans. She writes for the *Gazette* as Dorie Higginbottom."

So much for keeping a low profile. Oh, well. Chances were none of them were in communication with the O'Leary brothers of North End or the Boston DA's office.

"Lacy, you remember Virgil Cooper." Heather lifted a hand toward a thin, fiftyish fellow with a disastrous comb-over and a kind smile. "He runs the hardware store over on Elm Street."

She nodded a greeting to Mr. Cooper, who returned it in a slow, dignified manner.

"I knew your mother back when she was a Higginbottom, Lacy," he said.

That might be worth a private interview or two. Lacy's mom had never talked much about her early years.

"Next to him is Ian Van Hook," Heather went on. "He's our youngest member."

"Not so young. I'll be a senior next year," the boy protested.

Lacy grinned at the kid. Teenagers were always in such

a hurry to grow up. She wished she could convince him to enjoy his life now. There wasn't always an upside to getting older. He probably thought he'd be in more control of his life, but Lacy put the lie to that. She was the poster girl for unexpected pivots.

"Take a load off, honey." Ethel bustled around the tables and pulled out a chair for her.

"Thanks, Ethel." Lacy settled into her assigned seat and reevaluated her previous notion.

Ethel disproved the idea that there was no upside to getting older. The Green Apple's waitress was a whirlwind with feet, albeit one that twirled a little more slowly than most. Ethel obviously enjoyed what she was doing. The woman greeted, seated, and served. She even bussed tables for the grill's diners. And all with a smile on her wrinkled winter-apple of a face.

"How do you have time for all the things you do around here?" Lacy asked.

"Never you mind about that, sugar. If I don't have time, I don't have nothin'. Now, can I start you'uns out with some coffee?" Lacy cringed a bit at the local equivalent of "y'all," but "you'uns" was as much a part of Ethel as her casual endearments. Ethel lifted a pot from her rolling serving cart and filled all the cups in front of the gathered Warm Hearts in a jiffy. Except for the one in front of Ian. "It'll stunt your growth, sweetie-pie. I'll bring you some orange juice in a minute."

Before the kid could complain that he liked caffeine as well as the next man, she was off, pushing her cart back to the kitchen for the next orders that had come up.

The bells over the door jingled again. Heather waved at the newcomers. One was Marjorie Chubb, Lacy's fellow employee at the *Gazette* and captain of the Methodist prayer chain. The other was a woman in sheriff's office khaki. Her lustrous dark hair was so black it shone with blue highlights.

"You already know Marjorie," Heather said. "This is Valentina Gomez. She's the dispatcher over at the sheriff's office."

"Lacy, you're not here to do a story on our club, are you?" Marjorie eyed her notepad with suspicion.

"Well, yes, as a matter of fact, I am. Don't you want your good works to be a matter of public record?"

"I do not." Marjorie plopped into her chair with the force of an exclamation point. "The people we help, they might not appreciate their private business being plastered all over the media."

As if the Gazette *could be classified as media!*

"Anyway," Marjorie continued, "I'm not sure we want to shine a light on our activities. It might make folks hesitant to accept our help."

"Marjorie, you're the captain of the Methodist prayer chain. Don't the people you pray for get a light shone on their problems when you pass their information along the chain?" Lacy asked. "What's the difference?"

"The difference is it's God's light we're shining on the problems. And most of the people we pray for have *asked* for prayer themselves or else their family has requested prayer on their behalf," Marjorie explained. "And anyway, being prayed for is confidential. It isn't like being in the paper where anybody can read all about it."

"Wait a minute. When I first started writing for the *Gazette* you told me that you'd have some ideas for human interest stories based on the prayer chain."

"Only about *good* things. I was thinking I could share praise stories after answered prayer, not requests during times of trouble." Marjorie drew her lips together in a tight line. "Every time you spread gossip, it's a prayer to the devil."

"If that's the case," Lacy muttered, "Coldwater Cove must keep the old boy awfully busy."

"Easy now," Heather intervened. "Let's leave the devil out of it, shall we?"

"How about if I agree to leave the names and specifics of the people you help out of any article I write?" Lacy said. "Unless I get permission from all parties involved."

That seemed to mollify Marjorie. "We need to get the meeting started. Where's Charlie?"

"Oh, he'll be along," Valentina said. "I saw him talking to Alfred Mayhew in front of the Opera House."

"Then you'uns may as well go ahead and order." Ethel had reappeared beside their table before Lacy realized she was even there. "Charlie Bunn likes to talk folks' ears off. He's always the last Lutheran to make the lunch crowd on Sundays."

"Well, at least I'm not the last Lutheran in line for breakfast," came a rumbling bass from behind Ethel.

The waitress turned around and gave the tall older gentleman a playful swat on the shoulder. "Make a liar out of me, why don't you, Charlie. Sit down and I'll get you some coffee."

Lacy recognized Charlie Bunn from the year in her childhood when the Methodists and Lutherans had teamed up for Vacation Bible School. The gregarious Mr. Bunn had brought his lawn tractor to the churchyard, hitched a small wagon to it, and gave hay rides to VBS kids of all denominations. He even included those who just sneaked in for the fun stuff and intended to sneak back out before the teaching could begin. However, by the time they rounded the first bend in the track Mr. Bunn had laid out, he had all the children singing silly songs at the top of their lungs and very few of them skedaddled once the ride was over.

They were afraid they might miss something.

"How's the Royal Order of Chicken Pluckers going?" Ethel asked him as she filled his coffee cup.

"Fine as frog's hair."

"Royal Order of Chicken Pluckers?" Lacy asked, scenting a human interest story she might be able take to Wanda. "What's that?"

"Oh, it's just my little Warm Hearts project. We all take one on," Charlie explained. "For instance, Heather's is Mrs. Chisholm, though I don't know how she does it. That old woman is the poster girl for crotchety, bless her heart."

People could get away with saying anything about someone else so long as it was followed by some version of "bless their heart." "Tell me about your project, Mr. Bunn."

"Well, as you probably know, the Lutheran Ladies make and sell chicken pies to raise money for mission work. This year we plan to fund a new community well for a little town up in the hills that needs it yesterday."

"Best pies in the state," Ian said. "Just wish they were bigger though. I can eat a whole pie in one sitting."

"That's 'cuz teenage boys all have hollow legs. Hungry as wolves, the lot of 'em," Ethel said, and then quietly took Ian's breakfast order, promising to bring him an extra plate of toast and marmalade.

"Anyway, back to the Royal Order of Chicken Pluckers," Mr. Bunn went on. "Making pies is hard work and the ladies were bearing the brunt of it. I tried to get a few fellows to come help. Not to cook, of course. The ladies are great, but they needed some help lifting the big baking pans, boning the chickens, and doing general cleanup. But when I sent out the plea for volunteers there were no takers. So I decided, what if I could think up a way to make the work fun?"

Lacy always thought carving meat off the turkey at Thanksgiving was the worst job in the kitchen. "If you can make boning a chicken fun, my friend, you are a miracle worker."

"No, I'm just well acquainted with One." Mr. Bunn laughed. "However, you should never underestimate the power of silliness. I donned a paper crown one Sunday and declared that only a few worthy souls would be admitted to the Royal Order of Chicken Pluckers. After that, I had more volunteers than I knew what to do with. I gave all the jobs special titles—Lord High Bottle Washer, Mayor of Basting, Knight of the Wishbone—things like that. We even lured a few Methodists and Episcopalians into popping by to help when the ladies bake pies. The Chicken Pluckers are entirely ecumenical."

"But even so, what you're describing is a church ministry," Lacy said. "How do your Chicken Pluckers count as a Coldwater Warm Hearts Club project?"

"Ah. Well, you're right in part. The pies fund a mission. Thanks to the Lutheran Ladies, a little hamlet of about twenty-five souls will get a chance to enjoy clean drinking water. That's their ministry. But everyone needs an opportunity to feel useful. The Royal Order of Chicken Pluckers gives men the nudge they need to help and have fun while they're doing it." Mr. Bunn smiled. "Spreading fun is *my* ministry."

As if fun was something that could be broadcast like seeds. Maybe in Mr. Bunn's case, it was.

"I'd like to come over and take a few pictures of the Chicken Pluckers in action if that's OK."

"Sure. We're usually at the church by eight on Thursday mornings," Mr. Bunn said. "I'll make sure the boys all have fresh paper crowns to wear. They get a little wilted after a day of fetching and carrying, you know."

Ethel finished taking their breakfast orders while the other club members reported on their activities. In addition to Heather's work with fussy old Mrs. Chisholm, Ian had come to the aid of a kid who was being bullied at school. Mr. Cooper had mowed his recently widowed neighbor's lawn and changed the oil in her car, though he didn't want anyone to think he was sweet on her or anything like that. He was a confirmed bachelor and not likely to change at this stage in his life. Marjorie had volunteered at the senior center and taught a quartet of octogenarians how to play hand and foot.

"What's that?" Lacy asked. "Some sort of geriatric Twister?"

"Heavens, no. Twister would put us all in traction. Hand and foot is a card game that uses six decks," Marjorie explained. "Keeps the fingers nimble and the mind sharp."

Ethel was busy delivering muffins to some other patrons, so Jake came out of the kitchen with their orders. Lacy met his gaze and was relieved when he smiled at her as if nothing was different. Maybe that kiss wasn't going to make things weird between them.

"So I'm hearing that the only qualification for being a member of the Coldwater Warm Hearts Club is that you must do something nice for someone," Lacy said. "Someone who can't or won't necessarily return the favor."

Everyone nodded because their mouths were full. Once Jake put a plate in front of everyone, the delicious omelets, crepes, and breakfast scrambles were too yummy to resist.

He'd made waffles for Lacy, even though she hadn't ordered anything but coffee.

"On the house," he murmured as he set the steaming plate before her.

She grinned up at him. "I used to think carbs were better than men. Turns out they aren't better than *some* men."

He leaned down to whisper in her ear. His warm breath sent a shiver down her neck. "If I'd known you felt that way, I'd have brought you macaroni and cheese instead of meat loaf the other night."

Then he started to head back to the kitchen.

"Jake is qualified to be a member of the Warm Hearts Club," Lacy blurted out before he had a chance to make his getaway.

"Don't make a big deal out of it," he said. "It's just waffles."

"Not for that, though, believe me, I'm grateful." Belgian waffles were her kryptonite, but she'd willingly handicap herself with them. "I meant for rescuing Speedbump."

She told the group about how Jake had saved the little dog from traffic, cleaned him up, and taken him in. They all agreed that the good turn didn't have to be given to another human. Jake's kindness to Speedbump qualified him to be a member of the Warm Hearts.

"How did you get on with him last night?" Lacy asked.

"He snores," Jake said as he freshened everyone's coffee.

"Maybe you could move his crate farther from your bed," Lacy suggested.

"Wouldn't help. He'd have to be in the crate, and he's determined not to let that happen."

"Then where did he sleep?"

"He made himself at home in the middle of my bed."

"Finding a pet is a blessing, but it's even better when the pet finds you back," Charlie Bunn said. "Sounds like Speedbump has already made you his person."

"Well, he's over at Doc Braden's now," Jake said. "He'll make a good dog out of him."

That reminded Lacy of what her dad said about squirrels. The only good one was a dead one. "Oh, Jake, you're not having him put down."

"Heck, no." Jake frowned at her. "Speedbump's only there to have the sorry trim we gave him evened up, get all his shots, and . . . well, let's just say I won't have to defend my leg's virtue anymore after the doc is finished with him."

Jake started toward the kitchen again but Valentina Gomez called him back. "I'm proposing a new group project for the club today, Jake, and I think we'll need you for this. Will you join us?"

"OK." He folded his well-muscled forearms over his chest. "I'll help if I can."

"Good, because you know the target of this project, maybe better than any of us."

Target? That sounded like someone was about to be ambushed by a flurry of good deeds.

"Who is it?" Lacy asked.

"Off the record," Valentina said, lifting a perfectly shaped brow.

"Of course."

"It's Lester Scott," the pretty Latina confided. "He's an alcoholic and—"

"And an abusive husband," Marjorie interrupted.

"At one time, yes," Valentina conceded.

"As I heard tell, it was many times," Marjorie said.

"All right, he has a bad history, but that's just it. It's history. I looked up his records and he hasn't been charged with anything violent for the last ten years or so. I don't think he's beyond help." Valentina paused, but no one said anything. "Look. He's homeless and he's here among us. Are we going to ignore him?"

They had so far.

"Isn't that what Samaritan House is for?" Marjorie asked. "Why doesn't he go there?"

"A temporary bed is like putting a Band-Aid on an arterial bleed," Valentina said. "Samaritan House deals with immediate needs, not helping people find their way back into society."

"Lester may also be dealing with some mental illness. A high percentage of the homeless are," Heather added. "In fact, I wouldn't doubt it if that played a part in the abuse in his past."

"None of us are qualified to help with that," Mr. Cooper said.

"No, but I want you to think about it this way. What if he were sick with something else?" Valentina said, leaning forward for emphasis. "Say he had diabetes or some other chronic illness. None of us, except maybe Heather, would be qualified to treat him for that either. Would that mean we wouldn't try to help him?"

"Of course not," Heather said.

"He's a veteran," Jake said quietly. "He may be a drunkard and a lout and maybe crazy to boot, but we can do better by him than we have. Whatever you're planning, Valentina, I'm in."

Lacy watched in awe as one by one, the group agreed to join Jake in Valentina's "Project Lester." She was the visionary, but it took a leader to rap softly on their souls and make them open the door. Jake was just the man for that job.

Something glowed in her chest. She'd always been attracted to him. No sane woman wouldn't be. But now, she admired Jake, too. Compassion was a rare thing in this world. Jake had shown it for Speedbump, and now he'd shown it for Lester, who was probably just as lost and afraid as the little dog had been. Jacob Tyler was a good man.

As advertised, they were hard to find.

"I've already talked to Lester's attorney. I sort of have the inside track since I'm married to him," Valentina said with a wink and a grin. "Anyway, Tomas thinks he can swing a deal with Judge Preston if we have all our ducks in a row. Now, here's what we need to do."

Chapter 21

Whether it's giving a witness statement, speaking up for those who cannot speak for themselves, or giving someone a kick in the pants when they need it, too many people claim they don't want to get involved. What? Do they want to hide in a hole while others suffer around them?

What are we living for if not to get involved in the lives around us?

—Valentina Gomez, a wise Latina who believes
everyone is entitled to *her* opinion

Lacy made it a point to be present at Lester's sentencing that afternoon. She had no intention of writing anything for the paper about it. The bare facts would come out in the weekly report sent over by the courthouse. But the thought of adding to them . . . well, since Jake was involving himself in Lester's fate, the story felt too personal for her be objective. She wanted to see if Judge Preston would go along with the Warm Hearts Club's plan.

She was also there to give Danny moral support. Her stomach had stopped doing flip-flops whenever she thought about him. Something more like friendship had solidified in place of that fluttery feeling. Daniel was part of her life and always would be. He'd just never be that endless night sky again.

By the time the "Summer of Daniel" had happened, Lester was gone. His son had never wanted to talk about him back then. She figured he might now and if he did, he'd need a friendly ear. These proceedings could be the catalyst Daniel needed to lance that old wound.

Too bad he was a no-show.

The bailiff called Lester's name and he was led into the courtroom wearing an orange jumpsuit. After the charges were read, silence reigned while the judge studied the paperwork before him for a few seconds.

"Mr. Scott, I see that you were convicted of shoplifting in Tulsa six years ago." Judge Preston's gravelly voice reminded Lacy of Darth Vader with a head cold.

"Yes, sir. I was in a grocery store and I tried to make off with a box of Twinkies. In my defense, Your Honor, I was mighty sharp set at the time."

"Are you aware that upon a second offense, it is within my purview to fine you the sum of one thousand dollars?"

Lester's Adam's apple bobbed. "Sir, meanin' no disrespect, but that don't make no sense. If I had a thousand dollars, I wouldn't have had to steal something, would I?"

"No one *has* to steal, regardless of their situation, though hunger might be considered a mitigating circumstance in your first conviction. However, you did not try to steal food this time." The judge glared at Lester and then at his attorney. "Mr. Gomez, I suggest you instruct your client to limit his responses."

The public defender, Valentina's husband, leaned over to whisper something to Lester. The old man nodded and folded his hands before himself, fig-leaf style.

Jake slid into the row of chairs beside Lacy. "How's it going?"

She shook her head and mouthed, "not good."

But it was incredibly good of Jake to take time off from the grill to be present at Lester's sentencing. Granted, by three in the afternoon, things had slowed to a crawl at the Green Apple, but still . . . Lester wasn't anything special to him.

Except another veteran.

The judge cleared his throat. "The law grants me wide

discretion in these sorts of cases. By statute, you can be incarcerated for as long as one year."

"A year? For a teddy bear?"

His lawyer shushed him. Lester's shoulders slumped.

"Larceny is no small crime, no matter the value of the item in question. In light of your recalcitrant attitude, I'm inclined toward a year sentence to protect the hardworking merchants in our town," the judge said with an expression that would have served him well at a poker table. "So ordered."

He rapped his gavel smartly.

"A whole year." Lester's knees gave out and he plopped into the chair behind him.

"However," the judge said as he looked at another sheet of paper on his bench, "it seems there are those who believe you are worth saving. They have petitioned the court for leniency in your case."

Lester looked around in expectation, trying to figure out who might have spoken for him. Lacy spotted Heather Walker, Charlie Bunn, Mr. Cooper, Marjorie Chubb, and Valentina Gomez sitting in the back row. All the members of the Coldwater Warm Hearts Club were present except Ian, who was probably still in class.

But Daniel wasn't there.

Lester's face fell.

"Well, God bless 'em," he muttered. "Whoever they are."

"Here is what's going to happen, Mr. Scott," Judge Preston said. Lester's lawyer encouraged him back onto his feet. "You will serve thirty days in the county jail. Then the rest of your year sentence will be suspended, depending on your comportment once you're discharged."

"I'll comport the heck out myself, Your Honor," Lester said. "See if I don't."

The judge glowered at him. "I understand you are an alcoholic."

"I been known to take a drink."

"You won't for the next thirty days. While you serve time in jail, a representative from the local AA will visit you on a regular basis, and once your thirty days with the county are up, you will continue with the program."

"Not wanting to dispute your word, Your Honor, but ain't that sort of thing s'posed to be voluntary?"

"Yes. And you're going to volunteer," the judge said. "Otherwise, I'll reinstate the year sentence and you'll serve the rest of your time at the Oklahoma State Penitentiary in McAlester."

Lester shuddered. Doing time in "Big Mac" was no joke. The prison housed the most dangerous criminals in the state.

"In addition to remaining sober once you've served your initial thirty days here in the county jail, these are the other requirements for your continued parole. I've been informed that the Walker family has generously given a grant to the psychology department at Bates College to start a free mental health clinic."

This development had Heather written all over it. Lacy shot a quizzical look at her friend. Heather winked back. She might not be willing to accept a place to live from her parents, but belonging to one of the wealthiest families in the county did have its perks.

"By the time you are released from county, the clinic should be ready to accept patients. You will be one of its first," Judge Preston told Lester.

The old man scratched his head. "If you say so."

"I do. And you may no longer camp out on the streets of Coldwater Cove. You must accept housing."

"Reckon the main question on that point is what housing is going to accept me?" Lester said. "Samaritan House is good for a bed for three days, tops."

Charlie Bunn stood. "If I may, Your Honor, I'm in a position to offer Mr. Scott a place to live above my garage. It's not the Ritz, but the efficiency apartment there has all the essentials."

"I see from the petition for leniency that you intend to offer this situation to the defendant rent free?" the judge said as he continued to study the document before him.

"Not exactly, sir. I intend for Mr. Scott to pay for his rent in yard work and gardening." Mr. Bunn shot the judge a toothy smile. "I plant a mean vegetable patch every spring."

"Mr. Scott, do you agree to these terms?"

Lester nodded to the judge and then turned to Mr. Bunn. "Much obliged."

"Wait till you see the size of my garden," Charlie said as he resumed his seat. "Then we'll see how obliged you are."

"You must also have gainful employment," the judge said, ticking off the next item on the list before him.

"Well, now I'm sunk," Lester said. "Ain't nobody going to hire an old drunk."

Jake rose to his feet. "No, but I'll hire a recovering one."

"As will I," Mr. Cooper joined in. "Mr. Tyler and I have worked out an arrangement so that each of us will employ Mr. Scott part-time. He'll work a couple of days a week at my hardware store and a couple of days at the Green Apple."

"And one day a week in my garden," Charlie Bunn reminded Lester.

The homeless man's eyes glistened and he blinked hard several times. "Thank you. Thank you all kindly."

"And since these citizens of Coldwater Cove have come forward to help you, Mr. Scott, one of the conditions for this unusual arrangement is that you are hereby ordered to help someone else as well." The judge scanned the assembly. "I understand someone has a volunteer position for the defendant to fill."

Marjorie rose to her feet. "That's me, Your Honor. Mr.

Scott can join me at the senior center on Saturdays where he'll be playing cards with the patients there."

"A game of poker, maybe?" Lester asked eagerly.

"Good heavens, no. These are friendly card games. You'll play for the pleasure of conversation around the table and entertainment only." Marjorie started to sit, but then thought better of it and straightened again. "And he must be clean-shaven and dressed presentably when he arrives at the center or he will not be admitted."

"So ordered," the judge agreed. "Do you accept these terms, Mr. Scott?"

"Reckon I have to, Your Honor."

"Indeed, you do, Mr. Scott. Because unless you do, I'm compelled to point out to you that your life will only get worse." Judge Preston's face screwed into a frown. "The court fears you are not taking this seriously."

"Oh, no, Your Honor. I'm taking it dead serious. To be right truthful, if you was to tell me I was going to die if I don't do somethin' different, that wouldn't motivate me much. Dying is easy. It cures all ills, they do say," Lester said. "I sleep in an alley and eat out of trash cans mostly. It's hard to imagine something worse. But I figure you're a smart fellow, Your Honor. Wouldn't be sitting there in them fancy robes if you wasn't. When you claim things will get worse for me, I have to believe you. And 'worse' is not something I think I can face."

The judge nodded slowly. "Very well. Mr. Gomez will draw up the agreement for you to sign and if you adhere to the program outlined in court today, you will have a chance to change your future for the better, Mr. Scott."

"Thank you, Your Honor. I'm good to go."

"You'd better not. Leaving the area after you serve thirty days in jail will violate your parole. You are hereby ordered not to stray from this county until one year from today. I expect you to live up to your part of the bargain." The judge lifted his gavel again, poised to give the bench a sharp rap, but he stopped himself. "Mr. Scott, I am compelled to warn you that bad things will happen if you deviate in the slightest from the terms you have agreed to today."

"How 'slightest' we talkin'?"

"Miss a day at work or your volunteer assignment, except with a doctor's written excuse. Fail to keep an appointment with the Bates College psychologist. Do a poor job in Mr. Bunn's garden. Touch a drop of alcohol or any controlled substance, and you'll be arrested again," the judge said. "Trust me. You do not wish to appear before me a second time."

"You're too hard on yourself, Your Honor," Lester said. "I bet you'd be ever' bit as pleasant to meet a second time."

If the judge had been a teapot, he'd have been steaming like mad. "On the day that you appear before me again, your year sentence will be reinstated. You'll be sent to McAlester to serve the remaining time on your sentence without further recourse." He banged the gavel so hard, Lacy feared it might break. "Do you understand?"

"Yes, sir, Your Honor, sir. I think you just explained what 'worse' is."

Chapter 22

Miss Holloway's ninth-grade class will present
Shakespeare's Macbeth *in the high school*
gymnasium this Friday at 7 p.m. Don't miss this tragedy.

—from the Fighting Marmots Notes section
of the *Coldwater Gazette*

On Thursday morning, Lacy dropped by the Lutheran Church to take a picture to go along with her article on the Royal Order of Chicken Pluckers. It took longer to corral the members than she anticipated.

For one thing, it was hard to pull them away from their assigned "royal" duties. The men lifted heavy pans in and out of the ovens for the ladies, boned the baked chickens with willing hands, and mopped up after themselves when a whole platter of white meat was dropped on the way from one counter to the other. Snapping candid pics of them doing the work was no problem.

Setting the Chicken Pluckers up for a group shot, however, was a challenge. At first, Lacy made the mistake of asking them to arrange themselves by height. No one wanted to admit to being the shortest man there, so it turned into a back-to-back showdown with much surreptitious tiptoeing and stretching. In the end, she instructed half of the fellows to take a knee as if they were a football team posing for the high school yearbook.

Then once she got them all lined up for the shot, invariably after she snapped the shutter, someone would claim their eyes had been closed and she needed to take another picture. In the end, she took a full dozen shots and promised she'd print the one with the least number of visible eyelids in the bunch.

Then she dropped by the post office to mail a package. After studying the painting she'd bought at Gewgaws and Gizzwickies a week ago, she was still tantalized by the suspicion that it might be more than a clever imitation. She just had to know for sure. Neville Lodge, a colleague from her art institute days back in Boston, with art history credentials out the wazoo, had told her to send it to him for verification. He'd be able to tell if it was merely a copy of an Erté or—and Lacy scarcely allowed herself to hope—if it was something much more.

The value of a genuine, previously unknown Erté would go a long way toward retiring her loan to the O'Leary brothers.

So after her parcel was on its way to Beantown, Lacy's day off from the *Gazette* began in earnest and she headed out to meet Jake to work on his mother's lake-house chair. When she pulled into her parents' driveway at nine-thirty, Jake was already there. He and her dad were deep in conversation near the garage's open door. Her father handed him a steaming mug of coffee and, not having been forewarned, Jake accepted it.

Sorry, Jake.

Dad often claimed his coffee separated the men from the boys. He also maintained that keeping the wimps away from the door was a father's main task when raising a daughter. In this respect, his five-alarm coffee was better than brandishing a big stick. After taking a manly gulp, Jake didn't show any ill effects. Her dad smiled approvingly at him.

Evidently, Jake passed the "Trial by Caffeine" test.

Face it. Jake passes any test you want to throw at him.

He was still the Coldwater Cove poster boy for "tall, dark, and handsome." Lacy's chest constricted.

Down, girl. You just got out of man trouble in Boston with your fingers and toes barely intact. You seriously don't need more.

And there was no doubt Jake had the potential to be trouble. Even laying aside his player past, there was still the problem of those flashbacks. Until he got a handle on them, any romantic entanglements might just muddy the waters for him. She didn't want to be the distraction that kept him from working through his issues.

And the truth was, after Bradford's betrayal, Lacy was still guy-shy. She couldn't trust her judgment about men. Or her emotions.

Especially those fluttery ones. Just thinking about spending the whole day with Jacob had them kicking up a ruckus in her belly.

"I see you brought your mom's chair," she said, wanting to slap a hand over her own mouth at her grasp of the obvious.

"It's a dandy, isn't it? Surprisingly sturdy," her dad said. "Jake and I have just been talking about what to do with it. I'm thinking a good quality oil-based paint to liven things up. Maybe bright orange or—"

"George Evans, not another word." Tying a scarf over her head to save her coiffure from the breeze, Lacy's mom came into the garage through the mudroom off the kitchen. "You stop bossing those kids around."

It never failed when Lacy showed up at her folks' house. Now not only was *she* twelve again, Jake had been reduced to kid status, too.

"That chair is *their* project," Mom said, "not yours."

Well! That was a nice surprise. Lacy could have kissed her mom and did.

"I'm only trying to lend a hand," her dad said.

"That's nice, dear, but they don't need your hand. They have four of their own. However, since you're in a helpful mood, you *can* help me." Mom slipped a hand into the crook of Dad's elbow. "I signed up to sell tickets for the high school production of *Macbeth* and I've got ten left."

"Oh, Shirl, why'd you go and volunteer to do that? You know that play is bound to be rated PC."

"Politically correct?" Lacy lifted a questioning brow at her father.

"I wish." Dad shook his head ruefully. "PC means parental consumption. You have to have a genetic connection with one of the actors involved in order to squirm through it."

"Now, George, I'm sure the play won't be as bad as you think."

"No, it'll probably be worse," he said morosely. "I could understand volunteering to sell tickets if we still had a kid in high school, but we have *old* children now."

At last! Confirmation that I'm not, in fact, still twelve.

"Hush, George. Admitting to having old children makes us even older."

"I just mean, why do we have to sell tickets for this thing since we don't have a kid in it?"

"Because we want to be supportive members of the community," Lacy's mother said as she took his hand, led him out of the garage and down the driveway to their waiting SUV. "If you don't want to sell them, would you rather pay for the ten tickets yourself?"

"Yes, if it'll get me out of coercing our friends to buy them."

"Fine. We'll buy the lot, invite four other couples, and make an evening of it," Mom said brightly. "There's nothing like good theater, you know."

"I know. And this'll be nothing like good theater," Dad said with a frown. "Seriously, Shirl. Just because we pay for tickets, it doesn't follow that we actually have to show up and use them."

"If you buy the tickets, of course you have to go. Besides the fact that Miss Holloway's class has worked on the play for weeks, I was not raised to be wasteful."

Maybe that's why she never wants to throw anything away.

"Honestly, dear," Mom went on, "how will all those young people feel if Coldwater Cove doesn't support their efforts? They deserve an enthusiastic audience."

"They better hope for a forgiving one." Dad pulled his red Oklahoma Sooners cap from his back pocket and slapped it on his head. "All right, dear. Let's head over to the country club and see if I can corner somebody who owes me a favor. That's the only way we'll unload those things."

"Lacy, there's some fried chicken in the fridge and other picnic fixings if you kids want to head down to the park. I hear there's a band concert at one. If you're done here by then, of course," Mom called over her shoulder as Dad opened the passenger-side door for her.

Now who's trying to boss the "kids" around?

But it was kindly meant and her mother had neatly maneuvered Lacy out of having to accept her father's help with the chair. He had good intentions, but all his DIY projects ended up like the disastrous squirrel repellent.

"Thanks, Mom. A picnic sounds great." As her parents drove off, she could still hear her dad grumbling through the vehicle's open windows. Lacy turned to Jake. "Will that be okay with you or did you have other plans for today?"

Jake smiled down at her. "My only plan is to spend as much of the day with you as I can. Oh! And to make sure Speedbump isn't making a nuisance of himself."

"Where is he?"

"In the backyard with Fergus. I hated to leave him alone at my place. The little guy seems to enjoy company," Jake said.

"Will he be all right back there?"

"Sure. He and Fergus clicked like magnets. But we'd better check on him from time to time. I can't promise he's not a digger."

"Having a dog is sort of like having a furry child, isn't it? They need to be with you," Lacy said. "Having a cat, on the other hand, is like having a roommate. You can go your own ways with no repercussions. Well, at least not many. Effie has been known to sharpen her claws on the couch if I stay away longer than she deems appropriate."

Jake set his coffee cup down on her dad's workbench. "Let's see what we can get done on the chair."

They removed the cushions and donned safety glasses while they sanded the wood surfaces with fine-grain paper. It felt good to work beside Jake, to enjoy the way the muscles in his arms bunched and flexed, to catch a whiff of his clean masculine scent.

Remember, Lacy, just friends, she told herself. *We're just friends.*

Just friends who'd shared a kiss that curled her toes. She forced away the memory.

"Now we wipe the chair down to remove all the dust and then rub in some teak oil. Not much. It doesn't need more than a touch of oil," Lacy said. "I wouldn't use any at all if it was an outdoor chair."

"Why is that?"

"If it was outdoor furniture, you'd want the wood to darken from honey to gray, but since your mom uses this chair inside the lake house, a little oil will keep the natural wood tone fresh."

"You're the boss." Jake followed her instructions.

After he was finished and the chair was gleaming, she said, "Let's let it rest for about twenty minutes, and then see how it looks. Maybe you can check on how Fergus and Speedbump are doing in the backyard while I fix us some iced tea."

"Good idea. That little stinker may have burrowed half-way to China by now."

Speedbump hadn't. Instead, Fergus had taught him to patrol the perimeter of the fence, making sure the backyard was safe from squirrel incursions, no doubt.

Lacy watched out the kitchen window while she poured the tea. She almost didn't recognize Speedbump. Now that he was clean and professionally trimmed, he was terminally cute. Only his slight underbite saved him from looking like a total frou-frou dog. Jake tossed a ball for the dogs to chase across the yard. Sometimes, they fetched it back to him quickly so he could throw it again and sometimes, they played keep-away with each other.

Lacy noticed that Speedbump's right front paw was turned at a ninety degree angle each time he stopped and when he ran, there was a hitch in his get-along. Maybe that was why Jake had bonded with him so quickly. They both had mobility issues, but they weren't about to let that slow them down.

By the time Lacy brought out a tray with frosty glasses and a tall pitcher, Jake was sitting on the back deck steps, both dogs collapsed in panting bundles at his feet.

Lacy bent to give Fergus and Speedbump each a pat before she sat down beside Jake and handed him a full glass. Speedbump rolled over to present his tummy for her to stroke.

"He seems to be settling in with you pretty well," she said.

"I guess that's the charm of a stray. Speedbump is grateful for any scrap of attention." As if he recognized his name, the dog sat up. Jake reached down to scratch behind Speedbump's ear, setting the dog's hind leg thumping in sympathy.

"He's a good boy," Lacy said.

"Someone has spent some time training him. He's already housebroken. Not a single accident since he came to live with me," Jake said. "Makes me wonder if I should have you put another ad in the paper about him. He must belong to some-one."

"If he does, they weren't doing a good job taking care of him. And they aren't looking for him very hard. I checked some of the back issues of the *Gazette*."

"No one put in a 'lost dog' notice matching his descrip-tion?"

Lacy shook her head. "And he'd obviously been on his own for a while because he was in such miserable shape when we found him. Did the vet check for an identifying chip when he had his surgery?"

"Yeah. There wasn't one."

"Then I think you've done enough to find his previous owners," she said. "He may have a weird name now, but it comes with a good home. And that's the important thing."

"Hey! He likes being called Speedbump, don't you, boy?" As if to prove his master's words, the dog reared on its hind legs and did a happy pirouette, pawing the air. "This little guy is trying pretty hard to fit into my life and honestly, I'm glad to have him. He practically turns himself inside out to welcome me home when I'm done for the day."

"Hence the popularity of dogs," Lacy said. "If Effie is feel-ing magnanimous, she may lift her head to acknowledge my presence."

"Don't go maligning that poor cat again. She seemed to like me just fine."

"What's not to like?" Lacy grinned at him. "I guess I should admit that Effie and I are warming up to each other slowly. She actually curled up on my lap the other day."

"I'll be darned."

"And I didn't have a single sardine in my pocket."

"Well, that's progress," Jake said. "Maybe it's just the dif-ference between cats and dogs, but Speedbump is more eager to please. It's like he realizes he's got a good thing going and doesn't want to mess it up. Almost like he's been granted a miracle."

Lacy took a sip of her tea.

"You know, it was kind of like watching a slow-motion miracle the other day, the way you and the Warm Hearts Club stood up for Lester Scott in court. Do you think he'll realize he's been given a good thing, too?"

"I hope so," Jake said. "He's got thirty days in the tank to think about it. The miracle will kick in if he's able to meet the judge's demands. Lester is carrying a lot of baggage. This isn't going to be easy for him."

"I suppose not," Lacy said. "But being homeless is no picnic either. A place to live, work, and do some good for somebody else in exchange for staying sober. That seems like a good trade."

"From the outside looking in, it does," Jake said. "But who knows how it looks to Lester?"

"My uncle Roy—he's the real writer in the family—always says everyone has a secret and if you only knew it, it would break your heart," Lacy said. "I wonder what Lester's is."

Jake shifted uncomfortably, as if he knew more about Lester's baggage than he'd said.

"Well, he did lose his family all those years ago," Jake said.

"That's gotta hurt," Lacy said. "Especially since it was his own fault as far as I know. Daniel never wanted to talk about it."

Jake's knuckles whitened around his tea glass. She really shouldn't have brought up Daniel.

"The past is the past and nobody can change it," Jake said. "All we can do is the best we can from one moment to the next."

Lacy studied Jake's profile. He was a strong man. And his

strength wasn't just physical, though it was hard to ignore his well-muscled arms and broad shoulders. There was a strong spine of moral toughness in him.

Who knew he was also wise? He was right. The past was already written. What would happen in the future was a result of the present, so "now" was all anyone really had.

"Since Lester has no choice but to stay sober for the next thirty days," Jake went on, "maybe it'll help him believe his future can be different."

"Do you think people ever really change? Deep down, I mean."

Jake gave her a thoughtful look. "It depends on what kind of creatures you think we are. If we're just a product of heredity and environment, no one can be held accountable for their actions. We're only living machines, doing what we're programmed to do. But I believe people are more than genes and geography. We have free will. We are who we are because of the choices we make. If someone decides to change, they can."

"Is that your way of reminding me you've changed? That you're not a player anymore?"

He grinned at her, his dimple in full force. "That wasn't what I was thinking about, but I like that your mind is heading in that direction."

Her insides in full flutter, she looked away. No doubt about it. Her brief "Jake time" in fifth grade had not inoculated her from the power of the real thing.

"We can't force Lester to change," Jake continued. "Nobody can make that decision for someone else. All we've done is put him into a situation where it'll be easier for him to make good choices. That's the hope anyway. When it comes right down to it, whether this thing succeeds or fails is up to him."

"Looks like in thirty days, we'll find out which way he's going to go."

Jake downed the rest of his tea in a long gulp. "Good thing we don't have to wait that long to find out if that oil did its job. Back to the salt mines."

He stood and led the way back to the garage.

The chair looked terrific, the wood as warm and lustrous as the day the piece was made. Lacy showed Jake the fabric she'd chosen for the cushions, a crisp geometric pattern in shades of blue.

"I found an upholsterer who can do up the existing cushions in this material by next Saturday," Lacy said.

"Mom's going to love it. How'd you know blue is her favorite color?"

Lacy shrugged. "Blue is beachy and fresh, so it's perfect for a lake house. We'll pair it with a yellow throw and pillow to make it even cozier. Besides, blue is my favorite, too."

"How 'bout that?" Jake put an arm around her shoulder. His closeness was more intoxicating than Baileys in her dad's coffee. "Both my best girls like the same color."

Best girl. Jacob Tyler's best girl. It was the answer to many a Coldwater Cove maiden's prayer.

She just wasn't sure it was the answer to hers.

Not that she didn't care about him. She did. Too much, in fact.

But even if she opened up enough to let Jake in, how could she trust her feelings? After all, something very like this had steered her to Bradford Endicott, and look how that turned out.

Chapter 23

*Mrs. Chisholm is suffering from insomnia. She
requests prayer and a recording of Pastor Mark's sermon.*

—Marjorie Chubb, captain of the Methodist prayer chain

By the time Jake and Lacy reached the public park on the town-side shore of Lake Jewel, the blankets of hundreds of late-lunch picnickers dotted the green around the gazebo that doubled as a band shell. The park looked like a living patchwork quilt.

The air smelled of freshly cut grass. Jake drew in a deep lungful. Spring was his favorite time in Coldwater Cove. It was still too early for the humidity of high summer, but warm enough that every bush and tree had burst into full flower. Azaleas and lilacs, dogwoods and Bradford pear trees ringed the park. Best of all, the sunny weather had encouraged Lacy to rush the season and bare her long legs in a pair of shorts.

Why would a man want to live anywhere else?

The community band assembled in the gazebo and started warming up with squeaks and squawks and snippets of Sousa marches. Under the shade of a live oak, Jake picked a spot to spread out a worn blanket about halfway between the gazebo and the lake. That way they'd be close enough to hear the band once it started playing in earnest, yet not so close as to be bothered by the honks and caterwauling of the tuning up now.

"Kind of makes you want to break out the old kazoo, doesn't it?" he teased.

"It was a clarinet, not a kazoo," Lacy corrected. "And no. You don't want to hear me play it anymore. You'd have to move this blanket all the way down to the lake if I was in the band."

"That's OK. I'd rather have you on the blanket with me anyway."

Of course, they didn't have the blanket all to themselves. Speedbump was there. He was on a leash, but the little dog didn't test its limits. After playing with Fergus all morning, Speedbump was content just to curl up on a corner of the blanket. While Jake helped Lacy unpack the picnic basket, his unlikely version of man's best friend nodded off with a wuffling snore. Instead of running in his sleep, paws churning like most dogs' did, Speedbump's tail started thumping while his eyes were still shut tight.

"I've seen plenty of dogs chase rabbits in their sleep, but never one that wagged his tail," Lacy said. "He must be a happy little guy."

"They say dogs take on the attitudes of their owners."

"Are you trying to tell me you wag in your sleep, too?" Lacy said with an ornery grin.

He couldn't tell if she was making fun of him or flirting, but either way, Jake didn't care. Just being close to her made him happier than he'd been since he'd returned from Helmand province.

Lacy's picnic was a feast. In addition to the fried chicken, the picnic basket held half a dozen deviled eggs, carrot and celery sticks, and a crisp apple apiece along with chips and salsa. For dessert, there were a dozen peanut butter chocolate chip cookies that looked soft and chewy, just the way he liked them.

Before Jake popped one of the deviled eggs in his mouth, he sent a silent prayer skyward.

Lord, please don't let me mess up this date, too.

His iffy relationship with Lacy had survived a botched attempt at bringing her dinner when she was moving in, a disastrous day at the lake house, and a dog bath that ended with a kiss that made him grateful to be a man. For some inexplicable reason, the same kiss had sent her running. He didn't think he'd get another chance with her if today also went south.

Then the flavors of the egg burst on his tongue and he forgot all about how the date was going.

"Oh my gosh, what's in this?"

"Those are my mom's three-cheese deviled eggs."

"A plate of these on a bed of watercress would make a great summer special for the grill. I gotta have the recipe."

"No can do." Lacy shook her head. "It's a family secret."

"So you know it?"

"Of course. All the Evans women do. A girl isn't considered fully grown till she's learned to make three-cheese deviled eggs. It's a family tradition."

"Right up there with *not* cleaning fish?"

"Exactly." She nibbled a heavenly egg, too. "The secret recipe is held in as high regard as the family motto."

"OK, I'll bite. What's the Evans' family motto?"

"'If a little is good, a lot is a whole bunch better,'" she said in an exaggerated English accent pronouncing the last word as if it was "bet-tah." "My mom believes too much is never enough." Then her face scrunched into a frown. "Since I'm a minimalist, I'm not doing so well with that, am I?"

"Whatever you're doing, keep it up. I think you're really something special, Lacy," he said in all seriousness. "Everything you do. Everything you are."

"Careful, sir," she said, as if determined not to take his compliment seriously. "If you hope flattery will get you a deviled egg recipe, you are destined for disappointment."

"It's not flattery if it's true."

She chuckled. "Most guys use sweet talk to get a girl into bed. I've never had to defend the virtue of a deviled egg before."

Jake leaned toward her. "Is that your way of saying you'd like to sleep with me? If that's where this is headed, I'll give up on the recipe in a heartbeat."

"No, no, I didn't mean that." Her lips said no, but judging from the way her cheeks flushed and her pupils widened, she was thinking about tumbling into bed with him. Lord knew as soon as she mentioned it, it was all he could think about. "I was just trying to impress upon you how seriously my family takes its secrets."

"OK, so we'll take going to bed together off the table for now." Jake was disappointed by her sigh of relief, but they were still talking, still spending time together. He'd live to fight that battle another day. At the moment, it was time to focus on those eggs. Jake rubbed his chin. "But tell me, is there anything that would convince you to teach me how to make your family's soon-to-be famous eggs?"

"Hmm . . . I don't know. What did you have in mind?"

He fought the urge to admit the idea of taking her to bed still occupied most of his brain. And all of a certain part of his body. "How about if I name the dish after you on the Green Apple menu?"

Lacy frowned. "If anyone's name is on it, it should be my mom's."

"Done."

"Now, wait a minute. I didn't mean for you to think the Evans family eggs can be had for a nod in the Green Apple's menu." She cocked her head and gave him a searching look. "We're not that cheap."

"Never thought you were." Jake helped himself to another egg, willing his body to settle. "But it seems to me you've already agreed to share the secret with me. All we're dickering on now is your price."

"What price can you set on the best deviled egg recipe on the planet?" Lacy's blue eyes teased. "In addition to naming the dish after my mom . . . maybe I'd trade a secret for a secret. Back at my folks' house, I told you everybody had one—a secret that would break your heart if only you knew it." She cocked her head at him. "What's yours?"

Jake crossed his arms over his chest. "I don't have any secrets."

"Oh, that's right. You're a regular item on the Methodist prayer chain, so your life is an open book."

Jake laughed. "It was when I first came home from Afghanistan. I've been lifted up by the prayer chain in the past, that's for sure. And I needed it every time, but I don't think Marjorie and her gang are as worried about me as they used to be." He gave his prosthetic calf a slap. "I'm doing pretty good with my 'bionic' leg now."

Of course, he still hadn't been in a relationship with a woman since he'd returned from Afghanistan. His confidence had taken a beating, but he was working on it. That had to count for something.

Lacy's expression went suddenly serious. "Does the prayer chain know about your flashbacks?"

Jake shook his head. "You're the only one who knows about them."

"Me and that other vet you talked to, you mean."

He nodded. He hadn't exactly unburdened himself to Lester that day. Jake had done more listening than talking, but Lester was the only other person besides Lacy who'd ever caught him having a flashback, so at least the old man knew about them.

"Maybe you should try that new clinic at Bates College, too," she suggested. "They might be able to help. Why don't you see what they can do for you?"

"Is that your tactful way of telling me I'm nuts?"

"No, just pointing out an option for you that wasn't there before. But setting that aside, you can forget about getting my deviled egg recipe with a secret I already know." Lacy met his gaze steadily. "The day I first came home, you told me you'd been married once. What happened with that?"

Jake flinched. It had been months since Kim had even crossed his mind, but now the whole screwed-up mess flooded back into him.

"There's not all that much to tell."

"Let me be the judge of that." Lacy shifted onto her knees. "Who was she? Where did you meet? And most importantly, why did it end?"

"You don't want much, do you?"

"Neither do you." She popped the last bite of egg into her mouth and then licked her fingers slowly. "Talk or I'll take the secret of three-cheese deviled eggs with me to the grave."

Jake shrugged. "Okay. Why not?"

Contrary to Lacy's cynical suspicion that the point of a date was for a guy to work his way into a girl's bed, Jake wanted to use this time for them to get to know each other better. Of course, he'd rather she got to know him through his successes instead of his failures, but Lacy wasn't giving him much choice.

"I don't want you to have to shout, so you might want to tell me before the band starts playing." Then because he didn't answer immediately, she added, "while we're still young, please."

"Young, huh? That was part of the problem, I guess. We were too young. I met Kim in college when I was playing football. She was a cheerleader for the team, so we did some traveling together for games. Toward the end of my freshman season, we played UNLV in Vegas."

"So I'm guessing what happened in Vegas didn't stay in Vegas." Lacy popped the top on her Coke and took a long drink.

"Are you telling this story or am I?"

"Proceed, Mr. Tyler," she said in an imitation of Judge Preston's gravelly voice.

"Anyway, we whupped UNLV big time on the gridiron that year," Jake said. "After the game, Kimberly and I celebrated the win by hitting one of those cheesy wedding chapels on the Strip."

"So you got married, but you didn't really mean it?"

"Turns out, I did. Even if a wedding starts out as a joke, by the time you say 'I do,' well, the weight of the whole thing hits you pretty hard. All that bit about leaving and cleaving and 'till death do us part'—it's got to mean something." Jacob tried a bite of the chicken, which was juicy and crispy and perfectly spiced. Here was another Evans family recipe he'd need to finesse from Lacy sometime. "The vows meant something to me anyway."

"Not to her?"

"Oh, yeah. I think they did. At first. She had plans for us. Big plans," Jake said. "Kim expected me to go pro after we graduated. I'd racked up record-setting yardage in my freshman season and it wasn't over yet. I already had a few agents putting out feelers. But then I took some hard helmet-to-helmet hits and had a couple of pretty bad concussions back-to-back."

"Ouch."

"What can I say? A three-hundred-pound nose tackle can

really ring your bell. It made me pretty fuzzy-headed for a while." Jake took a drink of his Coke. "I could have kept playing once the team doctor gave me the green light. Guys do. But with all the talk of how multiple concussions in the NFL lead to dementia and other bad stuff, I felt like I was at a crossroads. I had two choices."

"And they were?"

"*Look* stupid by walking away from a full-ride four-year scholarship, or *be* stupid from recurring head trauma for the rest of my life," Jake said. "Like I told you, I need to keep all the gray matter I got."

"I'm glad you made that choice. I like the way your brain works in its present configuration," Lacy said. "But I take it Kim wasn't in agreement."

"Heck, no. She was furious. And she was even more upset when I joined up with the Marines. I tried to convince her it would be great for us. Depending on where I got assigned, we'd be able to travel the world together."

It had all seemed so exciting at the recruiter's office. Once the guy found out Jake was married, he hammered away at all the benefits offered to military families—from housing to shopping at the PX to the adventure of a possible assignment to Italy or Denmark or Japan with his hot young wife at his side.

"But Kim wasn't willing to leave the university." He'd known in his gut that was the beginning of the end, but he'd hoped they could work through it.

"She wanted to finish her degree?"

Jake shook his head. "She still had three years of partying left in her."

"So did she ever graduate?"

"Oh, yeah, she racked up enough credits to get a BA in something while I was in Afghanistan, but she was never what you might call a scholar." Kim's mind certainly wasn't the first thing Jake had noticed about her. He was choosier about women now. "A string of Ds can still add up to a degree, you know."

He went silent for a moment, reliving his last wrenching day with Kim. Lacy put a hand on his thigh.

"Jake, don't tell me she . . . she didn't leave you because . . . you were wounded, did she?"

"No. Kim had sent me a Dear John a couple of weeks before the incident. Turns out that old saw is right," Jake said. "Absence does make the heart grow fonder . . . for somebody nearby."

It was hard to make a long-distance marriage work. Harder still when one partner was in a combat zone, but having Kim cheat on him was a wound even the Taliban couldn't inflict on him.

"I know what it feels like to be two-timed." Lacy's brows tented together in distress and Jake remembered she'd been almost engaged to the lout who stole from their company and ran off with someone else. "I'm so sorry that happened to you."

"Don't be." He tried to brush aside her sympathy. He couldn't bear it. "Like I said, we were too young."

"Why do I get the feeling there's more to this story?"

There was, but he hated to talk about it. Still, when Lacy waited in silence, he felt duty-bound to fill the void. "When I woke up in the hospital in Germany, Kim was there."

"She wanted to come back to you?"

"No, not really." Kim told him she'd left the other guy. But Jake knew she was only at his side out of pity and that was harder to take than his injury. "The divorce wasn't final, so she said she wanted to give our marriage a second chance."

"But you didn't want to forgive her."

"No, it wasn't that. At least, not only that." He looked away from Lacy, feigning intense interest in the motorboat chugging across Lake Jewel. Even though his body was still in Coldwater Cove, his mind wandered back to the hospital ward in Germany.

It had been the sound of water that had made him open his eyes and realize for the first time that he wasn't in Afghanistan any longer. The overbright sun that bleached out all colors but dun and poppy red was in hiding. Falling in slashing torrents on the hospital windows, rain washed the whole world in gray.

Kim was there, sitting in a chair at his bedside in the bleach-scented ward. Her head drooped forward, her long dark hair obscuring her face. When she looked up and saw that he was awake, her eyes were red with weeping. At first, he was happy to see her, but then he remembered the letter. She'd cheated on him. The pain was still like a mortar to his gut.

She didn't love him anymore, so why was she there?

Then while she fussed over him and cranked up the head of his bed so he could sit up, he realized dimly that something else was wrong, too. The blankets draped over his body weren't lying right. They were flat where his left foot should have been.

He'd been wounded, Kim explained. Unconscious for several days because he'd suffered a head trauma in addition to . . . well, she wasn't able to finish the sentence. But she was there now. She'd come to take him home and, once they were back stateside, to take care of him.

It was pretty clear Jake was no longer the man she'd married. Heck, she hadn't even wanted him when he still was. The Dear John proved that. He wasn't about to let pity be the only thing that tied them to each other.

"I didn't want anything from her," Jake said softly, almost forgetting that Lacy was there. Kim hadn't seen him as a man any longer. He was a pathetic cripple and she'd cast herself in the role of the saint who'd stuck by him.

Not in this lifetime.

Then he met the gaze of the woman who didn't see him as an invalid. The one who still saw him as a man. And realized he needed to tell Lacy the whole truth.

"Kim didn't leave me because of my leg. I let her go because of it."

"I see." Lacy tugged absently at a loose thread on the hem of her shorts. "And do you still need to let the people who want to be with you go because of your leg?"

"No."

"Good." Lacy smiled at him. "Let's ditch the concert, go back to your place, and make some deviled eggs."

Chapter 24

Want to buy: a used camper trailer, the cheaper the better.
Don't have to be fancy or nothing. A title would be nice.
Call the Bugtussles at 555-0169. Ask for Junior.

—the *Coldwater Gazette* classifieds

Daniel was no judge of music, but he could have sworn the piccolo solo in "The Stars and Stripes Forever" wasn't supposed to sound like a gang of mice having their tails stomped off. Of course, it didn't matter much what sort of noise was coming from the gazebo because on the edge of the crowd, a group of teenagers was singing "Be Kind to Your Web-Footed Friends" at the top of their lungs, drowning out most of the band's mistakes.

Toward the end, all pretense of matching the right pitch was abandoned as the boys switched into screeching falsettos.

Daniel hid a grin as he walked by them. Once again, he was thankful to be in law enforcement in Coldwater Cove, where the worst youthful offenses seemed to be skateboarding in unauthorized areas, cruising around the Square too fast, and singing out of tune.

Loudly.

Coldwater Cove was a great little town. It was the best place in the world for his son to grow up.

If only Anne would allow him to be part of Carson's growing up again. He didn't blame her for limiting his time with the boy. Until he got himself together, it was the right thing for her to do. But knowing that it was right didn't make it hurt any less.

He'd been assigned to patrol the band concert on the off chance that there might be some drugs changing hands. The sheriff had heard that meth had found its way to Colton Springs, a town some fifty miles away. He wanted to make sure the drug didn't migrate up the highway and get a toehold in Coldwater, too. Daniel hadn't seen anything suspicious, but he did spot Anne and Carson on a blanket under one of the big live oaks that sprawled over the green.

Dan had been praying. He'd been working on his problem. He even swallowed his pride and drove all the way to Muskogee for a Gamblers Anonymous meeting on his day off. The hardest part was getting up in front of that roomful of strangers and admitting what he was. After that, he received nothing but support and a sponsor who was so committed to Daniel's recovery, he promised to be available to counsel him by phone anytime, day or night.

Maybe once Anne saw how serious he was about kicking his addiction—he could admit that was what it was now—she'd give him the benefit of the doubt. He screwed up his courage and headed her way.

Anne was still as pretty as the day he'd married her. And she was the best of mothers. He loved the way she held Carson's dimpled hands and clapped them together in time with the music. When the song ended she scooped him up and gave him a kiss on his chubby tummy. The child squealed with pleasure.

Watching the tender way she played with Carson made Dan's chest swell. They were his little family. His to love. His to protect.

He was so ready to do that again. All he needed was for Anne to trust him. To let him back into that safe little circle of love they'd once had so they could rebuild their life together.

Lester Scott's face swam in his vision. Dan rarely let himself think of the man as his father, but there was no denying the connection. Still, contrary to the old man's warning, he was not looking into a mirror, Daniel told himself. He didn't have to repeat Lester's mistakes.

Maybe Lester couldn't help his mental problems, but he hadn't tried to do anything about his mean-fisted drinking either. He'd given up any chance for a normal family in exchange for the worm at the bottom of a tequila bottle.

Daniel was determined not to do the same thing to Anne and Carson no matter how often a quartet of queens winked at him.

"Hello, Anne," he said, taking a seat on the quilt beside her before she could tell him not to. Gabbling a string of da-das, Carson crawled over to his lap. Dan hugged him close. "I see the boy's doing good."

She nodded, a smile drifting over her lips, there one moment, gone the next. "He misses you."

"Not as much as I miss him." He planted a kiss on the boy's temple and inhaled his fresh baby-powder scent. Dan shifted the boy up onto his shoulders so he could see the band over the heads of the people in front of them. Then he met Anne's gaze. "Not as much as I miss you. I do, you know. More than I can say."

Her eyes shone at him for a moment, but then she looked away. "I got the job."

"Oh?"

"At Walmart in the jewelry department," she said. "It's only part-time, but that's okay. I don't think I can bear being away from Carson more than twenty-five or thirty hours a week anyway."

"Is your mom taking care of him while you work?"

She nodded.

At least his son wasn't being watched by a stranger. Just

someone who sort of hated his dad. Still, Celia would take good care of Carson.

Daniel lowered the boy from his shoulders, leaned back and crossed his legs, turning his right foot into a horsey for Carson to ride. "If you let me know your work schedule, I could ask for time off some of those hours so I can take him."

"I don't want you to put your job at risk. Mom told me you've been giving her money and bringing over groceries to help with our keep," Anne said. "She's beginning to think you're not such a bad sort now."

Daniel chuckled. "If I'd known that was the way to Celia's heart, I'd have tried bribery sooner." Then he sobered. "What about you? Do you still think I'm a bad sort?"

"Danny, I never thought you were bad. Just . . . you just have a problem."

"But it doesn't have me," he corrected, putting Carson down to play on the blanket between them. "I'm dealing with it."

Her dark eyes seemed unsure. "I wish I could believe you."

Trust, but verify. It works for foreign diplomacy. Here's hoping it works in a marriage, too.

"Here. I'll prove it." Daniel reached into his shirt pocket and pulled out a much-folded scratch ticket. He handed it to her.

She stared at the piece of paper and then at him, her expression puzzled. "Danny, this is a lottery ticket. The only thing it proves is that you're still gambling."

"No, I'm not. Don't you see? The ticket hasn't been played," he said, pointing at the fading type. "Look at the date. I've carried it with me ever since then."

He'd bought it in despair at a twenty-four-hour convenience store the same day Anne left him. But then he realized that even if the ticket was a big winner, money wouldn't fix what he'd broken between them. So he'd folded up the ticket and put it in his shirt pocket without scratching off the surface to reveal whether or not he'd won. He kept it in his pocket, close to his heart, like a coiled viper he was trying to tame.

Resisting the urge to play the card was worse than the most vigorous exercise. It tested his will instead of his body. At first, hands shaking, he'd pulled out the card several times a day, always on the brink of peeling away the surface with the edge of a penny. Would he feel the rush of winning or the crush of loss? Each time, he forced himself to put the ticket away without answering that question.

Even after the drawing was past and the ticket was invalid, it still called to him, singing the siren song of winnings that were just out of reach. There were still ways to play the ticket for one of the state's "second chance" drawings, but he somehow always managed to refold it and stuff it back into his pocket.

"This must have been a terrible temptation for you," Anne said, turning the bedraggled card over in her hands. "You could have thrown it away. Why did you keep it?"

"So I could prove to you, and to myself, that I could quit." He decided to take a chance, the biggest gamble of his life, and reached for her hand. To his relief, she didn't pull away. "Anne, you are the most important thing in the world to me, you and Carson. I will never lose sight of that again. Ever. I promise."

Her chin trembled. "You mean it?"

"I'm betting my life on it. I'm no good without you, Annie. And I'll work hard. I promise. We'll have our own house again as soon as I can get a down payment together and—"

She stopped him with a finger to his lips. "This was never about the house."

It was to him. Losing their home had made him feel lower than a worm's belly. The little bungalow on Crepe Myrtle

Street had meant comfort. Stability. Permanence. A place to shut out the world and bask in the love of his family. He'd never had that as a kid. Now he was driven to provide it for his wife and son.

And he'd risked it all on the turn of a card.

Never again. Please God don't let me live to see another day when I don't put Anne first.

"Life doesn't mean a thing if I can't share it with you." He cupped her cheek. "Please. Give me another chance."

"I'll do better than that." She leaned into his caress and smiled up at him. He could live happy for a week on just one of those smiles. "I made mistakes, too. How about if we both give *us* another chance?"

His heart flooded with tenderness. It was so like her to shoulder part of the responsibility, but Daniel knew his weakness had caused all their problems. No more. He had plenty of reasons to be strong, but none were more important than the two he was sharing a blanket with at that very moment.

"My shift ends in an hour," Dan said, still hardly daring to believe he was being given a reprieve. "Can I come by tonight and move you and Carson back to my place?"

When Anne had left him, she hadn't taken any furniture with her except Carson's crib and high chair. Daniel had moved everything they owned from their little house into his rented duplex. Except for the nursery, everything was ready for his family to rejoin him. In a fit of hopefulness, he'd even put up Carson's swing set in the tiny backyard.

She hesitated, so he redoubled his efforts. He figured she deserved to make him grovel a little.

"Please, Anne, come home tonight." He drew her into his arms, not caring if any of the other picnickers were looking on. "I know the duplex won't be as good as the house was, but tell me you and Carson will move back in with me tonight."

"For the umpteenth time, I don't care about the house, Danny. I care about you. And wherever you are, that's home to me. But it won't be just Carson and me moving in."

Please God, don't let Celia try to move in with us.

Despite his frantic silent prayer, he managed to say, "Oh?" in a semi-neutral tone.

"Another little person will be coming home, too."

Wonderment settled over him as Anne took his hand and put it on her slightly rounded belly.

Daniel blinked back tears. Anne had forgiven him for the mistakes of the past. The folks at Gamblers Anonymous had told him he'd always struggle with his addiction. But his darling wife was giving him a new reason to keep fighting the good fight. He held her close.

Then she pulled away from him, tore the lottery ticket to pieces, and tossed them into the air like a handful of confetti.

"That's littering in a public park, ma'am," he said in a mock-stern tone.

"Then you'd better arrest me, officer," she said as she threw her arms around his neck. "And never let me go."

"That's a promise." Daniel kissed her long and deep. He didn't give a rat's rear end who saw them doing it in a public park either.

He'd been forgiven. He had a second chance.

Was there anything better in the world?

All afternoon and into the evening, Lacy and Jake played in his kitchen. She taught him how to make three-cheese deviled eggs and once he mastered that, he started improvising. Next it was deviled eggs with bacon and jalapeños that were so hot it made sweat bead up on Lacy's forehead. Then he concocted a cool mixture of chives and cream cheese to put the fire out.

"I've never done anything but the traditional relish and mayo and paprika deviled eggs before," Jake said as he sampled his latest creation. "I wonder how it would taste if I substituted mashed-up avocado for the mayo."

"I don't know. Call me a stick in the mud, but I think green eggs should only appear in a Dr. Seuss book."

"Or as a St. Patrick's breakfast special," Jake said, unaffected by her doubtfulness. "Might be worth trying next year."

"Oh, I know! Maybe you could approach one of the elementary teachers about taking a field trip to the grill. You could set things up for the kids to make their own eggs and end the event with a *Green Eggs and Ham* read aloud."

"Sort of tying good nutrition and books and creativity all together in one gooey project," he said. "I like it."

"Or you could do a cooking-with-kids class some evening to get the parents involved." Lacy recognized the burst of imagination surging through her. She used to get that same high when she discovered the right concept for a design. It felt good to know the old creative juices could still flow, even if it was in a totally different direction. "I know you've got a lot of regular customers, but surely you can always use more."

"That kind of thing would certainly pull in a different crowd." Jake filled the sink to wash up the bowls they'd used. "It would be great if families with kids wanted to come to the Green Apple to sit down for a meal instead of driving through a fast-food place."

"You wouldn't have to limit your cooking classes to parents and kids, you know," Lacy said. "In Boston, sometimes chefs would put on food raves that made for a great date night."

"With deviled eggs?"

"No, with much fancier entrées. It was a chance for foodies to learn to make a signature dish and spend some quality time in the kitchen with their partner, too. The taste, the aromas, the texture of the food—when you get right down to it, cooking is pretty sensual."

"Is this the voice of experience?" Jake said as he handed her a tea towel to dry with.

"Me? No. My friend Shannon dated a guy who was really into the culinary arts for a while," she said as she dried a bowl and stretched to place it back into Jake's neat cabinet. "Bradford Endicott wouldn't be caught dead cooking. He was never about doing anything for himself if he could pay someone else to do it."

She wondered if Bradford had burned through all the money he'd stolen already. Given the lavish lifestyle he was accustomed to, it wouldn't take long. Last she'd heard, his family had cut him off. He might well end up having to do things for himself. If he didn't come back to the States to face indictment, it would serve him right if he was reduced to washing dishes for the rest of his miserable life in some third-world beanery.

Somehow that image pleased her even more than picturing Bradford in an orange jumpsuit.

"Lacy, you're not still hung up on him, are you?"

"On Bradford? No." Even if he appeared before her in sackcloth and ashes, she had no interest in rekindling anything between them. And she certainly wouldn't trust him with her heart or her money any farther than she could throw him. "That chapter of my life is over and done with."

"Good."

While he made short work of the rest of the bowls, Lacy wondered what it would be like to do dishes beside Jacob Tyler for the rest of her life. It wasn't the glitzy world of high design she'd imagined for herself, but if the warm glow in her chest was any sign, it was a future with real appeal.

He pulled the stopper out of the sink and then caught

up her hand. "Let's let the rest of these bowls air dry in the drainer and head up to the roof. It's getting dark. The marina is going to have a fireworks display to kick off the boating season. My roof is a perfect place to watch them."

He took her hand and led her up a narrow set of stairs. Because the Town Square was built on a little rise, the park and Lake Jewel spread out below them to the northeast. In the deepening twilight, Lacy saw that Jake had spread out a blanket for them sometime earlier. A trail of loose rose petals led to it. The blanket was raised up from the decking by a couple of inches, far enough to suggest there was a foam pad under it for comfort. A handful of throw pillows were scattered over the blanket. A bottle of something sparkling was cooling in an ice bucket beside two stemmed glasses.

"You've been planning this for a while."

"Be prepared. That's my motto." He gave her the three-fingered Boy Scout salute.

"What makes me think you were never a scout?"

He took her hand and they sank together onto the blanket. "I'm not planning on being one tonight."

"That," she said as he bent to kiss her, "is something I'm counting on."

Chapter 25

*The Reverend Harold Hiney will be filling in for Pastor Mark
for our midweek chapel and the regular Sunday services.
Our visiting speaker invites us to call him
Pastor Harold. No one calls him Harry.*

—from the Methodist church bulletin

Lacy and Jake tumbled onto the blanket, mouths seeking, hands caressing. It felt so good to lie beside Jake, to be surrounded by his warmth, his strength.

Just kisses, Lacy promised herself.

Even so, her body thrummed to peak awareness. His every touch, every low groan—they moved her to her very core. She hadn't had a makeout session like this for far too long. Of course, she hadn't felt like this about a guy in . . .

Forever.

Bradford had been more a business decision, a merger, than a relationship. She'd been caught up in the glamour of his family name and prestige. The last time her heart had been engaged was eons ago, before she left Coldwater Cove for the first time.

But not even the "Summer of Daniel" came close to this.

She'd tried not to care about Jake. Really she had. She'd guarded her heart every step of the way, but there he was, firmly in the center of everything that made Lacy herself. All the empty places inside her, all the hurts, all the hopes, all her aloneness—he filled up every one.

And she ached to fill up those lonely places in him, too.

Holy So-Not Expected, I think I love him.

Jake rolled her over onto her back and, despite her best intentions, the night was about to spiral out of control.

Then the first screaming rocket exploded over Lake Jewel. Jake jerked away from her, chest heaving. He scrambled to his knees, thrusting her behind him.

Wild-eyed, he looked over his shoulder at her and ordered her to stay down. Then he turned back to Lake Jewel, where fire dripped from the sky and reflected up from the black water. It looked like fiery stalactites and stalagmites meeting in the dark. What must it seem like to Jake's combat-bruised psyche?

He's having another flashback.

"It's OK, Jake." She sat up and stroked his shoulders in small comforting circles. Although he was in a confused state, he was trying to protect her. "We're not in any danger. We're home. Look, there's the marina barge floating in the lake. That's where all this noise and flashing light is coming from."

A Roman candle began spewing into the night from the deck of the barge.

Tension drained out of his muscles and Jake slumped down on the blanket beside her.

"It's just fireworks," he said so softly he might have been talking only to himself. "I knew they were coming tonight. I should have been ready for them."

"Well, I think I was distracting you a little bit."

"Give yourself some credit." He offered a lopsided smile. "You were distracting me a lot."

"You're pretty good in the distraction department yourself." She gave him a thorough once-over. His eyes were back to normal now. His breathing had settled into a smooth rhythm. "Is the flashback over?"

"It's over, but that wasn't really what you'd call a flashback. It was more like, well, I just become hypervigilant sometimes."

"What's that?"

"It means I'm on high alert for a threat, whether there's one there or not," he explained. "You're not going to nag me to see somebody about this again, are you?"

She was tempted, but if he saw a therapist only to please her, all the counseling in the world would be useless. "You're a big boy, Jake. I trust you to make a good decision for yourself."

"Well, that's not good. If a girl won't nag a guy, it's a sure bet she doesn't give a flip about him."

"You're so wrong." She palmed his face and pressed a soft kiss on his lips. Tenderness made her eyes well up. "I actually give two flips about you."

"That's a relief. I was beginning to think I was losing my touch." He leaned back on his palms. "But I'm still ahead. I give seven or eight flips about you."

Was that his backhanded way of telling her he loved her?

Before she could ask him to explain what he meant by seven or eight flips, he grinned, splayed his legs before him, and patted the space between his knees. "Come here. I'll be your lawn chair while we watch the rest of the light show."

She slid into the space and leaned back on his chest, resting her arms on his muscular thighs. "You make a wonderful lounger."

"Just call me your La-Z-Boy."

Then they went silent while the fireworks from the marina's barge lit up the night sky. The crowd gathered along the lakeshore below *ooh*-ed and *ahh*-ed as each explosion became more spectacular. Occasionally Jake's arms tightened around her, especially after the screaming whiz-bangs and cherry bombs went off, but he didn't have any more moments when he lost track of what was really happening.

As the finale of pinwheels, Roman candles, and bursting shells faded and the stars came back into bright focus again,

Lacy decided she could help Jake deal with his PTSD. She could calm him whenever he had an episode. If she knew what to watch for, maybe she could even help him prepare for a flashback.

If she was stalling about committing to a relationship with him, it shouldn't be because of this.

Maybe she shouldn't stall at all.

As Jake's heart thumped against her spine, she wondered why she had. It had nothing to do with him, she decided. Jake was a great guy.

It was about her need for control.

Her life had descended into chaos in Boston. She'd felt so helpless when Bradford ran off and left her to deal with the mess of his embezzlement. If she didn't get mixed up with another guy, she'd never be at someone else's mercy again. Her hand would be firmly on the helm of her life.

But Jake wasn't Bradford.

Even in the middle of a flashback, his first instinct had been to protect those around him. She could trust him.

She *should* trust him.

"Jake," she said softly.

"Hmm?" He bent to nuzzle her neck.

"I was thinking you should come to my place for supper tomorrow night," she said. "And bring Speedbump with you."

"I thought you said Effie would kill him."

"I was exaggerating." She hoped she was. "Anyway, if you and I are going to be together, our animals need to learn to get along."

Jake gave her a squeeze and kissed the crown of her head. "You want us to be together?"

She nodded, not trusting her voice at first. Then she whispered, "But I think we should go slow."

"Slow is good. I'm a patient guy. I've wanted you since the day you walked back into the grill, but it's taken me a while to convince you. Slow is kind of my wheelhouse now," he said. "Speedbump and I will be over tomorrow as soon as I get the Green Apple closed for the night."

"Effie and I will be looking for you," she said, relaxing back into him. "But we'll keep a sharp eye on that cat. Just in case."

Fortunately, Effie the Unsociable only felt the need to box Speedbump's ears with her velveted claws once. After that, the dog was respectful of her personal space and they reached a fragile interspecies truce. Now that their pets were getting along, or at least tolerating each other's presence, nothing kept Jake and Lacy from seeing each other every evening.

Either she came over to his loft or he joined her at her place for dinner and a movie in. Jake was pleased to discover that they were both Trekkies and neither of them understood what had possessed Fox to cancel *Firefly*. Sometimes for a change, they went out to catch the late show at the Regal, where they necked like teenagers in the back row.

Once, they'd hit the Opera House when the big band was playing and after a jerking two-step that had them laughing together, Jake managed a creditable waltz with her. Holding her on the dance floor—any excuse to hold her, for that matter—made him thank God all over again for getting him out of Afghanistan. Even if he'd had to leave part of his left leg behind.

Days turned into weeks and the rhythm of Jake's life turned into the steady thump of counting the minutes until he could see Lacy again. When they weren't working, they were inseparable.

Jake even talked her into going to Wednesday-evening chapel with him. Twilight was giving way to deepening night as they walked back toward the Square after the service. Lacy was quieter than usual.

"Penny for your thoughts," he said.

"They're worth more than that."

Jake fished a quarter out of his pocket and offered it to her. The rest of his cash had been dropped into the collection plate. "This is all I've got on me."

"Better keep it, then. Looks like ice cream is on me tonight."

"Fat chance." He still had his debit card. Call him old-fashioned, but he wasn't about to let Lacy pay for anything when they were together. "Did you mind going to the service with me?"

"Not too much. Not as much as I thought I would."

"But you were uncomfortable." Sitting beside him in the pew, she'd been fidgety and her left knee had jittered through most of the short homily. But before and after the service, everyone had greeted her with hugs and smiles. "You grew up in that church. Why does it bother you to be there now?"

"It's not the church. It's me," she said. "It's been so long. I got out of the habit of going when I was back east."

"Not cool enough for you?"

"Wow, that doesn't make me sound shallow at all."

She stuck out her tongue and pulled an adorable face at him. He didn't know how she managed it, but Lacy even made being snarky seem cute.

"But maybe you're right," she admitted. "I was all about fitting in then and none of the people I knew in New England had much of a spiritual life—except for Shannon. She's Wiccan, but don't go thinking she worships the devil or anything like that. Shannon is good people. She'd give me a kidney if I needed one."

"So you weren't tempted to try the religious flavor of the month with your Wiccan friend?"

"No. Like my dad always says, I'm as independent as a hog on ice. Not going to church, or giving any other religion a try, was more about wanting to do things for myself instead of relying on someone else to help me."

"Someone like God."

"Yeah, Him or any of His close friends." She cast a glance and a smile up at him. "When I first came home, I had this weird, oh, I don't know, caricature, I guess, of church people in my mind."

"You thought we were all holier-than-thou bigots and homophobes."

"Something like that."

"I understand why you might think so. That's the rap we get, and sometimes we deserve it. We don't always live the love we're supposed to," Jake said. "The problem with the church is that it's just chock full of sinners."

She laughed.

"Most of us know that about ourselves," he said, "but sometimes we forget."

"I don't think you're a sinner, Jake."

"That's because you can't read my mind." He stopped and hugged her close.

"I might surprise you." Lacy stood on tiptoe and kissed him.

She was right. He had wanted a kiss. "Good guess."

"A safe one. You're a guy, after all."

But Jake wanted more than a kiss. He wanted everything with Lacy, every day, every night—all night—for the rest of his life. He just hadn't worked up the courage to ask her yet.

"But back to church people," Jake said as, still holding hands, they started walking toward the ice-cream shop again. "Have you changed your mind about them?"

She nodded. "However nosey the church folk in Coldwater are about the lives around them, the nosiness really is motivated by caring. I'd sort of forgotten that part of living in a small town."

"I know what you mean. When I came home from Afghanistan, it felt like I was being invaded at first, what with everybody interested in everything going on with me and my new leg," Jake said. "But then it started feeling good to know I wasn't alone. I was connected. I had lots of people pulling for me. Praying for me."

"It's hard to turn your back on people who care about you, isn't it? Most folks are so wrapped up in themselves, it's a total surprise to have someone invest their energy in you and your troubles for a change." She leaned her head on his shoulder as they walked. "Since I came home, I've been blown away by the unexpected kindness of this town—church people, my coworkers, the Warm Hearts Club, even total strangers. And I've learned that I'm not as independent as I thought I was." She started walking slower. "I've really made a mess of myself."

"You don't look like a mess to me."

"Well, I am. Like a duck, calm on the surface, paddling to beat thunder underneath," she said. "And I wouldn't mind being on the Methodist prayer chain so much anymore."

"Have you got a request you'd like put on the chain?" he asked, concerned.

"I probably should, but it's something I hate for anybody to know about."

He understood that. Pride still kept him from going to that free mental health clinic at Bates College. Somehow, saying that he had a problem with flashbacks out loud to someone with a degree on their wall would make it more real. He knew it was false pride, but he hunkered behind it anyway.

"Whatever this thing is you're dealing with, Lacy, you can tell me."

She sighed. Then she explained for the first time how badly in debt she was and why.

"My pay from the *Gazette* doesn't amount to much. It's all

I can do to make ends meet with what I bring home. I've been eating up the last of my savings to make the payments to the O'Learys." She sighed. "And just this week, I hit the bottom of that particular barrel."

"Lacy, let me help you."

"No way," she said, "Even if you had a hundred thousand dollars, I wouldn't take a penny from you."

Jake chuckled. "Well, I don't have a hundred grand, so no worries on that score. But I do own the grill and the building it's in free and clear. I'm sure Mr. Dutton over at the bank would give me a loan against that property, and at a much lower interest rate than you're paying those hoods in Boston."

"No, Jake. I love you for offering, but I can't let you risk your livelihood for me."

"You love me, huh?"

She swatted his shoulder. "You know what I mean."

Unfortunately, he did. She didn't love him. Not that way. *At least, not yet.*

Hadn't his dad always said a woman's "maybe" was what kept a wolf wolfing? He'd do anything for Lacy. He'd be willing to take the debt over entirely if she came along with it. He wanted her to trust him to solve this and make everything all right. It's what a man did for the ones he loved. "Getting a loan is no problem. Why don't you let me decide what I do with what's mine?"

"No. I mean it. I won't take money from you," she said. "I only told you because . . . well, I don't want it on the prayer chain, but . . . maybe *you* could pray for me."

He stopped and kissed her again. "I already do."

Chapter 26

Miss Holloway's drama students are looking for donations to fund their first annual field trip to a theater festival in Hot Springs. The freshman class is celebrating its final presentation of Macbeth. *If you want to support the end of high school drama, please contact the school office.*

—from the Fighting Marmots Notes section of the *Coldwater Gazette*

"Have you got that chili together yet, Lester?" Jake asked as he flipped a dozen burgers for the hungry lunch crowd that had gathered in the Green Apple.

"Almost," the old man said. It was Lester's first day out of the county lockup. More importantly, it was his first day on a job in decades. He was a little slow to complete the tasks Jake assigned him, but he tackled everything willingly enough. "I just need to stir in the jalapeños and then it'll be ready to simmer for a while."

School was nearly out for summer, but the folks in Coldwater Cove were huddling through an unusual cold snap. Thermometers struggled to reach the low 60s during the day and dipped into the 40s at night. Mr. Mayhew was worried sick about his "knockout" roses being shocked by the unseasonal temperatures. He wondered loudly to anyone who expressed the slightest interest, and even some who didn't, if the whole daylight savings time conspiracy wasn't responsible for the problem.

As if anyone can do anything about the weather, Jake bit back when Mayhew accosted him at the market. Mr. Mayhew would wish for a bit of this coolness once the dog days of August rolled around. But for now, a brisk wind swept mostly fussy customers through the Green Apple's door.

Jake decided to put his Lazy Man Chili back on the supper menu. It was sure to warm up their insides and it was an easy enough recipe for even a novice cook to throw together.

Lester Scott certainly qualified. He wouldn't know a pair of tongs from a ladle if they pinched him on the butt.

Having a parolee in his kitchen was more work for Jake than help at the moment, but he reminded himself a dozen times that morning that this arrangement was supposed to be for Lester's benefit, not his. The Warm Hearts Club experiment was the old vet's ticket from homelessness and alcoholism back to a more normal life. Jake was determined to do what he could to make sure Lester had a chance.

But it was still up to Lester to make the journey.

"Order up!" Jake rang the bell to alert Ethel to the Green Plate burgers lining the pony wall counter that separated the kitchen from the dining area. The harried waitress hurried to retrieve them.

There had been another snafu during the lunch rush. The Green Apple rib plate was always a little messy, but Lester had been extra heavy-handed when Jake allowed him to spread on the barbecue sauce. The ribs might taste great, but they were a serious danger to a diner's wardrobe. Ethel had trotted between the tables, making sure everyone who'd ordered ribs had a couple of napkins tucked under their chins and another draped over their laps.

"Aprons wouldn't be amiss," she'd muttered and then ordered customers to remove their ties or scarves and thoroughly cover anything they didn't want ruined. No doubt about it. The ribs were risky.

Jake made his way over to the stove where Lester was stirring the batch of bubbling chili in an industrial-sized stockpot. Along with premium ground beef and four kinds of beans, Jake's chili recipe called for sliced mushrooms, bell peppers in assorted colors, stewed tomatoes, and chopped onions along with a secret mix of spices.

"Looks good." *But the proof is in the tasting.* Jake dipped in a wooden spoon to sample the broth. When he barely touched it to his lips, they burned. "Whew! That'll open up your sinuses." If he'd swallowed a bite, he'd have singed his whole gullet. "Man, could you have used any more jalapeños?"

"Nope. I dumped in the whole can."

"The whole can?" Jake swallowed hard. "Lester, why didn't you follow the recipe?"

"I did." He picked up the directions and ran his finger along the appropriate line. "See here. It says 'Jalapeños, one C.' One can, right?"

"One C means one cup. You put in half a gallon." This chili was eight times hotter than Jake's usual batch. "Unless you've got a cast-iron stomach, it's inedible."

Lester's shoulders drooped. "First the ribs, now this. I screwed the pooch again, didn't I?"

"Big time," Jake said, not troubling to mask his frustration. There were several pounds of ground chuck in that chili, not to mention all the other ingredients. Fresh veggies were pretty spendy this early in the season. He hated to see it all go to waste.

"Want me to take it out to the alley and dump it?" Lester asked gloomily.

Chili this corrosive was likely to burn its way through the metal Dumpster.

It was also Lester's first attempt to cook anything by himself. Jake shouldn't have left him to his own devices. Now he couldn't let him fail just because he hadn't been able to give Lester the supervision he needed.

"No, let's not give up yet," Jake said, his mind churning furiously. "Maybe we can fix it."

"You think so?" A tentative smile stretched Lester's weathered face. "An army grunt and a jarhead, ain't nothing we can't do if we put our backs to it, eh, boss?"

Their backs wouldn't help this chili one bit. Jake had to put on his chef hat pronto. But before he could form a plan, he was interrupted by another round of orders from Ethel— two Reubens, a chicken club, and a chef's salad. He started working on them while he gave Lester instructions, starting with something simple. "Leave that chili on to simmer and start another batch. There are a couple more stockpots in the storeroom. But this time, leave out all the spicy things."

Lester scratched his head as he studied the recipe again. "Jake, um, which ones are the spicy things exactly?"

Jake took a Green Apple Grill pen out of his shirt pocket and crossed out onions, cayenne pepper, cumin, and freshly ground chili powder. "Instead of that, put in some ground-up cloves." The spice was known to numb the mouth a bit. "No, on second thought, I'll add that myself later."

If Lester had a hand in it, this new batch would be swimming with cloves. He'd probably end up with something numbing enough to prepare someone for dental work. Lester disappeared into the storeroom and reappeared with a second stockpot.

Jake layered corned beef on pumpernickel for the Reubens, cut them in halves, and arranged the sandwiches with chips and a dill pickle on a green plate. "Once you get a second batch of chili made, we'll combine the two and then freeze half of it."

The light of understanding dawned in the old man's eyes. "Oh, I get it. That way, each batch will be half as hot as this is right now."

And still four times hotter than Jake's usual Lazy Man Chili. How could he tone it down more?

"Put a can of condensed milk into both batches." Jake had read somewhere that dairy took some of the heat out of spicy foods. The milk would turn the base broth into something re-sembling creamy tomato soup. When they dished up the chili later, Jake decided he'd have to garnish it with a little freshly grated Parmesan for good measure. "How about adding a few dollops of sour cream to both stockpots, too?"

"Will do." Lester gave him a snappy salute and went back to work, whistling tunelessly.

Jake watched him from the corner of his eye while he filled the rest of the lunch orders Ethel had dropped off. By the time Lester had the second batch simmering, Jake had thought of another way to tone down the spiciness.

"Add a bag of frozen corn to both pots," Jake said as he rang the bell for Ethel to pick up another order. The grill was really humming, almost every table and booth full. At times like this, Jake wished he had six hands. Once Lester was trained, maybe it would be like having a couple more. For now, Jake was glad the old man at least did as he was told.

If he understands the directions . . .

"Well, would you look at that? The corn makes the chili even prettier, too, what with all them golden kernels float-ing amongst the beans and meat." Lester seemed inordinately pleased with his patched-up concoction. "Looks like a party in a bowl, don't it?"

A party that'll peel off the lining of your stomach, Jake thought. He nodded to give Lester encouragement anyway. Extra color was a plus in any dish, but his real goal was to add more starch. The corn should temper the hotness. He'd have to bake some bread that afternoon to go along with the chili. The supper crowd would need the extra carbs.

Lester began dividing both batches in half, ladling them into a third stockpot. Good thing Jake had an industrial six-burner in the grill's kitchen.

"Get a couple of limes and squeeze the juice into the chili," Jake said. The acid in citrus was supposed to tone down spiciness. Sugar was another cutting agent. "Chop up a couple of carrots into each pot."

The root vegetable was laden with natural sugars and would add another pop of color. If they somehow managed to make anything of Lester's mistake, the finished product was going to have lots of layers of flavor tracked through it.

Jake came over and sampled a spoonful. This time he swallowed. His eyes watered and beads of sweat popped out on his forehead.

"Well?" Lester asked.

"It's mighty hot," Jake said, "but I'm still standing."

"You know, when I was in Nam, the locals served up some pretty spicy stuff," Lester said, "only they ate it with rice."

"Lester, you're a genius." Jake slapped him on the back. "We'll keep this simmering all afternoon to thicken up the liquid. Then, instead of bread on the side, we'll ladle it over a bed of brown and wild rice for the supper crowd. If we pair it with a nice cool side salad, it can be the evening special."

"How 'bout that? I done made a new special." The old man clapped his hands together. "What'll we call it?"

"How about Lester's Take-No-Prisoners Chili and Rice?"

"Hot damn! That'll do, jarhead." Lester practically ran out to the chalkboard in the dining room to post the new dish that would be available on the supper menu that evening. "Yessirree, that'll do."

As Jake watched him, it seemed as if Lester grew a couple of inches taller. His shoulders no longer slumped. There was a sprightliness in his walk instead of a shuffle. It was the first step in a long journey. As victories went, Lester's unexpected creation of a new dish was a small one, but hopefully, it would lead to more.

It occurred to Jake that Lester was like that chili—almost irredeemable at first. But with a tweak here and a second chance there, he might just be able to make something of himself, after all.

Only rural residents around Coldwater Cove had curbside mail delivery. Almost everyone in town had a post office box. The rest picked up their mail at the general delivery window. Lacy was fairly dancing on the inside after she picked up hers.

She was eager to tell Jake about her good fortune, but it was the middle of the lunch rush. She couldn't interrupt him now and she was only on a short break from the *Gazette* herself. She decided her folks would be most happy about her news, so she drove over to their place.

There was also every chance she'd be able to shop in her folks' refrigerator for a sandwich. Her bank account was looking lean at the moment.

But that's about to change!

Seated on his Husqvarna, her dad was mowing his front lawn, turning tight, precise circles around the oak trunks. There was nothing unusual about that.

But wearing a football helmet while he mowed was.

As soon as Lacy pulled into the driveway, he cut the motor, climbed off the mower, and came to meet her.

"What's with the helmet, Dad?" she asked as he enfolded her in one of his bear hugs. "Planning on doing some racing with the Husky?"

"No, that'd be silly. I'm just trying to protect the old noggin from those rats with fluffy tails." He removed the helmet and shook his fist in the direction of the upper branches. "The darn things pelted me with acorns this morning."

Lacy looked up. The "rats" in question seemed not to be

paying them any mind, scurrying from one branch to the next. They were more intent on scolding each other than giving any attention to the humans below.

"Dad, I've never seen your squirrels do anything like that."

"Well, they did. Oh, I know they look innocent enough now, but . . . hey! What do you mean by 'your squirrels'?"

"Nothing. I don't mean a thing." She didn't know anyone who gave the rodents as much thought, time, and effort as her dad. It wouldn't be surprising if he felt like they were his, at least a little bit.

"Where's Mom?" she asked to change the subject.

"In the house," he said, still glaring up at the squirrels as if daring them to try something. "She's putting 'for sale' tags on some of her treasures."

"You mean the yard sale to end all yard sales is still on?"

Her dad nodded. Mom had set a date for the sale three times since Lacy had come home and each time, she discovered a conflict at the last minute that allowed her to cancel.

"I'd better get in there and help," Lacy said.

"Go easy, daughter. This is hard for her, you know."

"Yeah, I sort of do." She'd had a sit-down with Virgil Cooper over at the hardware store. Initially, she'd intended the interview to be about how he, as a member of the Coldwater Warm Hearts Club, planned to train Lester to work for him. But Lacy also had another agenda that had nothing to do with the *Gazette* article.

Her mom had never really talked much about her childhood, and Lacy's grandparents on that side of the family were gone before she was born. Since Mr. Cooper had mentioned that he'd known her mother before she married George Evans, Lacy quietly steered the conversation to his recollections of her mom when she was younger.

Shirley Higginbottom Evans didn't grow up on the wrong side of the tracks. There were no tracks at all in the little hill community where she was born. Her mother was raised in a two-room house with no running water. That circumstance didn't change until the Higginbottoms moved down to Coldwater Cove when she was ready to go to high school.

"But don't feel sorry for her. Lots of us grew up with nothing so far as the world can see. Myself included," Mr. Cooper had said. "Things are nice to have, but they don't matter in the bigger picture. If you're raised with love, that'll trump indoor plumbing every time."

It also explained why her mom's things meant so much to her. She'd never known any surplus until she married the man who would someday be Lacy's father. Now Lacy was ashamed of the way she'd fussed at her mom over collecting too many thingamabobs and doodads.

Lacy had been raised with love *and* indoor plumbing, so she was without excuse for her condescending attitude. She was determined to change that.

She gave her dad a kiss on the cheek before turning to go into the house. He slapped the helmet back on and prepared to engage in another skirmish in the War of Squirrel Insurgency.

"Mom," Lacy called out as she removed her shoes at the slate entryway.

"In here, dear." Her voice had a little quaver in it. When Lacy found her mom affixing stickers to a set of gold-trimmed collectors' plates, she noticed her nose was red. She'd been crying.

"Mom, don't do this."

"Whatever do you mean?" she said brightly, trying to blink back tears.

"If these things mean so much to you, you shouldn't part with them."

Mom cocked her head at her. "But you're always trying to get me to cull my things."

"Yeah, well, I've been known to be wrong. Often," Lacy admitted. "If you love them, you should keep them."

"But you're right, Lacy. I've been looking at the place with fresh eyes and I can see what you've been trying to tell me. That hutch is terribly overcrowded."

The shelves in the old oak piece sagged. Probably because it was crammed with two full sets of china, a dozen mismatched crystal goblets, and a couple hundred salt-and-pepper shakers. Shirley Evans would be hard-pressed to find room to add so much as a paper clip to the chaos.

"Will it make you happy to have the hutch less crowded?" Lacy asked.

Her mother ignored the question. "I have so many decorative items, none of them can be properly appreciated."

For the first time in Lacy's life, her words were coming out of her mother's mouth. The turnabout felt all wrong. "Mom, do *you* appreciate them?"

"I do," she admitted with a sigh. "Just knowing they're there, even if I can't see them all properly, makes me happy." Her chin trembled. "I can't help it, Lacy, I love my pretties."

"Then it would be wrong to part with them," she said with a hand on her mom's shoulder. "Keep the ones you love, Mom."

"What if I love them all?"

Lacy smiled. "Then keep them all. Remember the family motto."

"If a little is good, a lot is a whole bunch better," they repeated in unison, and then collapsed into a hug full of laughter. And a few tears.

What was a little intentional clutter if it made her mom happy? Design wasn't always about aesthetics. It was about surrounding yourself with things that lifted you up, things you loved, things that reflected who you were. Like a mossy stone, the house was filled with items her mom had collected as she rolled through life. This old Colonial, packed with all its bric-a-brac and whatnots and thingummies, was her mom down to the last frilly hand-tatted doily.

Far be it from Lacy to change a thing.

"Now, dear, I know you didn't interrupt your busy day just to watch me blub over a few treasures. What's up?"

"I got some wonderful news today," Lacy said, patting her jeans pocket. There was an envelope with a check for thirty thousand dollars in there. And it was made out to *her!*

Her contact in Boston had authenticated the painting she'd sent him as a genuine, heretofore unknown, Erté original. He wrote that he'd ship it back if she wished, but if not, the check was his offer to buy the piece from her. Lacy only had to cash it to agree to his terms. This would knock a huge chunk out of her loan to the O'Learys.

She had asked Jake to pray for her. It seemed God had listened.

"Mom, do you remember that painting I bought the day we went to Gewgaws and Gizzwickies together?"

"Sure."

She pulled out the check and explained what had happened. The pair of them danced around the room, hopping up and down. The check slipped from Lacy's hand and fluttered to the floor.

"Oops!" She retrieved it and quickly stuffed the check back into her pocket. "Don't want to lose that."

"I should say not. See? You never know when you'll find a real treasure in a secondhand shop," her mom said. "You should come shopping with me more often. First you help Jake's mom sell her Fiestaware for what it's really worth and now this."

Lacy had been giddy with joy over her windfall, but at her mom's words, her belly spiraled downward. Like Jake's mother and her soup bowls, the people who had consigned the Erté to Gewgaws and Gizzwickies, whoever they were, had had no idea what they were selling.

If Lacy didn't try to find the original owner, she'd be no better than those bargain hunters from Kansas City who were trying to make off with Mrs. Tyler's four-thousand-dollar bowl for a measly ten. It wasn't fair to take advantage of people like that. Even though she definitely needed the money, the check in her pocket suddenly felt like a lead weight.

What if the previous owners of the Erté also needed money? Wasn't this a little like buying Manhattan from the Indians for a song? Lacy had chafed under the unfairness of her settlement with the Boston DA. But how could she, in good conscience, pass that unfairness on?

And she realized, with a sinking heart, what she had to do.

Her mother's friend Gloria, who ran the consignment shop, would remember whom the painting had belonged to. Anyone who knew to the inch where a bunch of plastic grapes should be would surely recall the owner of a genuine Erté.

Chapter 27

*Bold font, all caps. We want this headline to really pop.
Nothing this unexpected has happened to a resident of
Coldwater Cove since Alfred Mayhew won a blue ribbon for
his roses at the state fair back in '96. Make it sing!*

—a note from Wanda Cruikshank to
the *Coldwater Gazette* typesetter and printer

As it turned out, the person who had consigned the painting to Gewgaws and Gizzwickies was Tina-Louise "Grandma" Bugtussle. The artwork had come to town wrapped in a holey quilt, part of a pickup bed full of odds and ends.

Gloria had sifted through the stuff and agreed to consign half a dozen items, including the Erté painting, which, thanks to the quilt, was undamaged. She judged the rest of the load to be of little value. Coming from a junk-shop owner, that was saying something. Since it was fit for nothing but kindling, Junior had hauled the remainder to the dump.

"Them old things was just taking up space anyhow. High time we was rid of 'em," Grandma Bugtussle told Lacy. "I been using the smokehouse for storage, you see, but after Junior bagged a wild hog, we had to clear out the place so's we could cure us some ham."

She couldn't remember exactly how the painting had come into the Bugtussle family's possession, just that she'd inherited it from her mother-in-law. Great-Grandma Bugtussle had been a woman of generous proportions who'd grown tired of seeing "that skinny womarn" on her wall.

Tina-Louise "Grandma" Bugtussle, who hadn't missed

too many meals herself, agreed that the lady in the painting was painfully thin. She hadn't really fancied the thing, but "when somebody gives you something, whether you like it or not, you'd best take it. No tellin' whether they might give you somethin' good next time."

So the painting was relegated to the smokehouse along with other items she considered of no earthly use. "But if I'd a knowed that skinny womarn was worth so much, I'd a hung her in the outhouse at least. That ways somebody'd be lookin' at her ever' day."

She thanked Lacy profusely for being honest enough to seek out the original owner of the painting and promptly offered to pay her back the twenty-five dollars Lacy had laid out for the piece at Gewgaws and Gizzwickies. After a good bit of rooting around for carefully concealed Mason jars that were secreted in various places in the Bugtussle home, Grandma was only able to come up with $17.50, but she promised she'd be good for the rest once she took that check for thirty grand to the bank.

Evidently, the idea of a finder's fee, or even the 15 percent per transaction Gloria charged at Gewgaws and Gizzwickies, never entered Grandma Bugtussel's head.

Lacy wasn't about to bring it up. She didn't trust herself to say much at all since it required every ounce of willpower she possessed to turn the money over to Mrs. Bugtussle. Heather Walker had always claimed she received more than she gave when she did a good turn for someone else.

So far, Heather was wrong. Lacy waited for the glowing I-did-something-right feeling to come.

Nothing.

Lacy took copious notes for her article for the *Gazette*, carefully omitting the part she'd played in this unlikely art find. Besides the fact that Lacy was still trying to fly below the radar and didn't want a mention even in a paper as obscure as the *Coldwater Gazette,* Wanda would want her to focus on the rags-to-riches human interest angle. So she asked Grandma Bugtussle what she planned to do with the thirty thousand.

"Land sakes, I ain't no Donald Trump. How should I know about high finance?"

After a few minutes' consideration, the old lady decided to use the windfall to replace the cinderblocks under the family home. The current ones had settled badly and the house had been a bit "shifty" all last winter. Then after that, if Junior could tinker with the old school bus that was parked in the front yard and get it running again, Grandma intended to take the whole Bugtussle clan out to California to see Disneyland.

"Guess it makes sense for us to use the money to pay a call on the second happiest place on earth," Grandma said.

"The second?" Lacy asked, wondering how the old woman had so mixed up Disney's claim to fame. "Where's the first?"

Grandma Bugtussle tutted under her breath. "Law, child, you ain't got the sense you were born with, do you? The happiest place on earth is home, right here in the hills around Coldwater Cove, o' course."

Lacy wasn't too sure about that as she signed the check over to Mrs. Bugtussle. She didn't have much cause to feel happy at the moment. "There are those who'd beg to differ."

"Maybe so." The old woman eyed her shrewdly. "But if where you are ain't the happiest place to you, then you ain't home yet."

Her words were a smack upside Lacy's head. They rolled around in her brain all the way back to the *Gazette* office.

Where was home? Boston?

Probably not.

If she still had her business there, she likely would have kept the Erté for herself, hoarding away her treasured find and enjoying it as much as her mom rejoiced in her ceramic chickens. It never would have occurred to her to seek out the painting's original owner. But that was more about the type of person she'd become while she lived in New England than the place itself. Lacy had been so inwardly focused—all about *her* career, *her* success—that she'd lost sight of how anything she did or said impacted other people.

Maybe that was why she'd been blindsided by Bradford Endicott's betrayal. She hadn't seen it coming because she wasn't looking. She'd never really considered Bradford a creative partner. That was her bailiwick. Even though he'd been almost her fiancé, she'd rarely had a romantic thought in her head about him. He'd been an empty suit, a prop, mere arm candy. His old-money name was the most appealing thing about him. She used it to bolster her design brand.

I used him, Lacy realized with dismay.

She'd never quite reached the Prada-wearing devil level of meanness, but her attitude had been despicable. Bradford must have felt it. How could he not?

Not that she was excusing Bradford's criminal behavior, but the way she'd behaved toward him must have made it easier for him to do what he did.

She'd made acquaintances in New England, associates and colleagues, but not real connections. It was all about the angles. What could they do for her and her business?

After living in Boston for ten years, she had one friend to show for her time there. Shannon Keane was the only one who seemed to realize she was gone, the only one who missed her enough to call every week.

Lacy liked to think it was because New Englanders were so reserved by Coldwater standards, but if she were honest with herself, she knew it was her own fault. She'd completed myriad design projects. She'd created beautiful things. But she hadn't invested in anyone else's *life* while she was in New England.

She hadn't shown herself friendly. Hence, no friends.

But she was trying to change. Being back in Coldwater Cove had pulled her out of her own problems a little. She was making tentative connections with others for the first time in a long time. She was surrounded by a growing circle of souls she cared about—her parents, Heather, her coworkers, all the members of the Warm Hearts Club, and even Effie.

And they cared about her. With the possible exception of Effie . . .

Then there's Jake. A jittery glow shivered over her at the barest thought of him. She still wasn't sure how to name what she was feeling for him. The intensity of it scared her even more than his flashbacks did. If she didn't guard herself, thoughts of Jake would consume her and she'd get nothing accomplished but mooning around over him all day. She almost didn't care so long as she could be with him, so long as she could help him, and maybe . . . make a life with him.

Was that love?

Perhaps. It might be only obsession and she'd end up using Jake like she'd used Bradford. She wasn't sure she could be selfless enough for love yet. Love meant putting someone else first. Always. She was woefully out of practice with that. Her heart was such a shriveled wreck of a thing, she wasn't sure she could manage love. But she was trying.

Didn't the way she dealt with the check for the Erté prove that? If she could put the Bugtussles ahead of her own interests, surely she could give Jake first place.

But if it was love she felt for Jake, did love make this little backwater place home? And if Coldwater Cove *was* home, why wasn't it, as Grandma Bugtussle had said, the happiest place on earth to her?

Lacy didn't have any answers.

As she pulled to a stop in front of the *Gazette* office, her cell phone rang. Caller ID on her phone let her know that the incoming call was from the district attorney's office in Boston. She didn't answer it. Once the ringing stopped, she turned off her phone without checking to see if whoever it was had left a voice mail.

Sometimes ignorance really is bliss.

She'd just given away thirty thousand dollars because her conscience wouldn't let her keep it. That ought to have bought her some good karma. After all, those funds would have held the O'Learys at bay for months. As things stood, she didn't even have enough to make one more payment on that hateful loan.

Now the DA was after her again for some reason. Shannon must have knuckled under and given that Hopkins fellow her new number. And on the first day she'd done something selfless for somebody else, too.

No good deed goes unpunished.

Chapter 28

The sermon topic next Sunday will be "Is Hell Real?"
Come early and listen to our choir practice!

—from the Methodist Church bulletin

Lester was at Jake's side that evening when he turned up at Lacy's place. Her belly fizzed with disappointment. She wasn't ready to share her time with Jacob with anyone, least of all with the fellow who was already claiming a good part of Jake's days. Still, her mother had raised her to be polite.

"I'll wait for you out here, marine," Lester said when Lacy invited them both in.

"I thought he was just working for you at the Green Apple," she said in a whisper once they were far enough from the screen door not to be overhead. Between giving up the Erté, having the Boston DA leaving urgent messages for her to return his call, and knowing she was about to miss a payment on the O'Leary brothers' loan, Lacy was feeling swamped. All she wanted to do was sink onto the couch beside Jake, drink a glass of Chianti—which she certainly couldn't do with a recovering alcoholic around—and have a little pity party.

"Do you have to babysit Lester for the whole evening?" she asked, ashamed of the whine she heard in her own voice.

"Not the whole evening," Jake said. "And we won't be babysitting. He wants to visit his wife."

Lester's family life had been as scary as tornado season.

And if half of what she'd heard was true, just as violent. A memory of Daniel, angry over his father's unpredictable viciousness, crackled through her mind like heat lightning. "Given Lester's history, do you think that's a good idea?"

"That's why he wants us to go with him. He wants to see her, but he doesn't want her to be afraid," Jake explained. "It might put her more at ease to have another woman there. Will you come?"

If Lester was thinking about how his wife might feel, that boded well. And if Heather and the Warm Hearts Club were right, it would do Lacy good to stop brooding about herself and her problems. "Let's go."

The three of them crowded into Jake's pickup and drove over to Glenda Scott's house. All the way there, Lester's knee never stopped bouncing with nervousness.

His wife lived in a little cottage on Chinquapin Street. Her lawn was about a week overdue for a mowing. A bleeding heart plant with dozens of strands of pink blossoms was about to overrun the steps leading up to the front porch. But the house's slate-blue shake siding and white trim were in reasonably good shape. There was a cane-bottom rocker on one side of the red front door and a porch swing on the other.

When Lacy and Jake knocked, a slender woman with gray hair and equally gray eyes came to the door. She was careful to keep the screen hooked, but her gaze kept darting past Lacy and Jake to where Lester waited, leaning beside the truck.

Lacy introduced herself and then Jake. "Mrs. Scott, you may not know it, but your husband is back in town—"

"I know."

"If you're agreeable to it, Lester would like to speak with you, ma'am," Jake said.

"I won't let him come into my house."

"He understands that and doesn't expect to be welcome in

your home," Lacy said. "But Lester wondered if it would be all right with you for him to speak to you here on your porch. Just for a little while, if you'll let him." Then Lacy hastened to add, "And he asked us to stay nearby if that would make you feel more comfortable."

"I think I know you." Mrs. Scott eyed her closely. "You used to go with my boy, didn't you?"

Lacy nodded.

Mrs. Scott cocked her head at Jake. "And you and Danny were friends in school. Played football together, if I remember right."

"Yes, ma'am. Our team took first in conference when we were seniors. Daniel was our quarterback. I was his halfback."

She nodded as if satisfied and looked past them at her husband again.

"Won't you two have a seat on the swing?" She stepped out to join them on the porch. Mrs. Scott motioned to Lester. "You can come on up."

Lester didn't have to be invited twice. He scrambled up the steps so quickly, Lacy was afraid he'd trip. She and Jake settled into the swing, wondering what the old man had to say that had lit such a fire under him.

For a surprisingly long while, he said nothing at all. Lester just looked at his wife and drew a deep breath, satisfied to be in her presence. It was as if she were the source of all that was good. She was the last summer day of his life and now she was gone. She'd slipped through his fingers like a warm breeze.

His scrutiny made her uncomfortable enough to cross her arms over her chest.

"You look mighty fine, Glenda," he finally said.

She sat in the rocker, leaving him to stand. "You've been known to lie about other things, too."

"I mean it."

Glenda shook her head. "I didn't invite you up here to tell

me pretty nothings. That's how you used to do, you know. First you'd tear me down and then you'd build me back up so I'd forget about how crappy you made me feel about myself until the next time. I'm not going to fall for it again."

Lester didn't say anything. He just nodded and let his chin droop, an acknowledgment that he'd heard her.

"Guess I should thank you," she said.

His chin jerked upward in surprise. "What for?"

"After you left, I made something of myself. I'm a CNA now, working at the hospital. I paid off this house and own it free and clear. Me. All by myself." She pointed an accusing finger at him. "You used to make me feel weak, but I found out I was strong."

Lester didn't try to defend himself. "That's good, Glenda. You always were the best part of us."

"Don't think you can sweet-talk me. Those days are long gone," she said. "*Jeopardy*'s about to start and I don't want to miss it. These kids tell me you have something to say. Say it."

"You probably know I been in jail for a bit and—"

"I saw the notice in the paper."

"Yeah, I 'spect you did." Lester nodded agreeably. "Well, what you didn't read in the *Gazette* is that I been seeing a shrink from Bates College. She visited me every week while I was in county."

Glenda eyed him with suspicion. "Did it help?"

"I think so. Some. I hope." Lester scratched his head. He'd used too much gel in his attempt to look nice for her, so running his fingers through his wiry hair only made it stand on end. "I mean to stick with the weekly sessions anyway and see can I get my head straightened out."

Mrs. Scott blinked several times. She welled up, but didn't let a tear fall. Her eyes were overly bright though.

She still cares about Lester, even though he hurt her, Lacy realized. No matter what he'd done, Mrs. Scott didn't have a toggle switch in her heart. She couldn't turn the caring off. Lacy was glad Mrs. Scott was smart enough to protect herself though. She still insisted on distance and control of the situation, as she should.

"I hope seeing a therapist works for you, Lester," Glenda said.

"Me too. Only wish I'd done it sooner. If I had, then maybe . . ." When she didn't say anything, he continued, "O' course, I been helped by some other things, too. I joined AA while I was in the lockup."

"So. You sobered up because you couldn't find a drink while you were in jail." Her features twisted into a scowl. "Are you expecting applause?"

Lacy had the feeling that Mrs. Scott wouldn't have been brave enough to be sarcastic if she and Jake weren't a stone's throw away.

"Reckon I deserve that. But one way or the other, I earned my thirty-day chip and I mean to keep up with it now that I'm out." He didn't add that he had to if he wanted to remain a free man. "Anyways, one of the twelve steps is that we have to give ourselves what they call a 'moral inventory.' I'm sorely lacking in the morals department, but I 'spect you know that better than anybody."

Mrs. Scott didn't say a word.

"Anyways, I'm wanting to get myself some, so I'm jumping ahead a bit to step eight. I had to list all the people I hurt while I was drinkin'," Lester explained, "and I guess it's no surprise to you that your name's at the top of that list."

Mrs. Scott looked away. Lacy tried not to imagine what she might be remembering.

"I done wrong by you. Whatever bad thing you're thinking about me, I'm worse than that and I know it," Lester said, his voice taking on a ragged edge. "And I'm here to tell you, I'm sorry."

"And that makes it all right?" she whispered. "Sorry just doesn't get it."

"No, I know it don't. That's why I got to make amends."

"Lester, you terrified me and our son for years." Glenda stood and retreated to the far corner of the porch, trying to put as much distance as possible between them. "How can you make amends for that?"

"I don't know. It may be that I can't. I'm not expecting you to forgive me. I wouldn't ask that of you."

"Seems like you are."

"Well, I'm not. I don't deserve for you to forgive me. I'm just here to tell you that when I look back on our life together, I want to kick my own butt."

As apologies went, Lacy didn't think it was very elegant, but it seemed to reach Glenda. Her lips twitched, but she kept silent.

"If knockin' my head against a brick wall would knock some sense into the old me, I'd do it in a heartbeat. All my meanness, all them . . . them hateful words I said, all the horrible things I did . . . God, I'd give anything if I could take it all back." Lester's voice broke and his eyes filled with tears. "But I can't and I'm heartsick about it, more than I can say. It fair eats at my gut."

Lester rubbed a hand on his concave belly, as if that would quiet his demons. "When you're on the street like I was, sitting through a sermon is the price you pay for a free meal more often as not. The preachers always talk about hell, all the time telling us it's filled with fire and brimstone."

"You think it's not?" Glenda said in a small voice.

"I know it's not. I been there, you see. It's a dark, cold place, and it's filled with regret. It's lookin' back and seein' yourself like you was somebody else. You're saying stuff and doing stuff you wish you hadn't, and you just keep seeing it happen over and over again. The worst of it is, you can't change a darn thing." He hung his head. "That's what hell is."

Glenda's hand lifted slightly in his direction, as if something inside her wanted to reach out and touch his shoulder, but then she pulled it back.

"Like I say, I'm not lookin' for you to forgive me," Lester said, still studying the boards between his feet as if they held the secret to life, "but I hope you'll let me make them amends. No strings attached. Ain't no way I can balance the scales either way. It's not much, but it's the only way I can think of to show you how sorry I am." He raised his head and met her gray-eyed gaze. "Will you let me?"

It was a little like watching a rosebud unfurl in slow motion, a minor miracle. Lacy could see the exact moment when something changed behind Mrs. Scott's eyes and she decided to give her husband a chance.

Not to undo their past. That was impossible, but at least she was willing to let him do what he could to make her present better.

"What did you have in mind?" she asked softly.

"Well, I owe you a ton in support. I thought I might start there. Thanks to some folks that call themselves the Coldwater Warm Hearts Club, I got myself three or four jobs now."

"You're working?" she said incredulously.

Lester nodded. "And two of the jobs actually pay me cash money. It won't make me no Rockefeller, but I was thinkin' I could give you half—no, make that three-quarters—of everything I bring home."

Glenda frowned. "If you do that, you won't have enough to live on."

"You let me worry about that. I been living on next to nothing for years. I don't need all that much, you see," he went on to say quickly. "For the price of doin' some gardening, I got myself a nice little place to stay. Jake lets me eat at the Green Apple on the days I work there. And he's been known to feed me even on the days I don't." Lester winked in Jake's direction. "Anyways, since I'm getting paid a little there at the grill and at the hardware store, even a quarter of what I make will have me feeling like a prince. I've had nothing for so long, I won't hardly miss what I give you."

"Well, that'll be nice, then, Lester," Glenda said, speaking slowly and choosing her words with care. "And I appreciate it. Might be I could put the money away for Carson." She clapped her hand over her mouth. "Oh. Maybe I shouldn't have mentioned—"

"It's okay, Glenda. I know we got a grandbaby. I seen him . . . from a ways off, you understand. I didn't like to intrude or nothin' where I'm not welcome, but I watch him and his momma at the park sometimes. He seems like a sharp little fella."

"He is."

"Then, too, besides the money, I was thinking I could maybe help you out around here on Sunday afternoons," Lester said.

"Doing what?" she said, her guard instantly up.

"Well, you've taken real good care of the place, but I could do odd jobs for you."

She took a step back. "You can't come into my house, Lester."

He nodded. "I understand. That's fine. But I could take over some of the outside chores for you. I could wash your windows or do the mowing. And I was noticing that the shingles on the garage are starting to curl. I could replace that roof if you want."

She arched a skeptical brow at him. "How would you do that?"

"I worked construction in Brownsville from time to

time," he said. "Long enough to learn how to pound nails into shingles. I could do it. Will you let me?"

"We'll see. It's time you were going now." She turned to Lacy and Jake. "Thank you for coming with him, kids." Then she glanced at Lester, stepped inside, and hooked the screen between them. "If you're serious about this amends business, I expect you to mow the yard on Sunday afternoon."

"I'll be here, Glenda. Count on it." Lester started down the steps, but then stopped himself and turned back to face her. "I can't thank you enough, babe."

"Don't 'babe' me. Just mow my yard," she said and shut the storm door with a hard click. Then through the door, Lacy heard, "And don't be thinking I'll invite you in when you're done."

Chapter 29

*Last season, the high school football team finished at
the bottom of the conference. "But with four returning seniors,"
Coach Campbell predicted, "the Fighting Marmots
should field a solid varsity squad next fall."*

—from the Sports section of the *Coldwater Gazette*

"Well, that was intense," Jake said after they dropped Lester
at Mr. Bunn's house and watched him climb the exterior stairs
to his studio apartment over the garage. Lacy slid across the
bench seat to take advantage of the breeze coming through
the open window.

Must get the AC on the truck fixed if I want her to sit close to me.

"I didn't think Mrs. Scott was going to let Lester do anything for her at first," Jake said.

"I wouldn't have blamed her," Lacy said. "It's a wonder
she even allowed him on the porch."

"The way she pulled herself up after he left is pretty impressive. You have to admire her for getting some training
and making something of her life."

"Guess it was easier without that deadweight."

Jake glanced at her sharply. Sometimes, he didn't find the
things rolling around in Lacy's head nearly as attractive as she
was. Of course, sometimes there were things in his head that
ought to send her running away screaming, too. He'd had another flashback last night, triggered by nothing more sinister
than a thunderstorm rolling through the area. He didn't want

to admit it, even to himself, but the episodes were becoming more frequent. And more intensely real.

"Why would you call Lester deadweight?" Concentrating on Lester helped Jake shove aside his own issue. He knew it wasn't doing much good trying to run from this one, but he wasn't ready to bare his soul to some stranger at the new Bates College clinic. Even if it was free for veterans.

"I know Lester is no prize," Jake said. "But he's still a person."

"A person who treated his family like dirt," Lacy countered. "Daniel didn't ever tell me much about what went on, but just from the things he didn't say, I know his father put him through a trial by fire when he was growing up."

Jake knew even better than Lacy how bad it had been for Daniel. It was a good thing Danny had told Jake about his plan to waylay his father that night just weeks before their graduation. If Jake hadn't been there to stop him once the beating began, Daniel had been out of control enough to have killed Lester then and there. And would've ruined his own life in the process.

But even though Jake was sorry about Dan's rough upbringing, he really didn't need an old boyfriend invading his time with Lacy.

"Are you still hung up on Daniel?"

"No, of course I'm not still hung up on Daniel." Lacy rolled her baby blues at him. "He's married, remember, and besides, I heard he got back together with his wife."

"Must have overlooked that bit of gossip."

"Aw, did you miss a call from the Methodist prayer chain again?"

"Cute." Jake grimaced at her. He wasn't on the chain's phone tree, but if he listened to his customers at the grill, he usually heard everything happening around town that was worth knowing.

"I do pray for people, you know." And whether he was on the prayer chain or not, he *had* prayed for Dan to reconcile with Annie. It was the best way to make sure Lacy didn't end up with her old flame.

"People besides me?"

"Besides you. You should try it sometime," Jake said. "You never know if it will help them, but I guarantee it'll help you. It's hard to dislike somebody when you're praying for them. Like Lester, for instance."

"You want me to pray for Lester? He's a pretty horrible person," Lacy pointed out. "At least, he was."

"You're right. He was a total loser, but 'was' is the operative word. Besides, if we only pray for people who deserve it, we won't pray at all," Jake said. "Lester is trying to make some changes now. That's hard for anybody and he has farther to go than most. How about cutting him a little slack?"

"All right. And if it'll make you happy, I'll pray for him, too," Lacy said. "I'm sorry to be so cranky. It's just, well, I've had a hard day."

"Want to tell me about it? I've got a good shoulder to cry on. It's yours for the taking." He lifted his arm to invite her to snuggle closer. She slipped off her seat belt and slid across the truck's bench seat.

Lacy sighed as she leaned into him. "I did something today that I should be feeling good about, something the Warm Hearts Club would approve, I'm sure. I know it was the right thing to do. Heather claims it makes her happy when she does something good for someone else, but to be honest, I'm kind of depressed about it. Does that make me a bad person?"

"Never. Whatever it was you did must have been hard for you. In my book that makes you an even better person. If we only do something good because it's easy, we might as well be bad."

"No worries on that score," she said with a chuckle. "I'm pretty sure it's the bad stuff that's easy most of the time."

"What was it you did?"

She sat upright and scooted back over to her side of the bench seat. "If I go through it all again, I'll just start second-guessing myself and there's no going back on this. I can only go forward and muddle through the best I can."

Jake pulled his truck into the small parking lot behind Lacy's building and cut the engine. "I wonder if that's how Glenda Scott felt when Lester left—like she could only go forward and muddle through."

"No," Lacy said after some thought. "To do what she did, she had to give up feeling bitter about what was past. She had to let it go."

Jake knew something about that. For months after he lost his leg, bitterness had threatened to unman him. Losing a limb meant going through a period of grief. Finally, he'd stopped asking why he'd survived when others didn't, or why he'd lost his leg when others came back from deployment without a scratch. Jake had come to a place of acceptance. Then he took stock of himself and decided what to keep and what to throw away. Bitterness was the first thing to go.

But while he had made good progress in his physical reha-bilitation, his mind was betraying him more often with flash-backs and periods of hypervigilance. In some ways, that was worse than losing the leg.

Jake squeezed his eyes shut, trying to block out the prob-lem. Back to Lester. That was the ticket.

"Do you think the fact that Mrs. Scott is letting Lester mow her yard means that in some part of her heart, she's al-ready forgiven him?"

"If she has, she's a better woman than me."

He reached over and stroked her hair. "Not possible."

"You silver-tongued devil, you." She flashed him a dazzling smile. "But you're wrong. I've been awfully bitter about what happened in Boston. I need to let it go if I want to move on."

He liked the sound of that if it meant she was moving in his direction. "Well, this is way too serious a conversation for a Tuesday night. I got some salmon steaks marinating and a bottle of Chardonnay chilling over at my place."

"Sure you want to cook after working over the grill all day?"

"As long as I'm cooking with you." Over the course of the last month or so, they'd developed a rhythm between them in the kitchen, a give and take that Jake hoped was a sign of good things to come in other parts of the house. "I'll even let you pick the after-dinner movie."

The on-demand feature on his satellite TV gave them tons of options.

Lacy climbed out of the truck, closed the door, and leaned on the open window frame. "What if I want to see a chick flick?"

"In that case, I'll sleep with my eyes open and try not to snore."

"Oh, poor you! And after I yawned my way through that soccer match last night. Hours wasted on guys chasing a ball around and it still ended in a draw." She came around the truck to the driver's side and punched his shoulder playfully through his open window.

"Hey!" After a bit of creative self-defense that involved using his beat-up atlas as a shield, he caught up her hand and kissed her knuckles. "Seriously. Whatever you want, Lace. A girl who made a tough decision she's not happy about deserves to get her way a little."

She gave him a heart-melting smile. "What I don't deserve is you, Jake."

"Too bad. You got me anyway."

She stood on tiptoe, leaned in, and kissed him.

It was one of those kisses. The kind she took her time about, the ones that had him thinking all sorts of wonderful wicked things . . .

Then she pulled away and headed up the iron stairs that led to her apartment. "I'll just feed the attack cat and be right over." She stopped on the bottom step. "Oh! And before we start supper, you need to water your plants. I noticed they were looking a little droopy earlier."

"My plants?" The only plants he had were in the pint-sized herb garden growing on the windowsill in his kitchen. Jake knew they were doing just fine since he regularly used snippets of them in his dishes.

"You know what I mean. The barrel of flowers the town put out on the corner near the grill. You're supposed to keep it watered and weeded. Remember? See you in a bit."

Jake watched until she disappeared into her apartment. Then he drove around to the alley behind the Green Apple on the other side of the Square and parked. Speedbump greeted him with a frenetic take-me-out-or-what-happens-to-the-floor-is-your-fault dance. Jake leashed up the dog, grabbed a bucket, which he filled with water for the flower barrel, and made his way around to the corner.

Most of the town's "beautification" barrels were filled with petunias that spilled over the sides in a red riot of fragrant color. For some reason, the barrel nearest the Green Apple got the nursery's leavings and instead of petunias, Jake's was planted with earthy-smelling geraniums and musty poppies.

Speedbump lifted his leg to the barrel.

"Yeah, buddy, that's what I think about it, too."

Jake's nose twitched. As he dumped the bucket of water on the petals, his vision tunneled and he felt it begin.

A red haze of poppies filled the bottom of the broad ravine. Jake peered over the edge of the ridge, his M40 clutched before him. The locals were harvesting the plants below, sending fumes into the air that made him yawn.

Jake gave himself a shake. He had to stay alert. Enemy combatants were reportedly hiding amongst the locals. The rest of his unit was waiting for him to single out the suspicious characters before they moved in. But how could he tell which, if any, of the workers might be concealing a Kalashnikov in their woven baskets filled with poppies?

An IED exploded at the far end of the ridge where the rest of the good guys were holed up. It was followed by the pops of small arms and then the louder, ominous thud of a rocket-launched grenade. Shouted orders echoed through the ravine, unintelligible from this distance, but packed with adrenaline-fueled ferocity.

Jake scrambled to his feet and ran to help his unit, bullets peppering the dusty ground around him.

Chapter 30

*The senior class is holdin the Annual Fihtin Marmots
Bonfire in the city ark near the azebo on the last day
of school. The ublic is invited to join the sin alon with
the hi h school choir. In other news, the hi h school
office would welcome a new com uter keyboard.
A letter or two is missin on this one.*

—from the Fighting Marmot Notes section
of the *Coldwater Gazette*

Lacy appeased Effie the Demanding with her evening allot-
ment of albacore and was rewarded with a brush of fur on her
calves as Effie made her regal way to the supper bowl. The cat
was definitely warming up to her.

She was barely out her apartment door when she heard a
kerflump-ing sound coming up the iron staircase toward her. It
stopped suddenly and was followed by a high-pitched whine.
She hurried down to find Speedbump straining against his
leash, which had become tangled in the iron fretwork on the
landing.

"What on earth!" She knelt to free him. "You naughty
boy. How did you get away from Jake?"

He couldn't have, Lacy realized. Speedbump might not be
at all the sort of dog a tough guy would be drawn to, but after risking life and limb to save the little bugger, Jake wasn't
likely to let him wander off. She glanced down the alley, but
Jake wasn't in pursuit.

Grabbing the end of Speedbump's leash, she trotted out
to the Square. Perhaps Jake was preoccupied with watering

the barrel of flowers nearest the Green Apple and hadn't noticed his dog had gone missing. The streetlights had come on, washing the Town Square in pools of yellowish light.

Jake was nowhere in sight.

She loped across the Square toward the grill, ignoring crosswalks and earning a honk or two from motorists when she failed to wait until they passed by.

Jake had given her a key to the back door of the Green Apple, but she didn't have to use it. The door was ajar. That wasn't like Jake at all. If Lacy had been in Boston, she'd have dialed 911.

Without hesitation, she picked up Speedbump and hurried inside, calling Jake's name.

There was no answer.

Instead, a sharp popping came from the apartment above her head. Even though she'd only heard something like it once back in Boston when she and Shannon had gone clubbing in a dicey neighborhood, she recognized the sound immediately.

Gunshot.

Speedbump wiggled out of her arms and flew up the stairs. Not to be outdone by a dog, Lacy followed. But she climbed slowly, ears pricked, dreading what she might find at the top. The sharp scent of a recently discharged weapon assaulted her nostrils.

The blinds had been drawn so only a few slender bars of light from the streetlamps filtered through. Jake's apartment was awash in shades of gray.

She didn't see him anywhere.

But she heard something. It was a wet noise, the gurgling, strangled sound of someone trying not to cry and failing miserably.

There in the dark, Jacob Tyler, the heartbreak of Coldwater High, was weeping like a lost child.

"Jake?"

"Go away." Then he loosed a string of profanity that made her flinch.

But Lacy was so relieved to hear his voice, she almost didn't care what he'd said. She felt for the nearest light switch and flicked it on. The place looked as if a twister had blown through it—chairs upended, lamps shattered on the hard-wood, books torn from the shelves.

Jake was sitting on the floor in the far corner, his Beretta still in his hand. Speedbump had crawled into the space be-tween his legs and, front paws on his chest, was trying to wash Jake's face with doggie kisses. Jake pushed the dog down and Speedbump curled into a quivering ball by his master's foot. Then Jake swiped his own eyes, schooled his features into a hard mask, and glared up at Lacy.

A stranger peered at her from behind his dark eyes.

"Jake, are you hurt?"

He shook his head.

"Then what happened? Was someone trying to rob the place and you interrupted him?"

"No."

For some unknown reason, his leg was off. The prosthetic was lying crosswise over his good knee. Since he was wearing his camo shorts, Lacy saw his bare stump for the first time.

The reddened skin was stretched tight over the knob. The rest of Jake was so strong, so vital, the missing limb seemed like an insult. A cosmic joke no one found funny.

But he was still Jake and his stump was part of him. She knelt down beside him, eyeing the handgun still in his grasp. "What's going on?"

God, I wish I knew.

Jake had been watering those darn poppies and then, with almost no warning, the whole world went sideways. He remembered desperate snatches of the episode, part of it in

Helmand province and part of it in a nightmarish version of Coldwater Cove, but after an image of glistening red petals, his next clear memory was the report of his own weapon.

How he'd gotten back into his apartment and opened the gun safe to retrieve his piece was a total blur. He'd trashed his own place without any of the destruction registering in his brain. Somehow, he'd even taken off his leg.

The "why" of any of it was beyond him.

And he needed to keep it beyond Lacy, too. "Go home."

"Not until I get some answers."

"There aren't any."

Couldn't she see that he was broken? Missing so much more than his leg. There were places in him that were darker than a moonless night, colder than freezing rain.

Oh, he tried to present a brave face to the world. He was a returning hero making the best of the poor hand he'd been dealt. But unlike his missing leg, no one could see the damage Jake had suffered on the inside. He couldn't control it and it was getting worse.

He despised weakness in others. He hated it in himself.

Jake had tried to gloss over the trauma, to pretend it wasn't there. But there was no prosthetic for his mind, no artificial patch to put over his wounded soul. And he had no way of knowing when that damaged part of him would lash out, when the past would intrude on his present with violence.

He didn't want to hurt the people he was supposed to love and protect, the way Lester had.

Jake had no idea what he was doing with the Beretta. What if Lacy had been with him when he'd fired his weapon?

It didn't bear thinking of.

She laid her hand on his knee, close to the spot where his flesh-and-blood calf stopped and his phantom limb began. "Jake, let me in. I want to help."

"You can't." Nobody could.

"Then I want to go through this . . . this whatever it is with you while you work it out."

Who said he ever would? The future was a long dark tunnel, and there was no light at the end of it. He brushed her hand away.

"No." He didn't trust himself to look at her.

"But, Jake—"

He swore a blue streak. "I said no. Now get out of here. Go back to Boston. It's where you belong anyway."

"No. I belong here. With you."

"Not anymore. Coldwater isn't for you. And neither am I. You outgrew both of us years ago."

She jerked back as if he'd slapped her. Her baby blues welled up.

It made him feel like crap to hurt her, but better this than to let her stay near him when even he didn't know what he might do next.

He held himself rigid, not daring to breathe as she slowly rose and walked toward the stairs that led down to the door to the alley and out of his life. He longed to call her back. Jake had taken his grandmother's ring out of his safety deposit box at the bank a couple of days ago, intending to ask Lacy to marry him. He ached to tell her yes, he wanted her to stay with him, please, God, not just for tonight, but forever. He'd only been waiting for the right time to pop the question.

Now the right time would never come. He let out the breath he'd been holding in a slow, measured stream.

Then she stopped at the head of the steps and looked back at him. He tamped down the wild hope that surged in his chest. He couldn't have it. Couldn't have her.

"I should have known, Jake."

"What?"

"That you'd break my heart. It's what you do. Love 'em and leave 'em. I should have remembered."

Couldn't she see it was for her own good? He didn't trust himself to speak. If he did, the words might pour out of his throat before he could get a handle on them and he'd be begging her to stay.

"You made me care about you," she said softly. "You made me love you. Made me let you in. I can't help it. I love you so much it hurts. Don't you love me back . . . even a little?"

He steeled himself not to answer, but she ought to know anyway. Of course he loved her. He loved her more than his next breath. She was everything he ever wanted.

And shouldn't have.

Which was why he had to send her away and make it stick. If he didn't love her, he'd try to keep her even though he was a dangerous man to be close to. He'd lean on her and use her to try to fill up that damaged place.

But he couldn't do that to Lacy. He loved her too much to chain her to a wreck like him.

"You'll get over it. You're a survivor," he told her. She'd blown off her attachment to Daniel easily enough. And that Bradford guy. Jake was under no illusion that he was any different. "It's what *you* do."

"Not this time. I'm done. There's nothing left in me for another go-round. You're the last man I'll ever love." As she started down the stairs, he heard her say, "Whether I want to or not."

Lacy trudged back across the Square toward her place, not sure she'd make it that far. By rights, her heart should stop beating by the time she passed the courthouse, but her feet carried her on. Her vision wavered with unshed tears. She made her way up the stairs to her place more by feel than by sight.

Love was supposed to be joy and flowers and strawberries dipped in dark chocolate.

No one told her it would be like this.

Her insides had been hollowed out. After Bradford, she'd thought she knew what rejection felt like.

His betrayal was nothing compared to this.

She'd been ready to give all that she was to Jake and to accept all of him—the good and the bad. But he didn't love her back. He'd tossed her away as if she were a used tissue.

As soon as her door closed behind her, she slumped to the kitchen floor. Her legs wouldn't support her a second longer. She covered her face with both hands and wept.

Effie meowed, her tail arched into a furry question mark. When Lacy didn't respond, the cat circled her warily before sidling up to her hip and beginning to purr. Lacy ignored her and continued to let the grief pour out of her eyes. After a while, the Siamese rolled onto her side and began kneading Lacy's thigh.

"Oh, all right, cat. If you're trying to say I still have someone who loves me, I get it." She relented and gave Effie a full-body pat, running her hand over the sleek head and on down to the tip of Effie's tail. "Can you blame me for hoping it would be someone who's a little taller? And doesn't shed."

Before Lacy had the chance to rise from the floor, her cell phone rang. She pulled it out of her pocket, expecting it to be the DA's office again. She'd successfully avoided taking no less than six calls from them. Instead, caller ID flashed the name Neville Lodge on the screen.

The guy who'd bought the Erté. The last thing she needed was a reminder of the other disaster this day had brought—giving up thirty thousand dollars to the Bugtussles. But it would be rude not to answer a call from someone who'd sent her a five-figure check.

"Lacy, darling, I called to thank you again for uncovering that marvelous painting." Neville's cultured New England accent didn't allow him to acknowledge the existence of Rs.

"I'm glad you're enjoying it."

"Oh, it wasn't for me, more's the pity. That check was written on the company account and FYI, we've already sold the Erté to a serious collector for triple the money."

"Great." Someone had skinned her like she'd almost skinned the Bugtussles. She understood that there had to be a markup in the art world. A business of any stripe couldn't stay afloat if it didn't make a profit. But three hundred percent seemed off the charts. Of course, she'd lost her business, so what did she know? "You didn't call to tell me I sold too low. What do you want, Neville?"

"To offer you a position with Boyleston, Quincy, and Lodge. When I told my partners you had such a good eye that you found the Erté in a . . . a thrift shop of all places, they decided we need to bring you on board full-time."

Then he named a salary that was double what she'd made in her best year with her own shop.

"What exactly do you want me to do for you?" *Donate a kidney?*

"We want you to find more undiscovered pieces. If Boyleston, Quincy, and Lodge develops a reputation for being able to provide our clients with heretofore unknown master-pieces, collectors will flock to our door. Art and high-concept design is a small and, fortunately, a very affluent world. A few more finds like your Erté and we'll be able to knock our European competition back on their heels." Neville giggled. Evidently even he had trouble imagining himself knock-ing anyone on their anything. "The position will entail a good deal of travel, for which you'll be well compensated, of course."

Her head was spinning while he went on to tell her about stipends and expense accounts. "We have one very avid Saudi prince who signed with us to replace the art in all his estates simply because we promised him we had a full-time expert actively acquiring new pieces."

"I haven't said yes."

"But you will," he predicted. "Let us fly you in to discuss it. You must be wild to escape that ridiculous little hamlet you've landed in by now."

Oddly enough, the idea of leaving Coldwater Cove was a lead weight that dropped through her heart and settled in her belly. It would mean giving up on Jake completely.

"I can't, Neville."

"Don't say no. Say you'll think about it. I'll send you the offer in writing. You can mull things over and give us the green light next week. Toodles."

The astronomical sum he'd offered to pay her orbited around her brain a time or two. If she was making that kind of money, she'd have the O'Leary brothers paid off in half a year—less, if she was frugal.

Even that much-to-be-desired outcome didn't raise her spirits. But she did feel oceans better about having returned the money from the sale of the Erté to the Bugtussle family.

"Evidently, there's something to that old sowing and reaping stuff," she told Effie.

Then her phone rang again. Hoping it was Jake, she answered before checking caller ID this time.

"Ms. Evans, this is Deputy District Attorney Ethan Hopkins."

Oh, shoot! He was probably calling to tell her new charges had been filed against her to appease Bradford's influential family.

"Are you still there, Ms. Evans?"

"Yes. Yes, sir, I'm here." Unfortunately, if he had her number, he probably knew where "here" was, too.

"I want to apprise you of new developments in your case."

"I thought my case was settled," she said shakily. After all she'd done to make restitution, how could the Commonwealth go back on the settlement like this?

"I suppose I should amend that. Some things have happened that have changed the disposition of your case."

"Is Mr. Endicott in custody?"

"No. To my knowledge, he's not even in the States. Besides, this doesn't concern him directly."

Oh, no. The Endicotts had managed to have all the blame for Bradford's embezzlement transferred to her.

"This has to do with your arrangement with the former DA and Thomas and Malcolm O'Leary." He went on to explain that his boss had been indicted for taking kickbacks from known organized crime types and was awaiting his own trial. DDA Hopkins needed Lacy to return to testify that the former DA had wrongly forced her to make restitution for a crime for which she was not guilty. Then the DA had put her in touch with the O'Learys so she could meet the financial requirements of the deal he'd made with her.

"You're not the only one who's fallen prey to this sort of arrangement," DDA Hopkins explained.

"If there are others, you don't really need my testimony."

"On the contrary, the weight of numbers makes a difference." DDA Hopkins needed as many of the old DA's victims to step forward as possible. "Besides, you're one of the few who is actually an innocent party. A jury will be especially sympathetic to you."

Lacy shakily agreed to testify.

"Oh, and just so you know, the O'Leary brothers were indicted as well and the judge ruled that all loans they made in conjunction with the DA's office are frozen until such time as a trial can determine whether said loans should be considered fraudulent. So in the meantime, you don't need to worry about repaying another dime."

All the air whooshed out of Lacy's lungs. Stunned, she thanked DDA Hopkins, promised again to appear in court when he needed her, and ended the conversation.

She'd done one good thing by turning the money for the Erté over to the Bugtussles, and now her whole financial life was turning around.

Sowing and reaping, indeed. Maybe Heather Walker and the Warm Hearts Club were on to something.

But being out from under the O'Learys' thumbs and having a fabulous job offer didn't make her happy. As long as Jake was suffering, she would suffer with him. But he wouldn't let her help him, and she wasn't sure what she could do even if he did.

So Lacy tried something she hadn't done in a long time.

She prayed.

Chapter 31

*Around here, it's always a slow news day. But that's
all right. My readers like to read slow.*

—Wanda Cruikshank, editor of the *Coldwater Gazette,*
who wouldn't trade it for some big-city rag on a bet

A week moseyed by.

Though most doings about town were overshadowed by
news of the astounding good luck of Tina-Louise Bugtussle,
a few things of note happened.

Deek Atwater, the sole member of the cyber team at the
Gazette, took first place in a chess tournament in Muskogee.
He credited the win to all the hours he spent playing against
the computer in his mother's basement. Who knew the time
spent in such a dank, musty place would amount to anything
except mushrooms?

Mrs. Paderewski's piano students presented their yearly
recital in the Catholic church fellowship hall. Mr. Evans
would have said the performance was rated PC—Parental
Consumption.

The town council voted to have a Most Beautiful Front
Lawn Contest to encourage folks to plant more flowers and
shrubs and generally spruce up their homes. Like most things
decreed by government, the competition had unintended
consequences. Lacy's dad overfertilized his lawn, which left
several patches of grass dry and brown. He fixed this with a

can of green spray paint and a promise from Lacy "not to tell her mother."

She also didn't tell her mother about the job offer in Boston. Or her dad. In fact, she didn't tell anyone except Heather and then only because she had to talk to someone. Her friend offered a sympathetic ear but no answers.

She'd been praying for Jake all week without receiving any answer, too. Finally, she called in the big guns and put him on the prayer chain as "an unspoken request." God would know who Marjorie and her gang were talking about, even if they didn't.

"Did you hear the latest news?" Lester asked Jake. The two men worked side by side flipping pancakes and making breakfast scrambles to meet the demands of the Tuesday morning rush.

"I'm not deaf."

Everyone in town had heard about how Grandma Bugtussle had turned an old painting she didn't even like into a big fat wad of cash. Not only was there a full-page article about it in the *Gazette,* the Bugtussles' good fortune was on everyone's lips.

Jake, however, had gotten the whole story from Gloria, the owner of Gewgaws and Gizzwickies, when he'd dropped by some pieces his mother wanted to consign. She thought it would be a good idea to have some of her wares in both consignment shops.

"Best not to put all your eggs in one basket," his mom had said. "It's good to spread things around."

Gloria evidently agreed. Without any encouragement on his part, Jake was told that Lacy Evans had bought the painting from the shop.

"In fact, she came back in wanting to know who it had

belonged to before, but don't tell her I said anything. My discretion is why folks trust me with their treasures," Gloria had said without a trace of irony. "Forget I said anything. If she'd wanted you to know what she did, she'd a told you."

But Lacy wasn't telling him anything. In fact, she'd gone out of her way to make sure their paths didn't cross. The Coldwater Warm Hearts Club was meeting for breakfast in the Green Apple as usual that morning, but Lacy was a no-show.

The club didn't know she'd given the biggest helping hand of all that week. Considering her debts, Jake figured Lacy's good deed was certainly more sacrificial than any of the other things the Warm Hearts did.

"To be honest," Jake said to Lester over a mess of frying sausages, "I'm a little tired of hearing about the Bugtussles and their plans to invade Disneyland."

"That ain't the news I'm talking about," Lester said. "Lacy Evans got herself a big job offer from some company back east. I overheard Heather Walker say something about it while I was bussing the table next to her group and—hey! Where you off to?"

"I need to top off some coffees. Ethel's running a little behind."

Ethel would have disputed that with her dying breath, but Jake had to have some excuse to leave the kitchen and find out about this job offer. When he'd told Lacy to go back to Boston, he never dreamed she'd actually do it.

His heart was pounding, but he tried to act casual. As he refilled the mugs around the Warm Hearts Club table, Mr. Bunn came in to the meeting late and had to be brought up to speed. It seemed Lacy had been offered a very lucrative position with a prominent New England art and design firm. They wanted her to start next week.

"Is she going to take it?" Mr. Bunn asked.

"She'd be a fool not to." Heather's nose twitched delicately and she glanced toward the kitchen. The smell of something burning wafted toward them. "How's Lester working out, Jake?"

He didn't take time to answer. Instead, he hoofed it back to the kitchen and sent Lester out to bus more tables before the old vet set the whole place on fire.

For the rest of the day, Jake was on autopilot. Cooking had a certain mind-numbing routine to it. He didn't really need to think about most of the prep work. Chopping veggies and measuring ingredients had become second nature to him. He really only needed to focus when he was dealing with a new recipe or the hot grill.

So while his body went through the motions of his day, his mind raced a mile a minute.

Lacy. Gone.

It was what he'd told her he wanted.

He'd lied.

A couple of days after that horrible night, he'd started working on a plan to dig himself out of the hole he'd fallen into. Jake broke down and went to the Bates Clinic to talk to a psychologist. It might take medication, he was told. It would certainly take therapy, but there was help for his flashbacks. He just had to be willing to accept the help and do the work.

It wasn't going to be comfortable. It wasn't going to be easy. If it meant he'd be safe for Lacy to be around, he'd do whatever was necessary.

But she might not let him. She might have come to her senses and realized he'd been right after all. She *had* outgrown Coldwater.

And him.

He wavered between letting her go and trying to change her mind. If he loved her, and he was sure he did, shouldn't he stand aside and let her take the dream job she wanted? All day long, his thoughts chased each other like squirrels circling the same tree trunk. Even once Ethel and Lester went home and he turned the OPEN sign over, he was no closer to an answer.

Jake looked across the Square to Lacy's windows. If she was packing to leave, she wouldn't have time to fix supper. The least he could do was take her something to eat. Surely after all they'd been through together, she'd let him feed her one last time.

Lacy wasn't packing. She hadn't decided whether or not to accept Neville's offer and in the meantime, she still had a job with the *Gazette*. She was working on an article about the college's summer term. While she made notes, she also decided to call her sister, Crystal, tomorrow. She was the dean of admission at Bates, after all. What better source for her piece? And it would be a chance for Lacy to actually talk to her sister.

The truth was, Crystal was just so poisonously good, Lacy had been avoiding her. Since she'd been home, she'd only seen Crystal and her family at a couple of "command performance" dinners at their parents' home. It was wearying to be in the presence of perfection and judge herself wanting by comparison. Still, she thought her relationship with her sister might improve with time.

If she went back to Boston, there'd be no time.

Yet another thing to regret if she took Boyleston, Quincy, and Lodge up on their offer.

But the main reason for staying in Coldwater was Jake, and he'd pretty effectively taken that reason away. If he wouldn't let her near him, why stay just to torment herself?

Someone rapped on the door. She went to answer it, thinking it was Heather. Her friend had often dropped by since Lacy had stopped spending her evenings with Jake. Instead, when she opened the door, she found Thomas O'Leary on the other side.

She tried to slam it shut, but he shoved the door all the way open and came in without being invited.

"What are you doing here?"

He shook his head and made a *tsking* noise. "That's not very hospitable. I thought people out here in flyover country were friendly sorts."

"Aren't you supposed to be in jail?"

He feigned shock. "Whatever happened to presumed innocent, darlin'? My brother Malcolm and me are out on bail. And speakin' of that, a little birdie in the DA's office tells us you're going to be the Commonwealth's star witness."

So that's how he'd found her, an informant close to DDA Hopkins.

Lacy took a step back. "I'm not the only witness."

"Maybe not, but you're the strongest. If you don't take the stand, all Hopkins will have to trot out are thieves, embezzlers, and con artists who got caught and pled out in exchange for their testimony. Jurors don't like that a lot," Thomas explained. "So that's why Malcolm and me are keen on seeing that you don't speak against us."

When she was younger, Lacy had read the Narnia books. In one of them, C. S. Lewis wondered if it was possible for men to go wild on the inside while still looking human on the outside. There was a glint in Thomas O'Leary's eye that made Lacy think he was one of Lewis's wild ones. There was no pity. No empathy. No recognition that she was anything more than an obstacle for Thomas and his brother to shove out of their way.

Permanently.

"Where is your brother? Back in Boston?"

"Oh, Malcolm will be touched you asked after him, indeed he will. But you'll soon see for yourself that he's just fine. He's waiting for us down in the car."

A lookout ready for a clean getaway. "OK. You win. I won't testify."

"Ah, now, why don't I believe you?" Thomas said with a charming smile that didn't quite reach his eyes. "Tell you what. You come for a little ride with me and my brother and we'll see if you can convince us."

"I'm not going anywhere with you." Now would be the perfect time for Effie to leap down in her wildcat mode, but she was cowering from her perch above the cabinets.

Thomas pulled out a small handgun that had been tucked into his jeans at the small of his back. "I hope you'll come quietly. If your neighbor should pop by unexpectedly, things could get . . . messy."

The hackles on the back of Jake's neck rose when he passed by the sand-colored sedan parked behind Lacy's building. He didn't remember seeing it there before. It had out-of-state plates, but he'd walked by it before he could make out the logo. Jake knew just about everybody in town, but he didn't recognize the guy drumming his fingers on the wheel.

Surely that wasn't enough to warrant the prickles on his spine.

No, God, please. Not another episode.

But he didn't flash. Instead, he focused. As he continued to walk, balancing the insulated caterer's bag in both hands before him, he thought about all the times in Afghanistan when that prickle had saved his life. It was a holdover, his CO had told him, from a time when people were less civilized. It was the same instinct that made a doe raise her head the instant before a hunter framed her in his sights.

There were still some pretty uncivilized folk in the world.

Jake couldn't shake the feeling that someone had eyes on him and without good intent.

At the bottom of the stairs, he heard footfalls on the iron staircase above him. Lacy was coming down with another man who had one arm around her waist, the other hand behind his back. Besides being so cozy with this stranger, there was something off about the way she carried herself—shoulders hunched, fingers bunched into fists. Her eyes went wide when she saw him, then she quickly averted her gaze. The guy cinched her closer to him.

Something was definitely up. Jake lowered his eyes as well, and started up the stairs, studiously not looking directly at the guy by Lacy's side. With the caterer's bag in his hands, he could pass as a delivery boy. He exaggerated his limp to present a non-challenging appearance.

When they passed on the broad staircase, Jake saw that the guy was holding a SIG Sauer pistol behind his back. Its muzzle was pointed in Lacy's direction. He shoved the caterer's bag between the man and Lacy, and made a move for the piece.

The gun fired, splattering meat loaf and biscuits and bits of insulated nylon everywhere. Lacy screamed as the guy gave her a shove that sent her over the railing. Jake launched himself at the man and they rolled down the staircase together, clattering to a stop at the bottom.

The man tried to wiggle away, but Jake wrestled him down, straddled him, and proceeded to beat the tar out of him. He'd held a gun on Lacy.

A beating was too good for him.

He heard the guy in the car shouting. Someone was coming toward them at a run, but Jake couldn't seem to get out of his adrenaline-fueled aggression. Then sirens blared and there was more shouting. Jake was vaguely aware that the other man had been subdued by a sheriff's deputy.

All his frustration over losing Lacy because of his own unwillingness to change, and then almost losing her for good because of this lowlife bleating under him, made Jake's blood boil. He just couldn't seem to stop pounding the man.

It took two men to pull him off.

"Easy there, marine." One of them was Lester.

The other was Daniel. "Come on back, Jake," he said softly. "It's OK. We got this."

Jake drew a shaky breath as the pent-up fury subsided. "I would have killed him."

"I know. But you didn't."

"Thank you, man."

"You did the same for me one time. Let's call it square." Another deputy lifted the man to his feet, cuffed him, and frog-marched him to the waiting cruiser to join the other guy in the back. Jake looked around for Lacy. She had been cornered by an EMT, who was checking her out.

"How did you know to come?" Jake asked Daniel.

"Lester called to report some suspicious-looking characters parked behind this building," Daniel said, giving his father a grudging nod.

"When you've people-watched as much as I have over the years, you get so you can spot the ones that are up to no good pretty darn quick," Lester said. "After I seen them guys hanging around, I hotfooted it over to the Regal and used the phone in the lobby to call it in."

"And you believed him?" Jake said to Daniel.

"Let's just say I gave him the benefit of the doubt this time," Daniel said. "Everyone's entitled to it once in a while."

Lester beamed. It wasn't a full-blown reconciliation, but at least father and son were on speaking terms now.

Jake left them to find Lacy.

As soon as she saw him approaching, she pulled away from the EMT who was trying to take her blood pressure and ran toward him. He hugged her close. It felt like a miracle that she was hugging him back.

"Jake, oh, Jake, you're hurt."

There was a cut on his temple that was bleeding like a son of a gun, but he didn't feel any pain. That would come later.

"I was bringing you dinner," he said, feeling stupid after the words came out. It wasn't at all what he wanted to say. Then he realized if he didn't say what was in his heart right now, he'd regret it for the rest of his life. "I was coming to tell you I'm seeing a shrink. I'll do anything to keep from putting you in danger. I'm going to get better, Lacy."

"That's not possible, Jake. You're already the best."

That was so far beyond what he'd hoped she'd say, it almost didn't register in his brain.

"I was coming to . . . to . . ." Words failed him. Instead, he fished around in his pocket and came up with his grandmother's ring. He should do this right. He should drop to one knee, but if he took the time to assume the position, he might lose his nerve. "I love you, Lacy Evans. I'll love you till they lay me in the dust. Don't go back to Boston."

"I love you, too." She leaned down and palmed his face. "As long as we have each other, Coldwater Cove is the happiest place on earth. I'm not going anywhere."

Epilogue

Re: Mr. Bradford Endicott

The defendant has been arrested by Belizean authorities for running a real estate scam on tourists in San Pedro. Mr. Endicott is incarcerated in the country's central prison while he awaits trial. The Endicott family's lawyer has indicated that they will no longer resist our efforts to extradite him to the U.S. to stand trial for embezzlement in the Commonwealth of Massachusetts.

How do you want to handle this matter?

—a note from Percy Junket, personal assistant
to Deputy District Attorney Ethan Hopkins

DDA Hopkins scribbled a note to his assistant, telling him to "misplace" the paperwork connected with the Commonwealth's extradition request. Hopkins would have Junket find them again in a year or so. By then, Endicott would be more than happy to face the music closer to home.

A Belizean prison was no day at the beach. Sometimes, the scales of justice balanced just fine without any help from him at all.

He couldn't have arranged matters better if he'd tried.

From the *Coldwater Gazette* Society column

Mr. and Mrs. George Evans are pleased to announce the engagement of their daughter Lacy to Jacob Tyler, decorated veteran and oldest son of the late Marvin Tyler and his wife, Mary, who survived him. Not that he was any bother, she says.

A November wedding is planned.

The bride predicts "a good time will be had by all."

Recipes from the Green Apple Grill

When I was first married, I didn't know how to cook. At all. I could set a table and throw together a passable chef's salad, but that was the extent of my culinary expertise. As a result, my poor husband received more than his share of burnt offerings that first year.

Likewise, Jake Tyler hasn't always been a great cook. He looked for recipes all over the place and then experimented and made his own tweaks. Here are some dishes that appear in *The Coldwater Warm Hearts Club*.

Belgian Waffles

Ingredients

2 cups cake flour (You can use all-purpose flour instead, but cake flour is finer and lighter. Fair warning: It requires sifting first.)
¾ cup sugar
3½ teaspoons baking powder
2 eggs, separated
1½ cups milk
1 cup butter, melted
1 teaspoon vanilla extract
Powdered sugar, sliced fresh strawberries, blueberries, or your favorite syrup
Nonstick cooking spray

Directions

Preheat your waffle iron.

Combine flour, sugar, and baking powder in a big bowl. In a medium bowl, lightly beat egg yolks. Add milk, butter, and vanilla. Gently stir into dry ingredients until combined. Do not overmix. Beat the egg whites with a whisk until stiff peaks form. Fold into the batter. Do not overmix! (*This is starting to be a theme, isn't it?*)

Spray your waffle iron with nonstick spray. Pour in batter and bake according to manufacturer's directions until golden brown.

Serve your waffles dusted with powdered sugar, garnished with fresh strawberries or blueberries. Or you can drown them in syrup if you like.

The recipe makes about 10 waffles and I'm sorry to have to tell you that two waffles have 696 calories. But Jake says if you enjoy them with someone you love, the calories don't count.

Happy Man Meat Loaf

Of course, men aren't the only ones who appreciate this dish. Kids love it, too. Moms like the fact that extra veggies can be sneaked into this one-dish meal and no one will ever be the wiser.

Jake decided it was the perfect "welcome home" meal to bring to Lacy when she was moving into her new place in Coldwater Cove. The meat loaf is warm and satisfying.

Just like him.

Ingredients

8 ounces tomato sauce (Try picante sauce for a Mexican flair. My husband likes Jack Daniel's Original No. 7 barbecue sauce in this recipe. Use your imagination and your family's preferences.)

1 small onion, diced

1 potato, coarsely grated (You can also add grated carrots or any other vegetable you want. I've even made this recipe with grated zucchini. Just add more meat and perhaps another egg to make sure the loaf holds together.)

2 pounds ground beef (Or ground pork, chicken, or turkey. This is a very flexible recipe.)

2 eggs

Sea salt and freshly ground pepper to taste

8 ounces cheddar cheese, coarsely grated

Directions

Preheat oven to 375 degrees.

Set aside ⅓ cup of tomato sauce. In a large bowl, mix onion, potato (and any other veggie you care to add), ground meat, ¾ of the grated cheese, the remaining tomato sauce, eggs, salt, and pepper. Roll up your sleeves and mix it together with your hands to form a loaf. Press the mixture into a loaf pan and top with the ⅓ cup of tomato sauce you set aside.

Bake at 375 degrees for one hour. Sprinkle the remaining grated cheese to melt on top, return to oven for another ten minutes.

Serves 4–6 with some left over.

My husband never minds leftovers. He says sandwiches the next day are the best part of having meat loaf!

Three-Cheese Deviled Eggs

Every family has secret recipes. The only way my sister teased the recipe for icebox rolls from my grandmother was to stand over her and write it all down as she made them. She was known to leave a few things out when she wrote a recipe down so no one else's rolls would ever be quite as good! ;-) My mother-in-law never did divulge the secret to her homemade chocolate sauce. We've cobbled together an approximation. It's good, but it's not the same.

Jake knew he was getting someplace with Lacy when she gave up the recipe for her mother's three-cheese deviled eggs!

Ingredients

6 hard-cooked eggs
¾ cup mayonnaise
2 tablespoons finely shredded Monterey Jack cheese
2 tablespoons finely shredded Swiss cheese
2 tablespoons minced chives, divided
⅛ teaspoon ground mustard
⅛ teaspoon pepper
2 ounces processed cheese, cubed (Velveeta. Yes, I know it's not considered haute cuisine, but we're feeding a family, not trying to win *Top Chef!*)
Dash paprika

Directions

Boil the eggs and let them cool. Cut eggs in half lengthwise. Remove yolks and set whites aside. Mash the yolks in a bowl. Add the mayonnaise, shredded cheeses, 1 tablespoon chives, mustard, and pepper.

In a microwave-safe bowl, melt the Velveeta on high for 1–2 minutes. Stir until smooth and then add to the yolk mixture.

Spoon into the egg white shells. Sprinkle with paprika and the remaining chives. Refrigerate until serving.

If your family is like mine, there won't be any leftovers. That way you don't have to worry about refrigerating them after the meal!

Sweet Cream Raisin Pie

This is a very old country recipe from "Tiny" Simon, of the very real Simon family of Oklahoma. Tiny is the oldest of eight children. She won't reveal her age, but her youngest sibling is seventy.

Here is Tiny's raisin pie recipe exactly as it appears in the Simon family cookbook. With a comment or two from me tossed in, of course!

Put 1 cup of sweet cream in a pan. Rinse cup with ¼ cup of milk. Add to cream.

Mix 1 cup of sugar, 1 tablespoon of flour, 1 teaspoon of cinnamon. Add to hot cream. (Okay, somehow the cream heated up. Use your imagination.)

Beat 3 egg yolks and add to cream. Also add 2 cups of cooked raisins. (I'd never cooked raisins before and Tiny doesn't share her secret, so I Googled it. Martha Stewart recommends soaking raisins for half an hour in hot water, laced with cognac or orange liqueur. Drain thoroughly.) Cook until cream thickens. (You have to stand over the pan stirring almost constantly to keep it from scorching.)

Pour into baked pie shell. (If you don't have a good pie crust recipe, check out Jake's Perfect Pie. The link is at the bottom of the Green Apple Grill page at LexiEddings.com)

Cover with meringue from 3 egg whites. (Tiny expects a lot of me. I had to Google how to make meringue, too.)

Thanks to my friend Jan Dold, who shared Tiny's recipe with us. Of course, as rich as this pie is, it'd be hard for anyone who eats it often to stay "tiny."

But everyone deserves a little sweetness in their life from time to time. It may not be politically correct, but at a very basic level, food is love.

Who's ready for a meringue-topped hug?

Acknowledgments

Coldwater Cove is a fictional town, but parts of it are real. It's a combination of every little wide spot in the road I've ever visited or called home. So if you see *your* town in it, you may well be right. I'd be remiss if I didn't acknowledge Marcy Weinbeck, my dear beta reader, who helped me sketch out a map of Coldwater Cove so my story would have a firm sense of place. Thanks, Marcy.

You may also think you recognize some of the secondary characters in Coldwater Cove: the fussy neighbor, Mr. Mayhew, or the Polish piano teacher, Mrs. Paderewski. Small towns are filled with interestingly quirky people, so I understand why you might believe I've been writing about someone you know. Actually, only one of my characters is based on a real person: Charlie Bunn, the founder of the Royal Order of Chicken Pluckers. Yes, it's all too real. I couldn't make that up! Thank you to my beloved friend, Kathy Bunn, for letting me use her dad's real name in the book.

It's said that it takes a village to raise a child. It takes a small town to bring a book to market. I'm grateful for Alicia Condon, my amazing editor at Kensington; and my tireless agent, Natasha Kern; and for the cover artist, copy editor, marketing team, sales staff, and bookseller who helped put this story into your hands.

Which brings me to you, dear reader. Without you and your imagination, my story cannot live. You breathe life into the words on the page and complete the conversation between us. Thank you for coming along for the ride!

If you'd like to know more about me and my books, I hope you'll visit LexiEddings.com.

THE COLDWATER WARM HEARTS CLUB

Lexi Eddings

ABOUT THIS GUIDE

The suggested questions are included
to enhance your group's reading of this book.

DISCUSSION QUESTIONS

1. Acclaimed author Thomas Wolfe may think "you can't go home again," but at the beginning of *The Coldwater Warm Hearts Club,* Lacy Evans is trying to do just that. Do you think going back home is hard? Under what circumstances would you do it?

2. Lacy has had her share of man troubles, especially with Bradford Endicott. What do you think drew her to him in the first place? Did she lose more than her business by hooking up with him?

3. To all outward appearances, Jake Tyler has adjusted to civilian life without part of his leg. Why do you think he hides the fact that he experiences flashbacks?

4. The relationship between a parent and his or her adult child is a tricky one. Do you think Mr. and Mrs. Evans treat Lacy like a twelve-year-old, or is it just her perception? How should they try to help her?

5. What would have happened if Lacy had decided she wanted to rekindle her romance with Daniel? How would that have changed the story?

6. Homelessness isn't just a big-city problem. Whose responsibility is it to see that people have adequate shelter? Government, either federal or local? Church and charities? What would have happened to Lester without the Warm Hearts Club? How would the group have responded if he had fallen off the wagon or been unwilling to make a change?

7. Beauty really is in the eye of the beholder. Lacy and her mom have very different ideas of what constitutes "art." How do the items we surround ourselves with tell people about us? What do you have in your home that shows others who you are?

8. At the beginning of the book, Jake makes Lacy her favorite waffles. He brings her supper while she's unpacking. Later, they play in the kitchen together when she teaches him how to make three cheese deviled eggs, an Evans family secret recipe. Could food be a metaphor for something else? What's going on in the relationship each time something to eat is involved?

9. Grandma Bugtussle tells Lacy "if where you are ain't the happiest place, then you ain't home yet." Is home a place? Is it a collection of relationships? Both?

10. Did the ending surprise you? Lacy was passionate about her career. What would have happened if Lacy had returned to Boston? Would Jake have followed her there? Could an Okie boy find happiness in Beantown? (Oh, wait, that sounds like another story, doesn't it? Maybe I'd better put that idea on the back burner and let it simmer for a while. . . .)

Thank you for spending time in Coldwater Cove with me. I hope you'll return often!

Happy Reading,
Lexi

Can't wait to spend more time in Coldwater Cove?

Read on for a preview of

A COLDWATER WARM HEARTS WEDDING

coming next May

Chapter 1

*Trouble makes us stronger, they say. It brings out
the best in us and shows what we're really made of.
But don't you just hate it when blessings come in disguise?*

—Shirley Evans, after she got the news
from her doctor about the Big C

"This was so not the time to take a surgical rotation,"
Heather Walker mumbled to herself as she scanned the lineup
of procedures for the day. Not that she didn't love assisting.
She did. It was rewarding to be part of the surgical team
at Coldwater Cove's small hospital. She went home "good
tired" every day. But it would be so much easier if she didn't
know her patients.

And Heather knew everybody in town.

Today was worse than usual because the mother of her
best friend, Lacy Evans, was on the schedule. Lacy pushed her
way past one of the curtains that divided up the surgical waiting area and made a beeline toward Heather.

"Mom was supposed to be in surgery an hour ago." Lacy's
nose was red, a sure sign she'd been fighting back tears.

"I know and I'm sorry, but it can't be helped. We had an
emergency appendectomy come in this morning." Heather
always tried to be calmly professional, however frazzled she
might feel on the inside. No one would be helped if she joined
them in barely suppressed panic. She strived to be detached
enough to get the job done. That was the goal anyway. It was
a hard line to walk when her friend was obviously holding

herself together with spit and baling twine. "Your mom is next on the list."

Lacy nodded. "Okay. Maybe it's just as well there was a delay. Michael's not here yet."

Lacy's fiancé Jake had called in a favor with one of his marine buddies in intelligence and between them, they'd managed to track down the elusive Michael Evans. Lacy figured her brother deserved to know what was happening, even though he'd shown precious little interest in his family in the past few years. Lacy had confided in Heather that she was relieved—and a little surprised—to discover her brother wasn't in jail somewhere.

"Are you expecting him to come?" Heather asked.

"No, but Mom is."

Her friend's black-sheep brother hadn't been home in ages. Hadn't called. Hadn't even sent a postcard. Mike Evans had been in Heather's class in school, but he ran with a totally different crowd, so their paths had rarely crossed. Her only sharp memory of him was when he christened her "Stilts" in middle school. Through no fault of her own, Heather had shot up to five feet, ten inches by her thirteenth birthday and she hadn't been finished growing yet.

The name stuck. She was Stilts Walker all through high school.

But even that indignity wasn't enough to account for the resentment simmering in her chest. According to Lacy, Michael had shamed his family many times over the years. If there was a way to go wrong, Mike Evans found it. Still, the frustration rising in Heather's chest was unproductive, so she tamped it down. Her relationship with her own parents wasn't anything to brag about. It was aloof rather than estranged, but in a pinch, she hoped the Walkers would come together.

Any guy who couldn't be bothered to show up when his

mother was facing cancer surgery deserved a swift kick in the backside.

Her friend Lacy's eyes went hazy for a moment. "She doesn't know how to swim."

"What?"

"My mom. Every summer she took us kids to the pool for lessons five times a week, and I mean *religiously.* At six-holy-cow-thirty a.m., we'd be hopping around by the side of the pool trying to warm up before they let us into the water." Lacy's voice trailed away. "Mom swims like a rock, but she made sure we all learned how."

"Maybe she can take lessons at the Civic Center as part of her physical therapy after surgery," Heather suggested. It was important for her friend to think positively about her mom's future.

"That's not the point," Lacy said with a sniff. "The point is she's a terrific mom and I never appreciated her like I should."

"She's still a terrific mom. Appreciate her now."

Lacy gave her a shaky nod. Ever since Mrs. Evans's routine mammogram had revealed a tumor and a needle biopsy confirmed cancer, Lacy had been pumping Heather for information about the diagnosis, treatment, and likely outcome. "But what will happen if—"

"Hush now." *Forget being professional.* Heather gave her friend a hug. "You're borrowing trouble. Until your mom has the surgery, we won't know if the cancer has spread. And until we know that, it's hard to say what treatment Dr. Warner will recommend."

Or if we caught the disease in time to make treatment worth the misery, Heather thought but didn't say. No point in rehearsing the worst-case scenario.

But Lacy had evidently been imagining it.

"Come on. I need to get your mom prepped." Pasting on

what she hoped was an encouraging smile, Heather led Lacy
to the surgical waiting room and drew back the first curtain.
The scent of antiseptic cleansers and bleached linen was second nature to Heather, but hospital smells put most people
on edge. Mrs. Evans wasn't troubled though. She was always
awash in a personal cloud of Estée Lauder. You couldn't have
smelled a skunk if it had taken up residence under her bed.

Heather's patient was sitting up on the gurney, trying to
wrestle a pillow away from Lacy's older sister, Crystal. Heather
wasn't sure what offense the pillow had committed, but Crystal was doing her best to pound it into submission.

Everyone deals with stress in their own way.

"Good morning, Mrs. Evans," Heather said as she edged
past Crystal to reach her patient. "How are we doing today?"

"Fine, Heather. Ready to get this over with." Mrs. Evans
gave up and surrendered the pillow to her daughter. She was
already festooned with electrodes monitoring her heart rate,
and the pillow fight had sent her pulse racing. An IV pumped
saline into her system. In a few minutes, Heather would add
a drug cocktail to prepare her for the general anesthesia to
come. Doc Warner called it the "don't give a darn" drug.

Only he didn't say "darn."

"I'll see what I can do to move things along," Heather
promised.

"Thank you, dear," Mrs. Evans said. "Crystal, for heaven's
sake, stop worrying that pillow."

"I'm not worrying it. I'm trying to give it a little shape. It
won't do you any good if it's all flat."

"Flat or fluffy, it's not doing me a speck of good if it's not
under my head."

"You heard your mother," Mr. Evans chimed in from his
seat in the only chair on the other side of the bed.

With a sigh, Crystal stuffed the pillow behind her mother's shoulders. Heather suspected Lacy's sister didn't fluff and

plump for her mom's comfort. She wasn't even necessarily doing it out of nervous energy. She was rearranging things to suit herself. Even back when they were kids, Crystal had had firm ideas about how everything should be.

Of course, everyone was entitled to their own opinion, but if they wanted to be right, they had to agree with Crystal.

Looking gray and stretched thin, Mr. Evans retreated behind the *Coldwater Gazette,* rattling the paper noisily.

A prime example of the ostrich-with-his-head-in-the-sand way to deal with stress.

Then he began to quote snippets from the *Gazette* whether anyone was listening to him or not.

"Labor Day is fast approaching," he read, "the traditional time for all graduates of Coldwater High to gather for their class reunions. Like lemmings rushing to the sea, we expect a number of Fighting Marmots will make their way home for the festivities."

"I did *not* write that," Lacy was quick to point out, though she did work for the local paper. "That's my boss all the way. It's not enough that our high school mascot is an oversized rodent, Wanda has to lump us with suicidal ones, too."

Heather had been a Lady Marmot once, a star power forward on the girls' basketball team back in the day. But she'd often wondered who had first decided it would be a good thing for the Coldwater Cove teams to bear the name of a glorified ground squirrel.

"Looks like our class is hosting a supper at the country club on Saturday as one of the reunion events, Shirley." Mr. Evans glanced up from the paper long enough to make eye contact with his wife before focusing back on the *Gazette.* "Think we'll be able to make it?"

Classic denial, Heather thought. If George Evans acknowledged that his wife was about to undergo breast cancer surgery, it would make it too real.

"Well," Shirley Evans said as Heather wrapped the blood pressure cuff around her upper arm and pumped it up. "I—"

"How can you ask that, Dad?" Crystal interrupted. "Mom will still be recovering this weekend. She might not even be out of the hospital by—"

"She might also like to answer for herself, if you don't mind," Mrs. Evans said with an arched brow at her oldest daughter. "I'd like to go, George, but we'll just have to see. Buy a pair of tickets anyway. The class always gives any excess to a local charity, so whatever happens, you know the money will go to a good cause."

Whatever happens . . .

Heather had to either lighten the mood or get things moving, preferably both. When she opened Mrs. Evans's chart, her heart fluttered a bit. No one had gone through the pre-op documents with the patient. Of all the aspects of her job, Heather rebelled against this part the most. She was a healer. She hadn't studied nursing to push papers. And especially not papers that dealt with some of life's toughest decisions. "There are a few things for you to sign."

"What sort of things?" Mr. Evans rose. Since he was a retired lawyer, papers were his life.

"First, there's consent for treatment." Heather explained the procedure Mrs. Evans was about to undergo, the possible risks, and the expected outcome. They'd heard it all before, but Heather was required to repeat it now. When Mr. Evans nodded, his wife signed. Heather drew a deep breath. She hated this next part, but it was absolutely necessary. "Then there are advance directives to consider. Have you made out a living will or durable power of attorney?"

Mr. Evans snorted. "I wouldn't be worth my salt as a lawyer if she hadn't, would I?"

"Dear George made sure we took care of all that a few

years ago when we were both healthy." Mrs. Evans patted her husband's forearm. "It's always easier to deal with the hard things when they seem a long way off, don't you think?"

Mrs. Evans gave Heather a tremulous smile. She was bearing up well for her family's sake, but it was hard to head into surgery not knowing if your worst fears were about to be confirmed.

"Lacy," Mrs. Evans said, "why don't you show Heather your wedding palette? I bet she hasn't seen it yet."

Heather *had* seen Lacy's colors. She'd even helped her pick them out one evening over a nice Merlot. Heather was Lacy's maid of honor, after all. But since Mrs. Evans evidently needed to change the subject, she asked to see the swatches again. Lacy pulled out her cell phone and brought up the navy blue, pale pink, and ivory palette.

"You'll be in ivory, of course, Lacy, and Jake and the male attendants in navy," Mrs. Evans said with a wistful smile, her gaze fixed on a distant point as if imagining the wedding party in their finery. "And the bridesmaids' gowns will be pink."

"No, Mom," Lacy said gently. "We discussed this, remember? Jake will be in his dress blues. He deserves to wear the uniform."

Since Jake had lost a leg from the knee down in Afghanistan, Heather agreed. He'd more than earned the right to wear the blues. Even though he was no longer in active service, Jake claimed, "Once a marine, always a marine."

Besides, nothing looked better in wedding pictures than a groom in uniform.

In my case, any groom would look good. No, wait. Scratch that.

No guy in her life was better than the wrong guy. Heather told herself she was single by choice. Lacy always argued she was "single by choosy."

While Heather prided herself on being choosy, it didn't put an extra place setting at her table. Or an extra head on her pillow.

"The bridesmaids' dresses will be navy, too," Lacy went on. "Pink is just the accent color."

Heather silently blessed her friend. A navy dress would help her blend into the background. As gangly as she was, a pink one would make her feel like an overgrown flamingo.

The curtain enclosing the waiting area ruffled and Mrs. Evans looked up expectantly.

"Michael," she whispered, but when she saw who it was, her smile turned brittle. Instead of her son, her future son-in-law stepped into the small space. Heather knew Mrs. Evans both liked and approved of Jake Tyler, but he wasn't Michael.

The one who isn't *here is always the one they want to see the most.*

Jake gave Lacy a quick kiss. "I overheard you talking about the wedding colors again. Isn't it settled yet?"

"The devil's in the details," Mr. Evans said morosely.

"I tried to talk Lacy into jarhead camouflage, but she insists on navy. *Navy,* of all colors!" Jake shook his head.

"Hey." Lacy gave him a playful swat on the shoulder. "I could always go army green, you know."

Jake shook his head. "It's enough to make a marine consider an elopement."

"I've got a ladder you can use, son," Mr. Evans groused. "This wedding is gonna cost the earth."

"Now, George," Mrs. Evans chided, "you know you'll love giving Lacy away in style. After all, she's the last daughter you have to walk down the aisle."

Heather had finished her nursing degree and moved back to Coldwater Cove to take a position at the hospital in time to be around for the wedding of the decade, the joining of Crystal Evans and Noah Addleberry. Years later, folks still talked about the event. The Addleberrys were one of the town's first families, so everything had to be just so. Mr. Evans had complained loudly and often to anyone who'd listen, and a few who wouldn't, that if the Addleberrys wanted to bankrupt someone over a wedding, they should start with themselves.

But the real driver of overspending was his own wife. Mrs. Evans got her way in the end and the wedding was elegantly excessive. Guestimates about how much the wedding had cost became a prime topic of conversation in Coldwater Cove. On the low side of the gossip scale, Crystal's wedding could have provided a substantial down payment on a house. If you took Mr. Evans's complaints into consideration, the amount would have run a small country for a week.

He disappeared behind his paper again. Lacy and Crystal and Mrs. Evans nattered on about the color scheme. Heather injected the sedative into her patient's IV and waited for it to take effect.

"It says here in the paper that Levi Harper needs a liver transplant," Mr. Evans told Jake. The young Sooner quarterback was a rising University of Oklahoma star and one of Coldwater Cove's favorite sons. Then he'd gone on a mission trip with his church group to some backwater country over the summer and come home with an exotic parasite that demolished his liver. Now he was forced to sit out his junior year.

"That's a shame." Jake had been an all-conference halfback himself when he was in high school, so following college football was second only to following Lacy. "If Levi gets a new liver, will he be ready to play next year?"

"Should be," Mr. Evans said. "Comes from good stock. Think the Harpers are related to the Walkers, aren't they, Heather?"

"Yes," she said. "Levi is my cousin a couple of times removed. His mother's uncle was my grandmother's first cousin or some such thing."

Levi was eight or so years younger than Heather, but she remembered him from the big Walker reunions. Levi had been the self-proclaimed leader of a whole gaggle of little boys that styled themselves the "Monkey Troop." They terrorized the great-aunts while they were trying to piece quilts and made off with the pies before the rest of the picnic things had even been laid out. No watermelon was safe from their predations. No jug of Kool-Aid stood a chance against their not-so-stealthy marauding.

No one held those youthful indiscretions against Levi now. Since he was family, Heather had been tested for a possible partial liver donation. Unfortunately, she was not a match. If he didn't get a liver soon, he'd have more to worry about than missing a football season.

Heather focused back on the patient at hand. Mrs. Evans was trying to referee while Lacy and her sister wrangled about whether the bridesmaid dresses should be tea length or drape to the floor. Heather was grateful that their argument was distracting their mother. Once the box was checked to indicate whether or not the patient was willing to be a donor, no one going into surgery should be subjected to a prolonged discussion about transplants.

Mrs. Evans was blinking more slowly now. It was time.

Heather told the family. The good-byes took a while because there was a lot of kissing and hugging involved. Through it all, Mrs. Evans assured them that everything would be all right. She stared at the closed curtain once more, as if thinking hard about her son Michael would magically summon him. Then she sighed. "I'm ready, Heather."

Heather pulled back the curtain and started pushing the wheeled bed down the hall.

Then Mrs. Evans waved her hand in the air and sang out

gaily, "If anything happens, give my liver to that football player!"

Behind her, Heather could hear the Evans family chuckling despite their tears. Shirley Evans was a wonderful human being. She so deserved the support of her entire family.

If Heather ever ran into Michael Evans again, she'd happily lock him in an examination room with a first-year proctology resident and let the new doc practice till he got it right.

However long it took.

Connect with U s

Visit us online at
KensingtonBooks.com
to read more from your favorite authors, see books
by series, view reading group guides, and more.

Join us on social media

for sneak peeks, chances to win books and prize packs,
and to share your thoughts with other readers.

facebook.com/kensingtonpublishing
twitter.com/kensingtonbooks

Tell us what you think!

To share your thoughts, submit a review,
or sign up for our eNewsletters, please visit:
KensingtonBooks.com/TellUs.